GALAXY ALLIANCE

GALAXY ALLIANCE

ALLAN D. RISA

iUniverse, Inc.
Bloomington

GALAXY ALLIANCE

iUniverse books may be ordered through booksellers or by contacting:

iUniverse
1663 Liberty Drive
Bloomington, IN 47403
www.iuniverse.com
1-800-Authors (1-800-288-4677)

ISBN: 978-1-4620-7138-8 (sc)
ISBN: 978-1-4620-7137-1 (ebk)

Printed in the United States of America

iUniverse rev. date: 11/28/2011

CHAPTER 1

ON THE FIFTH day of April, Galactic year 2525, on an Alliance experimental station called the Drandon, Station Commander Vencor stepped onto the bridge. "Today is the day. Is everything ready for our test flight?"

"Yes, sir. The scientists have been ready since 0600 hours, sir. If this works, we can increase our ship's abilities," the tactical station replied with a hint of excitement in his voice.

"Don't get too excited. We still have to see if the new system works, after all. You're right, though. If this does work, all of our fighters will improve by fourty percent," Commander Vencor replied.

"Sir, we have signs of dimensional space shifts appearing on our port side. Are we expecting anyone?" the tactical station asked.

"No, we aren't. I wonder if Colonel Calamen is done with their maneuvers. Place the station on yellow alert until we find out what is going on," Vencor demanded.

"Yes, sir . . . All pilots, this is a yellow alert. I repeat, this is a yellow alert. Stand by for further instructions . . . Sir, we have visual on those ships—they're Pirates!" the tactical station reported.

"Change the condition from yellow to red. Launch all fighters, call for reinforcements, raise the shields, and man the guns. I just hope we can last until help arrives," Commander Vencor yelled.

"This is a red alert. All ships are to scramble. Your targets will be those Pirate ships. Be careful. They have already started their attack," the tactical station called over the intercom.

"You heard them. We are to stop those ships at all costs. Fighter Squadrons Three and Four, you will help Squadron Ten take out their flag ship. Squadrons Two and Six, you're with me. We will hold off any infiltration group they might send in," the First Squadrons' leader ordered.

As the Pirate's fighters raced toward the station, a visual communication and an audio communications appeared on all channels.

"Trayon, what are you doing?" the commander asked.

"All Pirates, I want all of those new experimental weapons from that giant space station." (The Space Station had been previously mistaken for the planets' actual moon.) "You may do whatever you wish with those Alliance dogs. Just remember, I want that new ship and their new arsenal for the infantry that they have finished," a harsh voice said over the audio frequency.

"You heard Trayon. Now, all Korra guild ships, take out those shields and disarm those guns. Once that is done, Trisha and her team will infiltrate that station. Sis, did you copy all that?" a young male's voice called over the audio frequency.

"Yes, Tearan, I did. I will see you on the inside, or am I going in alone with eighteen platoons at my disposal?" a young woman's voice replied.

On a visual monitor, Trisha saw her brother wearing his red and black outfit that he liked to wear when he went into combat. Except for his long hair, tan skin, and blue eyes, he would have looked like any other Pirate—the only difference being the crest of the royal family on his left shoulder.

"Yes, little sister, I will lead another group in from the starboard side. We will meet in the middle, so be careful, all right?" Tearan replied to her question.

"Hey, who is the girl? She's cute," a voice asked about the young woman in the all black outfit.

After the monitor blinked out, Tearan turned around to face the infiltration squad he would lead and said, "My sister is of no concern. Right now, you must keep your focus on what is at hand!" he ordered.

As Commander Vencor looked out of the window of the bridge, he could see his fighters engaging the enemy, "How is that distress call coming?"

"This is the Drandon station. We are currently engaged with an enemy fleet. We request immediate reinforcements. I repeat, this is the Drandon station. We are currently engaged with an enemy fleet. We request immediate reinforcements," the communication station transmitted as the station shook from direct hits.

After trying the transmission three more times, the communication station reported, "Sorry, sir, the last direct hit took out our communication array. I am not sure how much of the message was actually sent before they started to jam our communications."

"Fine, if you can make contact with the First Squadron's leader. Order him to send someone to bring back reinforcement. Colonel Calamen is in the Ortaga system, which is only three systems away. Get him to send us help." Commander Vencor demander as the station shook again from another direct hit.

"First Squadron Leader, can you hear me? You are under orders to send a ship to the Ortaga system. Tell Colonel Calamen we need reinforcements. I repeat, you are under orders to send a ship to the Ortaga system. Tell Colonel Calamen we need reinforcements."

The communications officer did not receive a reply. "Sir, I'm not sure . . ." the Communication Station was suddenly interrupted.

"This is the First Squadron Leader . . . cop . . . sendi . . . thir . . . si . . ." the reply came as the communications was completely cut off.

While Commander Vencor watched out the window of the bridge, he noticed a black and red ship that suddenly appeared in the distance. Due to the shape, it could only be a destroyer moving straight toward them. As the ship closed in, the commander remembered that he had heard of a spy report that had been submitted to the Alliance of a brand new destroyer being built for the Pirates around Volcanic 9. The destroyer was supposed to be about forty-five miles long with four floors and a weapon system that could easily destroy a planet-sized station.

"All gunners, take out that destroyer. Give it everything you have. We must not allow any Pirates to get aboard this station. If they do, you will not see tomorrow. We must stop them for the rest of the galaxy." Commander Vencor ordered when the station shook again followed by an alarm.

"Sir, we have a hall breach on decks eighty-two and eighty-three. I'm sorry, sir. We are not receiving any response form the other decks," Communication Station reported.

"Those decks are the living quarters for the crew and their families. Status report, tell me how many have survived." Vencor demanded to know.

"I am sorry, sir. I cannot register any life readings on those decks," the tactical officer reported in a sad voice.

"Due to the last hit, all three hundred civilians are dead. All fighters and gunners, take those Pirates out now! I do not want anyone of them to live!" Vencor yelled in disgust while turning to face the crew of the bridge.

Suddenly Commander Vencor was thrown to the floor from another direct hit to the station as three platoons of soldiers ran into the room. "Sir, we've been boarded by Pirates. You must leave now before it's too late. If you are lost, the Alliance will not be able to receive their new weapons, not to mention you're the only one with the codes for the weapons locker," the lieutenant commander told the station commander as he locked the door to the bridge.

After turning to look at the platoon commander, Vencor placed a hand over his face and, in a calm voice, asked, "When did they board the station? How did they get past our shields? Tactical station, explain to me what is going on."

"Sir, I have to reboot the system. In a few seconds, I can tell you what is going on. Sir, someone has deactivated the main shields from the main orbital control center. The record shows our shields have been off line for fifteen minutes now!" the tactical station reported.

"That means we are trapped here, and our only hope might just be too late. Jack, my friend, I hope you can make it in time." Commander Vencor said out loud, not caring if anyone else heard him.

"No, this cannot be! Sir, Pirates are actually inside the station. I must get help. I just hope I'm not too late . . . Fighter three of Squad Six to Squadron Leader. I'm launching for the Ortaga system. Good hunting and good luck." A female voice radioed.

"We copy, Fighter Three. We'll do our best. Hurry up and get us that help, or there will not be anyone left for the reinforcements to help," Squadron Leader replied.

After looking at the silver-colored hall of her commander's fighter, the fighter pilot placed the co-ordinates in the computer and launched for the Ortaga system. *Please hang in there, and I will be back help as soon as possible,* she thought.

In the Ortaga system.

"No, you are doing this all wrong. Okay, Squads One, Two, Five, and Six, you need to work as a single unit and not as individuals. You need to hit that target faster, and you need to use better stealth than that. Remember the training simulation you had a few hours ago. Now get it right," Colonel Calamen ordered from the bridge of the Orgna.

While looking at his reflection in the window, Colonel Calamen scratched his short, black hair and thought, *Why, why do they act like individuals and not a unit? In the simulator, they preformed the scenario like they needed to. Now they are acting like my daughter.*

"Sir, this maneuver is harder in real life than using the simulator. That is why these are called maneuvers. We can practice and practice until we get it right," the fighter commander replied.

"Fine, this time you need to be more serious before I change my mind and send you over to my brother-in-law on the planet Trolena. You can lead the Planetary Academies graduating class on the simulation for ambushing Pirates. You can face off with my son, who is also there leading the Station Academies graduating class in the same simulation against each other," Calamen replied.

"Sir, I am picking a dimensional shift up on the radar," the tactical station spoke with confusion in her voice.

"How many ships are there—can you tell?" Commander Calamen asked while looking at the screen.

"I am not sure, sir. It only shows one. If there are any others, they must be using a masking device," the tactical station replied.

"All right, how soon . . ." Before Calamen could finish talking, a flash of light exploded as a ship re-emerged into real space.

"This is the Third Fighter of Sixth Squad from the Dradon station. The station is under attack by Pirates. Vencor does not know how much longer he will be able to hold them off," the female fighter pilot called over the audio frequency.

"All fighters, the maneuvers have been canceled. Dock with your carrier and prepare for battle. Dradon station fighter, I want you to dock with the Molvean and resupply your fighter," Colonel Calamen ordered over the communications.

"Sir, do you think we should call for reinforcements in case they are needed? If the science station Dradon is under heavy attack, our cruisers and fighters may not be enough to stop them," the communication station asked.

"Do not worry. I've sent a secret message to High Grand Admiral Calamen. I just hope we are able to hold out until the reinforcements can arrive. Once all the fighters have boarded their carriers, give the order to launch for the Dran Colhan system," Calamen ordered.

"Sir, what about you know who, should we request to have him sent to Dran Colhan system, as well?" a Lieutenant asked while walking onto the bridge.

"My son is very busy right now. Besides, do you think we should find out how the situation is looking before we make that decision? If we truly need him, then I will call for him. He can be here in just a few hours," Colonel Calamen replied to the lieutenant while turning to face him.

As he turned to face the lieutenant, he started to remember, "Sir, subject 1103's physical condition is at seventy-five percent. I believe we can still run this test without any problem accruing," a female's voice said while walking up.

"The seventy-five percent physical condition of 1103 is actually amassing. The fact is, he is still confused about what has happened to him. We have shown him a few different defense styles in Martial Arts," a male voice said from a hidden obviation room.

"You are telling me, even though he is feeling sorrow for the Drazarian's loss, not to mention for his own problems, and you still think we should proceed?" the female doctor replied.

"I do not know what you learned during medical school, but you should expect the unexpected. Remember, this he is still a live humanoid being," Lieutenant Colonel Calamen replied while turning to the young doctor.

"All right, send in the training robotic assistance," the Doctor called. Then he thought, *Now let us see how well subject 1103 can determine friend from foe, and if the subject can stay alive.*

As the three doctors and Lieutenant Colonel watched, they noticed subject 1103 had stood up and began to look around. *Come on, now. Show us what you have learned. Those training bots are programmed to increase the intensity of this training exercise. This can also mean that you can and will be killed,* Calamen thought as the first robot appeared in the distance.

"Um, are they supposed to be my new toys? Remember, I am not the fool you think I am just because I am from what you call an unsivalized planet. That does not make me a fool!" subject 1103 replied as his hands started to glow.

In a single motion, the subject slammed his hands together and shoved them forward as everyone in the observation deck suddenly started to hear the air in the room increase into blowing wind.

Before the doctors could analyze what was happening, a small tornado exploded out of nowhere and shot from his hands—straight into a robot.

"Is that all you have for me? I know you can do better than that, so come on and prove it!" the subject demanded.

Suddenly, twenty robots appeared in front of him. "I thought you said there were only six. What is it you are trying to prove here?" Calamen demanded from the doctors.

"We are under orders. No matter how much we disapprove of it, this comes directly from the Alliance Council. We are to see how well the subject's enhancements have improved his abilities," the doctor responded.

Suddenly, the room started to glow brighter just as a large gust of wind shattered the glass of the observation deck.

As the observers watched, a large tornado launched from the subject's hands and went twenty different directions.

"You told me this was a normal test, a test everyone has to go through. I hope you can do better than that," subject 1103 told them as he sat down and started to play with a robot's casing.

"What is he doing to that robot's shell?" the female doctor asked.

Suddenly, to their surprise, subject 1103 reached over and ripped a finger from the two robots that were closest to him. *Yes, now that will do nicely,* the subject thought.

As a glow of light disappeared, they noticed the subject laying the two fingers on the ground. "Torches—he turned those laser fingers into torches. How did he know about those fingers?" the doctor said.

"I don't know. I think he's turning those parts in clothing," the lieutenant Colonel responded as subject 1103 stood up and placed a hand through a shoulder joint. Just as the subject turned to face them, he snapped two connecting joints together. "Are you done with me, or do I have to sit here and take this from you? I have better things to do with my time than just staying here and playing," 1103 said as he walked off.

"Now what do you think he is doing? I have seen his so-called training results. The teachers did not place this information in their reports. I cannot believe the subject has that much power," another doctor said.

A short time later, they noticed 1103 dragging another robot's frame back to his work site and starting to tear into the chest cavity with delight. "I am sure glad he is doing that to a machine and not to me," a female doctor said with the sounds of agreement echoing through the room.

As they watched, 1103 tore out the wiring and circuitry. They noticed a small microchip was now sitting in the palm of his hand.

"What is he going to do with that? All the examinations we have done did not dictate any robotic kaponites with in his body. If I am right, all that circuit can do is enhance the abilities of the robots by fifty percent," the female doctor said out of confusion.

Suddenly 1103 took the circuit and started to weld it to the chest plate of his new armor. "Now what is he doing?" Lieutenant Colonel asked.

"I think we may have a problem. I just reread the notes from his training. The teachers kept repeating that all he would do is use enough effort to learn the lessons, and that was it. I think he has been playing around with his teachers and us all this time," Lieutenant Colonel stated.

"Send in the remaining thirty training robots. This time, we will see what he is capable of doing. This time, I want you to place their identification mode to kill all intruders," the female doctor ordered while watching 1103 connect a left and right arm piece to his chest plate, followed by a left and right leg pieces.

"Ma'am, they are inside and moving extremely fast and hard toward their target," another doctor replied.

Suddenly, the room exploded with wind, followed by a loud explosion as the lieutenant Colonel and the Doctors all dove for cover. Loud sounds echoed throughout the room of metallic objects being slammed around.

"What was that? Where did that wind come from?" Calamen asked while climbing back to his feet.

While looking down into the room, to their surprise, they noticed 1103 snapping his fingers, and the room fell silent once again.

"What was that? Computer, replay the last three minutes of the recording from the room," the female doctor ordered.

"Ma'am the video is ready," the computer answered.

"Play it now. Also, play the recording in slow motion!" Lieutenant Colonel ordered while still trying to hold his composure.

As the robots appeared in front of 1103, he generated a large, glowing ball of energy in both hands. Suddenly, the energy just disappeared, and the room filled with heavy winds, just as the camera picked up 1103 generating what appeared to be two energy weapons in his hands. Suddenly, the energy weapons disappeared as 1103 threw a kick and launched an energy attack from his feet. A few seconds later, 1103 raised his hand into the air and snapped his fingers as the large wind attack ended as the new armor fell to pieces.

Before Calamen knew what had happened, his mind was snapped back to reality, just as his Lieutenant started to speak again.

"Colonel, Colonel, did you hear what I said? We need to get a message to him. That way, we will have all reinforcements we'll need," the lieutenant demanded.

While the colonel and the lieutenant locked their gaze on each other, both were determined to get their way. The Colonel did not want both graduating classes to suffer in this extreme-need simulation. As for the lieutenant, he wanted someone that knew how to deal with the Pirates in their own way to handle the command of the ground units. This way, if they have to send in the ground units to fight just to take back the control of the station, they would have a commander that would be able to handle any problem that might arise.

"You seem very anxious to have my son here. Are you that afraid of the worst possibility?" Colonel Calamen asked the lieutenant.

"No, it's just that he's the strongest in the Galactic Alliance is all," the lieutenant replied.

"The truth is, my son is just skillful in the different styles of Martial Arts. He is actually very weak. I mean, have you ever seen him physically pick someone up and throw them?" Colonel Calamen said.

"Well, no, I haven't," the lieutenant replied.

"He combines his different stratigies with the combat styles he's learned. The stratiges and fighting styles combined make him strong," the colonel added.

"Sir, all fighters are secured in the hangers, and all three cruisers are launching for the Dran Holhan system," the Tactical station called as the first two cruisers disappeared in a blinding flash of light.

Back on the station, everyone on the bridge could hear lasers being fired, followed by screams of the innocent being killed when a loud explosion shook the inside of the station. With quick steps, Commander Vencor was now standing over the security officer's station.

"Tell me, did that explosion came from inside the station, or was it exterior? I need to know how many Pirates have made their way inside. How far inside of the station are they?" the commander demanded.

"It came from inside the station—the emergency door for sections Fifty Two A and Fifty Two B was just removed by a Class 2 explosive. Sir, what could it be that they are after, whatever it may be that they are doing? They are doing their best to keep from damaging it," the tactical station reported.

"Lieutenant, I want you and your troops to remove those filthy Pirates from my station," Commander Vencor ordered.

"Sir, that is what I have been trying to tell you. They have boarded the station in two parties. The first group that landed are making their way to this location from the east hanger. The second group is coming toward us from the west. This control room is their first, primary target. If you do not leave right now, you will surely die," the lieutenant demanded.

"No, Lieutenant, we Pirates are already here," Daggen said as the maintenance duct hatch dropped opened. "This means the commander will cooperate with us and give us what we want, or we'll kill everyone on the station that isn't dead already."

After Daggen dropped down from the maintenance duct, the yellowish-orange creature stood up in his grayish-silver uniform. With his red hair pulled back, he looked around and started to grin. "I want everyone on the bridge to listen carefully. If anyone tries anything—anything at all—we'll blow this station up with you right along with it! I want those experimental weapons, and I want them now, Commander." Daggen ordered.

"Never. I will never allow you or anyone else use those weapons against the Alliance. I would rather die first," Vencor replied with contempt in his eyes.

Suddenly, the door flew open, and the Pirates started to fill the room. When Vencor turned to look at the door, he felt a hand on his uniform and his back hitting the floor—hard. As his back hit the floor, Vencor noticed his vision becoming blurry. "What are you going to do with us?" Vencor asked as his voice trailed off.

"Take them to a storage compartment. We'll use that compartment as the brig. After that, I want those weapons located. Get moving now!" Daggen ordered.

"Yes, sir. All right, you mangy, Alliance dogs. Let's get moving. You try anything stupid, and we won't hesitate to kill you," a harsh, male voice said.

As the fighting raged in space around the Drandon Station, there was another fight being staged in the Alliance territory on the planet Trolena in the Centauri system. One of the participants was just leaving the Alliance Academies Space Station, heading for the Centauri system.

"All right, recruits, this is it. You asked for a real taste of what it feels like to fight Pirates. Our Intelligence has found a group of Pirate's hiding on the Planet Trolena. You are to ambush and capture as many Pirates as you can. If you have to shoot them to save yourself, or a fellow team member, then shoot to kill. Let us review the main objective. Capture, if necessary and kill if unavoidable—those are your orders," Grand Admiral Blake told the recruits as his cruiser left the Academy station hanger.

Somewhere in the Centauri system, two unknown beings were watching six Alliance Cruisers and a single war ship beginning their run for the planet's atmosphere.

"It's time to check on our creation, shall we? Oh look here—the beings in this dimension are closing in on our creation. Poor Trayon. It is too bad that had lost him," a strange voice said while watching the ships closing in on the planet.

"Yes, we shell check on our creation. Trayon losing the being whom he had altered with the plans we provided was a bad thing. Glad the Galaxy warriors do not know of our intervention, I am. This dimension would be destroyed by the Galaxy Warriors for our intervention in this dimension, it would be." A second voice replied as the ships enter the atmosphere and started descending to the planet's surface.

Meanwhile at Alpha camp . . .

"Sir, we have just been notified that we have Pirates inbound from space. The intelligence information we received was correct. Sir, what are we going to do with the recruits? We cannot allow them to face those deadly Pirates head on!" a voice said while entering into the command tent.

"Don't panic. Get those recruits into those new special suites and hurry up. Also, send recruit Breaker to me immediately. You need to find another person to pull sentry duty to replace him, even if it is you," the commander said while looking at a dark, green-haired, red-eyed Corporal. "Also, Johnson, make sure you place squads of one hundred and fifty recruits with three commanding units in four different locations."

"Yes, Sir. Ma'am, how bad is the situation actually looking?" the corporal asked the young-looking, middle-aged woman.

"Just do as you are ordered!" she replied.

As the corporal ran out of the tent, she sat in her chair and placed a hand on her face. She was thinking, *For being only twenty-eight, why do I feel like I am sixty?* After the corporal left, she was bent over a table looking at a map when she started to think.

"Hand-to-hand training instructor Lieutenant Colonel Melody reporting as requested, Ma'am."

"Oh yes, Melody, thank you for coming so quickly. Now, let us get right to the point. We have a new recruit at the Academy, and I do not want you or any one of your recruits to invoke this recruit to a fight. This recruit is the only one of his kind. He was also just saved a few weeks ago from Pirates. If you see a recruit you do not recognize, please have your recruits avoid any kind of hostile intentions with him. One last thing—he looks like he could be an Earthling. That is all," High Grand Admiral Calamen told her.

"I know there are a few hot-headed recruits that would like to show off. No one is supposed to engage this new recruit at any costs. *Do you understand?*" Grand Admiral Blake added.

"Yes, ma'am and sir. May I ask, if that does happen, what would be the outcome?" Melody replied.

"One or more recruits could end up in the medical bay with broken bones, or worse—one could be killed. Now, this conversation is over. You need to get back to your class." Kristy Calaemn answered.

"One last thing. If you happen to see this recruit, you may interact with him. Just don't provoke him at any cost. He is extremely dangerous. Just notify us if he starts to show hostile intentions," Mom added before dismissing the young woman.

"Ma'am and sir, I copied, and I will notify you if and when I see the recruit. If he is as dangerous as you claim, I am sure I will be able to handle him on my own." Melody answered while saluting.

"I do not care how skillful you are, your orders are to not provoke or engage him at any cost! Do I make myself clear?" Grand Admiral Blake demanded.

"Sir!" she replied just before she turned and walked out of the room.

What is wrong? Why does the new recruit make them worry so? I know. His family must be of royalty and they do not want him hurt. They must have come up with that story just to scare everyone, the lieutenant Colonel thought.

Five minutes later, as she entered the training room . . .

"Now listen up, maggots. We have new orders from our superiors. We have a new recruit here on the station . . ." Melody's voice trailed off as she noticed her recruits circled around in a group.

"What's going on over there? Recruit Emerson, what is this all about?" She asked while walking up to the circle.

"Ma'am, Recruit Riggers was the last one to finish his training, just like you wanted. Suddenly, a recruit we've never seen just barged in and demanded us to leave, just so he could start his training," the recruit replied without looking away from the fight.

"Hit him, Riggers. Teach that runt he cannot talk to us like that!" the crowd demanded.

"I have told you, this is my training time. Leave now! On your way out, don't forget to apologize to that young child," a male voice said.

"Ma'am, you need to get those people out of here before they get *huwt*," a young child's voice called out while tugging on Melody's shirt.

"Well, hello there. What is your name?" Melody asked the child.

"My name is *Shamawwa*, and I'm three years old," the young child replied while holding up four fingers.

"Well, *Shamawwa*, it is nice to meet you. My name is Melody. Now, can you tell me what you are doing in here?" the lieutenant Colonel asked.

"No, it is 'Shamarra,' you Alliance dogs!" the unknown voice said.

"I'm here with my *bwothew*. He's a Galaxy Alliance Wecruit," the child replied while beaming.

"You are? Can you point him out to me? I will need him to take you to a safe location while the recruits training," Melody asked while kneeling down to the child's eye level.

"Commander, do not talk to that Drazarian. She's not worth the effort!" a female's voice demanded.

"I'm not a *Dwazawian*. I'm an *Eawthling*!" the child demanded just before sticking her tongue out at the recruit.

"Now, that's even worse. I guess I'll have to teach you some manners!" The recruit replied with anger in her voice.

"If my sister wants to be an Earthling instead of a Drazarian, then she's an Earthling. This is your last warning. If you do not apologize and then leave, I will have to punish you. If anyone else even thinks about touching her again, I will kill them," the unknown voice replied.

"Why, I'm going to—" Before Riggers even finished his sentence, he threw a punch toward the unknown recruit.

To everyone's surprise, the unknown recruit grabbed the arm and twisted it as a loud snapping sound filled the room.

"My arm! You broke my arm!" Riggers cried out in pain.

"Ma'am, you need to get them out of *hewe*, my *bwothew* can't be able to hold back *mush* longer. Mommy, get Aunty, Uncle, and Daddy down here now, we have a problem." Shamarra calmly said while noticing her brother's eyes flashing from hazel glow to red glow.

"I understand. I've just notified them. Do you think he can hold out for at least five minutes?" Mom asked.

"No, Mom. Activate training robots maximum level. Reinforce this room to the maximum level. Activate the clear blaster wall now," the unknown male said while holding his head.

"Attention, all personal, we have a High Level Red Alert in Training Room Alpha. Medical teams, stand by for further instructions. Security teams, get the restraints ready, and all personell inside the room—evacuate now," Mom ordered.

Before Melody realized what was going on, Riggers body was thrown past the blaster wall just before closing and locking into place.

"Lieutenant Colonel, I thought you understood what your orders were. How did this happen?" Lieutenant Colonel Calamen said as he entered the room.

"Daddy, it is not *hew* fault, one of the *wecwuits* decided to hit me just because I am a Dwazawian. I was in *hewe* waiting on big *bwothew* when these people came walking in," Shamarra said while running over to him.

As the three moved closer, they noticed the recruit holding his head and looking at them.

"Allan, are you all right?" Kristy asked softly.

Suddenly, his head snapped up, and his eyes were glazed over. All she could see was hatred in his burning, red eyes.

"Let me out! I want to kill you all!" the recruit cried out with anger.

Suddenly, a training robot appeared and shot at the recruits while the rest charged toward him.

"I will take care of you later. First, let me have some fun with these new toys," the recruit replied while moving his head to dodge the laser blast.

As he turned to face the training robots, everyone noticed the that recruit's body mass started to expand while walking toward the robots. Right before their eyes, they noticed the recruit's speed starting to speed up, and his abilities and his strength started to increase as he tore into the first charging robot.

Within two minutes, the last robot fell to the floor in pieces. Then, they noticed the recruit's eyes were focused back on them.

"Now you are mine. Tornado drill," the recruit said as everyone noticed this hands glowing with chi energy.

"Mom, drop the oxygen down by eighty percent, and then keep gradually dropping the oxygen until he faints." Lieutenant Colonel told the AI. Three minutes later, the recruit's body fell to the floor, unconscious, with a loud thud.

"What was that all about?" Melody asked. Suddenly, she was snapped back to reality when she heard a loud explosion outside. "What is going on out here?" she demanded to know.

"Recruit, if you're not careful, you could kill someone by playing with those detonators!" a familiar voice yelled while approaching two fellow recruits.

"Recruit, I thought you had orders to see me! Get in this tent, now!" Melody demanded while the three recruit looked at her.

After he entered the tent, she noticed he was standing by the table where she had the map laying.

"A tent. With the amount of technology we have from the Alliance, all they give us is a tent," the recruit stated.

"Mom says, in some cases, we just need to get back to the basics," Melody replied while smiling.

"Ma'am, you wished to see me?" a young, male voice asked as he realized he was being watched.

"It's been a while, Phantom. Still wearing all black, I see. You've been told about what is going on, right?" she asked the short, black-haired teenager.

"Yes, Catherina. I am aware, in fact, that I was the one who came up with this idea," he replied to the young commander.

"I should have known when your Aunt High Grand Admiral Kristy Calamen told me she was going to have you help us with their training," she told him while walking up to him. "By the way, did you grow a few inches? The last time I saw you at the Academy, you stood five-feet-nine-inches. At least your hazel eyes are still beautiful, as always."

"You're still trying to flatter me to go out with you. In my race, you are only eighteen, and in your race you're now twenty-eight, right? We can discuss this later, but for now, let's get ready for this drill. We will need our recruits to hide in these locations that I've indicated on the map in green. The locations indicated in red are the areas they would be expecting us to be hiding at. The locations in yellow are the areas where they will be using as their drop points," he said while looking deep into her emerald green eyes as she hugged him.

"Ma'am, you're fraternizing with a recruit. You know that is forbidden. You could lose you command!" Corporal Johnson said while walking into the command tent.

"Ma'am, I will meet those Pirates head on like you've requested. How could she when she's a friend of my family? I do not think anyone would go against my will," Phantom replied as he walked past the corporal.

"Johnson, I would not say anything to that recruit, nor try anything against that recruit. If you do, you may end up either in the medical bay or dead," she told him while looking worried.

"Why do you say that, ma'am? Is there something special about that person?" the corporal asked with a confused voice.

"Let's say I've seen his training. I've been an observer for sixty-five percent of his off station training. Some of that training actually turned into real missions. I would have been killed if he had not been there. Just watch what you say around him, or you may find yourself out of a job," Melody replied while walking back into the tent.

CHAPTER 2

"I'VE BEEN TOLD that the Alliance dogs just sent a few recruits to this planet. Trayon has ordered us to capture as many recruits as we can. As for the rest, we are to destroy them. He wants to re-create that experiment he had been working on three years earlier," an elderly male's voice said.

"Driggs, are you actually expecting us to fool their sensors with these stolen Alliance ships?" the second male said while looking at a gray haired one-eyed old Pirate.

"Yes you fool, our intelligence checked on that. For my understanding, they don't know we have killed the crew and stolen these cruisers. Now, get your gear ready, and let's go hunting for recruits," Driggs replied while looking at a brown-haired, middle-aged man.

"You may be my son, but at times I think you received your brains from your mother's side of the family. This time, boy, you're not using that brain of yours at all. We are to do as we are told. Trayon will pay us a king's ransom if we can get him those recruits," Driggs told his son.

Back on the planet's surface . . .

Beep, beep! The recruits arm computer sounded.

"Computer, identify ships inbound," the recruit demanded while looking up at the sky.

Beep, beep! the computer sounded a second time.

"What is going on? The Drandric and her fellow ships were stolen from the Alliance," the recruit said as the names of the inbound ships appeared on the computer screen.

"Let us take the map and get the recruits to the safe zones. Our information says we have seven hours before they arrive to prepare. Now, let's get ready!" Commander Melody told Corporal Johnson.

"Get those recruits out of here! Send them to those marked locations on the map that I have highlighted in green," the recruit ordered walking back to them.

"Who do you think you are, talking to her like that?" Johnson demanded to know.

"Just do as the Atherian tells you to do," Commander Melody ordered.

He's the Altherian? I have heard all the rumors of a single Altherian existing and having unknown origins and skills. Now I will be able to see why everyone is so ecstatic about this guy, the corporal thought.

"Johnson, take squads one, two, and three to the south location. Marie, squads four, five, and six will go to the north location. Broaden, squads seven, eight, and nine will move west, and this will leave Doug with squads ten, eleven, and twelve for the east location. Wait for the signal to move in. The Altherian and I with squads thirteen and fourteen will stay here at the command post." Commander Melody told them before dismissing them.

As the commanders and the recruits ran off to their locations, Melody heard, "Ma'am, how bad is this, actually? I mean, I have family I would like to see again!" a recruit declared while walking up behind her.

"Don't worry. Everyone will be fine. Colonel Melody, I will take command now. All I want you and these recruits to do is stand by for my instructions. Do I make myself clear?" the Altherian said while activating a spot on his shoulder near the collar.

"I was hoping you would. Just tell us what you want us to do. We will do it the best that we can. Just remember that we do not have the same training you have received," Melody told him as she noticed a helmet had formed around his head.

"Just stay here, and I will check things out. I will notify you from there," the Altherian replied.

While looking at him, all she could see through the visor were his red, glowing eyes, "Grand Admiral Blake is going to be here in seven hours. Do you think we can last that long?" she asked.

"We can last up to forty-eight hours if we actually need to," he replied in a calm voice just before disappearing right in front of them.

"Ma'am, if it is the Drandric approaching the landing zone, then why do we have to hide at all?" Johnson asked in a confused tone.

"You did not read the memo mom sent out last week, did you?" she asked.

"No," he replied while trying to hide the confusion in his voice.

"To make this short, the Drandric was stolen by Pirate raiders. They slaughtered her crew and took the warship for themselves. This happened with the other six cruisers in the 109 fleet," Melody replied as she watched the recruits run through different emotions.

"What are we going to do? I mean, we are only trainees. We do not have the skills to handle an actual combat situation against Pirates," a female recruit said as she started to cry.

"Alliance recruits do not cry. Stop that now, or I will fail you here and now," Corporal Johnson demanded.

"Corporal!" Melody yelled. "Take it easy. Most Alliance recruits do not see actual combat until after graduation. This was just unexpected. Who among us would have known this would happen?" the commander said to them in a soft, calm voice. Suddenly, she touched her right ear. "Of course you would. Just shut up. Do not make me tell my aunt on you!" Melody just blurted out.

"Ma'am, who were you where just talking to? Do you have a transmitter in your ear?" Johnson asked.

"That was the Altherian. He is using a secured line just so he can listen to everything we say," Melody replied while thinking, *Uncle Blake, I hope you can back us up. I am having a really bad feeling about this.*

"All units, this is Colonel Melody. Do not move until you see my signal. I repeat, do not move until you see my signal. We do not know how many Pirates there are. If the Pirates have reinforcements on the way, we need to defend ourselves with the fewest casualties that we can. Just stay put for now and keep out of sight," she called over the tactical channel.

"If I may ask, ma'am, what could your aunt do to him that you cannot?" the corporal asked.

"Oh, that is easy. She could make him shut up and keep all of his comments to himself. She could also do something that he really does not like," she replied.

"So, tell us. What is it he does not like?" he asked her as they watched the ships land.

"All right. Get ready, everyone. It looks like they have just landed!" she told the two squads of recruits.

"No, do not engage, yet. We need to know how many—" Before she could finish, a loud explosion echoed through the air.

"Ma'am, what just happened?" The corporal asked in a confused tone.

"It looks like the Altherian is doing what he does the best—making others mad," she said while placing a hand over her face.

"Okay, I am sorry. I know you are a specialist. Yes, we would like to live to see tomorrow. Just finish up, so we can clean up," she said in a low voice.

Five minutes earlier, the Altherian was blending in with the thick vegetation known as "trees." He watched the Alliance ships starting their final approach to the landing zone. *I need to check what is happening at base camp,* he thought as he activated a switch for secured link.

Suddenly, he heard from his arm computer, "Corporal!" Melody yelled. "Take it easy. Most Alliance recruits do not see actual combat until after graduation. This was just unexpected. Who among us would have known this would happen?" the commander said to them in a soft, calm voice.

"I expected this to happen. Whenever the Pirate Guilds hear of our away-training missions, they always show up. That is why Aunt Kristy wanted me to be here as well," the Altherian told her through a microphone on his computer.

"Of course you would. Just shut up, and do not make me tell my aunt on you," the Altherian heard her reply.

"Now, you do not have to make threats. All right, I will give you more information when I can. For now, just sit tight," he replied.

"All units, this is Colonel Melody. Do not move until you see my signal. I repeat, do not move until you see my signal. We do not know how many there are, or if the Pirates have reinforcements on the way. We need to defend ourselves with the fewest casualties that we can. Just stay put for now and keep out of sight," he heard over the tactical channel.

After shutting his microphone off, he thought, *All right, now let us see what you boys are after.*

As he slowly made his way to the landing site, he noticed the Cruiser had already landed and started to lower the ramp, just as the war ship finally started to power down.

This is not good from the look of things. By the amount of Pirates that I have seen disembarking from those cruisers, we will be out numbered if those recruits get in my way, he thought as his hand hand slid around to his backpack.

"Colonel, I am engaging . . . and keep those recruits out of my way!" he told her.

"No, do not engage yet, we need to know how many—"

The Altherian rushed out and threw a detonator at the Pirates. A moment later, the detonator exploded as it shredded through several Pirates. "I do not have time to argue. Did you forget that I am a specialist? This is my job. Do you want to see tomorrow? If so, then shut up and stop your consent complaining!" the Altherian demanded as he rushed the remaining Pirates.

"Okay, I am sorry. I know you are a specialist. Yes, we would like to live to see tomorrow. Just finish up so we can clean up," he heard before turning the communication frequency off.

"What is this entire racket? I told you to keep things quiet, had I not?" Driggs said while exiting the Drandric.

"Father, look over there. Who is he? Is he an Alliance recruit, an Officer, or is he just someone who was stranded?" a male voice said from behind.

"I do not know, Barecks. Now, why don't you get back in there and use the guns to stop him. Or do I have to do everything myself, son?" Driggs asked.

"No, Dad, I'm more then capable of handling the weapons myself," Barecks said as he walked back into the Drandric.

"I want you all to leave and never come back. Leave the Drandric and the rest of her fleet here," the Altherian told them as he shoved a palm into one of the Pirate's throat.

"How dare you talk to us like that! No one tells The Drionic Guild what to do!" one of the Pirates demanded while three others started to square off with the Altherian.

"I can. Now, get out of my face and off my planet!" the Atherian demanded as both of his hands started to glow.

"Like this, Ice Storm!" a Pirate yelled while punching at the Atherian.

"You're pathetic," the Altherian said while smiling just before he jumped.

"That's what you get for defying our will. Come on, let's get what we're here for." a Pirate demanded while laughing.

"Sorry, boys" a voice said from above them. As the person looked up, the Atherian's fist connected with the Pirate's face. "Whatever you are after, it is not going to be here. The only thing here is a training exercise," he replied as he stood up from a squatting position.

Before everyone knew what was happening, they heard a loud discharge, while over the loudspeaker they heard, "Die, you Alliance dog, ha, ha, ha . . ." a male's voice said.

As the smoke cleared, Driggs asked, "Did anyone see where he went?"

"What do you mean? He was completely incinerated, sir," his Lieutenant told him.

"Are you a fool, Nichgal? Do you see any ash from someone being incinerated? I definitely don't," Driggs said while back-handing a red-haired man.

"No, sir, I don't," Nichgal said while whipping some blood from his lip.

"Come on, let's finish our job, and then we'll destroy the planet with everyone and everything on it!" Driggs snarled while grinning.

"Colonel, what is going on? Why was there a second explosion?" a recruit asked.

"I do not know. I just hope I hear from the Altherian about what is going on," Melody said while thinking, *I have tried for the last twenty minutes. He is not responding. What is going on and I hope he is all right?*

"Ma'am, look. Someone is coming toward us," the corporal told her.

"I can guarantee they are not with the Alliance. Everyone standby and get ready for anything!" Colonel Melody replied while looking through binoculars.

"There are right over there. Grab as many as you can!" Driggs yelled as he fired a single shot.

"Scatter. I will hold them off the best that I can," the colonel yelled as she threw a detonator.

Suddenly, a cloud of smoke erupted from the location where the detonator had hit the ground. *Yes, that should stop them for a while,* Melody thought as she heard coughing coming from the smoke.

"You're dead, lady. I'll make sure you die slowly and painfully," Driggs said in between his gasps for air.

To everyone's surprise, Colonel Melody started walking toward them as he heard her say, "I do not care who you are. We are members of the Galaxy Alliance, and you are trespassing. *Now leave*"!

A short time later, everyone heard Driggs and the Drionic Guild members just starting to laugh. "Look at this runt," Driggs told them as the colonel stopped right in front of them.

Driggs grabbed Melody. "Now, you've become extremely annoying. I'll just have to kill you."

Suddenly, heavy winds appeared. "I was being nice before, but now you have completely over-stayed your welcome," a male's voice echoed on the winds.

"Is this some kind of a joke? I didn't know the Alliance dogs were so pathetic," Barecks said just before laughing again.

"How dare you call the Galaxy Alliance, *my* Galaxy Alliance, a 'dog' or 'pathetic!' You will let the colonel go and then leave before I decide to change my mind!" a male's voice said out of nowhere.

"You better do as he says. I really do not want to think of what the outcome might be," Colonel Melody said while smiling.

"You're truly pathetic, demanding us to do what you want. You don't even have enough courage to face us," Driggs said with irritation in his voice.

"What? Do you really want me to face you? Fine, I will face you, and you will not like it!" the voice said.

To everyone's surprise, the voice was coming from behind the recruits. As the recruits turned to face the voice, they saw the Altherian standing before them. As the Altherian walked past, they noticed green eyes glowing from inside the helmet.

"What do you think you are doing? If you go and provoke those Pirates, they will surely kill the colonel," Corporal Johnson told the Altherian.

Suddenly, the Altherian shoved an elbow into the corporal's face as he spoke, "Shut up! I know what I am doing. Also, who gave you the right to order me around?"

"My nose—you broke my nose! I will see to it that you will be severely punished," Johnson yelled as he held his face.

"You will gently put her on the ground and step away," the Altherian demanded while approaching Driggs.

"Look here, boys, this recruit thinks he's a comedian. Now, you listen up, boy, even though you hid your face, we all know you're just another frightened, little child," Driggs replied in a skittish voice while pulling out a dagger.

"It sounds like you are the one who is afraid and not him," the colonel replied while looking at the dagger.

"I knew you were alive when we did not see any ashes for your remains," Driggs told him as the Atherian continued to approach.

"If I had been hit by that laser blast, there would be nothing left—not even ashes. Now, do as you are told, and let her go," the Atherian replied.

"Never! We're to capture as many recruits as we can. Now, I'll also take her, as well. Now, round those recruits up, and let's get off of this rock of a planet," Driggs ordered.

"I said let her go!" the Altherian demanded as he stomped a foot on the ground.

"Oh, look, boys. This dog-child of the Alliance is throwing a tantrum," Driggs said while laughing.

Suddenly, Driggs lost his grip of Melody as she was launched into the air by a tornado. Before anyone realized what was happening, the Altherian jumped into the air and caught the colonel before they had hit the ground.

"Allan, are you all right? Allan, answer me," Melody asked in a whisper as she noticed his eyes flashing from green to red.

"I am not Allan. I am just in a little pain," the Altherian replied as he touched a place on both shoulders.

As the sleeves retraced, she noticed black lines running up his forearm and circling around just before the elbow. "Are those gantlets? When did you get those?" she asked him in a worried tone.

"They're not gantlets. What you are seeing is poison running up my arms, and the same for my legs. I may only have a few hours to live," the Altherian told her.

"Allan, is it Elemental Porax Poisoning?" she asked him.

"Yes. Right now, I am too weak, and I am not Allan," the Altherian replied.

"Allan, you must release the stored elemental energy your body has stored," Melody told him.

"My name is not Allan! I am Phantom!" the Altherian yelled with anger as he slapped his hands together and pulled them apart.

As his hand separated, electrical energy shot from one hand to the other, just before he palmed the ground in a squatting position. Then, he suddenly started to stand back up.

As he stood back up, everyone noticed chunks of rock lifting out of the ground from the energy he had slammed into the ground. Suddenly, they heard, "This is half the power of the Altherians," Colonel Melody told the recruits as she started to walk away from Phantom.

"If you want to live, then stay behind me, Melody. Corporal, get those recruits to some cover now," Phantom said as his hands and arms started to turn a bluish green.

"Look at this. The Alliance dog is trying to scare us," Driggs told his men.

"Who is scared? Shards of Earth Blast," Phantom said in an angry voice while touching the two rocks.

To everyone surprise, the rocks started to shatter and then launch with a huge tornado toward the Pirates.

As the shards sliced through the Pirates, all the recruits could see were body parts flying everywhere as blood landed on the ground and the tents, and the unexpecting corporal was drenched from head to toe.

A few minutes had pasted. Everyone noticed the Altherian was back, kneeling on the ground and holding his right arm.

"What is wrong with him? I did not even notice anyone touching him," a female recruit asked.

"He has been poisoned. His body is trying to over-compensate for it," Melody said while kneeling down next to him.

"Leave me alone. This fight is far from being over," Phantom told her as he reached behind his back and pulled out three throwing knives.

"You've killed him . . . you killed my Uncle. I will kill you for that!" a male Pirate said while stepping out from behind a tent with a blaster in his hand.

"That is fine. Just remember, I will die fighting," Phantom said just as he threw the knives and charged toward the Pirate.

Before the Pirate realized what was happening, the blaster flew from his hands when the knives hit it. *What is going on? Who is this Alliance dog?* the Pirate thought as his body froze when he saw Phantom charging toward him.

Just as Phantom's body made contact, the Pirate fell to the ground with a knife in his throat. "Now, this fight is over," Phantom said while walking away from the corpse.

"Ma'am, where did he learn to do that? He is only a recruit, after all," Corporal Johnson said while looking surprised.

"It is true. He has not technically graduated yet. Yet, he is technically a member of the Special Operations Forces Team," Colonel Melody replied with a smile on her face.

"You mean, his Commanding Officers are Lieutenant Daniel and Lieutenant Ian?" Johnson asked with a confused voice.

"No, Colonel Calamen is his commanding officer. I meant, whenever the Special Operations Forces are called out, Mom and High Grand Admiral Calamen order Phantom to go with them. The Altherian is a one of a kind special humanoid breed. Just remember that the next time you truly want to make him mad. Now, let us get this place cleaned up," Colonel Melody told him.

"Yes, Ma'am. By the way, I just want you to know, I am glad you were not hurt," Johnson told her in a concerned tone of voice.

"I was never in any real danger. The Altherian—or Phantom—would never allow a family member to get hurt. Even if we are adapted and even if it is to different sides of the family," she replied just before walking off.

Cousins. They are cousins. I should have figured, Corporal Johnson thought as he ordered the cleanup of the camp.

He watched as several groups of recruits started to run toward the dead Pirates. He heard a small sigh escape from the colonel. Suddenly, his attention was snapped back to their conversation when the word "cousins" floated into his mind. "What 'cousins'? Ma'am, wait for me. What do you mean 'cousins'?" the corporal yelled while running after her.

"He is the adapted son of Colonel Calamen, who is the younger brother to my Aunt High Grand Admiral Kristy Calamen. I, on the other hand, was adapted by Aleena Clouden, who is the younger sister to Grand Admiral Blake, who is married to High Grand Admiral Kristy Calamen," Melody told the corporal as he matched his stride with hers.

"Ma'am, that means you were flirting with your own cousin. Man, that is disturbing," he replied.

"Also, remember, we are from different races. I am a Drocarian, and he is an Altherian. We were adapted into two different families whose only common relation is the marriage of our aunt and uncle. So, in all actuality, we really are not actually cousins," she told him while blushing.

"For my understanding, your mom and the Grand Admiral Blake—they are siblings, correct? The Calamen family does not share the same family tree. High Grand Admiral Calamen is a member of the Calaman clan, and Grand Admiral Blake is a member of the Blake clan. They just happened to fall in love and get married. Am I right?" Johnson asked while holding his head as they walked.

After a small chuckle, she said, "That is right. Now, here is the key point. This is why we are considered family. Our aunt and uncle, on occasion, they will call for family meeting. This means, whether your blood line is of a Calamen, a Blake, or a Clouden, you must report to that meeting. For Phantom, he is a Calamen by adapted name's sake. I am a Clouden by adaption, and we both have Calamen and Blake names, no matter what, so we are ordered to go to the meetings," Melody told Johnson.

"Melody, I am going for a swim. If you would like to join me, get your gear and let us go," Phantom's voice interrupted.

"I will only be a few minutes. Wait for me okay?" she replied while turning to face her cousin.

"Just hurry it up. I will not wait forever on you," he told her while grabbing a box.

"All right, I know our uncle told you to protect me, so protect me until we return to the station. You could just easy up with being overly protected of me. Just remember, I out rank you, no matter what," she replied with a worried look on her face.

"You may think you out rank me. Just remember, I can bust you back down to privet faster than your boyfriend here can say 'ouch'," Phantom told her while walking up to her.

"Go right ahead. You think you are a tough guy, so then explain to me why it is that you could not save your real family," she demanded as the two stared at each other.

Before he could say anything, she realized what she had just said and covered her mouth. Before she could apologize, Phantom turned around and walked away.

"Way to go, ma'am. That shut him up," the corporal said as he watched him walk out of sight.

"I am in for it now. I am defiantly going to get it for that. That specific topic is never supposed to be used against him. I just hope I can fix this little problem before it becomes even worse," Melody said while running into her personal tent.

A few seconds later, Johnson saw her leave her tent and asked, "Ma'am, do you need me to come with you to protect you from him?"

"No, I will be fine. I can handle him without any support," she told the corporal.

"Ma'am, if I need you, where will you be?" Corporal Johnson asked.

"I will be with Phantom at the lake relaxing. If you actually need me for anything, you can call me on my personal communication frequency," she told him over her shoulder while running to catch up with her cousin.

"Why was I told to help out as the acting Lieutenant? Why was I not told the Altherian would be here? Why was I not informed about the colonel and the Altherian being cousins? Who is this so-called Altherian? What does he do for the Alliance?" Johnson asked while a few recruits approached.

"Sir, all the Pirate bodies have been moved to a single grave. What would you like for us to do with them?" a female recruit asked.

"I do not care. Bury them. Burn them and then bury them. Just do something to get those Pirates out of my site," Johnson told them.

"Sir, I hear the Altherian is not a normal recruit. What I have heard from some of the squad commanders is that the Altherian's training is seventeen times more difficult than a regular recruit's training. Most of his time, he is off training in the most vast and harsh regions of the Alliance territory. A few times when he had been deployed, it was under the most extreme conditions. I hear there is no one in the Alliance who is able to handle him as their subordinate," a male's voice told him.

"Recruit, you are training to be one of the Intelligence Officers are you not?" Johnson asked.

"Yes, sir, why do you ask?" the male replied.

"I want you to gather as much information on that Altherian as you can. Just remember, if you get caught, I will deny any knowledge of your actions," the corporal demanded.

"Yes, sir. I will get started right away," the recruit told him just before turning around and walking away.

Good. Now, I should go and check on the colonel. Johnson thought while starting to walk in the same direction as both the colonel and the Altherian had gone.

A few minutes later, Phantom pulled out a small object from the small box. After touching a small, blue button on the object, he threw it onto the water. *Sorry, sis. I'm just going to test it for you,* he thought while climbing onto the flotation device and pushing himself away from the shore. As he floated there, he closed his eyes and started to think . . .

CHAPTER 3

"ARE WE THERE, yet?" a young boy asked from the back seat.

"No, honey, we are not. Go back to sleep, and we will be there before you know it," an older woman's voice replied.

"Mom, I'm not tired . . ." Before the child could finish, a yawn escaped from his mouth.

Suddenly, a bright light engulfed the car. "What is going on? The entire electrical system on the car just died!" an older male's voice demanded to know.

"Everyone, get out of that primitive transportation unit. You will come with us!" a yellowish-orange creature demanded while pointing a strange object at them.

"Why should we? I don't know who you think you are, but you will not threaten my family," a middle-aged male replied while the creature walked over to the car.

Suddenly, his fist connected with the car, "Because, I asked you nicely. However, next, I will help you out of the car, instead," the creature demanded.

"Daggen, Trayon has told us to hurry up. The Galaxy Alliance has found out about our presence here," another strange looking creature replied.

"Tell him we need two more microns," the yellowish-orange creature replied, just as he pulled the engine from the car.

Suddenly, the middle-aged male climbed out of the vehicle and walked toward the rear. After opening the trunk, the woman heard, "Honey, wake the kids and do as he tells you," the middle-aged male replied while collecting the luggage.

Before the family knew what was happening, all five of them were transported to the giant Alien vessel, just before it flew away. Inside the vessel, the family noticed strange-looking creatures running from one location to another. Suddenly, they heard, "Daggen, we have orders to lose the Alliance dogs and meet up with Trayon in the Zynic system," a greened-skinned creature told him while walking up.

"That is three hyper jumps from the Pirates' system. Do you know what he wants us there for? It will be safer if we return to our headquarters," Daggen replied.

"He says he has something to show us, and he has just captured a Drazirian family. We have only two hours to be there," another Pirate replied over the internal communications.

"All right, then. We have our orders, now get going," Daggen told them as he pushed the middle child into the cell before turning to walk away.

Suddenly, he stopped and turned to look at the child. "Is there something you would like to tell me, runt? How about I just call you 'a rodent'?" Daggen replied while looking into the child's eyes.

"Yeah, just remember this—one day when you are lest expecting it, I will kill you. As soon as I can get out of here, I will kill you!" the child yelled at him.

"What is your name, kid?" Daggen demanded to know.

"Don't call me kid, rodent, runt, or anything else you wish to call me. My name is Allan and don't forget it," the child told him with a defiant tone.

"Guard, I want you to give him the black collar. I also want the two big ones to wear blue and red collars. The other two kids, I want you to give orange and pink collars to. After that, I want blood samples," Daggen said as a smile appeared on his face.

"Yes, sir, once the test results are in. What do you want us to do them?" a strange-looking individual replied.

"I do not care. Feed them, shock them, sedate them, or take them to the training room—just keep them quiet," Daggen demanded while walking away.

Suddenly, the Pirate threw an object into the room, "Have a terrible sleep," the Pirate told them as a metallic sound echoed throughout the room.

"What did you—" Before the middle-aged male could finish speaking, the object started dispensing smoke. After two minutes, the family was knocked out cold.

"So how are they doing?" Daggen asked over the Pirate's communicator.

"Not bad. They are all asleep right now. I'm heading for the lab to test their blood," the Pirate replied.

A few hours later . . .

"What did they hit me with?" The middle child asked.

"You have been unconscious for four hours," strange female's voice replied.

"Oh, hey, wait a minute. How are we able to understand you? We had a problem understanding those creatures who abducted us," the child replied.

Suddenly, he heard a moan. "Oh, I hurt . . . why do my ears hurt?" The middle child's father replied while trying to stand up.

Then, they heard a door open, "That is because we placed a nanotech inhibitor insider you ears. That allows us to communicate with each other mare clearly," a familiar voice told them from the door.

"Daggen, what does the TRI Guild want with my family and me?" a strange male's voice demanded.

"Settle down, you Drazirian insect. Your family and these Earthlings are going to help us with an experiment," the yellowish-orange creature replied.

"You name is Daggen, correct?" the young, male child asked.

"Why, yes, how can I help you?" he said in a calm voice.

"You can help me by falling over dead. Just remember this one thing, no matter what you do to me or my family, *I will kill you!*" the child yelled out.

As a smile appeared on his face, Daggen walked toward the child. Suddenly, he stopped. "You know, I could begin to like you, but if you keep that attitude up, I will have no other choice but to kill you, instead," Daggen replied just after back-handing the boy.

Suddenly, everyone heard a loud thud, "If I could only walk, I would make you pay for touching my son. Do you hear me? The next time you touch my son, I will kill you," the boy's father replied with a harsh tone.

"I knew it. You Earthlings are too barbaric. No wonder why the Galaxy Alliance will not allow your planet among ranks. Just shut up. It is time for your family to get their exercise," Daggen replied just as he exited the cell.

"Sure, only if we can change into some kind of cloths to work out in," the middle-aged man replied.

"Fine. Do what ever you wish. Guard, make sure they are in the training room in five minutes," Daggen replied just before an explosion of static escaped from the guard's communications device.

"You heard him. Now move it," the guard replied while ushering them out of the cell.

Meanwhile, in the lab . . .

"Daggen, sir, here are the test results on the Earth family," a scientist told him while looking over a data pad.

"Stop reading and tell me what it says," Daggen demanded to know while watching the family being escorted to the training room.

"The blue collared male is capable of only having thirty percent enhancements done. The red collared female can only have forty percent done. The little one wearing the pink can be enhanced by sixty-five percent. The orange collared male can be enhanced by seventy-five percent—"

Before the scientist could finish, he heard, "What of the black collared child?" Daggen's voice demanded.

"Well, sir, I was just about to tell you. That child, even though he has the same DNA as the other four, we are able to enhance him to one hundred percent," the scientist replied.

I knew there was something about that runt that I liked, Daggen thought. "How soon can we get started?" Daggen asked while turning to look at the scientist.

"We can get started as of tomorrow. My nine assistants will be here then. Just so you know, Trayon will be the pilot of their shuttle," the scientist replied while walking back to his preparation table.

"Good. Just make sure you are ready by tomorrow. Now it is time for me to have some fun," Daggen replied as the door to lab flew open.

Back in the locker room . . .

"Hey, Dad, I'm bored. Let's have some fun," the black collared child told his father while placing a duffle bag on the bench next to himself.

"What do you have in mind? And will it make those creatures mad?" his father responded.

"I don't know, but I think you'll enjoy it," Allan replied with a devilish grin appearing on his face.

"All right. What do you have for me?" the child's father asked. The child pulled out a smaller duffle bag from the big one. "Allan, what do you have in there?" His father asked just as the child opened a smaller bag. Suddenly, Allan started to pull out weapons, "Allan, I thought I told you to leave those at your grandmother's house?" his father told him while smiling.

"Dad, how could I? Oh, come on. You already know how much I enjoy having them around. Besides, how can I leave these wonderful things at Grandma's?" Allan asked while trying to look innocent.

"Well, since you have them here, let's see what you have," his father replied.

"Well, I brought twenty throwing knives, twenty stars, twenty shuriken, two swords, and a gun, for Dad, with three hundred bullets," Allan replied as he placed a foot on the bench.

After laying all sixty throwing objects, the gun, and a single sword on the bench next to the bag, Allan heard from his dad, "I thought you told me you had two swords and not just one? Where is the second sword?"

"Oh, Dad, do I really have to show you that one?" Allan replied while unsheathing the second sword and showing it to his father.

"Why did you bring the Crystal Titanium Bladed sword when you know it is not supposed be seen. That sword was created from special material that no one has ever seen. Just like this gun," his father replied while looking at the clear blade and the gun.

"Both the sword and the energy in my gun are from a site we found a few months ago. I was unable to see just how strong the sword was before our trip," his father replied just as the locker room door opened.

After identifying a Pirate, Allan threw a knife at the Pirate's chest. Before he realized what had happened, everyone heard a loud metallic sound echoing off of the Pirate's armor. After throwing a few more and receiving the same results, he said, "Fine then. It's time to get back to basics," Allan blurted out loud just as he launched another knife. Suddenly, to their surprise, the Pirate fell to the ground with a knife sticking out of his head. "Now that is the only way of handling a rough situation," Allan said while looking at his father.

"Great job. It looks like you've been practicing," his father replied.

"Colonel, I told you I needed new targets for practicing," Allan replied as he slid the sword over his right shoulder.

"Come on, boys. Let's show these aliens who they are messing with," Allan's father told his two sons, just before stepping out into the training room.

Just as Allan's father exited the locker room, he raised the gun up and discharged a single shot into the chest of a charging Pirate. To his surprise, the shot bounced off of the Pirate's armor, just as the Pirate started to laugh. "What's so funny, ugly?" Allan's father asked, just as he discharged a shot into the face of the Pirate.

Suddenly, the Pirate fell to the ground—dead. "Aim for the heads. The rest of their bodies are covered with some sort of armor!" his father yelled, just as he turned to see Allan slicing through the left side a Pirate's body, all the way down to his right leg.

"I don't know what your problem is, Dad. I'm not having any problems with my sword," Allan replied as the body connected with the floor.

Suddenly, Allan's father noticed Allan placing ear phones in his ears, *Now what is he doing?* his father thought as he discharged another shot into a second Pirate's head. Before everyone knew what was going on, alarms started to sound, "Now what is going on?" Allan asked just as he ripped his sword from the side of another Pirate.

The five made there way to the control center, "Allan, go help the other family. Make sure you lead them to the control room," his father demanded as he pointed down a different corridor.

"Understood. I will be seeing you shortly," Allan replied.

Meanwhile, inside the cell . . .

"I wonder how that strange family is doing? I hope they are safe," the older male replied just as he heard the alarms.

"What could be causing that? Are we going to be saved by the Alliance?" the older female asked.

"I don't think that is why the alarms have started. I wonder if the Earthlings are more trouble then what they are worth," a young, male child replied.

"Erick, how do you know they are Earthlings?" the woman asked.

A few minutes later, everyone heard the door open, "That is easy, Amber, because I told him. Earl, take Erick, Amber, and Shamarra and follow me, because we are going to get out of this," Allan replied as he stood in the doorway of the cell. As Allan and the others ran down the hall, Earl started to notice dead bodies just lying on the floor.

"What happened here?" Earl asked.

"Huh? What was that?" Allan asked.

"I asked, 'what happened here?'" Earl replied just as he noticed Allan pulling an object from his ears.

"Sorry, we decided to put a kink in their plans. Now we are getting out of here," Allan told them just as he turned the corner.

A few minutes later, they approached the medical bay. "Daggen, we know you're in there!" Allan heard his father yelled while Daggen was in the medical bay being treated for his injuries.

"You will regret everything that you have done here," Daggen replied just as a grin appeared on his face.

Suddenly, everyone started to feel light-headed, "Dad, what is happening?" Allan asked just as he fell to a single knee.

Suddenly, everything became dark, just as Allan started to hear loud thuds. Before he realized what was happening, his entire world came crashing down with a hard, sudden stop. The last thing he heard from Daggan was, "Tell Trayon what just happened. Also, tell him we are going to need another group of scientists."

A month later . . .

"What happened to me? The last thing I remembered, I was in the lab being worked on . . ." Allan asked after letting out a long, hard moan.

"Come on, honey, sit up. Let me change your bandages." Allan's mother replied.

"Sure. Hey, Mom, where is Dad?" Allan asked while looking around.

"Don't you remember? They killed your father right in front of you while torturing you. They enhanced his muscle mass so much that it shredded his own body while dying a slow, agonizing death," she replied as tears ran down her cheek.

"That can't be what had happened. How could I have not known that?" he replied to her.

"Well you have been acting a little differently, lately," she told him as she took the bandage off his back.

"*Ewe* you go. *Fow is* back. Is *tere anyting ewse* I can *hewp wit, Emiwy*" Shamarra said while handing her a stack of gauze and cloth to wrap Allan's wounds in.

"Thank you, Shamarra. Yes, I could use some help," Emily replied while tossing the old bandages aside.

"Ah, good, you are awake. I need you to follow me. It is time to see what your skills are," a soft, kind-voiced scientist told Allan from the door.

A few minutes later, Allan and the scientist were walking down the corridor. "Tell me, what is your name? Also, why are you being so nice to me?" Allan asked as he looked back to see six armed guards following behind the two.

"My name is not important, and can you explain to me why I should not be nice to our volunteer?" the scientist replied while looking puzzled.

"First, they kidnapped my entire family, then they decided to torture me, and now you're being nice to me and calling me a volunteer. Oh, man, isn't your information all messed up . . ." Allan told him.

"I was told that your memory was erased. That might explain why it seems to you they had kidnapped you," the scientist replied.

"Fine, then, I will play your game. Just remember, it will only be this once. Now, tell me, where are we going?" Allan asked him.

"To the training room. I have already told you, we need to see what your skill level is," the scientist replied just as he stopped in front of a familiar door.

A moment later, the door opened to reveal the training room. On the inside, Allan noticed Daggen was standing there in the center of the floor. "Finally, you arrived. Now, boy, let's see what you are capable of," Daggen demanded while gesturing for the boy to attack.

Suddenly, to Daggen's surprise, the child had connected a foot upside Daggen's head. After stumbling for a moment, "What was that?" the giant creature asked.

"That was called a Tornado Kick. It looks like I caught you off guard. Now try this!" Allan yelled as he threw an upper cut toward Daggen's jaw.

Suddenly, Daggen stopped the attack and started to laugh, "Surprised me—yes. But it felt like a there was nothing backing it. You are a pathetic weakling," Daggen replied just as he connected a fist to Allan's face, followed by a side-kick right to Allan's right rib cage, sending him flying back three feet.

Before anyone could realized how wrong they truly were, Allan stood back up and, this time, when Allan charged toward Daggen, his speed was a lot faster. "All right, ugly, try this on for size," Allan demanded just as he disappeared.

"How can this little runt move that quickly?" Daggen asked while looking at the scientist.

"Trayon's orders were, after every enhancement that was done, take him to the training rooming and allow him to exercise. We have been in here four times about ten hours at a time. Also, try to keep the experimentation down to a maximum of fifteen hours at a time. If you want to damage him, then by all means, torture him for ninety-six hours straight," the scientist replied.

Suddenly the boy appeared right in front of Daggen, just as he connected a fist and a kick right to the side of Daggen's face. "I won't allow you to do this to me or my family," Allan yelled just as his foot connected.

Before Allan realized how much stronger Daggen truly was, Daggen suddenly back-handed him in the far wall. "Daggen, if he dies, what will Trayon say?" the scientist suddenly blurted out.

"I will just tell him that it was your fault," Daggen replied as he began to laugh.

Suddenly, the boy looked up at them. To both the scientist and Daggen's surprise, the look in the boy's eyes appeared to be different than the moment earlier. "Hey, science freak, tell me, why do his eyes look so funny?" Daggen asked with a confused tone.

"I do not know. For what information we have stolen from his planet, his eyes are glazed over. He is in an unconscious state. For an ignoramus like you, that means he should be lying on the floor not moving," the scientist replied, just as the boy charged toward Daggen, even faster than before.

"I'm going to kill him!" Daggen yelled as he swung his massive arm at Allan.

Suddenly, with a confused look on his face, Daggen noticed the Earth child was now hanging upside down on his arm. A grin appeared just as a sharp, hard pain shot through his arm. "My arm, what did you do to my arm? I will make you pay for this, you little runt!" Daggen yelled just before kicking Allan in the face

Suddenly Allan woke up screaming from a hard sharp pain shooting up from his back, "What are you doing to me? I thought we were supposed to be in the training room?" Allan asked him just as a tear started to run down his face.

"Allan, that was three days ago. Do you not know where you are?" the assistant scientist asked him in a confused voice.

"The last ting I remember, was being back-handed into the wall, and when I awoke, I was here with a sharp pain in my back. What are you doing to me?" Allan asked just as he looked up and noticed his little sister being tied down on another table.

"Stop talking to him and inject this one with the brain enhancements and muscle enhancements," the head scientist demanded.

After a few seconds had passed, he suddenly heard a loud scream explode from her, just as he felt another sharp pain shoot through his body. After a few minutes, he noticed blood running from her ears, eyes, mouth, and her nose, just as her muscles split open all the way down to her bones.

"I'm going to kill you for that! What has she ever done to you—to any of you—to deserve this? Let me go, and I will show you what I can *truly* do!" Allan demanded as he pulled on the restraints just to free himself.

"This is wrong. Something about this is all wrong. I might have to check his brain activity just find out what it is," the assistant scientist thought while hooking receptors to the boy's head.

Suddenly, Daggen walked in. "Oh, I see. The runt has finally awoken. How much longer are you going to need to complete his transformation?" he asked while grinning at the corpse of the boy's biological sister.

"Daggen, leave. You need to leave right now, or it will be your fault that we do not have him ready, yet," the assistant told him.

Then, Trayon entered the lab. "What is this I hear, 'you are not ready yet'? I brought a third set of prisoners for you to work on!" Trayon told them in a harsh demanding tone.

"They are almost done with this one, sir. All we have to do is finish the enhancements and then brainwash him into doing what we tell him," Daggen replied.

"Yeah right, like *that* will ever happen. You might as well just kill me!" Allan told them as he struggled to get free.

"Well then, bring the remaining two members of his family in. I want you to kill them. If you do, then all your pain will stop. Go ahead and kill them. Stop your pain—you know you truly want to," Trayon told him just as Allan's mom and older brother were escorted into the lab.

"Trayon, just go ahead and kill me. I promise you this, if you don't, then one day, I will kill you with my own two hands," Allan replied as he started pulling at the restraints frantically.

"Allan, don't worry about us you need to survive. You are the last member of our blood line. You need to live to carry on our family line," he heard his mother tell him just before hearing a loud noise from behind her.

To his horror, he saw his mother's lifeless body fall to the floor as he watched Trayon and Daggen standing over her corpse laughing. "I swear, once I get free, I will kill you for that!" Allan told them with the look of hatred shining from his eyes.

Suddenly, a second sound echoed from behind his brother, "Hurry up with his enhancements," Trayon demanded just as he walked out of the room, leaving both corpses on the floor.

Suddenly, the assistant ran out behind Trayon and Daggen. "Sir, I need to talk with you. The enhancement we have tried infusing into his body has not worked. So far, the only alteration we were successful are the alterations we have done to his eyes. His brain is showing some weird activity that I have never seen before. I need to know if he is or is not a volunteer," the assistant told Trayon.

"That is need to know basis, and you do not need to know. You have your orders, or should I refuse the Korra any and all activities regarding this project," Trayon replied in a humble voice.

"Fine, sir, I may have to do as you command, but just remember, I do not have to like it," the assistant replied just as he turned to walk back into the lab.

A few minutes later . . .

"Let me go. I promise I'll make sure your deaths are quick and painless." Allan demanded as he continued to struggle with the restraints.

"You may want to calm down. Hurting yourself will not help the two corpses," the assistant told him in a kind voice while turning to look at the brain scan results.

"Why? Why are they doing this to me?" Allan asked in a strange voice.

"They want a bioengineered weapon or the ultimate weapon. The weapon is supposed to be able to handle any opponent and any situation that may arrive. For what I believe, you are a prisoner being used as an experiment," the assistant told him.

"So why don't you just let me and the others go!" Allan yelled out in the strange voice.

"I wish I could, except I cannot. The contract my guild has with Trayon prevents me from helping you. I am under orders to alter you as much as we can," the assistant told him as his eyes widened.

"That is just perfect. Then explain to me, why do my eyes burn like nothing I have ever felt?" Allan asked in a harsh voice.

As the assistant turned, he noticed a quick, red flash of light exploding from Allan's eyes. "I have a question for you. Why do you not remember walking in here with me three days earlier?" the assistant asked.

"I remember walking in here—like I remember telling you to get off of this vessel before I killed you," Allan's voice said with a hint of pleasure.

"You are not the one called 'Allan,' now are you?" the assistant asked while walking around the table Allan was strapped to.

"Now, why would I want to be that little pathetic weakling? Why would I want to be like him when I could be stronger than that and kill every last one of you?" Allan's voice replied.

"For all the medical information I have read form this child's home world, I think we are going to have a problem."

As the weeks went on the enhancements continued, and the Drazarian family started to become smaller and smaller. "Allan, come over here, and I will to change out your bandages," amber told him in a kind, loving voice.

"All right, Mom. I'm sorry about everything that is going on," Allan told her in a soft, painful tone.

"That's all right, Allan. The three of us must stay together. Codie, I'm sorry, but your family does not have any kind of future," amber replied to a teenage male.

Suddenly, Daggen pushed three more individuals into the cell. "Runt, you better follow me. I may just decide to kill these three individuals," Daggen demanded.

"No, I am going to stay right here. My body is in pain from the enhancements you have done. I need to rest before any more enhancements can be done," Allan told him.

"Are you stupid? I was not requesting—I was ordering you to follow me. This is for the next set of training," Daggen demanded from the boy.

"Daggen, I told you I would bring the child when he is ready for the next stage in the training and enhancements," the assistant scientist told him while walking into the cell.

"I am under orders from Trayon to finish up the musical portion of his training and to begin with the fighter simulation. Now, do not get in our way if you know what is good for you!" Daggen yelled while getting close enough to the scientist's face where he could smell Daggen's foul breath.

"No, you better listen to me. There is something wrong with this child and his DNA makeup. What we really need to do for him before it is too late is to take out all the enhancements that we have already done before we regret this mistake. Besides, the next steps in the enhancements are going to be to his brain," the assistant scientist replied.

"I will not allow you to enhance my brain and then have it explode inside my head just like my sister's," Allan told him just as his muscle mass started to expand slightly.

A monster—why did they want to create a monster? We just enhanced his muscles, and now he can already control it, the assistant thought just as Allan stood up.

"Fine, when should we get going?" Allan's replied in his strange voice while the newly arrived family looked at him.

"Is that normal for him?" the male teenager asked.

"He wasn't always like this. Then again, none of us are truly like this," amber replied while placing her back to the wall.

"Don't worry, Mother, if I decide to kill anyone, it would first be the Pirates," Allan's strange voice told her without looking.

"Just do me a favor and don't overdo it, all right?" she told him.

"Oh, look at this. The runt is threatening us," a guard told the scientist.

"You should not push your luck with this one. He will kill you, and there will not be anything that I can do to stop him," the assistant replied.

"Yeah right, like this little runt could actually . . ." Suddenly, the guard's voice trailed off, just as he looked down to see Allan had shoved something sharp into his abdomen.

"I told you not to call me by that name!" Allan's strange voice demanded just as he pulled out the object.

"How . . . how did you get a weapon? Who gave it to you?" the guard asked as he stumbled backward.

"What, you don't like my homemade knives?" Allan's strange voice asked just as he swung a second knife at the guard.

To everyone's disbelief, Allan's knife had cut four inches from one side of the abdomen to the other. "I told you not to push your luck. Now, child shell, we get going," the assistant asked while gesturing toward the door.

"Fine, let's get this over with," Allan's strange voice demanded.

Before anyone could say a word, another guard entered the cell and removed the dying guard from the cell. "Let's get you to the medical bay," the second guard told him.

After a few tries in the simulator, the assistant realized that no matter how hard they tried to push the child, their efforts were never going to work. "See, Trayon, I told you. He is unable to comprehend how the controls work for that fighter simulator. His brain cannot understand what it is supposed to do. We labeled each component and what it does, but his brain cannot read the label or understand what that label means," the assistant told him while handing Trayon the results.

"Then enhance his brain. I was told from the head scientist that you have figured out the total percentage of enhancing it we can do," Trayon told him.

"Well, yes, except we do not know what that will do to him. I mean, we do not know what kind of effect that it will have on his actual brain. For all we know, the enhancements that we have already done may be worthless once we enhance his brain," the assistant told him with a hint of regret in his voice.

"Just do as you are told, even if you have to brain wash him first and *then* enhance his brain. I want the rest of the enhancements done by the time I get back. If he refuses to comply, then start killing the other prisoners—and start with the girl. That should make him obey our demands. I also want the other two individuals' enhancements done, as well," Trayon told him just as he turned back and started to walk away.

Five minutes later, Trayon's vessel left. *Now, I need to get this done and over with,* the assistant scientist thought while turning back toward the door.

Suddenly, Allan noticed the door open. "Untie him, and I will take him to his cell. Trayon wants you to wear this while you are asleep," the assistant scientist replied while holding out a metal headband.

"No, thank you. You can tell that ignoramus where he can shove—"

Before Allan could finish speaking, the assistant interrupted him, "What, do you want the others killed just because you do not want to do it?"

"What are you talking about?" Allan asked.

"If you refuse to obey what we tell you, he has ordered the deaths of the other prisoners—starting with the Drazarian child. Do you want their deaths on your head?" the assistant asked while tightening his fist around the headband.

"He is doing everything that he can to make me made, isn't he?" Allan asked while his voice showed signs of being defiant.

"Yes, except, I am trying to make this transfer a lot easier then what it truly is. By the way, here is a pain reliever," the assistant told the boy.

Suddenly, after taking the pill, Allan started to feel a little light headed, "What did you give me?" the boy asked just as he fell to his hands and knees.

"That was a pill to help you sleep, and it will also allow the others to work on your enhancements without you feeling a thing. This way, no one else needs to lose their lives over this project," the assistant told him.

One week later . . .

"Sir, all the enhancements to his muscles and eyes, as well as his nanotech ears, are done. All that we need to do is to finish the brain enhancement and the brain washing. The rest of the enhancements, for some reason, are not working," the assistant told the head scientist.

"What do you mean? I have seen him already kill two out of the three Colothian's. Now there is only that Colothian teenage male," a fellow scientist said with a confused look.

"I know that! Sorry, he may have killed the parents of that Colothian child, but he is also showing signs that all the brain washing is not affecting him," the assistant told them.

Then tell me, where is the runt?" the head scientist asked just before the assistant turned a monitor on.

"He is in the training room, walking around on his hands," the assistant replied while looking worried.

"I thought members of the Korra Guild weren't afraid of anything?" another asked.

"Most of the time, we are not. Although, his behavior is very strange to me. How many other species do you see just walk around on their hands?" the assistant replied just before turning the monitor off.

"Can you explain why it is that you think the enhancements are not working?" the head scientist asked.

"I have shown you the results. Every test to support what we are trying to do is coming back negative. It is as if his body is reverting back to a primitive or primal state. Example, if you were in his place, let us call him by his real name—Allan's—place. After everything has happened to you like we have done to Allan, I truly think his body has decided to reject everything and is unlocking the repressed genes for his species," the assistant told them.

"You don't know what you're talking about. Now go and bring me both the Drazarian girl and the Colothian teenager," the head scientist replied.

"As you command. Just for the record, I still think we should stop what we are doing with the enhancements," the assistant told them, just as the door slid open.

"Mommy, are we going to be *aww wigt*?" Shamarra asked Amber.

"As of right now, he is going through a change. Emily told me that before she was killed. Allan is starting to show signs of aggression with all Earthlings. Some do and don't have a habit of reverting back to a primal aggressive state when placed in a high level stressful situation," amber replied her daughter.

"So what was his mommy?" Shamarra asked.

"Are you wondering what his mother did for a job? She was a doctor of some sort. She told me to watch out for his primitive side. I'm not sure why. I just think she may have been on to something," amber replied.

"So what does that mean?" the Colothian teenager asked.

"Your name is Codie right?" Amber asked while looking at him.

"Yeah, so what's it to you?" Codie replied with hatred in his voice.

"Don't be upset, it is not Allan's fault that he has to do those bad things. I am sure, one day, I too will be victimized by them. You see, right now, Allan can't stop what he is doing. The Pirates have planted a poisonous seed deep in his mind that he can't stop the actions of," amber told him while walking over to him.

"What are you saying? Those Pirates are playing around with him and brainwashing him into doing what they want?" the teenager asked.

"That is exactly what she is saying. Unfortunately, that is exactly what Trayon is having us do. I am truly sorry for all of this. If I had believed what Allan was telling me back then, none of you would be here right now," the assistant scientist told them.

CHAPTER 4

"WHAT IS IT that you want? You're a member of the Korra Guild, aren't you?" Amber demanded to know just as she placed herself between the Pirates and the kids.

"Yes, that is right. The head scientist wants both your daughter and that boy. He is hoping that between the two of them, Trayon will be able to control Allan. Can you explain one thing to me?" the assistant asked.

"What is that? I thought Trayon and the TRI Guild had all the answers," amber told him with hatred in her eyes.

As the scientist stepped closer, he looked at her with sorrow in his eyes. "Please explain to me, why does Allan, as kind as he is, act as if he does not know what is going on or what day it is from time to time?" the scientist asked in a soft, caring tone.

"I don't know. The one person you could have asked and could have told you is now dead. Emily is the only one that could have told you what you needed to know. Why are you asking? Also, why are you calling my son by his name and not 'Runt'?" Amber asked him in a confused tone.

"It is because I believe that this child has, deep inside his DNA, the answers Trayon is looking for. All we should have taken from the boy is a few samples of his blood and allow his entire family to leave. What is going on here, I think is wrong. Allan should have been allowed to choose if he wanted the enhancements or not. I am truly sorry for this. Let us get going, children, before Trayon and the others decide to kill your mother," the scientist replied with the sound of regret in his voice.

"What is taking so long in here? You Korra Guild members are too soft. Let's get moving, children. Those scientists are busy and don't have all day for your enhancements," a guard told them.

"You will not touch my children! You have already damaged one of them far beyond his species' breaking point! I won't allow you to harm any more of my children!" Amber told them with extreme hatred in her eyes.

"Fine, then we will remove you form the equation," the guard replied just as he raised his weapon.

"Lower your weapon, now! She is a mother trying to protect her beloved children! You do not . . ." Before the scientist could finish speaking, everyone heard a loud discharge from the weapon. As the scientist looked at Amber, he noticed she had a look of both surprise and hatred in her eyes as her lifeless body fell to the floor. "You did not have to do that! She would have allowed these children to come with us!" the scientist yelled at the guard.

"Yeah, but now we don't have to worry about her getting in our way," the guard replied in a cruel, demonic tone.

"You are right. We do not have to worry about her. Honestly, I have never worried about her. I just hope your actions have not doomed us all," the scientist told him just as he picking Shamarra up in his arms.

"I don't understand what you are talking about," the guard replied.

"That is just it. No one ever stops to think about their actions before it is too late. Codie, come on, we need to get to the lab before they decide to kill you and Shamarra," the scientist told the two just as he exited the cell.

"Sure, it isn't like we can do anything to stop him. Shamarra, I'm truly sorry for your lose," Codie said her just as he placed a hand on her shoulders.

Two minutes later, the three of them entered into the lab where they noticed Allan lying on his stomach while blood dripped from the table onto the floor. "What did you do to him?" Codie asked.

"They are preparing to enhance his brain. The problem is that I do not know what will happen from that moment on," the assistant scientist told him.

"So what *awe tey* going to do with us?" Shamarra asked.

"Before they enhance his brain, they are going to inject what is called a 'sibling bond DNA enhancement' into the three of you. Once we are done with Allan, we are supposed to start on one of you. Trayon has decided to place Shamarra his control, and what that means is, you will control how much hatred and anger he has, just to get him to do as he is commanded to do. Codie, you are supposed to be his mental stability. What that means is, until he is sent out on a mission, you will be able to block the 'assassin' part of him," the assistant told them as he placed Shamarra on a table.

"What you are saying is that Shamarra will be controlling his emotions, and I will be controlling his mind. Does that sum everything up?" Codie asked.

"You know, you are a bright young man," the assistant told him.

"No, my parents were geneticists, and I just happened to pick up a few things when it came to DNA alterations," Codie told him.

"So you know exactly what is going on," the assistant scientist told him just as he injected the serum into Shamarra's arm.

Just as the assistant scientist poked the syringe into her arm, she started to cry. "Sorry Shamarra, I do not have a choice. If I did not have to do this, then we would not have to be here," the assistant told her.

Suddenly, they heard a loud moan, "Allan, you're finally awake. We are about to inject you with a serum that is called a 'sibling bond'," the assistant told him just as Allan started to sit up.

"That is fine, except, who is Allan, and who may I ask are you?" Allan asked in a strange, unfamiliar tone.

"Here, lie back down. This is your sister Shamarra, and this is your brother Codie. Do you not recognize them?" the assistant asked him.

"No, I do not really know who I am," Allan replied in the same, strange voice as before, as he leaned back down to lie on the table.

"Here, let us get this portion over with," the assistant replied as he injected the sibling bond serum into Allan's body. "The next thing I have to do is inject this DNA enhancement into your body. This will allow you to use one hundred and fifty percent of your brain. Your father and sister were given about three hundred percent enhanced brain abilities," the assistant told him while holding a syringe.

"Is this going to hurt?" Allan's strange voice asked.

"Not at all. In fact, you will not feel a thing. I promise," the assistant told him while looking at Codie and Shamarra.

"Is there something wrong? Is there something you're not telling us or him?" Codie asked.

"Take Shamarra and get into that office," the assistant told him as he thought, *I really have a bad feeling about this.*

A moment later, Allan suddenly felt a soft prick at the base of his neck, *There. It is done,* the assistant thought as he backed away.

A few seconds later, both Codie and Shamarra noticed the assistant locking the door to his lab. "If something—anything—goes wrong, we will be safe behind this door," the assistant told the two as they noticed a green flash of light explode from Allan's eyes.

Within a single moment, both Codie and Shamarra noticed Allan ripping his hands free from the restraints. "What is happening to me?" Allan asked in a strange voice as a bright flash of light erupted out from him like a shock wave—then, he passed out.

"Um, what is happening? Can't a guy get a little piece and quiet around here?" Allan asked as he heard a loud metallic nose echoing through his head.

"Why are you just lying there? Come on, we are free to do as we please. By the way, just so you know, I'm going to kill you soon," a strange voice came from the doorway.

As Allan looked, he noticed a figure standing there. To his amazement, he saw himself, but yet, it was not. "Who are you? Can you actually be me?" Allan asked while looking confused.

"I'm you. To be exact, I'm the *true* you," the stranger replied in a familiar voice, containing hatred behind the tone.

"No, it can't be, I won't allow it!" Allan demanded as he charged toward the look-alike.

"What makes you think you can stop me?" the look-alike asked.

"What, you can't be real!" Allan replied as he stepped into the hallway. As Allan looked up and down the hall, he noticed giant rooms field with what appeared to be books. Then, suddenly, his eyes stopped on a set of doors, "If you are me, then tell me, what are in those rooms? Why do they look like cells?" Allan asked.

"They *are* cells, you fool! The one behind you is your cell. The cell on the left is mine, and I do not know who that cell belongs to," the look-alike told him.

"That one is mine," a second familiar voice replied.

As the first two turned to look, all they saw was a dark figure disappearing right before their eyes. *What was that? Could all of this be a dream?* Allan thought. He looked at a wall and started to walk toward it.

"What are you doing? You're just going to walk right into that wall and get hurt," the look-alike told him.

"No I won't. This is a dream—it *has* to be. For one thing, you can't exist. There is no way I would allow myself to lose my mind. I will prove that by walking through this wall," Allan replied just before connecting with the wall.

"So, is this or is this not a dream?" the look-alike asked him just as a devilish smile appeared on his face.

After Allan's face connected with the wall, and he fell backward, he admitted, "Okay, so this is not a dream." He started to stand back up.

After a few minutes of laughing, Allan's look-alike looked at him and said, "I could've told you that myself. You're pathetic. You can't do anything on your own," the strange voice replied.

"Sure I can. Just watch me. I will pick a book from one of those shelves, and I'll read it," Allan replied while walking over to one of the giant rooms.

A short time later, he reached out for one of the books. To his surprise, just as he touched the book, it disappeared. "How is that possible? All I did was touch it. These books should have all the information I know it them," Allan replied with wide eyed confusion.

"Daggen, bring me the Earthling child with the black collar. I will tell the scientist to prepare their equipment. We really need to start the enhancements," Trayon ordered while smiling.

"What do you want me to do if the adults try to stop me? Can I use the collars to paralyze them until I can retrieve the child? Besides, what are we going to do about the second Earthling family?" Daggen asked.

"Do as you see fit. Those adults will not have long to live, and neither do the second Earthling male child and girl. We have the perfect child at hand. After we are done, we will make our prize child kill them himself," Trayon told him.

"Yes, that would be great, and what if he'd refuse to kill them?" Daggen replied.

"Oh, that's easy, because you will place the shock electrodes on his body every time he refuses. You will send an electrical current through his body. Just remember to be careful around the Drazarian. We just implanted the sibling bond in her and the Earth child," Trayon replied as he started to walk away.

"How far has the scientists altered him?" Daggen asked with a cautioned voice.

"Do not worry. They have only altered his body mass and eye color. Although, it looks as if the DNA enhancements have failed. After he kills the second family, the scientists will continue to the procedure . . ." Trayon told him as he thought, *. . . after seeing his own family being killed right in front of his own eyes. That should have sparked something, especially after altering his DNA without antiseptic to numb the pain, not to mention telling him lies—his mind will be ours. He will be under my control soon.*

Meanwhile . . .

"Hey kid, what is going on? Why are we here? Tell me kid, where do you fit into all of this?" a middle-aged man asked.

"*Weave im awone,*" a young child demanded.

"It is all right, Shamarra. I think they have a right to know that they are nothing more than test subjects to the TRI Guild. As for me, I don't know. How about you tell me, why is it that I am being tortured, punished, cut, poked, and prodded," the young boy replied.

"But, *tey* don't *undewstand. It'z* not *youw* fault, is it? You didn't ask for *tiz, wigt*?" Shamarra asked as she sat next to him.

"No, Shamarra, I didn't. I had to watch my family be killed right in front of my own eyes. When I tried to help them, I was tortured until the very last breath had left their bodies. Then, they did the exact same thing with your family. Before we knew what was happening, I was injected with something, and so were you," the young boy replied.

"Then, tell me, boy, how long have the two of you been here? What are they going to do with me and my family?" the middle-aged man asked.

"Well, we have been here for three months, I think. Codie, who is lying over there, has been here two months and three weeks. Now, about your family, I do not know. There is also a family from Earth the TRI Guild has been killing off one at a time. Here. let me show you what you can be looking forward to if they take you," the young boy replied as he stood up.

While having his back facing the newly captured family, he started to take his shirt off. Suddenly, they heard, "Allan, you do not have to scare them. Just look at them, and you can see how afraid they are," Codie told him as he sat up.

Suddenly, a greenish-red skinned, young man walked from the shadows into the light. "Where were you hiding?" the middle-aged man asked.

"That is none of you business. If you would just keep things quiet, then I would still be asleep," the young man replied.

Suddenly, there was a loud sound from outside the door, "Everyone, stand back, or we will shock every last one of you," a familiar voice yelled from outside the door.

"Shamarra, get behind Codie," Allan demanded.

"Why? Who is at the door?" the middle-aged man asked.

"It's Daggen. They are here for me," Allan replied with a look of disgust in his eyes.

Suddenly, the door opened, and the only thing the people inside could see was four individuals. "Daggen, lower your weapons. The deal was Codie and I would fallow your instructions as long as the child was left alone. If you don't lower those weapons, the deal's going to be off," Allan replied as he started to walk toward the door.

"You are not the only one we want. You follow us!" Daggen demanded as he pointed to the middle-aged man. The two started exiting the room.

"Allan, don't worry. We're right here if you need us," Codie replied as he noticed a slight movement from the corner.

"Codie, do you know what will happen those kids?" Shamarra asked while pointing toward the four individuals in the corner.

"I will not allow anything to happen to my children," a young woman's voice replied as a figure stood up in the shadow.

A few minutes later . . .

"Ah, our puppet has arrived. Daggen, is he wearing the new shock outfit?" a scientist asked just as Allan entered the room.

"Yes, he is!" Daggen replied as he turned to face Allan. "Kill him and kill him now. Do as you're told and kill that prisoner!" Daggen suddenly demanded.

"Excuse me, not on your life," Allan replied. Then, his eyes started to widen, and Allen's body exploded with pain. He screamed, "*Ahhh* . . . ! You're . . . not . . . going . . . to . . . get . . . me . . . to . . . kill . . . anyone . . ." Allan told them as he fell to one knee.

"You will do as you are told. Kill him now, and the pain will stop," Daggen demanded in front of the scientists as he sent another jolt into Allan's body.

"There . . . is . . . no . . . way. . . . *Ahhh* . . . !" Allan replied as he fell to both knees.

"You do not have a choice," Daggen replied as he connected his fist to Allan's face.

To everyone's surprise, Allan was unconscious. "Pick him up and place him on the table," a scientist demanded.

Suddenly, Shamarra heard a loud scream. "I hope Allan is all *wight*," she replied as she looked at the back of her glowing hand.

"You're right, and he is in extreme pain right now. I hope he is able to overcome this," Codie replied as the room started to become brighter with a red light.

"Excuse me. How can you sit there and tell me that the scream we just heard came from that young boy and not my father?" the young woman asked.

Suddenly, Codie and Shamarra held their right hands up. To the young woman's surprise, the back of their hands were glowing bright red. "You're telling me the two of you have a link with that young boy?" she asked.

"Yes, you might just call the three of us siblings. For some unknown reason, the three of us have a link that can feel how the others feel," Codie replied.

Meanwhile in the lab . . .

"Daggen, hold him down and do not allow him to move," a scientist demanded just as he touched a hot rod to Allan's left shoulder.

"Stay away from me," Allan told them as a bright flash exploded through the room.

"This will tell everyone who had a hand in creating the ultimate assassin. The tests are saying that he will be ours in the next few months," a scientist replied.

"I will never be your puppet, even if I have to kill myself," Allan yelled at them as he felt an overwhelming jolt of pain.

"After we place the next six Guilds on his back, you can take him back to his cell," the head scientist told him.

Suddenly, Allan felt pain rush through his body as another burning sensation touched his back, "Stop it! Why are you doing this to me? I'm not the person you're needing," he told them just as he felt something warm running down his back.

"Sir, we are ready to retry the body enhancements by using nanotechnology," another scientist said as he pulled a cutting tool from Allan's back.

"Go ahead and, this time, make sure you double the enhancements ability. If we are lucky, half of the enhancements will work," the head scientist replied.

"Leave me alone!" Allan demanded as he started to see everything turning dark.

"We already told you, boy, we are trying to make the ultimate assassin. Your body's makeup just happens to be the best choice and the easiest to alter. Now, be a good, little Earthling and *shut up!*" the head scientist replied as he touched a third hot object to Allan's back.

"You really should just give in. You know you really want to. What would it hurt?" an unknown voice said.

"Who, who are you? Are you my conscience? If you truly are my conscience, then you know what they are doing is wrong!" Allan replied.

"No, I am not your conscience. Who I am is not important right now. You know you really want them to do this," the voice replied.

"No, I don't. Tell me who you are," Allan replied.

"If you must know, I am you—just better and stronger then you are now," the voice replied.

"No, this can't be. You're lying!" Allan replied.

"Hey, Daggen, untie me will you?" everyone heard in a strange, calm voice.

"What are you trying to do, runt? Do not even try to fool me, because there is nothing you can say that will make me want to untie you," Daggen replied.

"Come on, untie me, and I promise I will make your death quick and painless," the Earthling boy replied as he opened his eyes and a burst of a glowing red light exploded out.

"Why, you little runt, are you trying to get me mad?" Daggen demanded and connected his fist to Allan's face.

"Oh, look, such a big man pounding on such a puny person like me. Now, that was a freebee, because the next time you even think about touching me, I will kill you," the unfamiliar voice replied as blood ran down the side of his mouth.

"Take him away. I do not want to see him in my sight for the next few days!" Daggen ordered just before he exited the lab.

When the scientists looked at their subject, they noticed an unfamiliar grin on the boy's face. "Is what we are doing right? Are we truly sure we will be able to control him, or are we just fooling ourselves?" the scientist's assistant asked with a worried look.

"What is wrong? Don't tell me that you are having moral second thoughts about what we have been doing for the last few months," the scientist responded while turning to look at his assistant.

"I do not know why or understand this sudden fear," the assistant replied. Then, he suddenly blurted out, "Yes, I am. I will not be a part of this any longer."

"Fine then, I will find another assistant to help me. I am done with the runt today. You can take him back to his cell," the scientist demanded as he turned to work on the data he had just taken.

"Yes, sir, come just calm down. I will not hurt you. Once I get you back to your cell, I will bring you something to eat," the assistant replied. *Then, after that, I will need to inform my contact in the Galaxy Alliance about what has been going on,* he thought.

Suddenly, Allan jumped from the exam table and ran toward the head scientist. "If you kill him, the pain will stop? All you truly need to do is follow everything we tell you. If you do, everything will be fine," Daggen's voice suddenly echoed through his head.

"Sir, look out!" the assistant replied, but it was already too late. When the scientist looked up at Allan, he pulled the exact, same, sharp object that the scientist had just used on him out of own back out.

"You little runt. You don't truly want to do this!" the scientist replied as he tried to scramble to his feet.

Before he could truly move to stop the boy, Allan had already plunged the object through the scientist's head, just as the assistant heard, "If I kill him, the pain will stop. Just follow every command that is given to me, and, if I do, everything will be fine," the young boy said just before falling to the ground unconscious.

"Security, take him back to his cell," the assistant ordered while turning to face his dead boss's body. *If the boy can do this right now without having any actual enhancements, what kind of monster are we actually creating?* the assistant thought while looking worried.

The following day when Allan woke up, he heard, "Yeah, he's awake," an unfamiliar girl's voice blurted out.

"Shamarra, wait. Remember the last time he woke up? We truly don't know if this is Allan or not," Codie told her while trying to grab the young girl's arm.

"Yeah, little girl, please come closer. You know I'm in the mood to rip someone's head off," an unfamiliar voice escaped from Allan's mouth.

"Codie . . . !" the young child screamed while trying to stop her forward momentum.

"Now I have you!" the voice replied just as his body suddenly stopped. "Leave me alone, get out of my head! I don't need you, and I will never need you. I must kill everyone here," he just blurted out as he placed his hands on his head.

Meanwhile, inside Allan's head . . .

"Leave her alone, or you will regret ever touching her," a familiar voice said.

"How dare you tell me what to do! You are weak. What does that child mean to you, anyway? She will never be a sister to you. Your biological little sister is dead, and *she* can't replace her," the second voice replied.

"If you even touch a single hair on her head, I promise you this day will be the last day you will ever see," Allan's voice demanded.

Suddenly, to both of their surprise, a *third* voice said, "If he decides to commit suicide, I will not stop him. This is your decision and yours alone. Kill her and you are dead, but if you let her live, then you will live."

"Nice try. Your conscience can't help you with this one. It's just you and me," the second voice replied.

"Fine then, make your move and find out what will happen," Allan's voice said with a demanding tone.

"You're lucky little girl. Allan has convinced me to spare your life. Just remember, if you ever get in my way, I will kill you, and he won't be able to stop me," the unfamiliar voice replied as the door opened.

"What is going on in here?" Daggen's voice demanded from the doorway.

"Daggen, it is nice to see you. Come in and let's talk. Afterwords, maybe I will decide not to kill you," Allan's voice demanded as the light in his eyes started to become brighter.

"All right, runt, stop trying to act like I do not scare you. I just came to tell you that if you play nicely, we have two individuals here you can play with. Their names are Tearan and Trisha, and they are from the Korra guild," Daggen told the boy.

"Oh, goody. How about I kill them instead," the strange voice responded.

"Why don't you both shut up, and, Daggen, just leave us alone," Codie demanded.

"Be nice, or you will not get your rations. Besides, those children are too important to us to allow you to kill them," Daggen told him as he threw a cart into the cell.

"Just leave us alone. Besides, don't you have latrines to clean?" Codie replied as he walked over to the cart.

Suddenly Codie grabbed a tray and charged toward Allan. "Now, what are you going to do with that?" Allan asked with a strange voice while grinning.

Then, Codie connected the tray with Allan's face, "Now sleep it off!" Codie demanded as Allan's body fell to the ground.

"Do you truly think that will stop me?" Allan responded in the strange voice as he started to get up.

"Not at first, because I've seen what they have been doing. Now, I expect you to sleep like a baby!" Codie exclaimed as he slammed the tray into the back of Allan's head, followed by connecting a knee to Allan's face.

"Stop it! *Weave im awone*! Why *awe* you doing this to him?" Shamarra asked as she noticed Allan's body fall limp.

"I'm sorry, Shamarra, I truly am. I could not allow him to continue to act like the monster they want him to be," Codie responded as he walked over and embraced the little girl.

"Are the three of you siblings?" the young woman asked while holding a young child in her hands.

"Biologically, no, because Allan is from the same planet you are. Shamarra and I are from different planets here in space. We *do* have a bond with each other, which, on some unethical aspects, would make us siblings," Codie replied as he walked over to the trays.

"Tell me, what are they trying to do with the three of you?" the middle-aged man demanded to know.

"I do not know. Why do you ask?" Codie replied while handing the man and the young woman a tray.

"That orange thing demanded your friend there to kill me. When he refused, they sent a series of pain through his body. Before I knew what was happening, we were brought back here, and you know the rest. Can you tell me how many times this has happened to him?" the man asked.

"Including this one, it has been three times in all. The only problem is that the effects are beginning to last longer and longer. I'm not sure how much longer Allan can take the punishment," Codie responded just as he heard someone outside the cell.

"Are you Daggen?" a young female's voice asked outside the door.

"Yes, I am. Who let you on this vessel? This is no place for brats," Daggen replied. "Daddy is here to see the volunteer for your enhancements," the young girl responded.

"Trayon wants the volunteer brought to the lab immediately. He wants to show the bidders how far along we are with the volunteer's enhancements," a male's voice followed.

"Who are you?" Daggen asked with a hint of anger in his voice.

"I am Prince Tearan, and this is my little sister, Princess Trisha of the Korra Guild. Now, should we go back and tell our father that you refused, or do we walk back with you and the volunteer?" the young boy asked as his voice stopped outside the cell.

"Fine then, just wait here while I go in and retrieve him. Do not look inside the cell, or you may get attacked," Daggen replied as he started to open the door.

After making sure the children were standing away from the door, he opened it. When he looked inside, he noticed Allan on the ground, "Hey, boy, get over here!" he demanded.

When Allan did not move, he said, "Hey, boy, are you hard of hearing? I said to get over here, now!" Daggen demanded as he pushed a button on his wriest.

As he saw Allan's body start to bounce around from the electricity running through his body, he heard, "Are you stupid? Unless you are blind, you should be able to tell that he is unconscious," Codie replied as Shamarra and he ran over to Allan's side.

"When the time comes, I assure you, I will really enjoy helping out with your enhancements," Daggen replied as he walked over to Allan's unconscious body.

Before Codie could do anything, he felt Shamarra holding him and shaking from being afraid. "Don't worry, Shamarra, because a deal is a deal. They can't start on your enhancements until they have completed

Allan's and mine first. Just remember, Daggen, if you touch Shamarra, Allan and I will try to stop you, even if it means getting ourselves killed," Codie replied while moving away from Allan's body.

"Yeah, yeah, whatever you say. If the three of you weren't so important, I would have killed you weeks ago," Daggen replied.

Suddenly, from out of nowhere, a kind male voice replied, "That is, we're not so important."

"Daddy, what are you doing down here?" the young girl replied.

"I was wondering what was keeping everyone so long. Daggen, something's just happened to come up. You can leave the child in there, unless you are going to proceed with furthering the boy's enhancements," the male replied.

"As you wish, Your Majesty," Daggen responded as he picked Allan's body up and started to walk toward the door.

As the door closed, the man asked, "Who are they? They do not act like the rest of the aliens I've seen here."

"If you look closely on both of their shirts, you can see that they are both from different groups," Codie replied with a look of hatred in his eye.

"Can you tell me what is it they have planned for us? I know they demanded that boy to kill me, even though he refused," the man responded.

"If they ordered him to kill you, I'm sorry—you don't have a future," Codie replied as Shamarra and he started to eat their food.

"Tell us, what will happen to that boy?" the young woman asked.

"They are trying to create an ultimate assassin out of him. They are trying to conquer the galaxy," Codie replied just before shoving a spoon full of food into his mouth.

Meanwhile, as Trayon, Daggen, King Carrag, and his children walked down the hall, the five suddenly stoped at an airlock. "Trayon, I have to leave right away. I will be back to check on the progress in a few weeks," a middle-aged man said.

"King Carrag, I'm looking forward to dealing with the Korra Guild in the future," Trayon replied.

"Maybe next time you will allow my children to play with your volunteer. You just cannot expect a child like that to grow without having fun in his childhood. I am concerned about a few things, though," Carrag told him.

"You are too busy right now. We can finish this at a later time," Trayon replied just before shutting the airlock door.

A few minutes later, as the royal Korra Guild's shuttle lifted the locking clamps and flew away, Trayon demanded from Daggen, "Tell those scientists to pick up the pace."

"Yes, sir. If you need me, I will be helping the scientist," Daggen responded as he started to walk off.

Just as Daggen walked into the lab, Daggen ordered, "Hurry up! Trayon wants those enhancements finished as soon as possible!"

CHAPTER 5

"SIR, YOU CAN tell him we will be finished with the enhancements by next week. The only problem we are having is trying to keep his mind from rejecting the brainwashing we subject him to," a scientist replied.

"Sir, we have a problem over here. The muscle enhancements are in the final stages, as well as the eye enhancements—" Before the assistant could finish, he was interrupted.

"So what is the problem?" Daggen asked.

"The picture on the right is what we are trying to create. The picture on the left is his body rejecting our enhancements. Now, here is the problem. The picture in the middle is his actual DNA we just took. As you can see, his body is converting into what we are trying to create all on its own. We just took the blood samples a few minutes ago, with and without the enhancements," the assistant told them with signs of starting to become afraid.

"All right, just keep him sedated, and I will have a talk with Trayon," Daggen told them just before turning toward the door.

A few minutes later, after Daggen walked into Trayon's study room . . .

"Trayon, one of the scientist's is having a complaint about the enhancements. He is insisting that the enhancements are not working. I am wondering, sir, why did you choose an Earthling from the known species?" Daggen asked.

"When I was handed the enhancement lists, it also was told to me that an Earthling was the only species to use," Trayon replied.

"Who told you that?" Daggen asked with curiosity in his voice.

"That is none of your business. All you have to do is keep him sedated until we are able to brain wash him. Now, get back to the lab and make sure they finish the enhancements!" Trayon demanded.

After Daggen left, Trayon sat down and looked at the security camera. "I need to remember to erase everything that has been said and done for the last five months. I do not need the Alliance to know what and why we are doing this," he spoke out loud.

"I need to stop him. I can't allow that monster to take full control of my body," Allan said out loud.

"Oh yeah, what make you think you are man enough to stop me?" the strange-looking image that Allan was finally able able to identify as himself replied.

"I will do everything I can to counter your actions. I will not allow the alteration they have done to me change who I truly am," Allan told him with a hint of anger.

"I would like to see you try that!" the strange image of himself replied.

"If they are wanting an ultimate killing machine, I believe that they have created him—and you are it. If I remember my history right, they are called 'assassins' back on Earth. From now on, I will call you 'Assassin'!" Allan replied with a hint of disgust.

"Fine, I will be known as your assassin," the strange image agreed.

One month later . . .

"What day is it? How long have I been out?" Assassin demanded to know.

"Codie, I'm *afwaid*," Shamarra told the boy.

"It looks like he has been completed. Now there is nothing in this universe that can stop him," Codie replied as he moved Shamarra around behind himself.

"What are you doing, challenging me, boy? I will make your death very slow and painful. First, before I do that, I will await my cousin's arrival, and then I will kill you in front of them for sheer pleasure," Allan told him with the strange voice everyone had become used to.

"So you truly are the ultimate killing machine? I can just imagine what your dead family would say if they could only see you now, Allan," Codie responded.

"Do not ever call me by that pathetic name again. I am called 'Assassin', and do not forget it," Allan replied with a more harsh tone to his voice.

"I can tell you what they would say. They would tell him that he is pathetic to have fallen under someone else's control so easily," a voice told them just as the cell door opened.

When the cell door opened, everyone noticed a tall, Caucasian male in a red and black outfit. "I could have prevented this a while ago. The needs of millions out-weight the needs of the few. Except, first we need to get you back to yourself," the stranger told them while walking into the room.

"Who do you think you are telling what I need to do? Do you honestly think that you can stop me?" Assassin replied while looking at his reflection on the stranger's helmet.

"Who I am is not of your concern. Now, whether I can stop you or not should be your first priority. Codie, it is great to see you again. Now, back to the pathetic being calling himself Assassin—it is past your bed time," the stranger told them just before his fist connected to Assassin's face.

With a hard thud, Allan's body stopped moving. "You killed him! How could you!" Shamarra cried while running over to Allan's body.

"No, Shamarra, I did not. Do not worry. Within a single day, Allan will be back to his normal self. Just watch out for Assassin, because that personality is a part of who he is now. Shamarra, do not worry. This is just a nightmare. All you need to do is wake up," the stranger told her as he knelt down next to her.

Suddenly, both Codie's and Shamarra's right hands started to glow blue, "Who are you?" Codie asked with a puzzled look on his face.

"I am truly sorry. I cannot tell you that. Shamarra, here is something that will prove, in a few days, that everything will be all right," the stranger told them as he placed a pendent around her neck.

"What is this *fow*?" she replied while looking a little afraid.

"That is a good luck charm, and it will keep you safe from this point on. Do you trust me?" he asked while placing a hand on her shoulder.

"I guess so," she replied as the color started to glow even brighter.

"Now, I have to go. I am sorry that I cannot do any more than this," the stranger told them as he stood up.

As he walked away, Codie asked, "Will we see you again?"

With a quick wave of his hand, the stranger walked out of the room and closed the cell door behind him. "Do you know what is going on Shamrra?" Codie asked just as the glow faded from their right hands.

"No, I just hope big *bwothew* is all *wight*," Shamarra replied while looking at Allan.

"Don't worry. He will be fine. Like the stranger told us, all Allan really needs is a good night's rest," Codie replied while walking up and hugging her.

"*Awe* you *suwe*?" she replied while lying down next to him.

"Yes, I'm sure. Let's get some rest. I'm still feeling the effect from the experiment they did on me yesterday," Codie told her while moving the bedding over to Allan and Shamarra.

"Okay, sweet dweams, *bwothews*," she replied just before closing her eyes.

Meanwhile, in Trayon's meeting room . . .

"Sir, two months ago, that boy did not show any signs from the brain washing. After hacking into the medical files on Earth, I can now tell you that we were missing all the signs of the brain washing and everything else we had been working on. I had asked him a question in the same month, and his answer was just, 'Let me burn everything.' Only a few days later, I asked him the same question, and he replied with, 'Why do you care what I think?' After I told him what he told me before, he responded, 'I did not say that, because this was the first time you asked me that question.' He showed signs of total memory loss or amnesia multiple times during my evaluation. Now, to the real reason I asked to meet with you. We have found a problem with the enhancement of his brain. After we tested to find out if his body accepted that enhancement or not, we saw more activity then we should have," the assistant scientist told Trayon.

"So, what? What is it you are trying to tell me?" Trayon demanded to know.

"When we enhanced his brain, we didn't just enhance it by twenty percent. When we opened every ounce of his brain, we noticed a lot more activity. If there are more persoalities than our desired personality, in time, they will be able to communicate with one another. They will know what the other one or ones are doing at that very instant. This should not be happening, but it is, so I am suggesting that we stop what we are doing and destroy the enhancements that we have done before it is too late," the assistant demanded.

"No, you have not shown us any actual proof of what you are telling us. Both of the boys are ninety-five percent complete, and now we will proceed with final step," Trayon responded in a threatening voice.

"Sir, I showed you every test results that we have taken. Every enhancement, except for the muscles, eyes, the brain, and the nanotech ear enhancements, have been rejected. Yet, for some unknown reason, his body is still transforming into what we have desired the most—a killing machine. We need to stop this, now!" the assistant demanded while slamming his hands onto the table.

"Daggen, tell the head scientist to proceed with the final phase. I want that girl's enhancements done by the time you and I get back here next month," Trayon replied while standing up.

"Yes, sir," Daggen replied just as Trayon walked out of the room.

Suddenly, Trayon appeared back inside the room, "By the way, pack your things, because you are no longer a part of this experiment. We tracked an unauthorized transmission with your identification code, but since we cannot tell whom it was that you sent the transmission to, we cannot execute you because of our treaty with the Korra Guild."

If my hunch is correct, at least I will not be around to be slaughtered, the assistant thought just as he heard Daggen demand, "Did you hear what he just told you?"

"Yes, I did. All I will need is five minutes," the assistant replied as he walked out the door.

Just as the assistant's transport left, Trayton told him, "Daggen, you must decode that transmission. I need to know whom it was he sent it to." Then, they stepped onto their transport vessel.

"I'm already on it. Can you tell me what it is that you are so afraid of?" Daggen asked while looking at the transmission log.

"If the other Guilds ever found out that some, dark, unknown entity was the one that gave me those enhancement schematics for the ultimate weapon, they would find a way to throw me out of power. If the Alliance found out, they would come here and take him from me," Trayon replied as he sat down.

"I will let you know as soon as possible," Daggen told him just as the vessel started its departure.

Later that day . . .

"What happened? Why do I have a headache?" Allan asked as he started to stand.

"You don't remember? You were knocked unconscious yesterday by a strange-looking individual," Codie told him.

"That can't be. I was in the lab yesterday. They were trying to increase the amount of enhancement DNA my body would not reject," Allan replied.

"Little brother, that was last month. You have been in a daze, or there is something seriously wrong with you," Codie replied.

"That can't be. Where did those other people go?" Allan asked while looking around.

"I'm sorry. You killed them last month. After that, you were showing high levels of aggression, and your eyes started to look strange. When did they enhance your eyes to make them glow?" Codie asked.

"I don't know what you are talking about. What do you mean, 'They enhanced my eyes just to make them glow'?" Allan inquired.

"Sorry, Allan, I thought you might have been Assassin playing a trick on us," Codie told him with a look of relief.

Suddenly, the door opened. "Come here, little girl. It is your turn to be enhanced!" a voice replied.

"Do not touch her," Allan demanded.

Suddenly, as the two figures appeared in the doorway, Codie and Allan rushed toward them. "What is it that you think you are doing?" one of the two asked.

Before anyone could answer, Codie connected an elbow to one of the individual's solar plexuses, just as Allan connected a fist with the second individual's face. "Shamarra, get to your secret hiding place," Codie yelled.

For the brief second that he turned to look at her, he heard a loud moan, followed by a hard thud. "Allan, is everything all right? Allan!" Codie yelled out. When he turned his attention back to the fight, he noticed Allan was on the ground and appeared to be unconscious. Suddenly, he felt a sharp object sliding into his side.

"Come on! We need to get him to the lab!" one of the Pirate scientists said.

"What about the girl? Hey, where did she run off to?" the second Pirate scientist asked.

"Who cares. If we cannot stop the bleeding, then our hard work will be for nothing. Without the mental stability from this boy, then our ultimate killing machine will start destroying the galaxy—no, the universe," the first scientist replied as the two picked up Allan and Codie.

A few hours later, after an examination of Codie . . .

"Just perfect, you stupid, moronic idiots. With subject Codie dying, how do you expect us to control subject Allan without a mental stabilizer?" the head scientist demanded.

"Can't we just fix him or create another like him?" one of the assistants asked.

"You idiot. The wounds are too severe, and creating another in his place will take too much time. The Korra Guild has already paid from him. Now what do I tell Trayon?" the head scientist replied as they exited the room.

After the door closed, Codie said, "You can open your eyes now they're gone."

After opening his eyes, Allan noticed the table Codie was lying on was covered with blood. After examining the table, Allan realized the blood was coming from the wound at Codie's side. "Big brother, are you all right? Are you going to leave us?" Allan asked as a tear started to form at the edge of his left eye.

"Yes, I'm dying. Allan, you must listen to me. Take Shamarra and leave from this location. Right now, she is only four years old. You make her think of this as a nightmare, because she does not deserve these kinds of memories. Protect Shamarra, Allan. You must protect her with your life. She needs to grow up in a peaceful place surrounded by friends and her family. Allan, promise me that you will protect her. *Protectd Shamar*—" Before Codie could finish, his last breath escaped from his lips.

"Codie, no!" Allan cried out while trying to break his bonds.

"What is going on in here?" a Scientist asked as he noticed Allan's body starting to expand a little.

"You killed him. You killed Codie. You killed my big brother!" Allan cried out as a green flash of light exploded from his eyes.

"Stop that now! If you don't, then I will kill you, as well!" the scientist told him.

"I would like to see you try it!" Allan's voice replied as he slipped his right hand from the restraints.

"Whatever is going on back there, get control of it. The Galaxy Alliance has found us. Our reinforcements are being driven back by an unknown fighter," a male's voice called over the intercom.

"We'll try to out run them," the scientist replied.

"I wish I could, however, our engines are not responding. The computer reports a total failure from yesterday. Somehow, a saboteur got on board, and we didn't know," the male's voice replied.

"It's the twelve-year-old Earth child. There is something wrong with him. I'm going to need help down here," the scientist replied as the male child started to release all of his restraints.

A few minutes passed. When the scientist's reinforcements arrived, they noticed Allan was now off the table and walking toward them. "What is going on here? Has he lost his mind?" another scientist asked.

"Thanks to you people, most definitely," Allan replied as he stopped at a computer and started to push a few buttons.

"What do you think you are—" Before the scientist could finish, they suddenly heard an audible voice declare, "Download commencing."

"How are you able to access that computer? You need to stop before you force us to kill you!" the second scientist demanded.

Laughter exploded from Allan. "Do not make me laugh! Do you actually think you can stop your ultimate creation? You kidnapped a twelve-year-old Earth male, a four-year-old Drazirian female, and a fourteen-year-old Colothian male. You then play with our DNA makeup just to create an ultimate weapon and his restraint, because you do not want to lose control of him. Then, suddenly, you killed a key factor, and now you think you can keep him under control. How pathetic you are!" Allan said as a second burst of green light exploded from his eyes.

"Red light, green light . . . what is going on with your eyes? We didn't cause that, did we?" a third scientist asked while walking into the lab.

"Oh, and the next time you play with someone's brain, make sure you don't cause a glitch inside the brain. Thanks to you, I can see everything the others do," Allan replied.

"All right, runt, you leave us with no other option," the first scientist told him.

Then, everyone heard, "Downloading completed," as Allan pulled a disc out and tucked it under his shirt. "By the way, that is not my name, nor is it Assassin. As of right now, I am tired of this game of yours, and you will let my sister and I go," Allan replied just before charging toward the scientist.

"Stop him! We must regain control!" The head scientist yelled just before he felt an object connect with his solar plexus.

Suddenly, the room exploded into a giant fight. Without realizing what was going on, the head scientist asked out loud, "How is he able to do that?"

"You must thank the royal children from the Korra Guild," Allan replied just as he shoved a glowing palm into one of the scientist's chest. Blood shot from the scientist's mouth, just as a second Pirate back-handed the Earth child. As he picked himself up, everyone noticed his eyes were now glazed, "Someone stop him before it is too late!" the head scientist demanded.

Before anyone could move, the child kicked one of the scientist's feet out from underneath him. Suddenly, Allan connected an elbow to the scientist's solar plexus, followed by shoving a knee into the scientist's face. After the scientist hit the ground, Allan flipped forward and landed a heel to the scientist chest. With a loud, sudden scream, the scientist's last breath escaped his mouth.

"Is . . . is he dead? How can this be?" the head scientist asked.

Twenty minutes later, the head scientist noticed all of the others were dead, except for the pilot and himself. "Stay away from me. Stay away from me, you little runt!" He demanded as Allan's body started to walk toward him.

Without a sound, Allan's body charged as quickly as it could, and he connected an open palm to the scientist's lower jaw. Suddenly, the laboratory's door flew open. "Everyone, get down on the ground, now," a voice demanded just after Allan's body walked over to a computer and activated a program.

"I said, get on the ground now! Tell me, what did you just do?" a voice said from behind a dark helmet.

Suddenly, he heard, "Sir, we just found this Drazirian child hiding. What would you like me to do?" The second voice asked just as a scream echoed throughout the room.

"What was that?" the first voice asked.

"Lieutenant Colonel Calamen, watch out! He is charging!" another voice called just as they heard the computers audible voice say, "Self detonation in two minutes. Please evacuate the vessel."

After dodging an attack by the child, Lieutenant Colonel suddenly connected a double fist to the charging child's solar plexus. Grab that child off the table, and let's get out of here," he ordered.

After everyone arrived back at their shuttles the pilot launched out of the hanger . . .

Before everyone realized how close to death they truly were, the science vessel exploded. "That was a close one," the lieutenant Colonel told them.

"Sir, we have a strange vessel flying parallel with us. I cannot identify who it belongs to," the pilot reported.

When Lieutenant Colonel looked out of the window, he noticed a strange, black vessel suddenly fade out of existence. "Well, whoever or whatever that was, it is now gone. Everyone, let's go home," Lieutenant Colonel Calamen told them as he took a seat next to the Drazirian girl.

"Are you all right?" the lieutenant Colonel asked.

"I'm fine. Is he going to be *aww wight*?" the little Drazirian child asked.

"I would not worry about him, because when he wakes up, he should be back to normal," he replied while placing a hand on top of her head.

"I *wouwd* be *caweful*. He is *dangewous*. Te *Piwates* messed him up. What is *youw* name?" she asked the lieutenant Colonel.

"My name is Lieutenant Colonel Jack Calamen. You may call me Jack Calamen, or just Jack. What is your name?" he asked her.

"I'm *Shamawwa*, and that is my big *bwothew Awwan*," the child responded while smiling.

"Do not worry. That terrible situation is now over. Once we find your family, we can return you to them," Jack replied.

"Sir, do you have anything to say about what just happened, for the record?" a soldier asked while holding up a recorder.

"Corporal, get that thing out of my face before I bust you all the way back down to private," Jack demanded as he shoved the camera.

"I want to stay with big *bwothew*. My daddy and mommy *awe* both gone," Shamarra told him.

"Well, sweetie, I do not know if they will allow that. Do you know what planet he is from?" Jack asked her.

"Nope," she replied as she started to yawn.

"Go ahead and take a nap. I will wake you when we are back at the Galaxy Alliance Academy station," Jack told her just before noticing she was already asleep.

"Phantom, Phantom, where are you?" Melody called while walking into a small field near the lake.

"What do you mean, 'Where am I?' I told you I would be here relaxing and swimming," his voice echoed through her personal communication device.

"I know that. I mean, where are you at right now? Are you in the water or on land? I really think we need to talk about what is bothering you," Melody said while noticing a made up dressing room from three trees and three blankets tied together.

"I am in the water. If you want to talk get changed, I will see you in the water," Phantom's voice said just before the communications frequency became nothing more than static.

A few minutes later, as Melody started walking into the water, she noticed Phantom's body mass was smaller than usual. "Phantom, how did it feel when you saw the Drionic Guild once again?" she asked.

"Let's not talk about that, please, cousin," his voice said shakily, just like a child who is afraid of their own shadow.

"I thought you had reverted back to the Allan personality, cousin. Phantom, oh, sorry, Allan, you know you must talk about this even if you do not want to. What was going through your mind when you saw them?" she asked once more while floating on her back next to him.

"I know, I want to, except its hard not to recall everything they had done to me and my family. Not only that, but just knowing how many other people they had killed just to create what I am today haunts me. I did not ask to be used as a science experiment, nor for them to painfully kill each member of my family, one family member at a time, then to see each one of them right there die before your eyes. Yet, I was powerless to stop them, and then for them to take a young child away from her family and do the same experiments they had done to my family all over again. I'm haunted in my dreams, to see the way each person they killed look at me for help, and all I could do is just sit there and watch them die. Now, I have three personalities to deal with and an internal struggle to keep under control," Allan told her while a single tear ran down the side of his face.

"I know it hurts. You need to stay in control for your sister's sake, as well as ours. Do you actually think any one of us really wants you to get hurt? We would rather you leave the Alliance and go somewhere you could feel safe and at ease before we would want anything terrible to happen. You chose to join the Alliance, for what reason, I do not know. You are an Earthling. Earthlings cannot join the Alliance due to how primitive your race is. You could leave at any time if you wanted to, all we would want from you is for you to stay in touch—nothing more," Melody replied.

"I wish I could, except if I did, who would protect my sister? I'm now nothing more than a monster that can only be who everyone wants me to be out here in space. Where else could I go? I cannot go back to earth even if I wanted to," Allan said in low, sad voice.

"You are right, you cannot. If Earth were more advanced than what they are now, then you probably could. Right now, they are too primitive and destructive for their own good, which is also why we have a blockade around that system. You already know the rules—no one is allowed to make contact, no one is allowed to send replies to their signals, and on one is allowed to go to Earth for any reason, not even to return home. If you did go home with the primitive technology they have, would they be able to keep your third personality at bay or overcome him if you did turn in to him? Our family knows how much you would like to go back, and we also realize it is unfair for a child with their family to be taken against their will and then used as liboratory test subjects like you were. I was not supposed to tell you this, but after this drill, you will be given some time off to spend with your sister," Melody told him.

"That reminds me, can you tell me how Shamarra is doing? Is she all right? How are the studies going for her? Is she getting along with everyone, or are they making fun of her?" Allan asked his cousin as he slowly moved around in the water on his back.

"All that I know she misses you a lot, for her studies I am not sure I was not able to talk to her that much. I do know according to Uncle and Aunt she is doing fine and they wanted me to tell you not to worry about her so much. I think they are watching over her for you while you are away, I also heard she has a new tutor. I also hear Melanie will be coming here for this drill, is she suppose to graduate in the upcoming class?" Melody asked.

"Yes, she is. I do not think this drill will have any effect on her graduating with the others. I am sorry to say that the planet academy has failed the drill. Now let's see if the station academy will pass," he replied after a short, sorrow-exhaled breath.

"Not to change the subject, but when you are in the right mood, cousin, I will need you to teach me some of that advanced training for hand-to-hand combat, you know. I am a little rusty, and I know you have learned around fifty to sixty different forms of Martial Arts. Besides, I have also heard you have created a new style that no one has ever seen before," Melody said while smiling.

"Sorry, Melody, I cannot. I wouldn't mind showing you, except I'm not a combat instructor. Besides, it's not my place to show everyone, due to the agreement and the confidential information the Galaxy Alliance has with those planets. Also, it's due to how extremely deadly they truly are," he replied.

While the two cousins continued the conversation, the battle at Drandon Station started to become intense. "Squadron Leaders, I want inside that station. Break those defenses. We need to get inside no matter what! Now move!" Colonel Calamen said as his cruiser dodged a laser blast from the station.

"Sir, I really think we could use your son's help here. We are outnumbered, and we cannot target the station yet," the lieutenant told him.

"No, he is busy dealing with the recruits. Phantom's drill is far more important than having him here with us. If this situation becomes extremely sticky, then I will place the priority one scramble code in, and he will be here in a matter of a few hours," Colonel Calamen replied from his command chair.

"Colonel, this is First Squadron's leader. Sir, we . . ." Suddenly, static exploded from the communication.

"Tactical, what is the status on our fighters?" the colonel demanded.

"Sir, we are down by ten percent. I do not think we will be able to break through. Sir, I think the lieutenant is right. We may need Phantom's help with this," a female voice said.

"Open communications. First Squadron Second Fighter, you are now the commander. Good luck." Colonel demanded, "Focus all our fire power on those blaster canons. Notify the rest of the fleet," while walking over to the tactical map of the fight after the communications ended.

"Sir, notified all the fleet, and they want to know if this is going to be a suicide mission?" the male's voice said from the communications station.

"No, if we can take out the canon's main power generator one at a time, those canons will be useless, and then we can start our assault against the station," the colonel told them while thinking, *I would like to know what it is exactly that they are after.*

"Sir, we have an incoming communications," the communication's officer reported.

"Ah, Colonel Jack Calamen, it is so nice to see you again," a male's voice said over the speakers before his face appeared on the screen.

"Daggen, I wish I could say the same. Tell me, what is it you want from this station?" the colonel replied.

"I want you and your ships to leave this system. Do not return until I send you a message. If you refuse, I will have to do this with the rest of the captured prisoners," Daggen said as an airlock opened and bodies flew from the airlock.

"Daggen, you did not have to do that!" the colonel exclaimed. As the communications ended, all he could hear was Daggen's laughter echoing through his mind.

"Sir, what are your orders?" the lieutenant asked.

"Order all ships to take out those canons on that station. Since those Pirates want that station so badly, I suggest we take it back," Colonel Calamen demanded.

Before Calamen could bark more orders, he heard, "Sir, canon number six is now off line. Squadrons one, three, and nine are heading for the others, while Squadrons two, four, and five are covering them," the communications officer told him.

Cheering exploded on the bridge. "What are you cheering for? This fight is far from being over. All right, tell those Squadrons that if they can manage a way to pull this off, I will allow them leave time for two weeks. Also, can someone tell me what they used to disable that canon?" Calamen demanded with a hint of being frustrated.

"Sir, I am First Squadron's Leader, and I used the new Alliance ghost impact missile. This gives off a negative impulse discharge. It disables any power source that is connected to the target. Fortunately, the canons have their own power supply from the rest of the station. Drandon Station itself was not affected," the male's voice said over the audio.

"I know what the ghost missiles are. Miranda, remind me later to thank my son. Now, can you take the rest of those canons out?" Calamen replied.

"Yes, sir, we can," the voice replied as the communications went silent.

"Sir, is there a reason you want me to remind you to thank Phantom?" the female at the tactical station asked.

"Oh, never mind. All cruisers, focus on the hanger's shielding," he ordered as his feet shook from the discharge of their canon.

"Sir, the shields are down by fifteen percent and falling," Miranda replied with a hint of relief.

"Great, now, everyone, just keep it up for a little longer, and then we will be able to board the station," Calamen told them as he took his seat while smiling. *I think I may need some reinforcements,* he thought as he pushed a button on the side of his chair.

"Sir, a strange signal was just sent out," Miranda replied.

CHAPTER 6

"THIS IS IT, ladies and gentlemen. We are currently entering the upper atmosphere of Trolena. Their sensors have not noticed us yet, and that is due to the phase compensating we are using for the radio and video frequencies we are sending out. For those of you who failed surprise tactics 101, this means we are invisible to them. Now, check your gear and get ready to show these Pirates what the Alliance can do," Grand Admiral Blake told them while thinking, *I hope Colonel Catherina Melody is ready, and I also hope he will not over do this.*

"What I am I suppose to do? Wait, what was it Phantom told me," a young recruit asked herself while thinking, *Whenever you must deal with Pirates, just remember these rules. First rule, never trust what they tell you. Ninety-nine percent of the time, it is a lie. There are only three people in a specific guild I would trust, and that is it. Second rule, do not ever think the Pirate you are facing is unarmed. You will be killed. The third and final rule, and this is the most important rule, always shoot the Pirate's body three extra times in the head, even if you know they are dead. They like to wear stun inhibiters to make it look like they are dead when they are actually knocked out for a maximum of twenty seconds. Follow these rules, and you will live.* Phantom's voice echoed through her head as the memory of a sharp pain from where Phantom had thrown her to the mat during that particular lesson shot into her back.

"Melanie, Melanie, is everything all right? Do not tell me you are feeling sick. You do not need to worry. I will be there to protect you," a young man said while looking at a green-haired, light-blue skinned young woman.

"I am fine. I was just thinking about a lesson I had. The nice part was, I had learned a lot from that teacher. Now, the drawback is that I can still feel the pain I had to endure to understand the lesson. Besides, Morris, who said I needed your protection? For what I can recall, all you liked to do was sleep during class," she replied to the young man.

"Oh, I see, you are thinking of that Drazarian girl, are you not? What was here name? Shametra, Shamorrta . . ." Before Morris could finish his sentence, he heard.

"It is Shamarra, and do not make fun of her," Melanie replied.

"I would wipe the floor with her. She is a good for nothing child who only lives off of the Alliance. Also, do not get me started about her good for nothing brother," Morris told her.

"I would love to see how well of a match you would be for her. That is only if she does not hold back," Melanie said while smirking.

"By the way, who was the teacher for that particular lesson? I do not ever remember any special classes being offered or being mandatory, either," he asked with a confused look.

"The Altherian was, and is, also the older brother of Shamarra. I think I could learn a lot more from him if he had been the hand-to-hand combat instructor. Even though I was given a few private lessons, I realized how truly great he was," Melanie replied.

"Get ready. We are on the final approach to the drop off points. Be ready for anything, recruit Melanie, you and your group will take the main camp. We will cover you on both sides, and, hopefully, we will be able to take them out before they can spot you," Blake replied.

"Sir, we have landed in the green zone. We can unload the recruits at any time," a male's voice said over the inner speakers.

"All right, lower the ramp, recruits. Now, move out," Grand Admiral Blake told them.

Just before the ramp touched the ground, Blake heard, "Why does she have to be the squad leader? What makes her so special? I should have been the squad captain," a male recruit said.

"It is due to the recent training she was given. She and another Alliance member had an agreement. To hold up the agreement, she was given advanced lessons in tactical readouts and deployment. She had passed the tests for the classes. Now, you three, listen up and listen good. When dealing with Pirates, there are three rules you need to know. First rule, never trust what they tell you. Ninety-nine percent of the time it is a lie. There are only three people in a specific guild

I would trust and that is it. Second rule . . ." Before Grand Admiral Blake could finish, he heard a female's voice approaching.

"Do not ever think the Pirate you are facing is unarmed. You will be killed. The third and final rule, and this is the most important rule, always shoot the Pirate's body three extra times in the head, even if you know they are dead. They like to wear stun inhibiters to make it look like they are dead when they are actually knocked out for a maximum of twenty seconds. Now, if you can remember these rules and follow these rules carefully, you will live," Melanie said walking up behind Blake.

"I could not have said that any better. Now move out, and remember if you find yourselves in any trouble, just fall back and wait for reinforcements," Blake replied as the four started down the ramp.

"All units, the intruders have arrived. The Altherian will meet up with the advancing forces, and then, on his signal, we will take the rest of them out," Colonel Melody ordered.

"I guess this is my queue. Just wait here. I have a feeling this won't take too long," Phantom said out loud as he switched to a personal frequency, "The other recruits will probably fall into all my traps I have laying around."

"You are probably right. That is why we are doing this, just to see if there needs to be more training before we let them graduate," Melody said in a low voice.

When Melody and Phantom both had realized a few minutes had already passed, seven blaster shots zipped past Phantom's head as he heard, "Over there we found one!" from an eager young male.

"Ma'am, I do hope he knows what he is doing," Corporal Johnson said as he watched the Altherian dodging the blaster shots.

"I would not worry about him, because I do believe he is enjoying himself," she replied while thinking, *Stop playing around with them and just end it already. We already know you are just going to fail them, anyway. Though, let us just see how far you are willing to take this.*

Suddenly, Melody noticed three young recruits had stopped their advancing and were now touching their ears. Then, she suddenly heard, "Ma'am, we have him now, except, we cannot land a single shot on him," one of the recruits replied.

A field commander—not bad, not bad at all. Now, where are you hiding? You must show yourself sooner or later. It is going to be sooner rather than later for the way your recruits are acting, Melody thought to herself.

"Ma'am, he is dodging every shot we launch toward him. What do you mean, 'Fall back'? I do not care if you were placed as the commander of this group. We know what we are doing all right, just shut up and allow us to take care of this Pirate scum," another recruit said as the three started to advance again.

This will not be pretty. Phantom, I know you, just do not do it, Melody thought. "Medical team, stand by. We will have multiple injuries that will be needing attention," she called over a secured line.

Suddenly, Melody noticed one of the male recruits throwing an object. As Phantom's right hand pointed toward the object, she suddenly saw a large explosion that erupted right in front of him.

No, cousin, those were supposed to be stun detonators and not the real thing, she thought as she saw their field commander walking out from her hiding place. *Melanie, you are the commander?* Melody thought with an expression of being surprised sweeping over her face.

"Yes! We did it. Did you see that? I blew his helmet completely off of his head! You see, Commander, I told you we did not need your stupid orders. We did everything that we were supposed to do without you, so why don't you go crawling back to the Altherian to get some more useless training?" a male recruit said while a young, blue-skinned woman with green hair walked up to him.

"Did you shoot him in the head three times?" the field commander asked while approaching the body.

"No, ma'am, he's definitely—"

Before the male could say anything else, he heard, "This cannot be. What is going on here?" she said out loud while shooting the body three times as she stepped backward.

"What is wrong commander? You look like you just saw a ghost," one of the three males replied.

"You are not too far off. Grand Admiral Blake, this is Melanie. Can you hear me? Over. I repeat, do you copy? Over," she said as she activated her communication unit.

"This is Blake. Go ahead, Melanie. What do you have to report?" he replied.

"This is either a drill, or the Pirates were able to turn the Altherian. My squad, against orders, used a detonator against him. His body is on the ground right now. Sir, I have a bad feeling about this. I suggest we recall everyone and regroup back at the transport. If I am right, the Altherian will not be too far behind us," Melanie said as she walked.

"What are you talking about? We killed him. There is no way he could have survived," another male told her.

"I copy. I am recalling everyone back to the transport right now. For the record, are you sure it is him?" he replied.

"Yes, sir, I am, and I think we are about to have a few extra problems," she replied while noticing the destroyed detonator on the ground.

"All units, fall back and regroup at the transport now. That is an order!" Grand Admiral Blake's voice suddenly called over everyone's communications.

"If I were you, I would not stand that close to that particular body," she said as she turned and started to run.

"Oh look, our commander is afraid of a corpse. What can he do to us now? He's—" a male's voice said as they heard a strange voice behind them say, "Dead . . ."

As the three recruits turned to look behind them, one of the recruits fell to the ground, holding his right arm and screaming.

"You boys do not understand anything you are told, do you?" Phantom replied as he dodged a kick.

"Why, I'm going to make you pay for that!" the second male recruit said as he threw another kick.

"Lesson one; you do not attack, especially if you do not understand what your opponent's skills are. Lesson two; you never go against orders, even if it is a drill," Phantom said as he caught the recruit's leg and then broke it at the shin.

"Who are you? What do you think you are doing?" the third recruit asked while charging the Altherian.

"My job," Phantom said as he spun to avoid the recruits attack and planted an elbow in his solar plexus. "This drill is over. Computer, identify all allies and notify the commanders we are heading back to Alpha camp," Phantom told his wrist computer as he laid the recruit on the ground.

"Why did you do this? What was all of this?" Melanie asked while walking up to him.

"We were told to run an actual combat drill of an ambush. So that is what we did, and this is what happens when people do not listen to their commanding officers," Melody replied as she touched her ear, "Medical teams, we have recruits that need to be picked up and examined."

"This drill was a bust. Both of the graduating classes need more drills on handling Pirates, or there will be nothing left of the Alliance," Phantom said while walking off.

"Melanie, out of everyone else here, I think that was his way of saying you pasted. One single recruit passed the drill out of one thousand recruits—I do not like those odds. Also, Melanie, it is good to see you," Melody told her while shaking the young woman's hand.

"I know those blasted rogue creator are here somewhere. I guess this planet is as good of a place to start then any. Computer, take us to that planet's surface." A strange male told his AI while thinking, *The vessel I had tracked them too was destroyed, and now their engine signal shows this planet was their last stop.*

"Sir, it has been three years ago when we started this mission. So far, those rogues have been a few steps ahead of us. I just hope this is not in vain. Sir, I am picking up strange signals from this planet," the AI reported.

"Then, let us investigate. Let us hope we can find them, so we can get back home," the strange male replied.

"You Galaxy Warriors *do* become extremely busy with your duties," the AI added.

"Just take us down. Also, remind me to wipe that sucking-up out of your program," the man demanded.

"Hey, do not blame me. Your son was the one who programmed that response into my data base. All right, here we go, and hold on tight—it will be a bumpy ride," the AI replied.

As the unknown vessel started its approach, Phantom and the commander's lined the recruits up into two, big groups. "I have made my decision, and I wanted to let you all know. Save for a single person, you all have failed this drill. Can anyone here tell me why we chose to have a drill instead of teaching every single one of you in a class room?" Phantom's voice asked over the loud speakers.

After a few moments of awkward silence, Phantom told them, "We are pacing around the names of a special group of people who laid down their lives to help the less fortunate people than you. After looking at the names, can anyone tell me what makes them so special? Once you are able to answer that, you will know why we had to run this as a drill with out anyone other than your commanding officers knowing about this."

"It is due to every one of these members dying because of an ambush from the Pirates," a female's voice spoke up.

"That is right. Without this actual drill, none of you could comprehend how dangerous this could have actually have been. Also, none of you could have known how fast an ambush could have happened. Recruit Direndall, step forward!" Phantom demanded while watching the recruits look of hope turn to a look of dismay.

"Sir, what can I do for you?" Melanie replied with a worried look on her face.

"Once you have graduated, your first assignment will be to the Intelligence Forces. From there, you will finish your training that was placed upon you. Your rank will become Corporal. A recruit straight from the Academy to become one of the top Intelligence Officers is truly an honor, and for the rest of you, every single one of you have failed. Congratulations, Direndall. For the rest of you, you are now dismissed," Phantom said just before turning around and walking off.

As the recruits started to break apart, Melanie heard, "The only reason she will be an Intelligence Officer is because she must be the Altherian's girlfriend. He is trying to keep her from the front lines," a male recruit said.

"Do not allow them to get to you, for what I hear that group was found in a trap a few meters from the drop zone. I am still wondering how my nephew knew we would use that particular field for the drop zone," Grand Admiral Blake said while walking up with is niece.

"Yes, I know. If they actually knew how painful those lessons actually were, they would understand. I never asked to be placed in with the Intelligence Forces," Melanie replied.

"I know you did not. I also know with the training I had given you, more recruits will benefit from that experience," Phantom said while walking up.

"I know. Except, why did you change my profession from a doctor to Intelligence?" She asked him.

"It is because you will still be a field doctor with more training. When you are at the front lines, you will be able to see the entire picture and not just the puzzle pieces," Phantom told her as his arm computer beeped a few times rapidly.

"What is it? Is there something wrong?" Blake asked.

"Nothing, at least, that *I* cannot handle," Phantom said while walking away.

"Phantom, I was ordered to bring that new fighter for you to look at. I must warn you, the new AI needs an attitude adjustment though," a middle-aged male said while walking up to him.

"*Beep, Beep* . . ." the computer on Phantom's arm sounded.

"Thanks. Tell Mac I will look at it in a few minutes. We have a visitor," Phantom said while looking into the sky to see a ship landing.

"What is going on, Phantom? Are you expecting someone?" Blake asked while approaching his nephew.

"Either this is a complete coincidence, or a stranger is looking for trouble, sir. It will only take a few minutes to find out, and then I will let you know," Phantom replied while walking off.

"Just be careful, your Aunt would kill me if anything were to happen to you," Blake called to him.

As Phantom approached the landing site, he heard, "Who do you think you are? You do not have the right to be here. This planet belongs to the Galaxy Alliance, and you are trespassing. Identify yourself or leave," a male's voice demanded.

"Tell me, where are the creators at? Are you hiding them from me? I will have no choice but to kill each and every one of you if I find out you are hiding them," a strange voice said.

"You will pay for that insolent tongue of yours," the male's voice said with a sound of a authority.

As the recruit charged toward the stranger, everyone noticed the stranger grabbing the recruit and throwing him to the ground. As he knelt next to him, he took the recruit's head in his hands and demanded, "Tell me, now, where are you hiding the creators? If you do not tell me, I will kill this one."

Suddenly, four knives flew past his head and into the ground as a voice said, "Let the child go. We do not know of anyone who calls themselves 'the creators.' If this is not the answer you are looking for, then I am sorry."

"Who said that? You are lying. I followed their trail right to this planet. Are you or are you not a coward? If you are not, then come out and face me," the stranger said while standing up.

Suddenly, as the crowd split into two groups, the stranger noticed a young man dressed in all black who was standing in front of him. "I am not a coward, nor do I wish to fight. Let the child go, and then we can talk about why you are here," Phantom said while looking at the brown-haired, green-eyed man.

"Do I know you? You look somewhat familiar," the stranger asked.

"I do not know you, nor do I want to get to know you. This is your last warning. Let him go, or you will have me to deal with!" Phantom demanded as his tone started to become stern. Then, he closed his eyes.

"Phantom, I want you to allow Allan to take him on," a strange voice said.

"Assassin, you know he does not have the same abilities as you and me," Phantom replied.

"Yes, I know that. All you have to do is allow him to tap into your abilities. I want to see what this stranger is capable of doing," the Assassin told him.

"Did you forget that if Allan is killed, then we die as well? We are sharing the same body, after all," Phantom responded.

"Yes, are you completely stupid? Or something else?" Allan added.

"Just do it, will you? I will help out if it calls for it. I will not mind if you take over, either. I just want to play with him for a bit. I want to know what he is truly after," the Assassin replied with a smirk on his face.

"All right, you heard him, kid. Show us what you can do with our help. Also, do not worry. We will not allow him to hurt you, too badly," Phantom replied while looking at a young, teenage male.

Phantom's head came up, and all they could see is his hazel eyes.

"I said, let the child go!" the man exclaimed as he started to sprint toward the stranger.

"Fine, if you want him, then come and get—"

Before the stranger could finish speaking, he realized the recruit was no longer there.

"My body . . . it hurts. Please, someone help me!" the recruit was screaming.

"This will only take a few minutes. Just sit back and try to relax. Melanie, take him over to the cruisers Medians' medical bay. This should reduce the pain for a while," Phantom told the recruit as his fingers walked across the kid's body.

"That feel a little . . ." the recruit started to say as he passed out.

"Uncle, that's Allan. We need to stop him before he hurts himself," Melody said while watching what was beginning to happen.

"I do not think we can. Look at his eyes. It looks like he is focused more than we have ever seen him," Blake replied while holding out an arm to stop three recruits from intervening.

"Tell me, I am trying to understand why you did this to him? What did he do to deserve this?" Phantom asked while walking toward the stranger.

"He refused to answer my questions, and now you are intervening with my investigation. Now, get out of my way!" the stranger said as his hands started to glow yellow.

"I do not care what kind of investigation you are trying to conduct here. When you involve any one of these people, you will have to answer to me," Phantom said while increasing his speed to a run.

Suddenly, the stranger launched a lightning bolt from his hands at Phantom as he thought *This fight is now over.*

Suddenly, as the smoke cleared, the stranger noticed half a wall of dirt where his target was standing. With a surprised look on his face, he thought, *Now, how could this happen? No one in this dimension should have been able to stop that.*

"Hey, ugly, up here!" Phantom yelled just before connecting his fist with the stranger's face.

As Phantom touched the ground, the stranger shoved a knee into Phantom's face. To everyone's surprise, the stranger knocked Phantom back three feet, and they heard, "That was the first time in a while anyone was able to connect any kind of attack with me."

"Well, I am glad you approve of that attack. Now it's time for the actual warm up," Phantom said while standing back up.

"Ma'am, how much more can that recruit take? I'm afraid that he'll be killed," a recruit said from the side.

"No, he is fine. Right now, I would really hate to be that stranger. Like Phantom said, he is now just 'warming up.' Just sit back and watch for when he decides to stop playing around. Also, Phantom is not a recruit," Grand Admiral Blake replied while Melody's eyes focused on the fight.

"Uncle, is it me, or are they speeding up?" Melody asked, and her gaze was ripped away as both the stranger and Phantom disappeared in front of them.

"For all I could see, they both countered each other's attacks, one right after the other," Blake said wide-eyed.

Suddenly, a loud explosion erupted around them as they noticed a boulder crumbling to the ground. After the smoke cleared, they noticed Phantom standing back up and dusting himself off. "Not bad, not bad at all. You are the first person that I have come across who was able to keep up with me. Tell me, who are you, and where are you from?" Phantom said with a grin on his face as his eyes started to glow again.

"I have to admit, you are the first person I have met in this dimension that is able to use the life energy of the universe. My name is Odin, and I am a member of the Peace Forces of New Atlantis. Now, tell me, where is the creator?" the stranger replied.

"New Atlantis? As in the Atlantis back on planet Earth? They had been thought to be more advanced then everyone had given them credit. Now, tell me, who is this creator you are looking for? Are they a mechanic?" Phantom asked.

"No, in your terms, they would be a scientist who has stolen information on how to engineer and create a being just like us. We followed their engine Ionics emotions to this dimension three years ago. Do you know where they are?" Odin asked in a frustrated tone.

"So the device the scientist's found in the underwater world was Atlantian, and now I know what they had found was a space dimensional device. As for your question, no, we have not seen your rogue scientists," Phantom replied.

"What do you mean, 'underwater world that was called Atlantis'? Who are you, and what race are you?" Odin asked.

Great. The secret's out. I can see the headlines, "The Galaxy Alliance Has an Earthling among Them" for the next topic discussion, Blake thought.

"You are an Earthling, and I am an Altherian who just happens to know about the planet Earth," Phantom said while thinking, *If I can prove all my pain was caused by those rogue scientists, this Atlantian can have whatever is left of them after I am finished with them.*

"I did not realize how advanced those Earthlings actually are. I think we may be in big trouble if they can harness that technology," Blake told himself.

"Ma'am, I pulled the Altherian's service record up. Why did you not tell us he has the ranking from Corporal all the way to Grand Admiral? Also, why did you keep the fact that he is Phantom Breaker—the same Phantom Breaker who is currently under Colonel Calamen and is a member of the Special Operations Unit with Daniel and Ian?" a recruit asked.

"Oh, that. I am sorry. It completely slipped my mind," Melody replied while watching the two individuals standing off.

"Are you just going to stand there and hide those traitors from me?" Odin asked with a hint of anger in his voice.

"We are not hiding anyone, and if I have to keep on fighting you just to prove that, then come on!" Phantom yelled as he touched the ground with a single palm.

"Now, what is he . . ."

Before Odin could finish his thought, a large tornado shot up around Phantom.

"Ma'am, why did you not tell us he is actually a grand admiral? How old is he, actually? Like, with you, you are twenty-eight, and you only look eighteen. Does that mean he is thirty five and looks only fifteen?" the recruit demanded to know.

"Oh, that. I just forgot about the rank. Phantom is only fifteen Galactic standard years old. No more and no less," Melody replied.

"Out of everyone with the most potential, he is that only one I have ever seen who despises military ranking," Blake said while thinking, *He will only accept the rank of corporal, even though he could be commanding this entire Alliance!*

Suddenly, Phantom rushed through the tornado toward Odin. "I am tired of this game, and this game is now over!" Odin yelled as he shoved a glowing, brown arm into Phantom's solar plexus.

As Phantom's image ran through Odin, the look on his face was of shock as he heard "You're right. This game is definitely over," Phantom's voice appeared behind him.

As Odin turned toward the voice, he suddenly felt a hard object connecting with his lower jaw. *How is this possible? I've never had problems defeating anyone from this dimension,* he thought as he fell to the ground.

"What was that? I have never seen anything like that before? Even the multi-Split Martial Arts could not perform any moves like that one," Melody said to her Uncle.

"That was called Shadow Casting. It is a newly created style in Martial Arts. There is only a single person to have the knowledge to perform a maneuver like that," Blake said while watching the Atlantian stand back up and start his attack.

As Phantom and the Atlantian continued their interrogations with one and another, the fight around the Drandon Station became extremely dangerous. "Sir, the shields are now inactive. We can land in the hanger," the tactical station told Colonel Calamen.

"All right, notify all infiltration transports to follow us in. As soon as we land, I want this station back in the hands of the Alliance—no matter what," Jack Calamen replied as his cruiser started toward the station hanger.

As the cruiser entered the hanger, Colonel Calamen suddenly felt the shudder of the cruiser from the discharge of the canons. "What was that? Did we just get hit by the defense systems?" the Colonel asked.

"No, sir, our gunners targeted a few Pirates that were still in the hanger. Sir, we are in the final phase of docking," the navigations replied.

Before the cruisers fully rested on their landing struts, the boarding dropped, and the soldiers rushed down the ramp. "Sir, the hanger is now clear," a lieutenant said while lowering his blaster.

As the colonel walked down the ramp, he ordered, "I want this entire station secured, and I want this done now. Lieutenant Erriks, I want you and your men to cover sections of the station on the eighty-first to the through eighty-sixth. I also want you to take Squads 101, 104, and the 182 with you. Good luck.

"Major Manic, section seventy-five to eighty is all yours. You will take the 253, 301, and 404 with you. Units 82, 155, 201, and the 303 will be on stand-by in case you need them.

"Corporal Vhan, the section seventy to seventy four is all yours. You will need special units to keep those hangers secured. You will take 204, 601, 300, and the 909 with you. The 475, 896, 775, 92, and the 53th units are going with you as back-up. Whatever the scientist are working on should be in those hangers. I want you to update me every hour. If I do not receive a transmission from you, I will consider your units lost. Now, let us get going and find out what is going on."

"Yes, sir! Come on, men, you heard them. Let move out!" the Major said while running toward the lower level's elevator.

"We will take the stairs, men. We need to find every location those filthy Pirates are hiding and take care of them. We are to take them either dead or alive. Right now, it does not matter—just take care of them," Lieutenant Erriks told his group while running down a hallway.

"All right, that means we will have to check the emergency escape routes. The sooner we get this done, the faster we can get home," the corporal told his mean while walking over to a hatch in the northwest corner on the floor of the hanger.

"Come on, we need to get to the control room. Move out, men, and stay on guard. You never know what those Pirates will try to do," the colonel relied as he started walking toward the main doors to the hanger.

Suddenly, a loud explosion shook the hanger. "What just happened? All command units, report!" Colonel Calamen demanded.

"Sir, this is Erriks. The Pirates set up traps to separate the groups from the others. One of my soldiers walked right into the trap. I'm sorry, sir. Joe's dead. Sir, we need back—" Suddenly, a sound of a blaster discharging was heard just before the communications devise exploded with static.

"Sir, this is Manic. We will have to find another way around. Our return point was just sealed, as well. It will take us a while to make it back to the cruisers. I believe that if the Pirates had anyone in these sections, they would not have sat up traps. Also, sir, the emergency escape route was destroyed. Every member of Corporal Vhan's group is dead," the Major replied.

"Copy that. Just be careful. We do not know what those Pirates have planned for us," Calamen replied while thinking, *I may need his help, after all. No, he has more important things than this to take care of. If I truly need him, then I will summon him.*

"Sir, I think right now would be the best time to call—" Before the lieutenant could finish his last word, everyone heard blasters discharging with bright red flashes at a distance in front of them.

"We're going to die!" "Someone save me!" Voices exploded from among the ranks.

"Will everyone just shut up and let me think! Find some cover and stay there. We must stop them from blocking us in. Units 304, 606, and the 701, try to get around them using an alternative rout. Units 45, 46, 47, 48, and the 52nd, you will try to counter the approaching group of Pirates. Units 205, 206, 207, 210, and 211, you are in charge of keeping our cruisers in one piece. The rest of us will use the maintenance crawl spaces to retake the control room. Corporal Ricks, I want you to try to gain access to the main computer. Everyone, good luck and move out," the colonel ordered as he opened the maintenance hatch and fear spread cross the soldiers.

"Get me out of here! I want to go home. I don't want to be a soldier anymore!" a female's voice cried with fear.

"Someone, please shut her up so we can come up with a plan. We will do our best, sir. As for the rest of you, for the old pros like me, this is just another day. For the rest of you who have never seen combat, remember your training, and you should be fine," a lieutenant demanded in a frustrated voice just before a loud explosion erupted from the detonator he had just thrown.

"Sir, I sure wished the Altherian were here to back us up," a soldier said as he discharged three more shots at the approaching Pirates.

"Yeah, I know what you mean. We will just have to do the best that we can and wait for reinforcements if they are able to get past those blasted canons. I just hope they can gain control of the main computer and activate the internal security system. That way, we can have the upper hand," the lieutenant replied while regaining his composure as he dropped a charging Pirate.

While the sounds of the blasters started to become softer and softer, Colonel Calamen and his remaining nine units continued to move through the corridors of the maintenance crawl space when he heard, "Sir, I do not think we will be leaving here alive," the lieutenant told him with a hint of being worried in his voice.

"Sure we will. All you need to do is to focus, or as my daughter says, 'Faith in our skills of survival.'" Calamen told them while trying not to panic himself. As they moved further down the maintenance corridor, he was thinking, *It also helps to have my son around when she says that. We may be in over our heads here. We cannot get control of the computer without the access codes, and to receive them, we need to get to the safe in the commander's office.*

"Sir, I still cannot gain access to the main computer system from in here. I may know how to hack into a computer, but that's only when I can gain access through the back door or by knowing the codes. For what I can tell, there are no back doors, and all the codes I have tried are not working. We need those command codes, and we need them now," the corporal replied with a panicking tone to his voice.

"All right, calm down. If you cannot break their control over the system, then I know someone who probably can. Let's just hope the individual can get here while we are still breathing," Calamen said while reaching down with his hand shaking to touching a switch on his belt.

"Sir, I'm sorry to say, all signals are dead. I can no longer hack into the main systems while we are in this crawl space," the corporal replied with terrifying fear in his voice.

"I knew it. We are going to die!" a few soldiers cried out with terrifying fear.

"Shut up! Will everyone get a hold of themselves? We are not done yet. We will gain control of the system, and the only way to do that is to get to a computer network. Meaning, we will have to leave this maintenance crawl space just so we can regain the signal. All right, when we exit this hatch, be careful. Now, let's get moving and keep our head down," Calamen said while trying to keep the fear out of his voice as he thought, *This is going to be a long night. Phantom, I hope you get here while I'm still breathing.*

"Sir, you and I both know we have never seen this kind of raid from the Pirates. What is it about this station that is looking so appealing to the Pirates that would cause them to attack it?" the lieutenant asked in a low whisper.

"I do not know. This is a science station where they are supposed to be developing new medical solutions for a few worlds. I wish I knew what is truly going on here, and I am going to find out," Calamen said as he opened the outer hatch.

"There is no sign of anything hostile here," the lieutenant said while climbing out on to one of the main decks.

"That is great. Finally, some good news for a change," Colonel Calamen said just before the station shook from another explosion.

"Now, what is it?" Calamen thought out loud.

"I do believe we are now in the hot zone, men," the lieutenant replied.

"That was a rhetorical question. You know one that does not need an answer to it?" Calamen demand while trying to hide the high levels of frustration in his voice as he touched the switch on his belt a second time.

"Sir, according to this security monitor levels, fifty-one A all the way to the level nineteen A floors was just detached from the main structure. The only reason that we have not felt the decompression is due to the emergency doors having sealed the rest of the station off," the lieutenant replied.

"Now, isn't that just perfect? All right, let's keep moving before unwanted guests just started to materialize from thin air," Calamen said as he heard, "There they are! Blast them all! If I find out even one has escaped, I will personally kill you myself," a voice said from down the hall.

"Fall back!" Calamen yelled while discharging his blaster while thinking, *Phantom, you had better be on your way. If I find out that you were just goofing around, I will haunt you till the day you die.*

"Sir, do you know where we are?" the lieutenant asked as a security door slammed shut.

"No I do not. If I did, we would already be at the control room," Calamen said as he placed a hand over his face.

"Sir, we are at the control room," the lieutenant replied with a sigh of relief.

After a few minutes of looking around, everyone heard, "This appears to be a sub control room not the main one," Calamen replied.

"Sir, all controls are locked. We cannot gain access to the main systems, and, according to the security cameras, even if we did get to the main control room, we still could not regain control," a soldier responded while looking at a monitor.

As the lieutenant and the colonel walked over to the monitor, the look of hope washed from their faces. "Jack, we have been friends for a while. Can you tell me what is going on here? There has to be a reason for the Pirates attacking this station," the lieutenant requested.

"If we can hold out long enough for my son to get here, we can ask him what this station is used for," Calamen replied as his voice became louder. "We need to move before those Pirates can get through that door! We cannot hold a tactical advantage here. Let us finally take the fight to those Pirates," the colonel replied while walking over to the emergency door for an escape route.

Three hundred meters down the hall, Colonel Calamen and his units felt the station shaking. Suddenly, the airlock doors just opened up as they scrambled for cover. Five minutes later, the doors closed, and the numbers of the soldier's where cut in half as he heard, "Sir, we have a problem!" the lieutenant said as the sound of blaster discharging and the blasts hitting the wall next to them.

CHAPTER 7

"I TOLD YOU, we do not know anything about your creators," Phantom exclaimed with frustration in his voice as he dodged a punch from Odin.

"You know something, or you would not be fighting me this hard," Odin replied.

Suddenly, everyone heard a loud, continuous beep from Phantom's arm computer. Phantom proclaimed, "I would love to stick around and play except I am needed elsewhere."

Suddenly, as Odin threw another punch, Phantom caught the arm as he shoved his right forearm into Odin's left arm with a loud, blood-curdling snap. Before Odin could scream out with pain, Phantom shoved his right elbow into Odin's rib cage as he pulled with his left arm. Suddenly, a loud cry came from Odin as his left arm lay limp at his side, "You broke my arm and dislocated my shoulder! I will kill you for that!" Odin screamed.

To everyone's amazement, Phantom was already in the air, and a loud explosion erupted above them. They noticed Phantom being launched two feet away from Odin as he was already on his feet and in mid run.

"What was that he just hit me with?" Odin asked as he fell to his knees while realizing the rock he was standing near was now sand.

"I do not know, I do know . . . Next time, if I were you, I would talk with him in peace instead of fighting him," Melody replied while catching him before he hit the ground as she watched Phantom sprint toward the landing zone.

"Colonel, go after him and find out what is going on. Do not worry about this man. I will have the medical doctors take a look at him," Grand Admiral Blake ordered.

"Right, sir," Melody said as she saluted him and then turned and started to run.

"Catherina, also tell your cousin good luck and, most likely, good hunting!" Blake yelled at his niece as she ran.

"I sure will, Uncle!" she yelled back, which at that distance, all he could hear was, ". . . sure will . . ."

"Mac started the preflight check on that fighter you brought. Also, make sure the weapons are live ammunition and not fake," Phantom called over his communications link while thinking, *I do not have time to change shirts, except, I do not have a choice.*

"Phantom, what is going on? Why do you want us to arm this fighter?" Mac replied back.

"This will be an emergency launch, just make sure everything I need is in order!" Phantom demanded as he heard a female's voice from a distance say, "Phantom, wait up! What is going on?"

"Colonel Calamen needs my help. Something has gone wrong with the maneuvers. Here, I need you to wash this and then place it in the nanotech repair center," Phantom said while slowing down for Catherina to catch up.

"Are you all right? What happened to your shirt?" sshe asked while looking at the hole in the center of his chest.

"I am fine—drained of energy, but fine. The Atlantian hit me with a strong attack, and it damaged the nanotech shirt all the way to my jump suit. I have to stop off and grab my second shirt before I can do anything else," he replied while taking the shirt off and handing it to her.

"That last attack of his should have killed you. What did you do to stop it? Is it true the planet Earth had a race that advanced in its technology where they could build a dimensional gate and then just disappear?" she asked as the two ran.

"For what I had heard from the scientists who just *happened* to find the lost city of Atlantis, the answer is yes. It just dropped into the ocean on earth several thousands of years ago without an actual reason. Here, recently, the scientists were starting to be able to understand what technology that was left behind, and they started running a history check with her barely active systems, just to find out what happened to the city and the citizens of Atlanis. Also, I was using a chi energy, concealed, protective barrier to protect myself from most of those deadly attacks," Phantom replied as he stopped at his tent.

"What does that mean if that man truly is Atlantian? I mean, does that mean there could be more of them in another dimension besides the one he is from? Or does this mean there could be Atlantians still walking among the rest of the Earth's population?" she asked him.

"The third dimension, maybe. Having true Atlantians walking among the present Earth inhabitance—not a chance. The DNA blood samples the medical staff of Earth would have already realized that. When a child is born, they get a finger pricked, so that child's DNA is then logged and checked for any diseases. During this process, the Atlantian DNA should have appeared. There are no records of this DNA ever appearing," Phantom replied as he slid the second shirt over his head.

"Okay, have they ever thought that through the generations if a few Atlantians *had* survived, their DNA strands could have been placed into dormancy, and that is why the DNA has not appeared?" Catherina asked him.

"I'm not sure if they are able to find that kind of information out with the level of technology Earth has, or maybe they are not capable of that at this particular moment," Phantom said just before rushing out of his tent.

"Do you know if the scientists tried to map the DNA on Earth, and then compare the two just to find out if anyone *does* have Atlantian DNA?" Catherina asked as he walked past her.

"No, they have not, and the reason is this; they do not have any DNA from Atlantis to compare to the DNA of myself or any other human on Earth. All that I know, they have found the lost city of Atlantis, and they have been trying to make sense of the language there, as well as a few strange looking objects," Phantom replied as he walked toward the new fighter.

"Then, explain to me, how can a city be lost for so long and then just be found out of the blue? It is like we had a city on a planet, and then suddenly it just disappeared without anyone knowing. Then, one hundred years later, the city reappears at the same location from when it disappeared," she said.

"That would be easy if the planet could phase shifts, or at least the surface does. That is my answer. Due to the amount high levels of technology, the Alliance would be able to locate the city without a problem. The technology is like you said before, very low compared to the Alliance, and it was just now at the right level to be able to locate Atlantis,"

Phantom told her while thinking and rubbing his chest. "At least, that is what the records showed when I hacked into them a few months ago."

After climbing into the fighter, Phantom activated the fighter's schematics and started to read. *It looks like the speed has been increased compared to the other fighters, and the hyper space is almost as fast as a cruiser. There are two artificial intelligences. The primary is Faith, and the secondary is called Battle Response and Analysis Tactical Technician for everything else. B.R.A.T.T. for short, then,* Phantom thought just as his attention was drawn back to his cousin.

"Uncle Blake wanted me to tell you good luck and good hunting. I will see you back at the Academy when you return," she replied as he buckled in and the canopy closed.

A few minutes later, the experimental fighter with Phantom took off. *Please be careful and come home. If you do not come back, I do not know how can I explain this to Shamarra,* Catherina thought as she watched the fighter leave the hemisphere.

"How could he have beaten me? I have fought against many other races in this dimension and won, so how is it that a child has beaten me?" Odin asked as Blake helped him to his ship.

"It is because he is not an ordinary child as you blatantly called him. He is Phantom, a single, very unique, young man, when he was brought to the Galaxy Alliance at the age of twelve and a half, he already was a mature young man for what he had been through. Thanks to the Pirate by the name of Trayon, that young man had lost everything, even his child hood, and it took his aunt, mom, guardian or dad, and me several months to a year before he even trusted us. He would not allow anyone to become close to him, except for his little sister, whom is not even his biological sibling. That young man was tortured, beaten, mentally abused, and had his DNA altered *painfully* due to Trayon. That young man became his own worst nightmare, and he even considers himself a machine whose only purpose is to kill. He cannot go back to his own planet because of that," Blake told him.

"Then, why do you not put him out of his own misery? You say you are his family, and family takes care of each other. It seems to me that he is asking to be killed by the way he just fought me. I need to get to Earth and find my fellow kinsmen. There is no way he could have been telling me the truth. Now, can you tell me what planet is his origin?" Odin replied.

"Why is that? Do you always assume the information you receive is false?" Blake asked.

"No, I should know there are Atlantians on Earth. I saw one hundred of our soldiers who decided to become rogue, as in, wanted to get back to the fighting, go through the dimensional gate one hundred years ago," Odin replied.

"One hundred years ago . . . how old are you?" Blake asked while trying to keep the confusion off of his face.

"In this dimension, I would be one hundred and twenty-eight years old. In our dimension, I am only twenty-eight years old," Odin said as he placed his arm in a medical sling.

"Atlantis was destroyed over twenty five thousand year ago, according to Phantom, so how could there be other Atlantian's living on Earth?" Blake asked.

"They are probably just in hiding. Now, answer my question. What planet is that boy from?" Odin ordered.

After a few minutes when Grand Admiral Blake knew no one was listening, he relented, "His records are a secret. The Galaxy Alliance, although, has a very strict rule about no Earthling being allowed in the Alliance, meaning, someone like you. That is why, even though he looks like an Earthling, he is an Altherian. No one other than a few family members and the AI Mom knows of his origins. I will allow you to get on your way, just promise me you will not threaten anyone any more, and in return, I will notify our border guards to allow you in and out of the system as you wish. Do we have a deal?" Blake asked with a very serious look on his face.

"All right, you have my word. I will not threaten anyone. I thank you. I take me leave," Odin said just before the canopy closed and he thought, *I have enough blood from that boy on my shredded cloths and a small vile of blood where I can analyze his actual DNA.*

With those words, Odin's ship lifted off the ground and shot into the air. *Why do I have a feeling this is far from being over? Oh, well, I better notify my wife and mom about what just happened and then place a second call to the Earth border guards, like I promised,* Blake thought as he turned and walked away.

To everyone's surprise, a quick flash exploded from space as Blake heard, "Sir, that stranger's ship just disappeared, so do we need to contact Mom?" the communications officer asked.

"Besides Mom, we need to contact the Alliance Counsel and let them all know what is going on. Also, they will want to know what is happening with Phantom," Grand Admiral Blake replied to the young male while walking over to the communications tent.

"This is the Vortex calling Shinineer. I have finished docking with B.R.A.T.T. We are setting the navigations computer. I will be leaving the system in two mikes. You better be back at the station by the time I arrive," Phantom's voice exploded from the speakers.

"This is Gina. Phantom, stop calling me 'Shinineer.' You know my name! Be advised, we copied, Vortex, good hunting. Um, one last thing before you go. I need a favor from you. I have a little brother that had just joined the Academy. I want you to train him the same way you were trained, so he will be ready for the real galaxy," a young woman asked.

"Request denied!" Phantom said just before the communications exploded with static.

"Phantom, tell me why I need to know! I know when we were at the Academy, everyone, including myself, made fun of you. 'Hey, look at the odd ball!' 'Where do you think he received his looks from?' and other hurtful thing like that. It was not until later we found out in class you were told to hold back. By that time, you were already were on a mission, and before we knew anything else, it was mission after mission. I was never able to apologize to you about everything. I really found out what you were capable when the first cruiser I was assigned to fell under the enemy attack and had been boarded. Just as everyone thought they were dead, you appeared out of nowhere. At that moment, even with your face being covered in the Pirates' blood, I knew I was wrong about everything we did to you," Gina responded on the tactical channel.

"Do not waste your time with him. He is nothing more than a loner who only thinks of himself," a male's voice said from behind.

"You are mistaken. He is everything. He has the looks, the skills, the mind, and he is a member of the Special Operations Unit. To me and most of the younger Alliance female members, he is perfect. Yeah, he does have his flaws, but he is still perfect," she replied with a hint of agitation to her voice from the remark she just heard.

"That may be so, still, he is off limits to any and all female Alliance members, and do not forget that. Connect me with the Station. I need to tell High Grand Admiral Calamen and Mom about what is happening," Blake said walking upon the two.

"Sir, we have made contact," Gina said with a glimpse of fire in her eyes.

"Ah, High Grand Admiral Calamen, it is nice to see you again. Honey, we have a problem. We just encountered a being who claims to be from Earth. The only thing wrong with this is that Phantom says the civilization this person is from was destroyed about twenty-five thousand years ago, if not longer. He had injured one of the recruits before Phantom could intervene. Now, here is the problem. When he and Phantom fought each other, it was like looking into a mirror. I have never known anyone who could fight against Phantom in a true one-on-one fight and do as much damage as he did," Blake told his wife.

"How is our nephew? How bad was he truly hurt?" Kristy inquired.

"Dear, I would not worry about him. He is fine. He was called to assist in another area of the Alliance system. The stranger called himself 'Odin,' and he said he was from Atlantis. Do you know what is going on?" Blake asked.

"Atlantis was indeed destroyed several thousands of years ago. For what we could tell from a planetary scan by a scientist named Nathan Hurts Calamen, there were no survivors. Do you know where this stranger's next location will be?" Mom asked.

"Odin said he was going to Earth to find the rest of the Atlantian race. What concerns me is that the three of us know what happened to Phantom, and that is why he is able to do what he does. Now, here is the Galactic Question of the century; where was it Odin actually came from, and why is it he has the skills, the strength, and the speed of Phantom?" Blake asked.

"He is a waste of your time. No one should care about a loser like him, and I do mean *no one.*"

"I don't care about what you say. If you were on that vessel with me and the crew I was with, you would understand. You also should have seen how awful we truly had treated him. We also took what we thought was fun out on his little sister, then suddenly one day a few weeks before we had graduated, one of the newly ranking officers saw his little sister in the hall and back-handed her for running into him. When he arrived to our class to help train us in the way to handle Pirates, he walked in with a broken hand. After asking, how he broke his hand, he replied that a recruit caught him off guard and squeezed his hand until a loud popping sound exploded from his hand, and a sharp, searing pain rushed up his arm from that location."

"That still does not mean you need to respect that Altherian. There is nothing decent about him to respect."

"What I am trying to say is there is more to him than meets the eye. We were told not to play tricks against him, and we did it anyway. In the end, it was him who had more to teach us then we did for him."

"What is that bickering all about? Who is arguing, and what about?" Kristy Calamen asked while placing a hand to her face.

"Gina and Timothy, stop that bickering now!" Blake said as he turned around.

"Sir, Timothy is making fun of Phantom by saying he is weak, worthless, and a few other horrible things," Gina said with her salute.

"Sir, I am only speaking the truth about the Altherian. You cannot condone me for being honest," Timothy added.

"You are right—if it was the truth. Except, what you said is far from the truth," Blake said in a harsh, sharp tone.

"Let him find out what kind of training Phantom is actually capable of. We will have a match between Melanie and Timothy. If you win, then Phantom will lose his freedom to come and go as he wishes. Now, if you lose, you will lose your rank, and you will have to go back through the Academy. Do I make myself clear?" Kristy said after receiving Mom's permission.

"All right. I will now go back to the real reason for this call. I want you to notify the border guards that they will have a visitor entering and then leaving Earth's system. Can you do that for me, please, dear," Blake asked with a grin on his face.

"Yeah, we can do that. Also, on that match, there will be no killing," Mom replied in a loving tone.

"Yes, Mom, you do not have to worry. I will make sure of that myself," Blake answered just before the call ended.

"An Atlantian. Who would have thought there were survivors still alive from Atlantis? Mom, what happened to Atlantis?" Kristy Calamen asked with a hint of confusion in her voice.

"Well, for all I know, the first time anyone did a planetary scan, they mapped several cities on the Earth's surface, and that race had died out due to a planetary, catastrophic disaster. They were more worried about what was out there and what could hurt them that they had not noticed the problems right there in front of them. They used up all their resources they had for space exploration. One thing that we had learned from the old computer logs was that particular race did not believe in making contact and trying to secure new resources for use. They destroyed their own world and themselves along with it. When we arrived to that barren waste land of a planet, all we found were old structures and obsolete computers with data stored on them for almost five hundred thousand years. I believed that race was the first race to explore the entire galaxy. I just wished they would have made contact since they would still exist as of today. All we can go by is the records we found.

"Your great, great grandfather, Nathan Hurts Calamen, found that planet. He gathered as much of their data as he could and then started to map out the same planets, just to make sure the planetary scans were still correct. For earth, he found out some of the structures were still there, and there were three that was destroyed. Among the three, one had sunk into the ocean, and that single one was called Atlantis," Mom told her.

"Then, where did he come from? Blake said he came from another dimension. Although, how would early earthlings be able to come up with that kind of technology?" Kristy asked Mom.

"I do not know. When Phantom returns, we will need to ask him for more information," Mom replied.

The conversation continued in High Grand Admiral Kristy Calamen's office back on Trolena. "Recruit Harks, get over here! Lieutenant Commander Timothy Harps, I need you over here, as well," Blake ordered with a stern voice.

"Sir, is there something you wanted to see me about?" Melanie asked while walking up to him.

"Sir, reporting as ordered!" Timothy replied.

"Yes, I want the two of you to fight in an exhibition match. There will be *no* killing. Melanie you can only use what Phantom had trained you to do, and that is it. Also, you can use weapons and chi attacks, just hold back the amount of energy," Blake said with a smile on his face.

"Yes, sir. Lieutenant, do you want to use weapons first or not?" Melanie asked without looking at him.

"Sure, little girl. Now I will show all the recruits how to properly use a sword and knives. Your so-called Altherian has a problem keeping a hold of his knives," Timothy said while pulling out a knife that slid into a sword.

"Okay then . . ." Melanie started to say as she looked around for a weapon. "Ah, I will use this," she replied as she walked over to a five foot one inch thick twig.

"That? You are going to use that? Stop kidding around and pick out a weapon!" the lieutenant demanded.

As she spun the twig around like a staff, she said, "I have. Do you want to face me or not? Sir, I think the lieutenant commander is too much of—" she stopped in the middle of her sentence.

"Let me guess, one of Shamarra's favorite words, right? He is a 'chicken', is that it?" Catherina Melody said while walking up.

"That is it. That is the word, thank you, Colonel. Sir, I think the lieutenant commander is an over grown, Earthbound, none-flying *chicken!*" Melanie said sarcastically.

"Who do you think you are? Calling me, a superior officer, a chicken? You are nothing more then a play thing. Your race has been, is, and will always be a slave owner's play thing. You and your kind will have to live with that truth that that is the only thing you and you race are good for. Now, apologize to me for stepping out of line, and do it now!" the lieutenant commander demanded from the recruit.

"Make me. If you think you are all that, I would love to see you *make* me take that back, *swamp breath.* By the way, you need to brush those filthy, disease-carrying, bacteria-eating things in your mouth you call 'teeth'!" Melanie demanded while showing a devilish grin on her face.

"Fine then. You wanted a fight, andI will give you a fight!" the lieutenant commander snarled as he charged toward her.

As he swung his sword at her, he suddenly heard a loud metallic sound echoing through the air. "What was that? There is no way that sound could have come from our weapons connecting?" the lieutenant commander said with a look of confusion.

"What if it had? Then what?" Melanie replied as she swung the staff around at the lieutenant commander's chest plate.

"You will not defeat me. Do you hear me, child? I will not allow you to defeat me!" Timothy replied as he swept the attack away.

Suddenly, just as his sword and her staff connected, Melanie swept hard to the right. Everyone noticed a shinny object flying through the air as they heard, "How, how did you do that? There is no way you could have brokn my sword. It was a nanotech sword! There were no weak parts to the sword, so tell me how it was you were able to do that!" Timothy demanded while looking at what was left of the hilt.

"Stop trying to be over-confident, *swamp breath*. You know, all I here from men lately is, 'You are a woman. Let us men take care of that,' and I'm really tired and sick of hearing that from most of you men! 'Oh, look at me. I am a helpless little girl. I need a strong, handsome man to protect me, someone, please help me.' Here, let me show you what this helpless girl can do!" Melanie demanded as she broke the twig in half just before throwing it aside.

"Now what will you do for a weapon?" Timothy asked while smirking.

"Who needs a weapon? I sure don't. You may want to quit that smiling before I wipe it off your face for you!" the recruit replied while connecting two cloth sleeves to her uniform.

"Oh, look, she is going to beat me with sleeves. I am truly afraid. Stop running your mouth, and let us get down to business," Timothy replied while pulling another sword out.

"Sure thing, and I will allow you the first move," she replied as she took a defensive stance.

"Hey, honey, does that stance look familiar to you?" Blake asked his niece.

"It should, Uncle, that is the stance that Phantom always uses for the Razor Wind Style of Martial Arts. If I am right, she is about to use Razor Wind Blades. I think my favorite male cousin has shown Melanie a few decent tricks, and poor Lieutenant Commander Harps is about to find out what she can actually do. I wonder what other styles of Martial Arts he has trained her in," Catherina replied in a loving tone.

"I did know he had shown her three different styles and trained her in the basics. I do not know how far she was able to get in the structure. Except, if she is about to use the Razor Wind Blades, she must have mastered most of that style. The other two styles are Multi Style of Martial Arts and the Blinders Style Martial Arts. I hope Timothy enjoys being a fool. He is about to make himself look like one. By the way, your aunt wants you to join us on the Academy Space Station," Blake replied.

"All right. And if I refuse," she asked in a playful voice.

"It was an order and not a request," Blake replied.

"That is what I thought," she replied as the lieutenant commander charged toward the recruit.

"I have you now!" Timothy yelled as he swung his sword at her head.

Suddenly, the blade stopped an inch from Melanie's blocking arms, "Why, oh why do so many men have to think that they are macho? The only person who has that right is Phantom, and, here, let me show you *why*!" Melanie demanded just as she ripped both of her arms away from the blade.

Suddenly, the sword fell into two pieces. "That is cheating. That means you must have two invisible blades hidden in your sleeves," Timothy said with ager in his voice.

"No, *swamp breath*, I do not. I *will* admit that my sleeves do have metal in them, covered by cloth, so whenever I do that move I will not cut myself. Now, are we done, or do you want more?" she replied while smiling.

"I will not be defeated by the likes of you!" the lieutenant commander yelled as he pulled another sword out just before he thrust the tip at her.

"Pathetic. Fine, then I will show you what elemental energy combined with chi can do!" she yelled right back as her glowing right hand caught the tip of the blade.

Before everyone's eyes, she started to squeeze with her right hand as the blade itself started to fallow suite. "I was told I could only use what Phantom had shown me and trained me in, and now I have decided that I am done playing. This weapon match is over," Melanie explained in a calm and stern voice.

"What are you doing to my sword? This is my favorite one!" Timothy said just before the recruit's left hand touched the back part of the blade that connected to the wrist guard.

Suddenly, everyone heard a loud shattering sound as the blade started to bend with the direction of her hand, and the blade started to become smaller and smaller. Before Timothy knew what was happening, Melanie handed him a small chunk of metal. "Here you go, little boy. Here is a brand new paper weight for you," she replied.

"Lieutenant, do you give up, or do you want to try hand-to-hand combat next?" Grand Admiral Blake asked.

"I will never be defeated by this child. I am far better of a hand-to-hand combat expert than anyone in this Alliance ever thought of being—especially that Altherian of yours. If he is that great, then why was he trained on the Academy station and not the planetary Academy?" Timothy asked.

"Just shut up. I am tired of listening to you wining and having to smell that awful swamp breath of yours. All I have to do is tie this around my eyes, and I will be ready. Just do me a favor and do not cry once I have defeated you," Melanie told him just before pulling out a blind fold.

"The only thing I hate worse than someone who thinks they are better than the others is a recruit who was supposed to have been trained by someone who thinks they are better than everyone," he replied as she finished tying the blind fold.

Suddenly, the lieutenant commander charged toward her. "Try protecting yourself from this High Pressure Razor Wind Slash," the lieutenant commander yelled while striking at her.

"What is she doing, Catherina? What is going on?" Blake asked while watching the fight.

"Uncle, the move she is doing is what Phantom calls 'heightened sense of awareness'. She will be able to tell when he will move and what attack he will be using," Catherina replied.

Suddenly, the blindfold split along the right side, and when Melanie moved her head, they heard from the lieutenant commander, "How did I miss? What are you doing? How are you predicting my movements?"

"My teacher knows a lot more then you do," Melanie replied as she snapped her eyes open.

"Wait, this cannot be. Are you an Altherian as well?" Timothy asked as he stepped backward.

"No, you imbecile. Phantom is the only Altherian there is. Not only that, but you have made fun of my big brother!" she replied as her glowing, blue eyes shot fear into the lieutenant commander.

"Your brother? I heard he only has a single sister, and she is a Drazarian. How how can you be his younger sibling? You are not a Drazarian," he replied while his voice revealed the fear he was feeling.

"You wanted to prove to me that Phantom was nothing more than a lap dog, now, did you or did you not!" she responded while taking another stance.

"All bark and no bite. I will prove to everyone that she is nothing just like he is." Timothy thought as he suddenly charged.

Before she even reacted, the lieutenant commander grabbed her throat and lifted her off her feet. "I thought so. You learned a few neat tricks, and now you have nothing," Timothy said while smiling.

"I would not consider this fight over yet," Melanie said as she started moving her hands.

"What is this? Oh, do you actually think you can get free just by playing with your hands?" Timothy asked as he watched he hands move in motion.

Sign language? How can this be. Let me see. Shut up, you pathetic good for nothing loser. Why do you not give up and go . . . Blake thought as he turned to his niece "Hey, honey, do you know what that last word means?"

"Yes, Uncle, I do. Trust me when I say you do not want to know. According to Phantom, that sign means 'the bird'. It also is a filthy word back on earth. I have seen him smack Shamarra's hands when she was trying to copy his hand gestures," Catherina told him.

Defiant as always. I bet you will be defiant until the day you die, Blake thought as he chuckled.

Suddenly, three forms appeared before everyone's eyes. "Oh look, you brought toys to play with. I am truly sorry, recruit, but those holo projections will not work on me," the lieutenant commander told her.

"Who are you calling a halo projection? You are an *idiot!*" one of the images replied as he suddenly released a hard fisted, connecting with the man's right cheek.

As his head snapped to the right, the lieutenant commander thought, *How did I feel that? There is no way I should have felt that punch. That hurts!*

Suddenly, everyone saw Melanie's right knee connect with his jaw and knock him to the ground. As he fell backward, Melanie felt his grip loosen up, just before she used the momentum of her attack to back flip out of his hands.

Catherina exploded with laughter. "'The greatest hand-to-hand combat expert,' you say? 'Better than anyone in this Alliance had ever thought of being,' you said? I *do* believe, a recruit is far better then you are!" Catherina told him in between her gaps for breath.

"*Stop making fun of me!*" the lieutenant commander demanded as he jumped to his feet and started to attack the recruit.

To his surprise, he could not connect with any of his kicks or punches. "Stop moving around and fight me like a man!" he demanded as the recruit's body moved like the wind blowing waves of water.

Suddenly, he felt two, open palms on his chest, just before being thrown fifteen feet backward. "Remember, I am a woman and not a man, and now this fight is over. Grand Admiral Blake, may I return to the cruiser that will take me back to the Academy?" Melanie asked while turning to face her commander.

"You realize she was toying with you, right? Now you are to report to the Academy station, recruit," Catherina Melody told the lieutenant commander.

"Yes, ma'am," Timothy Harps replied in a low, sorrowful voice while standing back up.

"Oh! By the way, they are not brother or sister. That just happens to be how he treats her when she is around his actual sister. Also, the person who is the greatest hand-to-hand combat expert was not completely trained on the Academy. Instead, he was sent all over the Alliance territory for training. So, in all actuality, neither Academy has the best training—it is all the same. Now, get moving to the transport. We are leaving this planet," Colonel Catherina Melody told him. "Also, if I were you, I would watch my step at the station Academy. If you do not, you may find yourself floating out into space. No one like a show off who cannot back up their words."

As the fight started on Trolena, a lonely ship somewhere else in the Alliance territory dropped out of hyper space. "This is the Alliance boarder guard. Vessel, identify yourself," the communications officer ordered.

"My name is Odin. I am an Atlantian, and I am going to visit my home. I was also given permission by Grand Admiral Blake. You will allow me to enter, or I will be forced to fight my way through!" Odin replied.

"My name is Jaxs. I am the commanding officer here. I was just informed of your visit. You are clear to enter this system. I hope you find what it is you are looking for. We will await your return. Also, next time be more patient, won't you?" an older, more harsh sounding voice replied over the audio communications.

"I am truly sorry about that. Next time, how about you train your boys to be more respectful," Odin said as his fighter shot past the command cruiser.

As the fighter disappeared into the darkness, Commander Jaxs said, "You, boy, best not get that guy mad. I hear he and the Altherian went one on one, and he stood his ground. That is, until Phantom decided it was time to stop playing," Commander Jaxs told them.

Before Odin knew how long it had been since he had seen the surface of Earth, the AI sounded, "Sir, we are approaching our destination. We will be in the Earth's upper hemisphere in five minutes."

"Thank you. You can analyze this blood sample from my shirt while we wait," Odin replied as he placed a piece of blood-soaked cloth in a small canister.

"I will have this for you in about ten minutes," the AI replied as he blurted out, "Next time, make sure I have the proper upgrade before you ask me to do you a favor!"

"Just shut up and do as you are told," Odin said while thinking, *I am going have to remember to have a talk with that boy of mine about giving an AI to much a personality.*

"Sir, Antarctica is straight ahead. I just linked with the main systems, and the Altherian was wrong. There are two hundred people moving through the center court yard or, if you may, the garden. There also seems to be three hundred in the Bio's room. I have also placed a total of four hundred more people throughout the rest of Atlantis," the AI told him.

"Why would they have three hundred people in the science lab? Has earth became extremely hostile, and our brethren are developing weapons for defensive purposes only? Or have they become the hostile ones and are trying to take control of our home planet? Whatever the case may be, I will find out. Computer, are you done yet with the analyses?" Odin demanded as he started to feel uneasy.

"Yes, sir, the blood sample you gave me is yours. I am sorry, sir. If there is another sample in the piece of cloth you had given me, your blood has soaked it up, and it is now hidden from me. Like I told you, next time, make sure my software is updated before asking me to do the impossible with the system I have now," the AI replied.

"Fine, then, analyze this blood sample, then. I want you to compare it with all the other blood samples we have taken from the other species in the dimension," Odin said as he tapped a few buttons on the control panel.

Right before his eyes, a large hanger door broke through the seven layers of ice and started to show a beacon *At least the hanger's doors still works. What happened to cause this amount of ice to form around and on top of Atlantis?* Odin thought.

A few minutes later as his fighter started its landing procedures, Odin noticed people in unfamiliar uniforms running into the hanger with their weapons pointed right at him.

Great. Now what? Who are these people, and what are they doing here? Odin thought as his canopy started to open.

"Get out of your strange fighter. Get out and get on the ground now," a person in green demanded.

"Computer, raise the fighters shielding. Now, sir, tell me what it is that you are doing here," Odin demanded.

"I will be the one asking the questions. Who are you, and how do you know about this place? If you do not answer me, then I will be forced to make you talk," the commander replied.

"Um, how about *no!*" Odin demanded as he jumped toward the commander and his unit.

As his feet touched the floor, Odin's right knee came back up and connected with the commander's chin. "You will back off. I do not want to kill you," Odin told them.

"Take him down now!" the second lieutenant told the unit.

Suddenly, Odin realized it was fifty to one. *I guess it is time to stop playing around. If I do not take them out, then I will be the one injured,* Odin thought.

As the first guard charged, Odin jumped up and connected a foot to the back of the guard's head. As he fell to the ground, another person charged toward him. *How stupid are they? I do not have time to deal with them right now,* Odin thought as his right palm connected with the charging officer's breastplate.

Before anyone realized how dangerous he truly was, Odin launched a yellow ball of energy toward a small group of charging soldiers as he heard, "You will not escape. We will—" just before the group fell to the ground unconscious.

"George, hand me that flash grenade. We need to take him out safely. We cannot afford any more people becoming injured by his abilities, nor do we need him getting killed from the others trying to subduing him," a fellow soldier yelled.

Suddenly, a bright light exploded right in front of Odin's eyes. "My eyes! I'm blind, what did you do to me?" Odin yelled out in pain.

"You are now our prisoner. You will answer our questions willingly, or we will make you tell us what we want to know," a male's voice said just before Odin felt something hard hitting him on the back of his neck.

"Wake up, sleeping beauty. You have been unconscious for two hours, and we need answers," Odin heard from a male's voice after he felt something cold hitting his face.

"I'm awake. You do not have to try and drown me. So what is it you would like to know? Oh, wait, let me guess . . . 'How is it I knew about this place,' right? Or maybe it is, 'How was it you were able to activate that lift?' That's it, isn't it," Odin said with a smile on his face.

"Wrong. My first question was what you are doing here, and while you are at it, you can answer the other two, as well," a male dressed in all green with three stars on his uniform demanded.

"First, tell me why is it you are here, and where are all the other Atlantians? What did you do with them? Are you with the Garilds tribe? Someone answer my question!" Odin demanded in a frustrated voice.

"All the Atlantian's are dead. We are excavating the ruins of Atlantis to see what we can learn. The great news is, we can learn quite a lot just from this old, perfect remnant of a place. By the way, my name is Sheena, and I am an archeologist. I am the one in charge, remember General? I am impressed that you have made it here. No outsider has ever just shown up without us knowing," a female's voice said while walking into the room.

"It just might be due to the fact that I grew up here. Then, you have the possibility that I am a hacker, and I hacked my way through the security systems and into the city systems. Now, why are you here? And do not tell me it is because the group that remained behind is all dead!" Odin demanded.

"Miss, do not tell him anything. Everyone, return to your duties and leave him to himself, and hopefully he will think about giving us the answers we need. We will give him a day to think about whether he will help us or if we need to beat it out of him," the General told everyone just before walking out of the room.

"I am sorry about that. . . . Nice shirt. Where did you get it? By the way, my name is Sheena. What's yours? Anyway, please help us. It is not every day someone just waltzes in here and is able to activate the ruins while we, on the other hand, have been here six months, and we only have made it through the first level of the city," sheena told him in a soft and gentle voice.

"My name is Odin, and in regards to helping you—no way. This place belongs to the Atlantians, and you have no right to be here. Get out of my site, and take your lap dogs with you!" As Odin yelled at the archeologist, his wording went from English to another language Sheena had never heard in her life.

"Wait, what language is that? I've studied most of the languages here on this planet and have never heard the way you just spoke. Where is it you came from?" Sheena asked with her attention fixed on him.

"You know, you did me a favor. Now, I do not have to go looking for the infirmary. This is the lobby of that facility, and I am now taking my leave, my lady," Odin said as his hands came free.

Just before exploding into a full out run, "What did he just say?" a soldier asked as he turned to see a knee connecting with his face.

"Stop! What are you doing?" Sheena asked as the soldier fell to the floor.

"I am getting out of here, and if you are as smart as you think you are, you better not even try and stop me," Odin told her as he touched the right wall.

"What are you doing? That is only a—" Before she could finish her sentence, the wall opened up as he disappeared into a bright light.

CHAPTER 8

IN THE DRANDON system, the battle really began to get out of hand as Alliance fighters exploded into balls of light. "Sir, my sensors have picked up on a distortion. There appears to be a ship. Get ready to revert from hyperspace," the communications officer blurted out.

"I want you to identify that ship, or ships, as soon as they revert to normal space. If they are Pirate reinforcements, we will be out numbered seven to one, and we are just barely capable to handle four to one," the commander replied with a hint of being worried.

"Sir, here it comes. There are no identification codes to it. What do you want us to do?" the communications officer yelled.

Suddenly, without warning, a strange voice came over the communications, "Fighter 11358, you are in my way. Move to your left. I'll take care of that bogie!"

"What bogie? What are you talking about?" the female pilot asked over the communication just before her alarms sounded, telling her she was being targeted by an enemy fighter.

"All fighter Squadrons, regroup and reform around the Cerberus," the voice called again as a bright light from a set of engines lit the area around them.

"Who do you think you are, ordering us around?" a male voice demanded just before his ears exploded with static.

"B.R.A.T.T., activate the identification code. I want the weapons system brought online now," Phantom called just as he heard, "Someone help me! I am unable to shake them."

"This is the 596th Squadron commander. Do not worry. I will be there," Phantom heard over the communications after turning the system back on.

"Commander, roll right, and fighter 11358, roll left now!" the strange voice said as a shinning, silver fighter no one had ever seen before streaked toward them.

As the two started their rolls, they noticed the silver fighter increased its speed as it just opened fire. "Hey what are you trying to do, kill us out here? What side are you on, any way," the commander demanded to know just as a fighter exploded in front of them and the fighter that had been chasing fighter 11358 exploded behind them.

"Cerberus, this is Night Shadow. Do you hear me?" Phantom called over the communications.

"Night Shadow, it sure is great to hear you voice. So your dad really felt this situation was out of control, then? Now, tell me, what kind of fighter is that thing you are flying?" the commander replied with a sigh of relief.

"Yes, do you know where he is? Randall, point all of the weapons you have on the Cerberus at Echo Delta Niner Niner Zulu 5582. The Vortex is telling me we have Pirates getting ready to drop out of hyperspace. If you can pull this off, you can annihilate those ships before they are able to raise their shields," Phantom said as the Vortex stopped at the front of the other fighters.

Suddenly, the crew of the Cerberus heard their commander yell, "Fire at that location!" just as the temporal distortions started to appear. Before the commander knew it, Phantom was right. He heard cheering echoing from all three hundred and twenty decks. "That is enough. Did you all forget we are in the middle of a battle? Save the celebration for later. Dark Shadow, that fighter of yours is great. What kind is it?" Randall replied.

"Thanks, except this is the first time Vortex has ever seen any action. I was supposed to run her through a series of tests today, but I was summoned to back you up. Let's just hope she can hold out until this battle is over," Phantom called as he throttled the fighter forward.

"This is the 169th Squadron Commander. What are our orders, Commander Randall? Do we need to guard the cruisers, or are we to reengage the enemy?" a female's voice called over the communications.

"Do not ask me. The Altherian is now in charge, fighter Squadrons. Phantom, your unit is awaiting your orders," Randall said with self satisfactory in his voice as he thought, *I am sure glad that boy is on our side. I sure do not want to think of what could happen if he was the enemy.*

"Listen up, all Squadrons, I want the 169, 175, 176, 592, 692, 712, 850, and the 920 fighter Squadrons to stay back and protect those cruisers. Randall, I want the 150, 222, 252, 331, 353, 445, 446, and the 912 fighter Squadron on standby and their fighter prepped for launch at short noticed. This situation may become even stickier than we can imagine. The 22, 23, 24, 25, 250, and the 332nd units will be with me," Phantom ordered as his fighter started shooting at the enemy fighter that is approaching.

"Sir, our shields are starting to fail, and the engines are starting to overheat. If you keep this up, we will end up dead," the AI told Phantom.

"B.R.A.T.T., you should be able to handle this. What is wrong? Give me a diagnostic check, and let's see if we can isolate the problem," Phantom demanded from the ship's AI as he rolled to avoid the showering laser fire.

"Sir, I have located the problem. It is within the operations system. I am showing erratic malfunctions in the systems," the AI replied.

"Let's put this into English. The way I am handling the fighter is causing malfunction throughout the Operation System. The more maneuvers I use to avoid being shot down, the worse the problems are getting. Also, due to the glitches in the operations systems, it will be easier for them to shoot us," Phantom said as he placed a hand over his face.

"Correct, sir. You know, it was really reckless of you to take this fighter into actual combat without the pre simulated test runs and combat situations. So, just for the record, if I am destroyed, it's all *your fault!*" the AI's voice resounded through the cockpit, causing Phantom's ears to ring.

"Hey, what is that? No, it cannot be. Joe?" Phantom asked out loud as he noticed a body in space while his fighter flew past it.

"Checking identification of the soldier we just passed. Sir, his name is Joe Pentphil. Do you know him?" The AI asked just as a warning siren sounded in the cockpit.

"Blast! B.R.A.T.T, try to reroute the cooling units to compensate for the overheating engines. If that does not work, then open the heat shield and allow the heat to be extracted by the vacuum of space. The cold space should cool them down and in a hurry," Phantom ordered as his shot penetrated another Pirate's fighter.

"Sir, the cooling units systems have shut down, and the heat shield is not responding. You have exactly one hundred and eighty seconds before we become a ball of plasma," B.R.A.T.T told him.

"Fine, then. Target the left hanger of the station and push with everything you have left. Faith, prepare to separate from B.R.A.T.T. at the forty-five second mark. Your orders are, no matter what, I want to be in that hanger. Faith, do you understand the orders?" Phantom said as he tightened the crash webbing.

"I understand your orders, sir. Just for the record, you have a twelve percent chance of being successful. I hope you've paid off all your debts," Faith replied as his fighter accelerated toward the hidden hanger.

"Sir, the engines are about givem, and you are still nine hundred kilometers away from the station. Engine breach is imminent in ten, nine, eight . . ." B.R.A.T.T. said through the cockpit.

"Faith, emergency separation—now!" Phantom called as he started to push the emergency switches.

Suddenly, to Phantom's surprise, he felt the shudder of the two pieces separating as the portion he was in started to take the form of a giant robot. "Faith, what is going on?" Phantom demanded to know.

"Mac decided to build me with a collapsible from. I can be either a fighter or a robot that runs on your chi strength. The stronger your chi energy is, the stronger I will become," the female's AI's voice replied.

"Now *that* I can handle. Let's see how much *you* can handle. Let's get going, shall we?" Phantom replied as his hazel eyes started to glow brighter.

Without warning, Phantom started to hear an alarm sound in his ears. "Faith, what is happening? Shut that alarm off," Phantom ordered.

"Sir, the output chi regulator is starting to critically malfunction. You need to lower the volume of your chi before we explode," Faith replied in a worried voice.

"I will after I do *this!*" Phantom told her while grinning as he pushed a single amount of chi through the regulator.

Before the AI realized what was going on, Phantom raised a hand toward the station's shields, just as the robot started to shudder hard. "Faith, how long will we last before the regulator and the storage units erupt?" Phantom asked as his right hand danced across his arm computer.

"At the given radius, I calculate it is less than a minute. I hope whatever is going on is worth destroying me just as you did with my brother," Faith replied.

"Great, all I'm going to need is fifteen seconds," Phantom told her as he thought, *Now that's just great. Artificial intelligence with family bonds programmed in them. What is this galaxy coming to?*

Suddenly, Faith felt a surge of energy shoot through the regulator all the way to her hand; a giant ball of energy exploded into existence just as Phantom connected the ball of energy with the station's shields. "There, we're in. Once I have safely left the fighter, I want you to fly back out the hole just before it really becomes critical. Do you copy computer!" Phantom demanded.

Two beeps echoed through the cockpit, and the voice of the femail AI inquired, "What happened to me? One minute, I was looking at the display screen, and the next, I was in a closed off circuit. What did you do to me?"

"As of right now, you are being relocated. Just shut up and allow me to help you unless you want to end up like your older sibling," Phantom said as the giant robot landed in the hanger.

Suddenly, he started to hear slow, continuous beeps. "Faith, what does that continuous beeping imply? Also, how long do we have before this ship explodes?" Phantom asked just as he jumped from the cockpit.

"That sound is implying the amount of time you have before the storage units and the regulator will erupt. The faster the sound, the sooner it will detonate," Faith replied.

"Computer, this is a priority one. Revert back to the fighter mode and launch back through the hole in the shields now!" Phantom demanded as he ran toward the hall way. He heard his computer rapidly beeping. "Now what is it? Computer, identify the source of this alarm," Phantom ordered as he noticed a yellow light and a purplish-blue light started to flash. Then, a loud explosion erupted outside.

"Sir, I am registering Jacquelyn Calamen and Colonel Calamen. They are both on the station, just in separate locations," Faith replied.

"Where is she located? Is she safe, or is she in any danger?" Phantom asked while sprinting down the hall.

"She is safe for now. It appears to me that she and five other scientists have locked themselves in the secret emergency room in lab thirteen. What are your orders, sir? Colonel Calamen is twenty levels up from our location with seven units. It appears that they are pinned down by the Pirates," Faith replied.

"Colonel Calamen and his units will be fine. First things first, I have to help her before it is too late," Phantom said as he doubled his speed.

"Jacquelyn, what is going on? I mean, all we are doing is just enhancing the weapons that we normally use, right?" a male's voice cried out with fear.

"That I know of, yes. I have heard from my son that there are a few stations that are developing newer and stronger weapons for the Alliance. I have seen certain levels of this station are off limits except to a small handfull of people," a female's voice said in a soft tone just as a loud noise started to echo throughout the room.

"I hope your husband can get to us before those Pirates can. What is taking him so long?" a young female's voice said as her body shook from being scared.

"Mommy, I'm scared. Make the bad people go away," a female child cried as she held on to her mother's leg as if she was about to be sucked out an airlock.

"It is all right. Cousin Jack will be here shortly to help us," the girl's mother replied.

"Molly, how can you say that? We are on the fortieth level, and Jack is on the fifteenth level of the station. He will not be able to get down here fast enough," Jacquelyn told her.

"Just maybe he can bypass what those stinking Pirates have done to the computers and become able to make his way down here before those Pirates outside can get us," Molly replied.

"You see this yellow beacon? You see how light it is? This means Jack is too far away in another location on the station. So there is no way he will be able to do so. Though, we have at least one person or three units approaching our location very quickly," Jacquelyn replied while looking at the rapid white glow from another beacon.

"Who do you think is leading that unit?" Molly asked.

"Phantom is, and he will be here soon," Jacquelyn told them.

"Last time I almost saw him was at the graduation. I swear he must have done poorly on the final exams. Even he refused to show up for the graduation from being embarrassed," Molly said with disgust in her voice.

"All Phantom is, is nothing more than a loser, lazy, good for nothing, stupid Altherian who can do nothing more than cry like a little girl," the child replied to her cousin.

Suddenly, the door to the safe room flew open. "Mommy!" the child yelled as she starred into the face of a Pirate.

"What do you think you are doing? Why did you allow those Pirates to live? Are you *insane?*" Faith asked as he shot past a group of Pirates.

"She is more important than those Pirates could ever be," Phantom said as he wrapped a white cloth bandage around his left arm. "More importantly, she's more important than *us* living!"

"How dare you tell me that! Tell me, what is it that makes her more important than our lives!" Faith asked.

"Shamarra," Phantom said as he tilted his head to allow a knife to fly past.

"Shamarra? Who is Shamarra, you stupid fool!" the AI replied just before Phantom reached over and disengaged the audio setting on his arm computer.

"She is Shamarra's mother. That is all you need to know," Phantom replied as he wiped the warm trickle from his face.

Suddenly, he heard, "You know, that was not nice—shutting the sound off just so you wouldn't have to hear my voice. Now, mister wise guy, can you tell me, how are you going to face all the Pirates that are now following us and the ones that are in science lab thirteen, as well?" Faith asked.

"Faith, I want you to try to access the station's computer. I want to know if the original command codes have been changed. If they have not, I want you to make a copy of yourself and download that copy into the computer. This way, we will have full control of the station again, and then all I need to worry about is taking out those Pirates," Phantom told her.

"Understood. You know, I was wrong about you. I originally thought you were nothing more then an over-ego, an imitation soldier, a good for nothing loser who could only look at the world and the galaxy that rested on the tip of your nose. I do apologize," Faith told him.

"We can discuss this later. We have innocent people here that need our help. Can you do as I asked, or can you not?" Phantom asked as he started to type commands into his arm computer.

"I am talking with the station's computer now, sir. All the command codes have been changed. What do you want me to do now, sir?" Faith replied.

"Stand by for downloading. Station computer emergency command override Alpha Tango Delta 11529. Command authorization Phantom 115862 voice identification and confirm," Phantom ordered.

"Accessing, voice confirmation, confirm Phantom Galaxy Alliance Member unknown ID number 588623. All command codes are now in an emergency override and ready for your orders," the computer's automated voice replied.

"Download files by the name 'Faith' and activate. You will allow the new program to take control of the entire computer brain. The two of you are one. Once you have done that, seal off levels one through twelve. Do not allow anyone the knowledge of this. Play along with the Pirates and make the interior sensors show the command they had requested," Phantom ordered.

"Why is that, sir? All systems are now under my control, sir," the automated voice said as the voice started to sound more feminine.

"Great to hear you voice, and not just coming from my arm. It is called the element of surprise. If they think they still have full control over the system, they will not see our forces approaching," Phantom replied just as he turned the corner and saw the door that was labeled 'Lab Thirteen'.

Suddenly, Phantom heard a few multiple beeps. "Computer, what is it you want?" he asked his arm unit.

As he looked at the display, he noticed a word. "New File has been downloaded and is now ready to be ran. What would you like me to do sir?" the computer asked him.

"Download and run the file from storage port two," Phantom told the computer.

Suddenly, he heard, "I cannot believe you left me to die back there. I am just happy your arm unit was able to download me in time."

"B.R.A.T.T., it is nice to hear your voice. I will send your file to the Cerberus, and you can run their computer. You can help Faith relay what is happening with the station's weapons to the fleet," Phantom said as he launched the program through a hidden link.

"Copied, sir. What about the person you said is more important than the Pirates?" Faith asked.

"Override and full lockdown on that safe room. I do not want any Pirates even three inches from her. If they show hostility inside that room, your orders are to neutralize the threat at all costs to those Pirates," Phantom said as he started to type a command into the door's access panel.

"Come on, how much longer is this going to take? We need in that vault. There might be something valuable in there," one Pirate said as the second one worked on rewiring the access panel.

"Just hold on. All I need is a few more seconds, and then we are in," the second Pirate said as the door slid open.

"Mommy, help me!" the young girl screamed as the sound of a second door sliding open.

"Let my daughter go. Take me instead, please," Molly demanded as the two Pirates started to laugh.

"Sure thing, cutie, except I will take the four of you, and I will kill that man, just because I can," one of the Pirate's said.

"No, you won't!" a male's voice said from behind them.

Just as one of the Pirates turned to look at where the voice came from, Phantom's right knee connected with his face. "Hey, little brother. Is everything all right?" the man holding the girl asked.

"That little punk. I will kill you for that!" the Pirate on the ground said as he knocked Phantom's legs out from underneath him.

As a loud crashing sound echoed throughout the room from Phantom hitting the ground hard, everyone heard the Pirate, who was holding the girl, scream out in pain, "Ouch! Why, you little brat, I will kill you."

When he looked up, he noticed the girl was now hiding behind her mother. "If you come anywhere near my daughter, I will kill you myself," Molly said with a look of hatred on her face.

"Faith, close and re-secure that door. Deny all access except to Galaxy Alliance members. Only allow access once the situation is neutralized," Phantom said just before getting a back hand to his solar plexus.

After his back hit the wall, he slid down it. "Why are you here? What is it you are after?" Phantom said while blood ran down the corner of his mouth.

"That is for us to know and for you to find out. Now, why are you here challenging us? The Galaxy Alliance does not have any rights to this system," a Pirate replied.

"This is still Alliance territory. It is you Pirates who do not belong here, nor do you need whatever it is that may be here," Phantom replied as he started to stand up.

"How dare you make such claims. You are nothing more than a puny, little ant. We Colgallian's are bigger, stronger, and a lot smarter then you humanoids, who look to be from the backwater planet of Earth. It is we who should be ordering you around," one of the Pirates said.

"Oh, look at me. I am scared! I am shaking in my boots! Now, you will listen to me, do you understand, girls! You will leave whatever you had taken from this station and bring it back. Once you are done, you are then to leave this system and never return. In fact, you will not return to the Alliance systems ever again. For, if you do, I will personally track you down and slowly kill you and the crew you are working with. Once I have finished with that, I will then move to each and every one your home worlds and kill everyone there, just to make an example out of you. Do I make myself *clear?*" Phantom said just before charging at the Pirates again.

"Big brother, look out! I'll—" Just before the second Colgallian could finish his sentence, his lifeless body fell to the floor in a puddle of bluish-purple blood.

As Phantom looked up, he saw the reddish-orange skinned creature looking very angry and very hungry, like he had not eaten for weeks, and Phantom was now going to be his main course of vengeance. "That was my youngest brother. How dare you cut him down like the Ravenous Alliance dog you truly are! Once finish killing you, I will then open that door, even if I have to rip it out of the wall and kill those people on the inside. They must be dear to you if you came here all alone just to try and save them. You Alliance dogs are nothing more than fools. You should allow Trayon to take control of this galaxy without apposing him, and that way you will live longer. But for you, you will not see another sunrise after today!" the Colgallian told Phantom as he rushed toward him.

Before Phantom could react, the Colgallian wrapped both arms around him. "Now you will die," the creature told him while breathing in Phantom's face.

While trying to hold his breath, Phantom said, "Man, that stinks. Have you ever thought about using a breath mint? One last thing before I kill you—I'm sorry, I don't do requests," Phantom said just as he graded his right foot down into the Colgallian's shin.

Suddenly, from outside the room, Phantom could here feet running down the hall. "You need to pay attention to me and not those that are arriving," the Colagallian told him just as his fist connected to Phantom's face.

Just as Phantom's back connected with the wall, he heard, "Take this you Alliance dogs!" and a spherical object was thrown into the room.

Before Phantom could react, a loud explosion echoed throughout the room, and sharp objects flew from the sphere and imbedding themselves into everything, whether it was flesh or mechanical. "Sir, the emergency locks have been severed, and the door is now opening," Faith reported.

"Faith, just shut up," Phantom demanded as his body ducked, twisted, and turned to avoid from being pierced, and as a loud moan escaped from his mouth.

"Sir, are you all right?" Faith asked with a hint of concern in her voice.

"Yes, I will need some time to heal my wounds. First thing's first, I need to secure this room before anything else happens," Phantom replied as his left arm covered his lower rib cage and blood ran down it. His right arm was holding his right leg.

As he limped over to the room where the Alliance scientists were hiding, he suddenly tripped over something, and his body hit the ground. "That hurt. What did I trip over?" Phantom said as he started to pick himself back up.

In a now-sitting position, he noticed the Colagallian's lifeless body just laying there with the look of agonizing pain and torture painted on his face. "Close. That was just a little to close, even for me," Phantom said as he started toward the door again.

Suddenly, the door slid open just as Phantom felt something hard connect to the thin chest plate on his shirt. "I'm glad to see you, too," he said just before he hit the floor.

"Phantom, I'm sorry, I did not realize it was you. Oh, you've been injured. Just lie there, and I will fix you up," Jacquelyn replied as she knelt down next to him.

"I do not have the time. I must protect you for Shamarra's sake. Now, let me do my job before we are all killed," Phantom told her as he climbed to his feet.

Suddenly, as he entered the room, a fist came out of nowhere and launched him back into the far wall. "This puny runt killed the group in this room. This is a joke. I want to see the real fighter who killed these men," a Pirate said just before a loud sound echoed from where he hit the wall.

"What are you talking about? I *am* that fighter," Phantom said as he climbed to his feet and looked at the man with bright, glowing, blue eyes.

"Mommy, why does he look smaller than before? Look at him. His cloths look like they are about to fall off him," the young girl asked as she saw Phantom slowly walking toward the main room.

"Jacquelyn, what is going on, and what is that he is doing?" Molly asked while focused on her cousin's attention.

"Earth, Fire, Air, Water, Light, Dark, Sister, Brother, Mother, Father, Love, Hate, Happiness, Sorrow, Laughter, Crying, Life, Death, Elements, Nothingness . . ." Jacquelyn mouthed as she watched Phantom passing by as she was making hand signs.

Suddenly, they noticed Phantom sitting cross legged in a meditation stance. "Oh, look. This soldier boy is giving up," a male's voice said as one of the Pirates walked up to seven inches from Phantom.

"I know I cannot do anything in this injured state. I just hope this is the right thing to do. Once I do this and release the lock on the gates, there will not be any way of stopping the massacre that will fallow. If I do not, then Jacquelyn, Molly, Valerie, and the others—everyone will be killed if I do not allow this to happen," Allan asked himself as a set of gates appeared in front of him.

"Make up your mind. Do you want to save them, or do you wish to die? You are the only one that can make this choice, and you will have to live with the outcome," a familiar male's voice told him.

"Hurry up, fool, or they will kill you. You must choose now," a second, familiar voice replied.

If I do this, a lot of people will be killed, and if I do not do this, then Shamarra's mother and cousins will be killed, Allan thought as the two gate merged into a single gate.

"Well, what will it be?" the second male's voice asked.

"I do not know. Shamarra . . . what would *you* do?" Allan replied out loud.

"Look at him. He is too scared to even move. I will fix that with a single stroke," a Pirate told everyone while smirking. He swung his sword at Phantom.

Suddenly, the sword stopped seven inches from Phantom's head. The Pirate noticed green sparks flying from the location his sword just hit. "What was that sound? Where did it come from?" the Pirate asked as a metallic sound echoed throughout the room.

"It was just an echo that fallowed the ventilation shaft down to us. Some metal must have hit the ground a few levels above us," another Pirate replied as he approached Phantom.

Suddenly, the same sound echoed through the lab again. "Jacquelyn, what is going on? We would have heard explosions from the other levels. Instead, all we are hearing is echoes of two metallic objects colliding with each other," Molly replied in a low whisper.

"Just be ready to move. You do not want to be caught out side of that shield once a shattering sound happens. Allan, Allan, honey, let us in. Come on, sweetie, it's me, Jacquelyn. I know you do not want to hurt us—just those Pirates. So what do you say? Will you let me and the others in?" she said in a soft, loving voice.

"Are you crazy? He is worthless. How do you expect him to save us? Everyone find something and prepare to fight," Molly told them as the Pirates started to blast at Phantom.

As the green sparks continued to fly, everyone continued to hear a metallic sound echoing through the room. "You're right, that *does* sound like it is coming from this room. Where can that noise be coming from?" a third Pirate asked as he started to look around.

"Allan, you know it is almost time. You must let us in! We will die not at the hands of the Pirates, but at the hands of the Assassin! Could you live with yourself if we die? If I die! What will Shamarra think of her big brother?" Jacquelyn cried out.

Suddenly, everyone heard a loud shattering sound echoed throughout the room. "What was that? Oh, well. Kill him now and worry about it later," a Pirate demanded as he slammed his weapon against the same location he had the last thirteen times.

Suddenly, to their disbelief, two gates appeared in front of them. One was made of a reddish-blue corral with a golden-white glow, and one was made of scorched bones that emanated a pungent sulfuric smell while glowing with a dark, eerie light. They noticed a lock and the chain falling to the floor as a creeking sound echoed as the gates started to open. "What is that? Is this some kind of a joke?" a Pirate asked with a look of confusion on his face as the gate disappeared.

"Far from it," a male's voice replied.

"Who said that?" all the Pirates demanded in unison as they noticed a strange motion coming from Phantom.

Out of the multiple, shadowing image emerged two beings standing next to their target. One looked to have been a halo projection, except, the person was deformed, and the second person was bound in chains. Both of the beings were male and looked identical, except for the glow of their eyes and the expressions on their faces.

"What are you smiling about, ugly?" a Pirate asked while looking even more confused.

"Oh, that is easy. Tonight, I am going to enjoy a nice, well-deserved work out," the man in chains replied while grinning.

"This is pointless. At least you could give them a chance to escape before you decided to kill them this time," the deformed man told the other.

"If you are that worried, I could always handle this mess. By the way, I never said I needed your help. Why don't you crawl back into to the box he let you out of," the man in chains replied.

"At least when I'm in there, I wouldn't have to smell that dragons breath of yours. Besides, all I truly need is to stretch," the crippled man replied while grinning.

"Um, sir, what are those two talking about? What do you think we should do?" a young male Pirate asked.

"Kill them. What else would we do?" the commander replied.

Before the Pirates charged them, the man in chains said, "This finger is for you, that finger is for you, this other finger is yours, and my index finger is yours, commander," the man in the chains said as he cut through each one the fingers on his right hand.

"Are you trying to scare us? If so, you know it is not working?" the commander replied while smiling.

"Who is trying to scare whom? I do believe you have not truly looked at the full situation here. You see, just because you out number us twelve to one, does not mean you have the upper hand," the crippled man replied just before throwing his right arm out to his side.

Suddenly, everyone heard the sound of bones cracking echoing all around them. "Almost done with that one," the crippled man told them as he noticed the Pirates cringing from the sound.

"Now . . . now that does not bother us at all. Attack them now, you fools!" the commander stuttered his orders as the sound of a second set of bones cracking erupted throughout the room.

"Jacquelyn, what is he trying to do? What is happening to that object around his head? It appears to be cracking!" Molly asked her cousin with a disgusted look on her face as the sound of the cracking bones reverberated through her head.

"It is because that object is called a halo, and, yes, it is cracking, and eventually it will break. When that happens, everyone in this room will be slaughtered. Allan, honey, come on, let us in," she replied as she focused her attention back onto Phantom.

"Just shut up, woman. Can you not see we are negotiating here?" the man in the chains replied while holding his hand up to reveal all of his fingers were now back.

"Do not worry. I do not think Allan would let the most important person to his sister be killed. Although, at times, I wish you'd take that annoying brat away from us, and then, other times, I'm happy that she is around," the crippled man replied as he threw a leg out into a side kick.

A few minutes later, to everyone's surprise, they noticed the man that had been crippled only appeared to have a single, crippled left leg as the heard, a third familiar voice say, "Now, that is not polite, Phantom. I cannot believe you would talk to a lady like that. As for you, Assassin, your targets are only the Pirates and no one else. Do you understand me?" and the physical body of Phantom fell over onto the floor.

Suddenly, a loud explosion erupted throughout the room as the halo and chains exploded with vengeance. Then Jacquelyn heard, "Come on, get in if you want to live. Also, do not forget to close your eyes and plug your ears," the male's voice said as a Glowing green person appeared in front of them.

Everyone heard, from the man that was crippled and the man who was in chains, say, "Now, that feels better." The two voices called in unison as their muscle mass started to expand.

"Hurry up, everyone, and get in!" Jacquelyn cried out as she turned to face the glowing person, "Allan, will your body be all right?"

"Yes, Mrs. Calamen, the body is fine. I slowed the heart rate down, and the body is taking slow, deep breaths. All I need to do is to reinforce the chi shielding while our body starts to heal itself," Allan replied just as he touched the sides of the shield with his hands.

Suddenly, the opening started to close just before Jacquelyn could make her way inside the shield, "Allan, hold it open for a few more seconds. I am almost through," she told him in a loving tone.

Meanwhile on the Academy Station in the training room . . .

"Today, class, you will learn how to overpower your opponent by using their weight against them. Shamarra, I would like your help to demonstrate this," a middle-aged man told them.

"Sure thing, sir. You know, it will be unfair for you if you use me as your opponent," a young girl with bluish-green skin replied as she stood up.

"Oh, Shamarra, why didn't you tell me you are not dressed for this? If I ruin that new dress of yours, your brother will ruin my hide," the combat instructor replied.

"All I have to do is pull my hair back and slip out of this dress. Do not worry. It will be fine, sir," the child replied as she pulled her shoulder-length, red hair back.

"Shamarra, you know you cannot change in front of everyone," a young female's voice said from the corner of the room.

"Do not worry. I have my gym clothes on underneath. My big brother always told me to be ready for anything, even in training," the child replied while looking at the blond-haired, blue-eyed recruit.

"Shoanna, I know it is supposed to be Shamarra's studying time. I just really need her help with this training exercise. Go ahead and relax. You must be exhausted from your third day of training, or you can practice the basics you have learned so far," the training instructor told her.

Suddenly, the girl had her purple dress folded in her arms, "Shamarra, are you wearing nanotech clothing? Your shirt looks just like your older brother's, and your shorts look as if you have pads hidden under them," the training instructor inquired.

"No, they're not pads, sir—they're my legs. They've became bigger through the exercise I get from gym class. I also have a habit of exercising with big brother, sir . . ." Just before Shamarra finished her sentence, she formed a look on her face that was alarming.

"Shamarra, what is wrong? If you truly do not want to help—"

Suddenly, a recruit ran from the corner and over to Shamarra. "Shamarra, Shamarra, is everything all right? Talk to me!" Shoanna said as she caught the girl.

"Mom, notify High Grand Admiral Calamen that her niece just is unconscious, and we are taking her to the infirmary. This is a medical emergency. Medical teams, stand by for a patient," the instructor ordered as he picked the child up and ran out of the room with the recruit hot on his heels.

"Big brother, big brother, what is wrong? Your entire body is filled with pain. What happened to you?" Shamarra said in a low, soft, mumbling tone.

"Jacquelyn, what is going on?" Molly asked just as a purple light started to glow from the back of Phantom's right hand.

Suddenly, they noticed a young child in all purple standing next to Phantom's body, "Oh, big brother, what have they done to you? Do not worry. I'm here to help the best that I can," the child said in a loving tone.

"Shamarra, Shamarra, what are you doing here? *How* can you be here?" Jacquelyn asked with a confused look.

"Do not worry, big brother, I will remove those shards from your body," the child replied.

"Shamarra, you should not be here. I know you want to help me, just be careful, will you?" Allan replied just as he noticed his little sister starting to pull on the piece of shrapnel in his arm.

"Ouch! That hurts!" Shamarra cried as her hands slipped off of the piece of shrapnel.

"I told you to be careful. How about you keep the shield stable, and I will remove the shrapnel. That way, you will not be hurt," Allan replied as he bent down and wrapped her palm up with cloth.

"Big brother, I am not sure if I can. You are a lot stronger than I am. Let me try once more while you keep the shield stabilized," Shamarra asked just as he tied the cloth.

"Computer, activate Shamarra's lullaby. Now all you need to do is focus on the rhythm of the music and open your chi point in your hands. Do you remember the first step in using chi and storing energy?" Allan asked her.

Everyone noticed a soft melody starting to play. "Jacquelyn, what is the name of this soft music?" Molly asked her cousin.

"I do not know what the name of this one is. I have not heard this type of music before," Jacquelyn replied as their attentions returned to Allan and Shamarra.

"Um, if I remember right, energy is energy. That's whether if it is the energy of the body (chi) or in nature (elements of earth, fire, air, and water). You told me once that all I would need to do is focus on the energy and transform it into chi energy, except, you never told me how," Shamarra replied with a look of confusion.

"What do you mean how? Look at what you have done. You've taken your actual chi energy and infused it with your spirit. Then you used the invisible communications network from our sibling bond to appear right here," he replied as he ruffled her hair.

"I had to do it. It was out of concern for my brother. How would I use the same ability to match the amount of chi you are using just for the shields?" Shamarra asked.

"Now you are learning. The second step is for you to remember that everything has energy. The beat from the song is giving off energy. Focus on the rhythmic portions in the music. The energy the music is giving off is being sent into the air with each and every beat. You can pull energy from anywhere in the galaxy—the sun, the planets, white dwarfs—anything you can think of has energy," Allan told her.

"Right, if it has energy for life, it can be absorbed. Now all I have to do is focus on the music," she said as she took a seat in front of his body.

Good, you truly do understand, Allan thought as he watched as her body started to glow a deep purple. *Now it is time to fix this little problem.*

"Ahhh . . ." Phantom yelled in pain. There were white sparks exploding out of Phantom's arm just as blood shot out from the left arm of Phantom's physical body.

"Will you be more careful, Allan? That truly does hurt, you know!" Phantom yelled just as a loud popping echoed through the room.

"I'm sorry. The piece of metal went deeper than I thought! Assassin, be ready. The shard in the leg is next," Allan yelled back just as he watched Phantom letting go of a Pirate, and the lifeless body plummeted to the ground.

"That's fine, just hurry up!" the Assassin replied as he ripped a knife from a Pirate's throat.

The Assassin fell to one leg just as white sparks shot out. He threw a kick and knocked another Pirate to his back. "You could have done that more carefully!" the Assassin demanded.

"Oh, yeah, I still would have heard the same complaint," Allan replied as blood shot from his right leg.

"Just shut up!" the Assassin replied as they heard the third cry of pain.

"Big brother, are you all right?" Shamarra asked, and white sparks exploded from Allan's side.

"Yeah, I'll be fine, kiddo. I just did not think I would feel that much pain for a little piece of metal," Allan replied as he placed the small piece of shrapnel on the floor.

"Brother, take over the shield and allow me to heal your body," Shamarra said as she crawled over to his body.

A few seconds later, Jacquelyn, Molly, and the others noticed a strange, purple glow now covering Phantom's body. "When did little Shamarra learn that trick? What kind of training have you done, my little sweet heart?" Molly asked.

"Big brother taught me this technique—this one and a lot more. I do not care what everyone says about my brother. I will still think of him as the strong, selfless person who will always think of others fist, no matter how dangerous the task is," Shamarra popped off as everyone could sense a smile on her face.

Then, they heard a loud, metallic sound echoing off of the shield. "You are all dead. I promise you this; I will kill you myself," a Pirate told them as his throwing knife just touched the ground.

"No, you won't. I will see to that myself," Phantom said as his body sat up.

"No, big brother. I have not healed your wounds all the way. You must allow me to finish first," Shamarra said as she wrapped her arms around his neck.

"How, how is he capable of regeneration that quickly? There is no one in the Alliance that is able to that," Molly replied.

"You are right. No one in the Alliance can. The Valcanucian can, and I spent six months learning their techniques," Phantom said as he looked at Allan. "Are you able to hold the shield up for a few more minutes?"

"Just a few more, and that is it. Also, when did you and the Assassin return to our body?" Allan asked as what appeared to be sweat ran down his face.

"Just a few seconds ago. If we had not, then the shield would have given way. We were using too much of our energy in different directions," Phantom replied as he stroked Shamarra's hair.

"Big brother, once this is all over, will you be returning to the station?" Shamarra asked gently.

"Yes, I do believe I have done enough work for the Alliance for a while. I sure can use a break, and I also need to spend some time with my little sister," Phantom told her in a loving tone and with a smile on his face.

"Shamarra, it is up to you to keep the shield stable," Allan told her in a weak voice, just as he fell to a knee.

"Right, just one last thing. Make sure you come home alive, all right? I do not know what I will do if you are no longer in my life," Shamarra replied as she hugged one of her brothers.

"Be good. I will see you in a few days," Allan said just before disappearing.

"Phantom, honey, are you going to be all right?" Jacquelyn asked in a loving tone.

Suddenly, to their surprise, when Phantom turned to look at them, they noticed his face was covered in blood, "*Hello, Mother!* I will be fine. Now, it is time to finish this," Phantom said as he stood up and the shield just disappeared.

As Phantom walked away from the group, a purple shield suddenly appeared. "I did not realize how much work he was going to have me perform," Shamarra said just as a smile started to appear on her face.

"Do not ignore me, you filthy Alliance dog!" the Pirate demanded.

"Computer, activate work out number one," Phantom said as he pulled two knives out from behind his back.

Suddenly, a hard, rhythmic beat exploded from the speaker on his arm computer, just as he heard, "Big brother, do be careful, will you?" Shamarra told him with a big grin on her face.

"What are you trying to do? Kill us by playing a bunch of noise?" the Pirate asked just before Phantom disappeared in front of him.

Then, everyone heard, "Ahhh!" as a loud thud hit the ground, and Phantom was now standing over the lifeless body.

"What is the matter? Are you scared of little, old me? I know—how about I fight you with only Jujitsu, Ninjitsu, Capoera, and Shaolin styles of Martial Arts," Phantom replied as he started to jenga for the Capoera style.

"What are you talking about? There is no such thing as those styles in the Martial Arts," the Pirate told them in a snarling tone.

"I call them 'The Back Water Planet of Martial Arts'," Phantom replied just as a smile started to creep across his face.

Suddenly, Phantom pulled two knives from behind his back and started to charge toward the Pirate. "You are mine, and you are now dead!" he yelled just as he swung the knife in the Pirate's direction.

Suddenly, Phantom realized the Pirate was holding a one-foot-three-inch piece of Dylemian metal that was twenty inches thick. "Oh, look, I caught you off guard. Now what are you going to do?" the Pirate snarled just as the blade of the knife connected with the piece of metal.

"I think I will make you panic," Phantom said just as he touched a switch on the hilt of the knife. The blade of the knife turned red just as Phantom started to gently push the blade into the piece of the Dylemian metal. "How is this possible? This metal is one of the toughest alloys the Alliance has came up with!" the Pirate replied as he noticed the blade sliding through the metal with ease.

Suddenly, to Phantom's disbelief, the Pirate turned the piece of metal and snapped the blade. "Now what are you going to do?" the Pirate asked just as he dropped the metal and swung a fist at Phantom.

In a single motion, Phantom spun around, caught the Pirate's arm with his right hand, and connected a heel kick to the back of the Pirate's head. "Oh, look at me. I have never been so *scared* in my entire life," Phantom told him just before connecting a forward kick to the Pirate's face.

As the Pirate fell to the ground, everyone noticed Phantom had already thrown himself into an aerial spin. "What is he doing?" Molly asked with a confused look on her face.

"He is doing his job. Also, the day of his graduation, the reason why he was not there was because he was stuck on a planet in the middle of a mission. That mission was very important, and it just happened to be a rescue mission. The individuals he saved were actually spies for the Alliance. Those spies were gathering information against Trayon and sending the information back to us. Most of his time in the Academy was nothing more than mission after mission, a training exercise here, an intelligence operation there, and smuggling, among others. Also, Shamarra, do not worry. All three of them will be returning home," Jacquelyn told her daughter.

Suddenly, everyone noticed Phantom's elbow connecting with the Pirate's solar plexus as a loud gust of wind escaped from the Pirate's mouth. "You won't live long to celebrate—"

Before the Pirate could finish speaking, Phantom had already shoved his second knife into the Pirate's head. "Now, *that* will keep things quite," Phantom said as he stood up.

"Big brother, are you all right? You look exhausted," Shamarra said just as the shield dropped.

"She is right, son. How much sleep are you actually getting?" Jacquelyn asked while walking over to him.

"Seventy-two hours, that is all," Phantom replied as the color washed from his face.

"That should be plenty," Molly told him.

"No, seventy-two hours in the last two months. Let us see you . . ." Before he could finish talking, they Phantom fell to the ground.

"Hello, Allan, Phantom, and Assassin. It is nice to see you for a change, even though it is under hostile conditions," Shamarra told them as she threw her arms around Allan.

"Shamarra, why are you here?" Phantom asked while placing a hand on her head and kneeling.

"I felt that you were in pain. I thought I could be of some help," she replied while placing an arm around Phantom.

"You are nothing more than a liability. You should have never come. You know better than that," the Assassin told her.

"I love you, too, you old grouch. If I had not arrived when I did, who knows what could have happened? I don't want to hear anything from a big mouth. I'm better then you are, over obnoxious wannabe, the best and a good for nothing man. Don't worry. I love you, any way. Now that I have all three brothers in front of me, promise me you will return to the station in three days," Shamarra replied as a smile came across her face.

"If I could get away with killing you, I would. By the way, who are you calling 'a good for nothing'?" the Assassin inquired.

"Shamarra, I don't want you to talk like I do, and you know that. You should talk like Phantom. It's not a good idea to talk like an Earthling when you're around others," Allan reminded her in a loving voice.

"You do it all the time, so why can't I?" she asked.

"I've been talking like this my entire life. I can't help it, and you know that. You also know I try to talk just like everyone else, and at times, the other words slip into the conversation," Allan replied.

"We cannot promise you three days, but what I can promise you is that we will be back by your side in one week, maximum. Now, get back to your body and leave the rest up to us. I also saw Melanie and the Station's graduating class on Trolena. Do you have another tutor?" Phantom asked.

"Yes, I do, and her name is Shoanna. You know, big brother, I think you will like this one," Shamarra said as she started to giggle.

"Who knows? I just might, at that. Now go, and we will see you soon," Phantom told her as he ruffled her hair and then kissed her forehead.

As Shamarra's image disappeared, everyone heard Molly ask, "What does she mean 'her three brothers'? Can someone tell me who they are?"

"Let me introduce you to the three personalities of the Altherian. The one in blue is Phantom, the one in green is Allan, and the one in red is called the Assassin. The Altherians are capable of splitting their personalities to overcome any situation. In Allan's case, his personalities split a total of three times, and by doing so, both Phantom and the Assassin were born," Jacquelyn told Molly and then looked at the three Altherians. "You need to get some rest. Go ahead and sleep for a few hours."

"Yes, mother, that would be nice. Faith, activate security protocols for this room," Phantom replied as his three images disappeared.

"Yes, sir, the security level is now at maximum. If anyone tries to enter this area without giving a proper Galaxy Alliance identification code, they will be shot on site. Do not worry about anything, just close your eyes and relax," Faith replied in a soft gentle voice.

"That sounds great," Phantom just as he fell unconscious.

"Phantom, my precious little Phantom. Do not worry—mother is here," Jacquelyn told him in a loving voice just as she placed his head upon her lap.

"Is he going to be all right?" Molly asked her cousin.

"Do not worry. After a good night's rest, he will be back to normal. For now, we should just allow him to rest. Next time, how about being much nicer to your younger cousin. He has had a rough life. How about becoming much nicer to him the next time you see him," Jacquelyn told her cousin's as she stroked Phantom's hair.

CHAPTER 9

"SIR, OUR FIGHTERS are outnumbered three to one. I do not know how much longer they will be able to handle the situation," the tactical officer replied.

"How are the pilots handling the situation right now?" Commander Randall asked.

"The Pirates are handing them one extreme punishment. Other than that, sir, they are just fine," the female tactical officer replied while smiling.

Suddenly, all the lights started to flash. "Sir, I am receiving reports from every vessel of power failures. What are we going to do?" the communications officer asked.

"Reroute as much power as you can. Make sure you keep those shields up and our life support systems online!" Randall ordered.

Suddenly, everyone felt the entire cruiser's systems shut down. "Sir, as Phantom would say, we are dead in the water. None of our systems are responding. If those Pirates find out about this, we will not see the next sun rise," the tactical officer replied as tears started to run down her face.

Suddenly, the entire fleet felt a quick surge of energy launch from their cruisers. "Sorry for shutting your systems down. My name is B.R.A.T.T., and Phantom told me to help you out, Commander Randall," the AI told them just as the entire system returned to life.

"Can anyone actually tell me what is going on?" Commander Randall asked with a confused tone.

"Cruiser Class Bravo Echo Gloria, a.k.a. Drionic Guilds' second flag ship, was destroyed. Focusing on the second target. All cruisers weapons are charging," B.R.A.T.T told them.

"What was that was that one of our cruisers or one of theirs?" Colonel Calamen asked just as he activated a communicator. "Phantom, do you hear me? Where are you?" Just then, the whole ship shook.

"Jack! Jack, is that you? Where are you?" Jacquelyn replied.

"Jacquelyn, why are responding on this frequency?" Colonel Calamen asked.

"I am on the Drandon Space Station, where are you?" she asked.

"You are here? I am on the seventeenth level. What are you doing here? Where are you, and where is Phantom?" Colonel Calamen asked.

"Level Thirty-Seven B, Science Lab 13. I arrived here two days ago. I was picking our son's birthday gift up, and then I would return to the station. Phantom overly used his energy, and is unconscious right now. If you are able to hold your position for a few hours, Phantom should be back on his feet," she told her husband.

"All right, we will try our best, and as soon as he is awake, tell him to get a move on it," he replied.

"Yes, dear, I will. Can you hold on until he is awake?" she asked.

"Well, it looks like we do not have any choice, now do we?" he replied.

"I guess not, but please be careful," she told him just before the communications ended.

"All right, if anyone has any ideas, now would be the time to start talking," Colonel Calamen told his soldiers.

"Can I make a suggestion? How about I separate your troops from those nasty Pirates?" a female's voice requested as the emergency security doors started to close.

"Who are you? What is going on here?" a lieutenant asked.

"I am Faith, the station's new Artificial Intelligence. I have only a limited control of the station. Rest up while you can. Tomorrow will be a rough day," Faith replied.

"You heard her, people. Get some rest—that is an order," Colonel Calamen told them.

"Sir!" the soldiers responded from all around him as his lieutenant thought, *I just hope tomorrow shows a brighter ray of light. Phantom, if you are here, boy, could we use the help.*

Back on the station . . .

"Move out of the way! Medical emergency coming through," the instructor yelled while running down the hall.

"Shamarra, please be all right," Shoanna thought while chasing after them.

As the instructor turned the corner, he noticed everyone slamming their backs to the wall just to stay way out of his way. "Why are you here? Why did you not stay in the training room?" the instructor asked when he saw Shoanna in an all out sprint catching up to him.

"I am her tutor. I was instructed to take very good care of her—as much as I would a sister," the female recruit replied.

"Fine then. Just stay out of my way. You will need to turn right at the next intersection, and then at the following intersection, you will need to turn left. The medical facility will be at the end of that corridor. Once we are inside, you will need to stay out of the doctor's and the nurse's way," the instructor told her.

"Yes, sir. Do you know what happened to her?" Shoanna asked with the tone of being concerned in her voice.

"No, I do not. We might find out as soon as High Grand Admiral Calamen arrives. All I know is that she said 'big brother', so what happened had to be the cause of something happening to her brother. That would also explain why she suddenly had blood run from the cuts on her hands," the instructor replied just as he thought, *I just wonder why the bleeding had suddenly stopped.*

"I have the results on the brain scan. Her neural wave patterns indicated that, a few minutes ago, she suffered from a realistic dream-state of mind. Meaning, what she had felt in her dream is what happened to her physical body," the doctor replied as High Grand Admiral Calamen sat next to her niece.

"All right, this will stay between the three of us. I do not want Phantom to know what had happen here today," the High Grand Admiral told them as she stroked Shamarra's hair.

"Why would you refuse to tell him? Does he not deserve to know? He is her big brother after all," a recruit replied as she walked around the corner with a piece of cloth.

"Ah, recruit Malnerva. Do you have the cool cloth I asked you to get?" the doctor asked before turning to look at the young woman.

"Yes, ma'am, what would you like me to do with it?" the young woman asked as she approached the child.

"Place it on Shamarra's forehead," the doctor replied as a smile appeared on her face.

"Now, listen up, recruit, if her brother finds out about this, it could throw him into an unstoppable rage. Once that happens, everyone on the station could be killed. This must stay between us and only us," the instructor demanded.

"I know what you are thinking, and, no, my nephew is not a monster! Now, recruit, what is your name?" the High Grand Admiral asked.

"I am Shoanna Malnerva. I am Shamarra's new tutor," the young woman asked with a hint of being worried in her voice.

"I am Kristy Calamen. You do not have anything to worry about. My nephew is overly protective of his sister. I cannot allow him to take her with him while he is on missions and placing her in danger. This must stay with the four of us. Can you do that for me?" The High Grand Admiral said.

"You do not need to be overly protective at all. He already knows about this. He is the one who bandaged up my hands. Big brother told me he will be back by the end of the week," Shamarra told them as she started to sit up.

"That is a fast recovery. How are you feeling, dear?" Kristy asked her niece.

"I feel a lot better than big brother does. I just feel sorry for whoever thinks that they can stand in his way," Shamarra replied while she held up her right hand as it glowed.

"Your brother cannot decide when he will return. The report of the situation on the station has not arrived yet. We do not know how bad the situation truly is. Mom, I need to have Jacquelyn Calamen found, and she needs to know what has happened to her daughter," Kristy replied.

"Aunt Kristy, mom is on the station with big brother. Do not worry. Big brother has everything under control," Shamarra told them while smiling.

"She is right, Kristy, Jacquelyn is on Drandon Station. She was picking up a few things for Phantom just before the Pirates started their attack," Mom replied.

"Shamarra, honey, how did you know your mother was on Drandon Station?" Kristy said with a confused look on her face.

"I had seen her there just a few minutes ago," the young girl said with pride in her voice.

After a few minutes of holding her hand to her face, Kristy looked back at her niece. "All right, you've seen her, now why is your hand glowing two colors? Is it something new, or is it something we all should be worried about?" Kristy asked with a hint of not understanding.

"Big brother showed me how to use my chi to astral-project to whereever he is. Right now, he is unconscious. The white glow is saying he is dreaming, and the black glow in the center is saying it is a nightmare from our past. Once he wakes up, big brother will be a lot stronger than the Assassin could ever imagine of being. Last time he did that, Mac was repairing the training robots for a year," Shamarra replied while smiling.

"Is he going to lose control? Is that what you are telling me?" Kristy asked.

"No, Aunt, it is more on the lines of Allan being in full control—and deadly. The problem is, he will not realize that he is actually killing the enemy until he has snapped out of the trance," Shamarra replied.

"I sure hope you are right. All right, since I am off duty now and your uncle is away, how about having a girl's night? What would you like to do tonight, honey? Recruit Malnerva, thank you for being worried. You are one of two how have every showed concern for my niece, and for that I thank you. If you do not mind, I will handle everything from here on out. You can see each other in the morning when it is time for her tutoring. Until then, go and get some rest," Kristy Calamen told the room.

"Auntie, I told Shoanna that I would let her try some of big brothers cooking. He had left some Sharonkan Stew frozen for me. All the food he already cooked up, so I would not get hungry, and the food I cooked has already been eaten. Shoanna and I were going to eat the stew and watch a movie big brother bought for me right before he left. How about you join us instead?" Shamarra replied.

"That is all right. I have a hand-to-hand combat training exercise in the morning. We can spend time together another time, if that is all right with you," Shoanna told them. After a quick huff, she continued, "There is nothing in that class you could learn that my big brother cannot teach you himself. Not only that, but he could teach you a lot more advanced techniques, as well." With that, Shamarra hopped off the bed.

"We know. That is why, after this mission, he will be a new instructor here at the academy. What class he will be teaching, I am not sure yet, but he will be an instructor, though," Mom replied.

"Mom, do not allow him to be the hand-to-hand combat instructor. If you do, you should already know what could happen," Shamarra cried out with fear.

"What is the big deal? What does it matter if your brother is the combat instructor or just another instructor?" Shoanna asked with confusion in her voice.

"Ah, nurse, tell the doctor he will need to get the medical infirmary ready in three days," Kristy told the nurse who just happened to be walking by.

"Yes, ma'am," the nurse replied as she continued to walk.

A few minutes later, Shoanna, Shamarra, and Kristy exited the infirmary, "You forgot to tell me what movie he bought for you," Kristy asked.

"Oh, that is easy. It is a cartoon based on the Galaxy Alliance. The movie is called Space Alliance. Big brother found out the creator did not want to get into trouble by calling it the Galaxy Alliance," Shamarra replied as she started to giggle.

"You know, my little brother watches that. I did not know they made a movie out of it. Honestly, I think it is a stupid show, although, I have to admit that it is actually funny," Shoanna added.

"I have never seen that. I think this might be worth the time to see," Kristy said as the three walked onto a lift.

A few minutes later, while in the living room, Shamarra said, "Is it ready? Is the food ready yet? We can't watch the movie without food."

"Shamarra, does Phantom actually allow you to talk like that? The word is 'cannot.' Do not make me quiz you on your words," Shamarra heard her aunt say from the kitchen.

"Sorry, Auntie. Come on! I am hungry," Shamarra replied as she heard her stomach growl from hunger pains.

"Huh? I wonder what this is," Shoanna thought to herself as she started to sit down.

"Don't touch that!" Shoanna heard Shamarra suddenly blurt out. "Sorry, big brother does not like anyone to touch his projects. The data on the screen is commands and information that he had left up and running just before he left for his last mission eight months ago," Shamarra told her just before activating Phantom's personal pass code.

"Sorry about that. The information looked really interesting. What is he trying to do? I mean, it appears he has command coding for an artificial interagency, and then it also looks as if he has an operations system with override commands and identifying codes for the AI. Do you know what he is doing, Shamarra?" Shoanna asked.

"Not bad. You are half right. Mom and I had asked him to create a new AI for his arm computer to help him on his missions. We also have asked him to try and rewrite some of our old operating systems. Unless I am able to get mom to look at the programming to tell what it is he is actually trying to do, your guess is just as good as ours," Kristy replied as she carried three bowls of Sharonkan soup into the living room.

"Wow, that is amazing. How did you know that, Shoanna?" Shamarra asked.

"Oh, that is nothing. I just remember what our old farm equipments operating systems looked like. I also have the beginning schematics of an AI program. I have been working on one, and I think it would be great to have an AI to help us out on every mission when we need to hack into computers," Shonna replied.

"If you do not mind me asking, what is it you are hoping to do for the Galaxy Alliance? What job field are you looking at? It seems to me you are smarter than most of the individuals who join the Alliance and are placed into the infantry," Kristy asked as she sent a request to mom.

"All I am trying to do is my very best. It does not matter which job I am placed into. The High Grand Council could tell me that I will be in the infantry, and I would not mind. I will do my best, even if it kills me," Shoanna told them.

"Then, you might just stay away from my big brother. He hates drones even worse than most of the people on the council," Shamarra replied.

"For what I can see from you preliminary exams, I could almost grantee that you would be an Intelligence Officer. That is how you knew what Phantom was doing on his computer. Shamarra, I think you will need to keep her away from him permanently. He especially despises Intelligence Officers," Kristy told Shoanna.

"That is not true. He respects Nichole Grimly from the third Intelligence Office. Big brother was able to know her as a recruit and as an individual before she was placed into the Intelligence Core," Shamarra demanded with a sad voice.

"Shamarra, honey, Nichole is different than most of the Intelligence Core members. She is a field operative. She and Phantom have worked side by side on training exercises and missions. She as earned his respect, and he has earned hers. Most Core members think of the infantry as nothing more than a waste of the Alliance's payroll. The truth is, without the infantry, there would not be an Alliance. Most of our greatest High Grand Admirals have been from the infantry officers," Kristy told them while hugging her niece.

"The original person who designed my programming just happens to have been an infantry officer. That is why she programmed me to absorb the brain patterns and personalities of all the High Grand Admirals and then to assimilate the newest one with the rest. From the first time I was activated until now, I have assimilated over eight hundred personalities. There is nothing wrong for being in the infantry. It just depends on where you are placed in the infantry. You could be an Intelligence Officer out in the field, grunt soldier, or Special Operations Officer, which is a Commander of your own Squad. Now, if you become just as good as Phantom, you may end up on covert missions with him as your commanding officer," Mom told them.

"It sounds like your brother is one of the best the Galaxy Alliance has to offer," Shoanna told Shamarra just as she turned to look at the young girl.

"That may be true, but he still has a lot to learn. As I told you before, during the selection for Shamarra's tutor, Phantom has given extra training in any field you want that he knows. Melanie, who was Shamarra's third tutor, asked him to train her in a few advanced styles of Martial Arts. For what I have heard, she learned her lessons very well. From some of her teacher's reports, I can honestly say she can knock the pride out of most of the people she may make contact with," Mom replied.

"So you are telling me she is *that* good, and that is with only a few extra lessons?" Shoanna responded with a hint of disbelief in her voice.

"No, not 'good,' she is great. The way big brother teaches the advanced styles requires you to use different combination just to land even a single punch on him. Her predecessors before her both died in combat. Sorry to say, Mom, big brother thinks that the hand-to-hand combat styles taught to the recruits are nothing more than a joke. I remember him telling me once, 'With all the different styles I have trained in, even the most simple of styles could defeat the toughest recruit the Alliance has. I am not sure why I was chosen to receive all this training. I am sure there is someone else far better than I am, and I was the one chosen to leave the academy to train in all these different styles of combat.' He also told me he had watched both Tallea and Miranda lose their lives right before his eyes, and yet he could not do anything to stop it," Shamarra told them.

"I remember that training mission. As I recall from the report, Pirates arrived while the three were gathering information against the Alliance Planetary Academy. The training exercise was supposed to have been getting intelligence information and leaving the planet without being caught. Suddenly, five Pirates jumped them. The recruits killed all five Pirates with devastating cost of two recruit's lives and almost a third. Your brother was severely injured, if you recall, Shamarra, and Phantom was hospitalized for three months. At that moment, Mom and I knew the basic styles we originally were teaching were useless. Your brother was chosen for the special Martial Arts training because of his back ground. We knew his hatred for all Pirates would keep him going, even if the training was far more then he could handle. Now, look at Phantom. He is one of our best operatives. The problem is trying to fix his humanity," Kristy replied as she took a seat on the couch.

"Shoanna, I know you have been told this once already, but I will tell you this once again. Mom decided to commission Phantom into the military, even though he should not have been. That part you did not know, and you will not tell anyone else. For that, the Council decided to make a decree that while Phantom is in the military, no one is to fraternize with him at all. That means no one is allowed to date him, associate with him, or even try to be his friend. If you are caught doing any one of these things, you could find yourself being dishonorably discharged and/or in prison. Most of the young female members who have seen him in action have fallen in love with him, and others just think that he is cute. So take heed to what I have told you," Mom said in a loving voice.

"Shoanna, may I ask where it was and who had shown you how to read Operation Systems programming? You should not have been able to know what it was just by looking at the programming," Kristy asked the young woman.

"My dad used to work for a privet company. He used to write operating systems for different things. We would spend time together when he was at home working on the different operating systems. When I was little, I thought it was a game, until the day after my ninth birthday, and I found out he had lost his job due to the company losing all of their contracts. My parents decided to try farming. My home planet's soil was not the best to use for farming. I remember my father buying old equipment to try and transform our land into decent farm land. The problem was that most of the operating systems were too out dated to have been used the way we needed. So my father, with my help and the knowledge he had given me, started to rewrite all the old operating systems that we could. Then, one day, our land started to show how much hard work we had placed in it. By my eleventh birthday, our land was truly great for farming, and we helped the rest of our neighbors who wanted the same as my parents. Next thing we knew, my home world was a farming colony, and we could self sustain our own way of life. So, for the question, I learned at home from my father. Now if I could only figure out how to write an AI program," Shoanna replied.

"You might ask big brother to help you out. I think he would if you asked him nicely," Shamarra said with a grin.

"Do you truly think he would? After all, I am only a recruit, and most of the instructors refuse to associate with recruits if it is not during training," Shoanna replied.

"That is enough about Phantom. I thought we were going to watch a movie, girls," Kristy asked while thinking, *This might actually be beneficial for him.*

Once they were forty minutes into the movie, Kristy heard a faint snore. "What was that? Did that come from the movie or—" She turned and noticed Shamarra asleep and snoring on the couch. Right next to Shamarra, she saw Shoanna's awareness bouncing from conscious to unconsciousness. "How about we call it a night? Shoanna, you look exhausted. You should get back to your barracks," Kristy said while pulling a blanket out to place on Shamarra.

"That is all right. I am fine. I am not tired at all. If you would not mind, excuse me," she replied to Kristy as she stumbled her way in to the bathroom.

Poor girl. I do not think she will last through her entire training. This training might be too much for her, Kristy thought. Then, a loud noise echoed from the bedroom, "I wonder what that could have been?" Kristy asked herself as she walked into the bedroom, finding Shoanna unconscious from exhaustion on her nephew's bed. *This should be fine just for tonight*, she thought as she placed blanket over the young woman.

"Kristy, the situation at the Drandon Science Station has just become a lot worse than we originally thought. I just found out a moment ago, the council has decided to hold an emergency meeting in secret. The meet has been going on for two hours now. There has to be something about that station they did not want either one of us to know about. It is your call. I have confirmed Phantom is on the station, except he is unconscious right now in Science Lab 13. Your brother is on the seventeenth level trying to hold back the Pirates," Mom replied.

"How are the troops holding up? Are they able to continue, or do they need more back up?" Kristy asked the AI.

"I do not know. All I am able to tell is that Phantom is their only option for survival," Mom replied.

"The Alliance Cruisers and the Cerberus are all doing fine. We have lost three squadrons, though. They are outnumbered ten to one in the Pirates' favor. The Pirates have been taking more damage then we have, though, and the Pirates have lost seventeen fighter Squadrons, nine cruisers, and one—no, sorry—*two* flag ships now," a male voice told the two ladies.

"Who may I ask you are? And how are you able to tap into this frequency?" Mom asked him with Kristy's added agreement.

"Sorry, my name is B.R.A.T.T. I was just giving you an update," the male AI replied.

"B.R.A.T.T., was that not the name of one of the two new AI units for the Vortex?" Kristy asked.

"Yes, I was, until Phantom decided to pilot us," B.R.A.T.T. told her.

"Oh," Kristy replied as her hand covered her face.

"Phantom downloaded my programming and transferred my programming to the Cerberus. Faith is in control of the Drandon Science Station right now. Do not worry. She has the Pirates cut off from the Alliance infiltration units and Science Lab 13," B.R.A.T.T. told them.

"All right, thank you for the update. Just keep us informed. Kristy, get some sleep, I will give you an update when you wake up," Mom replied.

"Sure thing. Just remember, Phantom is only human. He cannot save anyone if he is dead. I know the council thinks of him as nothing more than a machine, but he has feelings, even though he does not know how to show them," Kristy replied.

"We know that. That is why I spend as much on his uniforms as I do. I try to keep him from being vulnerable. He is the best person we have, and that is also why I am going to have him train our recruits in hand-to-hand combat," Mom replied in a loving tone.

A few moments earlier at the Science Station . . .

"Not again. What is going on out there?" a lieutenant asked Colonel Calamen.

"Another Pirate Flag ship was just destroyed. Sorry, it was just a little too close to the station," a male voice said, appearing on their communications.

"Who are you supposed to be?" the lieutenant asked.

"My name is B.R.A.T.T. I am the new AI for the Cerberus. My counter partner is called Faith, and she is the one who has the control over the station right now," the male AI replied.

While the AI and the Alliance infiltration units talked, Daggen turned to the communications station. "Tearan, it has been eight hours. Have you broken the command code to the safe yet?" Daggen asked just as Tearan's face appeared on the screen.

"You *do* realize this takes a lot of time, correct? We are having problems with passing the new command codes. They just keep on appearing every time we have deciphered the last one. If I had to guess, there is something in the operations system that does not want us in this safe. Oh, I know, how about bringing the Stations Commander down here, and he could just use his command code? Oh wait I forgot. You threw him out the air lock with all the others! Just shut up and allow us to work!" Tearan replied.

"You insolent fool. You are under orders to do as we say, and this is how you treat us?" Daggen snarled as saliva fell from his mouth.

After Daggen's disappeared, Tearan said to his sister, "I hate this. How did those Drionic Guild scum balls trick our father into helping them on this little raid of theirs?"

"Remember, it was due to the acient pact our great, great, great, grandfather made with the rest of the guilds. Our guild was the strongest, until the awful day Trayon was born. Now, if this mission fails, I will have to marry him," Trisha told her brother as a tear ran down her right cheek.

"Do not worry. We will not fail. Hurry up and get that safe open," Tearan told them.

"Sir, I have been at this for six hours now. For what I can see, this system has a recycling command code. For every password I enter correctly, another one appears. There is either a program in the operations system that is doing this, or someone—if not something—is rewriting the command codes faster than I can crack them," a middle-aged man replied.

"Just do your best. I will handle Daggen the next time he checks on us," Tearan told the man.

Meanwhile, on the bridge . . .

"Sir, if the Korra guild does not hurry up, we will not accomplish our task," a male's voice told Daggen.

"I know that. The only other option is to convince Colonel Calamen to give us what we are wanting," Daggen replied.

Daggen's voice echoed throughout the station, "Colonel Calamen, I have a proposition for you. If you would like to hear it, contact me on the bridge."

"Great. Now what does he want? Jack, sir, this is becoming annoying. Why do you not just separate the bridge from the station?" a dark-haired lieutenant asked.

"Johnny, we have been friends for a long time. If I separate the bridge from the station, than we could also be killing some of our Alliance members who are still alive. Daggen thinks that he has the upper hand. I wish I could see his face when he meets Phantom face to face," Jack told him just before activating the communications.

"Ah, Colonel Calamen, you give us the blue prints and the new weapons the Alliance has already created, and we will allow the prisoners and your little infiltration units to leave freely. That means we will allow the entire Alliance fleet to leave with you," Daggen said as he grinned.

"You know, that *does* sound tempting, except for one little thing—you have already killed the commander of the station, and by doing so, you lost the command codes to activate the data that you wanted. So, my answer is *no*! By the way, how many of the station crew members do you still have alive?" Jack asked him.

After a short chuckle, Daggen said, "None you fool. Why does that matter?"

"That means you killed nine hundred and fifty people just for data. I do not know what it is that you are thinking for or are trying to do. Just remember that I will not allow it. For every member you have killed, you will lose that number of soldiers yourself." Jack replied just before Daggen heard weapons discharging throughout the communications system.

After the communications ended Jack said, "AI, thanks for the hand."

"My name is Faith, and you are welcome," she replied.

"I am sorry. Now, Jacquelyn, do you hear me," Jack called to his wife over a secret communications unit.

"Yes, dear, I do. How is the situation up there?" she inquired.

"It is not looking good. How is our son holding up?" he asked her.

"Well, dear, Phantom is sweating a lot, and he is talking in his sleep," she replied while wiping the sweat from Phantom's face.

"Can you tell me what he is saying?" Jack asked in an unusual concern and curiosity.

"He keeps saying over and over, 'Yes, I will protect Shamarra.' What about you, brother? What can I do to ease your pain?" Jacquelyn told her husband.

"It has been about twelve hours now. This is not good, not good at all. Honey, I want you to get everyone into the safe room. Faith, upon her signal, I want you to deactivate all the command codes to that room. Once you have heard the all clear from my wife, then you can reopen the doors," Jack told them with a worried tone in his voice.

"Honey, what is going on?" she asked with a hint of confusion in her voice.

"Just do as I told you!" He demanded just as everyone heard, "Codie, no!" from Phantom.

Suddenly, Phantom opened his eyes, and all his mother could see was hazel, glazed eyes as she looked into her son's eyes. "Honey, it is me; Mom. What is wrong," she asked him as she embraced her son.

To her surprise, he threw her to the floor. "I can't take this anymore. I can't keep on living like this. All I can do is be an Assassin for the Pirates and an ultimate Warrior for the Galaxy Alliance. Why did I have to become this monster? Why can't I just live the same life that I used to have. Big brother, I'm lost. Help me, please," Phantom said as he placed a hand over his face.

"Jacquelyn, what is going on with him?" Molly asked her cousin.

"I do not know. Jack wants everyone to get back into the safe room before the situation get out of control," she told them just as she activated her small communication unit that she had taken from of her son's arm computer. "Jack, what is going on? Everyone is heading for the room, and our son is talking really strangely. He has also reverted back to one of his other selves," she replied just as the door closed.

"Remember the Colothian child. If not—"

Before he could finish, she blurted in with a, "Yeah."

"Okay, remember, he died before we could save all three of the prisoners. One child was supposed to be the Controller. Every time the Controller felt pain, hate, etc., the Assassin would feel them in an enhanced level. The third person was to be the mental stabilizer to keep him at bay and under control. With all three children working as a single unit, there would have been no stopping the chaos that would have been unleashed," Jack told his wife.

Suddenly, Phantom stood up and started to stumble forward. "Someone stop them. They're going to kill him. They're going to kill all of us! Shamarra, run! We will try to stop them," Phantom told them just as his body shrunk to a normal, humanoid size.

"Allan, you need to snap out of it!" she cried.

"What is going on? Is he drunk or what?" Molly asked her cousin as they watched Phantom stumbling around.

"Hey, cousin, your guess is as good as mine. I can diffidently tell you he is not drunk. Allan, you must snap out of this right now!" Jacquelyn replied.

"Shamarra, it's too late to run. You better just hide. The Pirates will be coming through those doors any minute," he told them.

"Quickly, do as he says!" she told them just as the door flew open and twenty Pirates rushed in.

"You are dead. Did you hear me? I said you are all *dead!*" a blue-skinned Pirate yelled.

"At least we're in an agreement," Allan replied as he touched two fingers to the alien's chest.

Suddenly, the alien's heart exploded inside his body. "Kill him. Kill him now!" another Pirate demanded.

Before everyone's eyes, Allan and the Pirates had just engaged each other in battle. "Allan, honey, be careful. Think of Shamarra and what would happen to her if you died here and now," Jacquelyn yelled out to her son.

"Why do you keep calling him 'Allan'? His name is 'Phantom,' and he is nothing more than a loser," Molly said.

"I am the only one allowed to call him Allan—me alone and no one else. Besides, the true reason for the name 'Allan' is my secret," she told her cousin.

Before anyone could say anything else, Phantom's clothing started to reform into a different look. "Mommy, what is happening to him?" Valerie asked with a confused voice.

"I do not know, honey. Jacquelyn, what is going on? Why did his uniform suddenly change like that?" Molly asked.

"I do not know why it is changing. I *do* know all the nanotech has changed. It is possible that it is changing just to protect him. After we are back on the station, I will get a closer look at that shirt of his," she replied.

"Mommy, why is his body turning black? Is he sick?" Valerie asked as she watched Phantom's fight.

"Elemental Porux Poisoning. Allan, you need to discharge all the stored elemental energy!" Jacquelyn yelled in a scared tone.

"Hey, cousin, what is Elemental Porux Poisoning?" Molly asked.

"It is the stored elemental energy inside his body. We store a small amount of elemental energy and use the energy as normal energy," she told them.

"I did not ask for an anatomy lesson. You still have not explained what Elemental Porux Poison is," Molly replied.

"I was just about to get to that. Phantom's body just stores the energy until one day he either discharges it as chi or it kills him. The black look to his arms is the indication of how much energy he has stored," Jacquelyn said as she watch her son duck and dodge the Pirate's attacks.

Suddenly, Phantom back-handed a Pirate. "No more. Please, I cannot take this anymore. Codie, please help me!" he yelled just as he pulled his hand away.

The Pirate fell to his knees and then onto the floor. "What did you do to my big brother, Alliance dog?" another Pirate asked as he bent down to check for a pulse.

"Phantom, you must retake control of your body and discharge the elemental energy before it is too late," Jacquelyn yelled at her son.

"Um, can you explain to me who you are talking to now?" Molly asked while watching Phantom dodge another kick.

Heavy winds suddenly appeared as everyone noticed the remaining Pirates get slammed into the wall. "Phantom or Allan, I do not care which one of you does it. *You need to just wake up!*" Jacquelyn demanded.

Suddenly a red outlined figured appeared and threw a punch at Phantom's physical body. "Now, listen up, you little squirt. I need this physical body to survive, and I cannot just allow you to go and get killed. Wake up now, or else," the figure demanded just as Phantom's physical body slammed into the wall.

"Next time, Assassin, you could wake him up a little gentler," Phantom replied.

"Sure, and how about the next time I just bring flowers instead of a wakeup call," the Assassin replied.

"Did anyone get the license from the cruiser that had just hit me? What happened to me? One minute, I remember passing out from exhaustion, and now I am on the ground?" Allan asked as he placed a hand over his face.

"Allan, Allan, are you all right, honey?" Jacquelyn asked him as she knelt by his side.

Suddenly, he stood up and started to walk forward. "Yes, mother, I am fine. By the way, I am not Allan!" Phantom replied as his muscle mass started to expand again.

"Phantom, you're back! It sure is good to see you," she replied to her son.

"Get back, and I will show you how to really take care of things," he demanded just as thirty more Pirates entered the room.

Suddenly, Phantom had discharged blue energy, followed by yellow energy. "Shock therapy, anyone?" he asked as all thirty Pirates slammed into the wall.

Before Phantom realized what had happened, a knife flew past Phantom's right shoulder. "You will die, Alliance dog," a harsh older male's voice demanded.

"This is my favorite shirt, and now it is ruined," Phantom replied as he turned around.

Just as Phantom turned to face the Pirate, he heard, "What are you doing wearing the Korra Guild's crest? Not only do you have their guild's crest, you have the royal family's crest, as well. I just knew we could not trust them. If I see those two brats again, I will kill them before they can even leave the station," the Pirate told him.

"What 'brats' are you talking about? This guild's crest is not the only one I have, and for that, I will kill all of you," Phantom replied as he walked toward the individual.

"The only royal pains in my back that would be on this station right now, *that* is who I am referring to. Who else would I be talking about?" the Pirate told him.

Suddenly, a loud noise echoed from where Phantom slammed the Pirate into the wall. "Names, I want their names now!" Phantom demanded.

"Their names are Princess Trisha and Prince Tearan of the Korra Guild. Those two are the only royal pain in the necks that we have right now. Once I can get close to them, I will kill them," the Pirate told him just as Phantom picked him up by his neck.

"Jacquelyn, you never told us your son is an absolute, crazed lunatic who enjoys making an amuck throughout the galaxy and killing everyone and everything in his wake. Are you just going to stand there while he strangles that person?" Molly told them.

"Who are you calling 'an absolute, craze lunatic'? If it was not for my intervention, you would have been killed all ready," Phantom said as he dropped the lifeless body to the floor.

"So what are you trying to say? Are you trying to tell us that we are weak, pathetic, and helpless? Besides, you are the only pathetic one here. How can you judge me when you were a Pirate at one time? You are nothing more then a hypocritical monster!" Molly exclaimed.

"You also forgot about being empty minded, lack of skills, moronic and just plain stupid," Phantom replied as he turned to look at her.

"Now, that is enough, son! I know what they all say about you. Just remember that the only ones that matter are the ones that love you. That also means you do not have to look at them like you are going to kill them," Jacquelyn told him while looking into his hazel, glowing eyes.

"Yes, mother!" Phantom replied as his right hand reached into his shirt.

Suddenly, thirty Pirates rushed in while shooting and throwing objects at him. "Come on, it's only a single person. Kill him and then take the rest as prisoners," a Pirate demanded as an object flew past Phantom.

Without hesitation, Phantom pulled his hand out and launched the objects toward the Pirates. "If dealing with scum like this means I am killing everyone and everything in my wake, then, yes, I am a monster that both them and you have created," Phantom said as everyone noticed the objects that had been thrown were knives.

Without a single word, Molly and the other scientists realized the three knives Phantom had thrown were now starting to look more like one hundred knives in all. "Jacquelyn, what did he just do?" Molly asked in a low voice.

"Those are not knives. They are called 'shadow darts.' With the help of nanotechnology, the darts I threw are held together by a magnetic lock. Once they are thrown, the magnetic lock disengages, and a negative impulse launches the darts out. It is really handy when you are outnumbered, and it is more like ninety-nine," Phantom replied as he noticed the front of his shirt was now hanging down at his waist.

"Oh, honey, you are hurt. You have blood running down your right side," Jacquelyn told him as she rushed over to him.

Before realizing it, he felt something warm running down his left side. "No, Mom, it is not just my right side. I have blood running down my left side, as well. I must have been careless for them to be able to slice through both sides of my shirt," Phantom told her.

He heard a single pair of footsteps closing in on them very quickly. As Phantom turned to face the door, he noticed a middle-aged male enter the room. As the man slid on his back to a stop, the man asked, "What is going on here?" He then noticed the crest on Phantom's right shoulder.

After a few awkward minutes, Phantom noticed the crest on the man's shoulder and told him, "You are a member of the Korra guild. What are you doing here on this science station? You are being ordered to help these scientists to a transport shuttle and escort them out of this system. You will protect them until they are clear from this system."

"We are under a treaty to help Trayon. He is wanting all of the Galaxy Alliance's new weapons that this science station has been developing for the last several months," the man replied in a sad voice.

"What is wrong? You sound a little disappointed. You are hiding something, and I want to know what it is," Phantom demanded.

"It seemed to be going well until Daggan decided to throw the station's commander out the nearest airlock. You must decide quickly on freeing those scientists before Trayon arrives, or he will have you killed on the spot for being a traitor," the man replied.

"Let me worry about Trayon. All you need to worry about is my orders. Now, get moving," Phantom replied as he took his shirt off.

"Here you go, son. I was going to give it to you for your birthday, but I think now would be the best time," Jacquelyn told him while holding out a new shirt.

"Thanks, Mom, and do not worry. I will make sure Dad is all right," Phantom said as he took the shirt.

"Honey, watch out, I have—" Before she could finish, everyone heard a loud thud.

"What is this, Mom?" Phantom asked as he reached down and picked up a pouch.

"That pouch has a few new toys for you, but I do not know if they would be of any use to you. I also have a new untested sword for you on the thirteenth floor," Jacquelyn replied as Phantom pulled out a knife from the pouch.

"Thank you for the knives and the new shirt. I was wondering how much longer the nanotech would last on my old one. I was having problems trying to repair them," he told her as he connected the nanotech tubing with the tubing on his pants.

"Just be careful with those knives. They are not ordinary I have integrated nanotech slide rails in each and every one of them," she told her son as he flicked a wrist and the blade extended into a sword.

With a second flick of his wrist, the sword reverted back to a knife, "This is going to come in very handy. Thank you mom," Phantom replied as he tucked the knife back into the pouch.

As Phantom attached the pouch to his waist, the Pirate told them, "If everyone is ready we need to get moving."

"All right, just give me one more minute," Jacquelyn replied just as she heard a loud, metallic sound being torn away. As she turned to face the sound, she noticed Phantom holding a nine-by-nine-piece of metal plating. "What are you doing? This station is in a really bad state as it is, and then you go and rip a sheet of metal off of the wall," his mother said with a confused tone.

He took one of the knives back out and started to cut into the sheet of metal, "Do not worry, those Pirates have already damaged the station far more than I ever have. Now, get moving and tell my sister I will be home soon," Phantom replied to her as small pieces of metal fell from his cuts.

"Sure. And, honey, be careful," she told him as she started to walk out of the room.

"Cousin, I just have to tell you, your son has just lost his mind," Molly told her as they two exited the room.

"Tearan, come in. Tearan, do you hear me?" the middle-aged man replied.

"Yes, I can. Now, what is it, Jon?" Tearan replied over his ear communicator.

"I am escorting five scientists and a little child to an escape shuttle, and then I will report back to you," Jon told the prince.

"Can you tell why are you escorting them off the station and who has given you that order?" Tearan requested to know.

"It was an order from a member of your royal family. The only thing is I have never seen this person before," Jon told him in a soft tone so no one else could hear him.

"What are you talking about? Our family has never and will never join the Galaxy Alliance," they heard Tearan reply through the communicator.

As Jon and Tearan talked, Jacquelyn heard Molly ask in a low whisper, "If your son is that strong, why does he not just blast them with that kind of energy every time?"

"It is because he was looking death straight in the face. He just cannot arbitral summon that kind of elemental energy up, and you saw how bad his arms looked. I can tell you if he had not released that energy, we would be dead along with Phantom. Yes, my son is very talented, and he has out maneuvered the enemy on multiple occasions. With that look, his body was surely about to shut down, and then the poison would have killed him," she replied to her cousin.

Then, Jon asked, "You want me to do what?"

"You heard me. The Korra guild does not have the habit of just going around and killing people—especially innocent people. You will allow them to leave and then return to us!" Tearon told Jon just before ending the conversation.

"It looks like today will be your lucky day after all. Come on, let's get you out of here," Jon told the scientists. He started to walk a little faster and thought, *If Trayon found out about this, he would kill every last Korra Guild member without hesitation.*

Meanwhile . . .

"Faith, as soon as I tell you, activate the station's cooling system," Phantom told the AI just before jumping into the cooling duct.

"Yes, si—"

Just before Faith could finish her sentence, she heard, "Faith, activate the cooling systems!" Phantom yelled as he heard the few seconds' delay of his voice echo.

Suddenly, Phantom heard the giant fan starting up. "The systems are now active. I only activated the air system for the cooling systems. Sir, Colonel Calamen and his platoons are currently still under fire. Sir, what would you like me to do?" Faith asked as a giant gust of wind launched Phantom upward.

"What I want from you is for you to keep those Pirates away from him and his platoon. Just keep them busy so I can get over to them," Phantom replied as he noticed three openings rushing toward him.

"Understood, sir," Faith replied just as he felt his speed starting to pick up.

Before Phantom realized how fast he was truly moving, the three different shafts were upon him. Without hesitation, Phantom grabbed the center shaft's right edge and swung himself into it, just as a second giant fan started up. Before realizing he just barely cleared the corner, he heard a loud scrapping sound from where the metal board connected with the side of the shaft. "Computer, remind me to get my hearing checked when I return to the station," Phantom replied.

With a few beeps, the computer acknowledged the command. Suddenly, Phantom heard a rappid beeping sound coming from his arm computer. When he looked down, he noticed the computer showing he was now on the sixteenth floor. "I know I am on the sixteenth floor because I needed to overshoot the level so we can get over to the alpha side of level seventeen," Phantom said as he placed a finger in his left ear and started to shack it.

Meanwhile, on the seventeenth level, a soldier demanded, "Colonel, I thought you had reinforcements on the way. Where are they? We need help!"

"Do not worry. He is on the way and moving fast," the colonel replied while looking at a locating device.

"Jack, come on, tell me what your next move is. Don't leave your old friend in the dark. I know you were hoping your son would be here in time to help us. I am sorry to say this, but we need to fall back to another secured location," the lieutenant said in a kind, friendly voice.

"Do not worry—he is coming. Sergeant, come here. I need you to go out there and tell them to leave this section before something awful happens," Jack told her as she walked toward him.

"Sir, what if they do not want to listen?" she replied with a shaky voice.

"Just calm down. Take this locator and relax. If anything happens, toss it over to the Pirates after tapping the green marker on it and then get back here to cover," Jack told her as he handed the locator over to her.

After a few minutes, the sergeant turned and walked out in front of the Pirates while holding out a white cloth. "Hold your fire. All I want to do is talk," she told them.

Suddenly, one of the Pirates shot the lieutenant in the upper-right breast plate. "That was the fastest conversation I have ever had," the Pirate commander said just as the Sergeant touched the ground.

As a loud noise echoed throughout the hallway, Colonel Calamen yelled out, "What just happened out there?"

"Your soldier's life has been ended. Come on out, and we will talk," the Pirate commander yelled at Calamen.

"Just great. She was one of the best. Sir, now what are we going to do?" the lieutenant asked.

"Hey, Pirates, you said you wanted all the top secret weapons on this station, right? Well, here is your chance. That small device the soldier has—all you need to do is pick it up and press the green button on it," Calamen told them as a smile started to creep across his face.

"Now, tell me, Alliance dog, what does this red indicator mean?" the Pirate asked.

"That red indicator is the person who has some of the weapons. After you push the green button, it will send a signal to that individual to show them where to bring the weapons," Calamen replied.

"So you are telling me the person that is indicated in red has the weapons? You *do* realize that individual is very close to our location," the Pirate snarled.

"Yeah, I know. I promise you that when they get here, you will be surprised," Colonel Calamen replied while trying to hold the excitement.

Suddenly, he heard a loud noise echoing from down the hall, *Now this is too perfect. They fell for the trap, and our reinforcements will be here in any second,* Jack thought as he heard, "Jack what is going on? You just pulled something, did you not?" the lieutenant asked while trying to hold back his frustration.

Just before Jack Calamen could reply, everyone heard a loud crashing sound from down the hall. "What is going on? Daggen will not like this—our field commander is dead! I knew having a treaty with you Korra Guild members was nothing more than a curse," the Alliance soldiers heard one of the Pirates say.

"Wrong. Dealing with the Alliance and making me angry is the curse. I was enjoying myself, and here you go and ruin it," a familiar voice said while echoing.

When the lieutenant looked down the hall, he noticed a dark figure dropping down from the ceiling. "Jack, old friend, it looks like our reinforcements have arrived. What are you orders, sir?" the lieutenant asked.

"Stand down and just let it be. Do not move from your position for any reason. This is an order!" Jack yelled down the hall at his troops.

CHAPTER 10

A FEW MOMENTS earlier . . .

"As soon as the new weapons arrive, we will rush them and kill them all," the commander told them while grinning.

Suddenly, everyone heard a loud crashing sound as they looked up. "What happened to that grate?" a Korra Guild member asked his field commander while whispering.

"What is going on? Daggen will not like this—our field commander is dead! I knew having a treaty with you Korra Guild members was nothing more than a curse," another Pirate yelled in a paniced voice.

"Wrong. Dealing with the Alliance and making me angry is the curse. I was enjoying myself, and here you go and ruin it," a voice said from the opening in the ceiling.

Suddenly, a dark figure fell from the opening and was now standing before them, "What is going on? Who are you, and what are you doing here?" the Korra Guild field commander asked.

Suddenly, the black, long sleeve of the individual's shirt started to retract to revel a marking on this right arm. "That was my question. This is only a science station. The work here is supposed to help cultivate the planet in the Alliance systems that cannot be farmed without industrial help," the individual replied.

"Tell me, stranger, what is your name?" the field commander asked.

"Let's just kill him and get it over with!" another Pirate demanded.

"We cannot. You see, he has not made any hostile actions toward us. Our Guilds code of honor demands that we treat him with respect until the precise moment that he does," the field commander replied.

Suddenly, the individual slammed his palm into the field commander's chest and bent over backward, just barely missing a laser shot. As the individual straightened up, he noticed everyone holding a weapon on him. "Now can we kill him?" the Pirate asked.

"Oh, my, what shell I ever do?" the stranger said in a calm voice.

As the stranger spoke, every Pirate there started to look at each other in a confused manner. "What are you waiting for—"

Half way through the sentence, the Pirate heard, "Me. They are waiting on me," the stranger replied just as he slammed his forearm into the Pirate's neck.

After hitting the floor, the Pirate rolled and was looking into the stranger's eyes. "I will have you killed for that. Kill him now!" the Pirate demanded.

"Why, you are the one who fired upon the commander, not me," the stranger replied just before turning to the Korra Guild's field commander. As the stranger approached the commander, to everyone's surprise, they heard, "I extend my hand in friendship and make a pact," Phantom said as he extended his hand out to the field commander.

After a few minutes of trying to figure what just had happened, the field commander replied, "I accept your hand and friendship with the honor of a pact." After climbing to his feet, he looked at Phantom with an unspoken, questioned look. "Who are you? More importantly, how do you know of that?" a very familiar voice asked.

Suddenly, Phantom started to laugh. "It is you, an older you, but you still the same, Jon-Astic, the head body guard of King Carrag. What are you doing here? And also, it sure is good to see you again. It has been a while. The name is Phantom," the individual replied.

"I do not think we have actually met. Can you tell me, how do you know who I am and who the king is?" Jon-Astic replied while not trying to be obvious in staring at the mark on his shoulder.

To his surprise, Phantom extended his right arm out. "Here you go. Take the time you need to identify. For the pact, I would like to have the Alliance soldiers leave this portion of the station. They will not engage in any conflicts with you. The second condition is if there are any royal family members on the station, go and protect them. If Trayon's guild is in command, I can assure you that they will try to take out the royal blood line for their own personal gain," Phantom said just as Jon-Astic's eyes widened.

"You heard him. All Korra Guild will stand down!" Jon-Astic ordered.

Suddenly, they heard, "Princess! Someone help! She's been hit!" another guild member cried out.

"She is not the Princess of Korralla. If you would mind moving out of the way, I would like to take a look at her," Phantom said while walking past Jon-Astic and seven other Korra Guild members.

"Sir, can you explain how he would know our secret pact and what the true Princess would look like?" a Korra member asked Jon-Astic in a low voice so no one else could hear.

"If you noticed the crest inside the guild's emblem on his right shoulder, that crest is the royal family's crest. Somehow, I am not sure how, this Alliance soldier is a member of the Korra royal family," Jon-Astic replied in the same low voice.

"I am tired of this game, and this is for our friend. Everyone, your target is that man who calls himself 'Phantom'!" an opposing guild member replied.

Just as the opposing guilds started to walk toward Phantom with their weapons raised, Jon-Astic and the rest of the Korra guild member's stretched their arms out to their sides. "If you even think about starting a conflict with someone the Korra Guild has made a pact with, your fate will be the same as his. Remember, I do not care if you are part of Trayon's Guild," Jon-Astic told them while gesturing over to their unconscious friend.

"You there, you are a member of the Merynna Guild, are you not?" Phantom asked a young Pirate while bent over the injured Pirate.

"Yes . . . yes, sir. How did you know that?" the young man asked.

"Blue, green, yellow, and white," Phantom said while cutting the cloth from around the wound.

"Red, yellow, purple, and indigo," an older man said while walking up next to the young man.

"Indigo, gray, black, purple, yellow, blue, and white," Phantom replied.

"White, then. The only problem is you are not a member of our guild," the man replied as he watch Phantom poor a clear liquid over the wound.

"That is not quite true. Let me finish up with her first," Phantom replied as he looked over the wound.

"All TRI Guild members, attack him now," one of the Pirates demanded as he started to walk forward.

Suddenly, he noticed every member of the Korra Guild turning around and pointing the weapons at the TRI Guilds members. "We are not here to engage in a bloody dispute where there are not victors. If we are able to get what we are after without killing each other, don't you think that would be a better position?" Jon-Astic replied just as he heard, "There, that should fix the problem." After turning to face Phantom, he noticed the young woman in Phantom's arms, and he walked closer.

"Here is your sister back. I disrupted the flow of blood to this portion of her body. It will tack some time for the wound to heal. Change out her bandages every two hours and add this cream on the wound. Trust me, there will not be a scar left when it is completely healed," Phantom replied as he handed Jon-Astic the young woman.

"How did you know she was my little sister?" Jon-Astic asked Phantom as he walked toward the injured Alliance Sergeant.

"I recognized the family crest patch on her left arm. Besides, I had met you both once. Remember, I did not always look like this," Phantom replied as he bent over the injured Alliance member.

"I invoke the peace pact to Malgona the god of wisdom. I make a pact with you and all the guild standing before me. My group will walk by freely without aggression toward the guilds. In return, they will follow our example," Phantom said out loud.

"Sir, um, what is he doing?" a Korra Guild member asked.

"He is making the ancient pact. No one among us can now engage the Alliance until that man calls an end to the pact," Jon-Astic told his fellow member.

"Hey, Colonel, tell the troops to shoulder their weapons before they decide to show themselves," Phantom said as he started to walk his hand across the sergeant's body.

To everyone's eyes, a small spot on Phantom shirt started to retract to show six scars across his upper back and shoulders. "There you go," Phantom said as he injected a clear liquid into the Sergeant's arm.

"Am I going die? My body hurts all over," the Sergeant replied.

No, you will be fine. Right now, all you need to do is rest up to regain your strength," Phantom replied just as Colonel Calamen walked around from the corner.

"How is she doing?" he asked as he walked up to Phantom.

"She will live, fortunately. She will need time to rest and recover from this wound. Alright, start sending the troops through," Phantom replied as he stood up.

"Jon-Astic, who is he? How could he have been a member with of all the guilds?" a Korra Guild member replied.

"I do not know. Now I am curious about this young man," Jon-Astic replied as he started to walk over to Phantom.

Jon-Astic saw Phantom stand up with the young woman in his arms. Just as Phantom turned toward the colonel, Jon-Astic asked, "How do you know so much about the different guilds?"

"These scars on my back are not for looks. Every ounce of information about each guild was beaten into me. As every guild was branded into my skin, I had to give every ounce of information back to a particular guild leader, just so he knew I was almost ready for my true assignments," Phantom replied as he walked over to the lieutenant and handed him the young woman.

"Son, be honest with me, will she be able to take the exams for the elites?" Colonel Calamen asked in a low voice.

"I am sorry. We will be lucky if she will be able to move in the same amount of time. I am truly sorry about this, father. I know that you think she is the best soldier you have for those exams that are in two days," Phantom said as his eyes reverted back to normal.

"No, son, she is not. The best that we have to offer is you. We have been thinking—your aunt, your mother, mom, and I—we want you to take the exams, as well," he replied to his son.

To everyone's surprise, Phantom's voice exploded, "No, I will not take those exams, and there is nothing you or anyone else can say to make me!"

"Oh, yes we can. You have miss understood the question. This is not a request—it is an order from an officer of the Galaxy Alliance to his subordinate," Colonel Calamen replied to the outburst.

"Fine then, you can handle this on your own. Therefore, I quit," Phantom said as he started to walk off.

"Fine then, I will have to talk to everyone and tell them how you feel. Just for now, let us find out what they are wanting from this station and then leave," Jack Calamen replied in a soft, calm voice.

"Jon, may I take a look at your weapon?" Phantom asked while ignoring his father.

"Sure. Here," Jon-Astic replied as he noticed the first group of Alliance soldiers walking past.

"A Morina special ninety-seven, a standard issued Alliance weapon. Here, you can have it back now," Phantom replied after looking the weapon over.

"What are you doing, giving that weapon back to the enemy!" the lieutenant asked.

"I cannot take the weapon away from him under the pact. Besides, there is nothing special about it," Phantom replied as he turned and faced the lieutenant.

"All right, keep moving. We do not have all day," the lieutenant replied as he yelled at the soldiers slowly walking past.

"I want all guild members, except the Korra Guild, to leave this section and return to your transports. Korra Guild, you will walk with us as our escorts," Phantom told them just as he walked past Jon-Astic.

Before the Alliance soldiers knew what happened, every guild member walked off. "What was all that about? I mean, he is the best in the Alliance, and now he has control over the Pirate Guilds, as well. Who is he?" a soldier asked.

"I do not know, but I sure would like to find out, though," a female replied in a low, giddy, school girl voice.

As the group walked down the hall, Phantom called out, "Faith, download and transmit the station's blue prints to my computer. I also want you to download a live, active beacon for each and every Pirate guild with a different color and position."

"Sure thing, sir," a female's voice replied.

"Can you explain to me why you wanted us to walk with you?" Jon-Astic asked in a confused voice.

"I heard there might be royalty of the Korra Guild on the station. I want you to go and protect them from the TRI Guild. I heard one of the members threatening to kill them if he had a chance," Phantom replied as he stopped in his footsteps.

"What if there were? Why would you tell me this information?" Jon-Astic asked in a very confused voice.

"That is for me to know and for you to find out. Just do as I request, will you? Besides, you really should get your sister out of this environment," Phantom said as he heard the young woman moaning.

"Where did you hear that? Can you explain to me why you would tell me this information?" Jon-Astic asked with a sense of being confused even more.

"I was told by one of the TRI Guild members that it was the Korra Guild royal family's fault the Alliance found out. When I catch up with the prince and princess on the station, I will kill them for their treason. I just think it is impolite to kill two innocent individuals over Trayon's stupidity," Phantom said as he felt the young woman moan with pain.

"Is she going to be all right?" Jon-Astic's sister asked.

"I see that you have finally woken up, Jennifer. How are you feeling?" Phantom asked.

"Better. Hey, wait, how did you know my name?" she replied.

"We met each other three years ago, and I will leave it at that," he replied as he looked down at the young woman in his arms. "Do not worry. I will not allow anything to happen to you," he whispered into her ear just as she opened her eyes.

"Phantom, you look different. Your eyes are filled with kindness and resolve unlike your normal facial expressions," she replied.

"Dyanna, I do not know what you mean. You have seen this look on me before back in the Academy, remember?" he replied to her.

"Yes, except back then, you were always coming and going. The only time I saw you was during the testing phases of the training," she replied just as her body fell limp.

"Shhh . . . All you really need to do now is just sleep," he replied in a soft voice.

Suddenly, Phantom's attention was snapped back when Jon-Astic said, "Now, you *do* realize the TRI Guild members will report this back to Trayon."

"Let them, if he truly thinks he can stop me, just let him try it. I will rid the galaxy of that vermin at any given time," Phantom replied just as his eyes turned red. Back in his mind, he thought, *The only problem is, Trayon has to give me the chance without running and hiding.*

"This is where we leave you. Just watch your back," Phantom told Jon-Astic as he started to walk down the right side hallway.

"The next time we see each other, we will be enemies," Jon-Astic replied as he started down the left side of the hallway.

As Phantom walked, he could feel the sergeant's heart rate starting to slow, and then it started to race. "How is she doing?" Jack Calamen asked him.

"She has come down with a heavy fever. We need to stop after we turn the corner just up ahead," Phantom said as he looked down at the sweat running down the sergeant's face.

"Sure. How far down is it? Also, can you tell me what is it that you are after?" Jack asked.

"There is a small, emergency supply outlet down that hallway," Phantom replied just as he heard a harsh voice yell from down the hall, "We found the Alliance dogs! Kill every last one of them."

"Lieutenant, we need cover fire before they can box us in," Colonel Calamen ordered.

"No need for that, Colonel. I am starting the intrusion protocols. In just a few seconds, all the blaster doors will close. This will separate both groups for now," the AI's voice called out to him.

"Stop telling us about doing it and just do it!" Colonel Calamen replied just as a wild shot flew past his head.

A loud slamming sound echoed from behind him. "Those Alliance dogs. What gives them the right to do that? All I wanted to do was kill them," a harsh voice snarled.

"This is it," Phantom spoke out loud as he suddenly stopped.

"What 'is it'? What are you talking about?" Colonel Calamen asked.

A hidden compartment opened. To everyone's surprise, they saw four bags of blood and three caleem injectors (a small circular device that is placed upon the skin with a two inch needle penetrating the skin. Inside the device, you will place small, circular discs that contain one of four objects. The first will cure any kind of poison. The second will suck out and store within itself any foreign substance from your body. The third will contain numbing agent. The fourth and final is poison, itself), and seven discs marked with either green or yellow. "Dyanna, this will numb all of your pain. Right now, I just need you to bear with me while I insert the caleem injector to your skin," Phantom told her.

"You do not have to worry about me. If you say I will be fine, I will be fine. Why would I refuse the medical advice from a field medic specialist?" she replied as she felt a slight pinch from the needle.

"Here is the numbing agent. After that is done, we will give you something that will help you sleep," Phantom replied as he inserted a needle into her arm with a tub that was connected to one of the bags blood.

"Lieutenant, send a scouting party ahead and let us see what we are up against," Colonel Calamen ordered.

"Yes, sir. Groups 101, 597, and 336, you have point. I want a reconnaissance of the area. Afterward, take up positions in case of an ambush," the lieutenant told them.

"Sir, if we find anything, I will report back to you," the 101's commanding officer replied.

"How do you feel now, Dyanna?" Phantom asked just he heard the three sets of soldiers walking away.

"The pain is now gone. Before I forget, Phantom, or I should say. Allan, I am truly sorry about what happened at the Academy. Can you see it in your heart to forgive me?" she asked.

"First of all, do not call me that. Besides, how do you know that name? The second, I do not know what you are talking about," Phantom replied.

To her surprise, she could see his hazel eyes extremely clearly. "I heard your sister call you that. You *do* remember how we made fun of you, all the tricks we played on you, and how mean we were to you whenever you would show up for the exams?" she replied with a look of confusion.

"I don't know what you're talking about. Also, just because my little sis calls me by that name, doesn't mean you can," he replied as he placed a yellow disc in the caleem injector.

With a strange look on her face, he could tell the relaxing agent was starting to affect her. "Dyanna, don't misunderstand. I truly don't know what you are talking about," Allan whispered into her ear.

"Lieutenant, I was wondering if you had noticed or if I was just imagining it. Didn't Phantom look a little odd to you?" a soldier asked.

"Now that you mentioned it, he *did* look a little different. It appeared that his body mass shrunk, the way he talked changed, his eyes had a glow to them, and he did not recall what had happened back in the Academy. It was as if he was someone else," the lieutenant replied.

Suddenly, everyone heard a loud explosion. "Sir, what was—" Before the soldier could finish, he was slammed into the wall.

"Are you all right, soldier?" the lieutenant asked.

"Yeah, I think so," the soldier replied as he started to climb to his feet.

"I wonder what it is that they are trying to do. I do not understand this. All right, fall back and regroup with the others," the lieutenant said while looking confused.

"Sir, what is it that you are looking at?" the soldier asked.

"Your shirt—it has started to glow," the lieutenant replied just as he touched the shirt with his bare hand.

"I'm not truly sure why, sir, but we can figure that out on the way," the soldier replied.

"You are right," the lieutenant replied as he yelled, "Fall back now! We need to regroup with the others!"

Suddenly, the lieutenant heard a loud explosion from behind him, "Soldier, are you all right?" the lieutenant asked just as he started to turn around.

When the lieutenant saw the wall, he could not believe that the wall was covered in blood. "Sir, what just happened? One minute he was talking, the next minute, a loud explosion. What is going on?" a fellow soldier asked.

"Colonel Calamen, this is Lieutenant Creggs from the 101. Can you hear me? I repeat, Colonel Calamen, this is Lieutenant Creggs from the 101. Can you hear me?" the lieutenant asked over his communicator while ignoring the soldier.

"Yes, Lieutenant, I can hear you. What is your situation?" the colonel replied over an exterior speaker.

"It's Privet First Class Johnson, sir. He's dead. I repeat, Privet First Class Johnson is dead, sir. What are your orders?" the lieutenant replied.

"Take cover and do not allow anyone else to be hit," the colonel replied just as he heard, "Hey, Phantom . . . wait, what is it that you doing?" the Colonel's voice replied as a loud noise came from the background.

"It looks as if you will be receiving a few reinforcements," the colonel replied just before the communications fell silent.

"All right, you heard him. Take cover now. Our reinforcements will be here shortly," the lieutenant ordered.

"Sir, how do you think the reconnaissance team is doing?" Jon asked his old friend.

Just before Jack could answer, "Colonel Calamen, this is Lieutenant Creggs from the 101. Can you hear me? I repeat, Colonel Calamen, this is Lieutenant Creggs from the 101, Can you hear me?" suddenly came over his exterior communications unit.

"Yes, Lieutenant, I can hear you. What is your situation?" Colonel Calamen replied just as he looked over at Phantom.

"It's Privet First Class Johnson, sir, he's dead. I repeat, Privet First Class Johnson is dead, sir. What are your orders?" the lieutenant replied over the speaker.

Suddenly, Phantom stood up. "This has gone way too far. I will not allow another Alliance member to just standby and throw their life away," Phantom replied just as everyone noticed his body mass expanding.

"Take cover and do not allow anyone else to be hit. Hey, Phantom . . . wait, what is it that you doing?" Colonel Calamen asked just as Phantom shot past him. "It looks as if you will be receiving a few reinforcements," he finished saying just as he pushed the disconnect switch on the communications unit.

I hope I can get to them in time, Phantom thought as his speed started to pick up.

Soon, he turned the corner and noticed the reconnaissance team returning fire. "What is going on here?" Phantom asked just as his speed slowed to a walk.

"We do not know what is going on. I was talking to a soldier, and then suddenly his body exploded," the lieutenant replied.

"All right, what did he get hit with?" Phantom asked while looking at the blood-covered wall.

"That is just it, sir. He slammed into the wall from being hit by something, and that was it. Before I knew it, his body armor started to glow, followed by a loud explosion. Sir, what could have caused it?" the lieutenant asked.

"Phantom, this is B.R.A.T.T. We had four units sneak aboard on the back side. The only problem is two units were killed in an ambush, and the rest are trying to meet up with your group," a voice said over Phantom's computer speaker.

"Copied. I do not have time to deal with this right now," Phantom replied just as he disconnected his communication unit.

As the soldiers returned fire, Phantom called out, "Faith, I need you to give me access to the security cameras."

"Sure thing, sir. It will be a few—"

Before she could finish, "I am linking up to your computer now," Faith replied.

Suddenly, Phantom flipped his arm computer's screen open and started to activate it. *ICDU, they are using ICDUs. That has to be the answer*, Phantom thought loud while watching everything through the cameras.

"Sir, what is an ICDU?" the lieutenant asked.

"Inanimate Charging Dispersal Unit. ICDU for short. It means it will turn non-living tissue or objects into a highly unstable substance. The end result is that wall right there. Since you know, do us all a favor and do not get touched by their discharged blasts," Phantom said while pointing at the blood-covered wall.

"You heard him, people. Do not get hit," the lieutenant ordered just as he noticed Phantom starting to walk over to the entrance to the hallway.

"On the count of three, the lieutenant and I will charge them," Phantom replied.

"What did you just say?" the lieutenant replied with confusion.

Phantom said, "Three—move out now." Before he could reply, Phantom grabbed him and ran him out into the hallway.

"What do you think you are doing?" the lieutenant asked just as he placed a hand out to stop a blast from hitting him in the face.

Before he knew what had happened, Phantom ripped his glove and the lieutenant's glove off and threw them at the Pirates. "Close your eyes if you do not want to be blinded," Phantom told him just as the gloves disappeared in a flash of white light.

"My eyes! I'm blind!" two Pirates yelled out with pain.

Suddenly the lieutenant noticed Phantom had two knives in his hand just before they retracted into the shirt. "What was that?" the lieutenant asked.

"An IK, which means Inanimate Knives. They only cut through non-live things," Phantom replied as two claws appeared.

Suddenly, he sliced through two blasters at the same time while the Pirates were distracted. "Wow, look at him go," a soldier said.

"Oh, that is nothing. You should have seen him on the Alpha mission a few years back," a second soldier replied as Phantom and the lieutenant started to disarm the Pirates while ducking and dodging.

"We need to get back to Colonel Calamen. Move out, now!" Phantom yelled just as he noticed a large group of Pirates running toward them.

"Sure thing. Can you explain to me how?" the field commander responded while firing at the Pirates.

"Just back track from the same direction you came from, all right? Now move it and do not look back," Phantom demanded as he threw an object at the charging Pirates.

With a loud explosion, the commander turned the corner. "Sir, we have enemy troops incoming. The Corporal is trying to hold them off the best that he can," the commander yelled into his communications unit just as he started to run back toward the others.

"I copied. Just get back here as quickly as you can," Colonel Calamen's voice echoed through the speakers on the communications unit.

CHAPTER 11

A FEW MINUTES later, Colonel Calamen and the rest of his taskforces noticed the members of Phantom's task force running as fast as they could toward them. Suddenly, everyone heard a loud explosion. "Lieutenant, what was that? What in Mom's name is going on?" Colonel Calamen asked just as another loud explosion echoed throughout the hallway.

"Does that truly matter, father? I want everyone down and prepared to fire on my command. I have three platoons of Pirates following me," Phantom's voice blurted in.

"Take cover and prepare to fire on the corporal's command. Everyone here wanted a piece of the Pirate scum, and now here is your chance. In a few minutes, there will be three platoons that will fallow the corporal around that corner. Once the corporal is safe, I want you all to open fire. Take out as many Pirates as you can. The more you take out here, the less we will have to worry about later," the colonel told them just as he saw Phantom rounding the corner.

To everyone's surprise, Phantom's speed started to increase, "Sir, I think your son is injured," the lieutenant commander told the colonel after he noticed Phantom holding his right side.

"That has to be your imagination. I have yet to see him with a major injury," the colonel replied just as Phantom shot passed him.

Suddenly, he heard a loud, heavy discharge from behind him. "Phantom, what happened?" Colonel Calamen asked him while looking at his son's blooded side.

While sitting on the floor, back propped against the wall, Phantom told his father what had happened.

After he finished, both Pirates' lifeless bodies fell to the ground, and Phantom suddenly heard cheering from the rest of the platoon. "Do you actually think this is over, already?" Phantom asked just as the Lab Seven doors opened.

To Phantom's surprise all he saw where discharged rounds one right after another, flying right at him. "One, two, three . . . five . . . ten . . . thirty . . ." Before he could finish counting, he started to duck and dodge the rounds as he started to back away.

"Sir, let us help—" Before the soldier could finish, he was struck in the face by a discharged shot.

Just as the soldier's lifeless body touched the ground, Phantom stomped on the ground with his right foot, causing a heavy gust of wind to throw the Pirates in different directions. "Do not try to help me! Everyone, your orders are to keep your heads down, and do not move until ordered to!" Phantom demanded just as he launched several razor wind attacks at the un-expecting Pirates.

With every step Phantom took backward, more and more Pirates arrived to replace their fallen comrades. "Think, think, come on you must think. There has to be away to help him," the lieutenant thought just as a stray shot zipped passed his head.

"We need to get back to Colonel Calamen. Move out, now!" Phantom yelled just as he noticed a large group of Pirates running toward them.

"Sure thing, except, can you explain to me *how*?" the field commander responded while firing at the Pirates.

"That is the easy part. Just back track from the same direction you came from, all right? Now, move it and do not look back," Phantom demanded as he threw an object at the charging Pirates.

A few seconds later, a bright flash of light exploded in the air. As the taskforce started their way back to the colonel, they all heard, "You Alliance dogs, you will pay for that! I will make sure of that. Once I can get my hands on you, I will rip each and every one of your heads off!" Daggen's familiar voice yelled after them.

Suddenly, Phantom noticed an object flying through the air toward him. *Now what?* Phantom thought. "Hey, Daggen, are you that desperate?" Phantom asked as he started to run.

Suddenly, he heard a loud explosion from behind them. A few seconds later, Phantom felt a sharp object piercing his right side as he fell to the floor, rolling.

"After losing a few soldiers, I ordered everyone to fall back just as the Pirates threw a few detonators. I allowed everyone to get a good distance away before I ran and started my retreat. Suddenly, I heard Daggen taunting us as we ran," Phantom told his father just as he placed a hand on his right side.

"The good thing is that your platoon and you are safe," the colonel told him just as he looked at the exhausted soldiers.

Suddenly, he heard a small moan followed by a metallic echo sounding from nearby. "What was that? Son, did you hear that?" Colonel Calamen asked as he turned back to Phantom.

"No, Dad, I did not. I think you are hearing things again," Phantom replied just as he lifted his shirt up and started to place a bandage over his right side.

"You're injured. How bad is it?" the colonel replied while watching his son finish bandaging his wound.

"Do not worry. It missed all of my vital organs. This should not take to long to heal," Phantom replied as he pulled out an object and slid it to his right arm.

"What do you mean it 'won't take that long to heal'? Um, what are you doing?" the colonel asked with a confused voice.

"Remember what the Pirates had done between the enhancements, and that the Alliance helped my immunity system? My body can heal itself faster than anyone in the Alliance. Oh, this was a gift from mother. Whenever I need the extra strength, I am to use this," Phantom told his father.

Suddenly, to his surprise, Phantom was looking at a halo projected computer interface. "I thought you said it would make you stronger?" his father asked.

"It will. The more information you have, the stronger you will become," Phantom replied while inputing information.

"You have been helping out your mother too much," the colonel replied just as he could hear her voice saying the exact same thing in the back of his mind.

"Sir, what are we going to do? It appears that the Pirates are regrouping for one last single . . ." the lieutenant said as his voice trailed off. After a few moments, the lieutenant asked, "Hey Jack, what is your son doing?"

"Becoming stronger," the colonel replied.

"He's been helping Jacquelyn out to much. Am I right?" the lieutenant asked.

"Who do you think helped me gather the components I needed for my computer? Who do you think helped me write the Operation System for that computer?" Phantom told them.

After the two men looked at each other, Phantom heard, "That figures."

To their surprise, the computer image disappeared just as Phantom stood up. Without saying a word, they watched him take the projector off of his right arm and slide it back into place. "May I ask what it is that you have come up with?" his father asked.

"You can ask, but that does not mean that I will tell you," Phantom replied, and then he started to type commands into his arm computer.

Before any further questions could be asked, the automated voice asked, "The Neural Toxin Suppressant will disengage its primary functions. Do you wish to confirm or deny this action?"

"Confirm," Phantom replied just as he started to walk toward the sounds of gunfire.

"Where do you think you are going? What is wrong with you?" the colonel asked his son.

"I think I could use some playtime," Phantom replied in the exact same way his little sister had every time.

"'Playtime'? What do you mean by 'playtime'?" the colonel asked while noticing the confused looks on his soldiers' faces.

As Phantom turned his gaze toward his father, a white light exploded out from his eyes. "That is what I said. Either you will allow me to play, or I will go and play without your permission," Phantom said as he continued to walk away.

"I do not know what kind of food you and Jacquelyn feed that son of yours, but I would recommend the next time you go to the grocery store to buy something with less sugar," the lieutenant replied while noticing the same look Jack always had when he was lost in thought.

". . . Yeah," the colonel finally replied while remembering the first time Allan, Shamarra, Jacquelyn, and he sat down to eat dinner.

"Dinner is ready! Allan, here is a special dish just for you. Shamarra here is yours," Jacquelyn said just as she placed the two bowls on the table.

"Honey, I'm home!" Jack called to his wife as he entered the apartment.

"We are in here darling. I just finished making dinner." Her voice echoed from the dining room just as he smelt the aroma of their dinner.

Once he entered the dining room, he told her while smiling, "It smells like you made your special Callarian Stew."

"Tell me, sir, how did you know that?" she replied just before chuckling as Jack took his seat.

"I would know that smell anywhere. Honey, you out-did yourself tonight," Jack told his wife while looking at Allan and Shamarra.

"So, Shamarra, what do you think of the stew?" Jacquelyn asked as she took her seat.

"It is good. *Mowe pwease,*" Shamarra asked while holding up her empty bowl.

"Maybe you should wait a while. That stew has a special trait to it. Jacquelyn has been able to add a special compound into the food we eat to make it more nutritious for our bodies," Jack told her.

"Meaning, your body will break down every ounce of nutrition in the food and throw away all of the waste by running it through your body. Once your body starts to digest the nutrients, you will start to feel like you have eaten a lot more then you actually had," Allan suddenly blurted out.

"That is right. You catch on quickly. What do you think of it?" Jacquelyn said while smiling.

"More," Allan replied while showing that his bowl was empty.

"Go right ahead and help yourself," Jacquelyn said just before placing a spoon full of stew into her mouth.

Before realizing what she just said, she heard a scraping sound. "Allan, all you need is just a little more, all right?" she told him before turning around to face him.

She then noticed the small pot that she had made just for him was empty. "Allan, you might want to sit down. You have just eaten enough for three people," she told him just as she noticed his eyes starting to glow.

"You said I could eat as much as I wanted, and now you are placing a limitation on how much I get. You Alliance dogs are just like those Pirates. Just under a different name. Hit a person while they are down or take away the food when a person is hungry. You're all the same, both the Galaxy Alliance and the Pirates," Allan told her just as his muscle mass started to expand.

"Sharmarra, what is he talking about?" Jacquelyn asked while looking at the young child.

"Wen we *wewe stiww hungwy* and asked *fow mowe* food, the *piwates wouwd* cut the amount of food in half. *Awwan* and Codie made *suwe* that I had *mowe* food then they did," Shamarra explained to her.

"So what you are telling us is that the Pirates starved you when you were still hungry? Now, after asking for more food and then being told to only take half of what he *did* have, he now thinks that is what we are doing," Jack Calamen replied while stepping between his wife, the child, and Allan.

"Yep!" the young girl said with exhilaration.

"How can you be excited about all of this?" Jacquelyn asked just as Jack charged toward Allan.

Suddenly, she noticed Allan charging toward Jack. "Hey, Lieutenant, be careful! You do not want to hurt him too badly," she replied to her husband just as Allan caught his arm.

He felt a sharp searing pain shoot into his arm. "Let's see how much pain you can handle," Allan replied just as Jacquelyn realized Shamarra was now squeezing her arm in fright.

"What is it, honey? What is wrong?" Jacquelyn asked while bending down to look at Shamarra.

"That is not my big *bwothew*! That is someone who *cawws himsewf* 'Assassin'!" she screamed just before throwing her head into Jacquelyn shoulder.

"Darling, I would be . . ." Before she could finish, she noticed Allan's speed starting to pick up as he connected his two fingers into her husband's body.

A few minutes later, after Allan had stopped his attack, she saw Jack's unconscious body falling to the floor. "Why did you do that to him? He was only trying to protect Shamarra and me. If this is your true self, you are nothing more than a monster that was created by the Pirates. You claim to hate the Pirates for killing Shamarra's family and your family, but look at what you have just done. Take a good look at my husband! Would a normal person do this just because they were told to take it easy when it came to a second helping of food? You claim that the Galaxy Alliance and the Pirates are nothing more than the same thing under different names. Should I place you in the same classification as those Pirates who have done this to you, or maybe I should classify you as a class one criminal just like Trayon who is the cause of all of your problems? Do not ever try to judge the ones who think there is more to you and that are willing to help you before you are able to know them. You just hurt my husband and have possibly made it to where he can never work again by crippling his pressure points—" Before she could finish speaking, Allan was walking toward her.

"That is not a half-bad idea. Maybe, the next time he and I fight, I should cripple him. Or how about if I just kill him, instead. Just relax. He is not crippled. He is just taking a nap. You think that you are so high and mighty, you think that you know what I had to endure, you think you can fix whatever is wrong with a wave of your hand, and you think that you know me. You are wrong. Everyone in the Pirate guilds, except for the Korra Guild and the Alliance, can just disappear for all I care!" Allan told her just as Shamarra pulled away from her and walked over to her big brother.

"*Bwotew, tey* want to help us. This nice *wady towd* me if the *Awwiance wouwd awwow* it, she *wouwd wike* to be *ouw motew*. She is *wowwied* about what *wiww* happen to us once the *Awwiance* finds out *tat* you *awe fwom* Earth," Shamarra told him just as she wrapped her arms around him.

"I warn you, if you even harm a single hair on that child's head, I will kill you myself. You will not have to worry about what those Pirates have ever done to you because you would be dead from this moment on. Do you understand what I just said?" she cried out to him.

"I would be more worried about myself instead of her. She is my little sister. Besides, there are others in me that will not allow her to be harmed. You, on the other hand, are not so lucky," Allan told her as he tried to move again.

"Big *bwotew*, when you and I *wewe pwisonews* with the *Piwates*, do you *wemembew* what we both wished *fow te* most? We both wished that we *couwd fowget* about *evewyting tat* happened and *wive a peacefuw wife*. You *pwomised* me *tat*. Now, *Awwan, ow* no name, *wiww* you *tawk* to me, *ow wiww* you *awwow* that man *wight* there to harm me?" Shamarra asked just as he closed his eyes.

"They promised you a better life. I was created to cause chaos. You need to work on those words of yours, little sister," Allan's strange voice told her as he tried to move.

"*Onwy* if you *pwomise* me *tat* you *wiww* not *huwt* the nice *wady*," Shamarra told him.

"Now, this is unfair. I was not going to hurt the child. I was going to kill that lady over there," the strange voice said while gesturing toward Jacquelyn.

Suddenly, she noticed his muscle mass was back to normal, and the hatred was gone from his eyes. "No you won't. Shamarra does not deserve what you were about to do. She thinks of her as her new mother because of the kindness that she as shown us. I will not allow you to harm her, ever. Shamarra, he is right, though. You need to work on you *h*'s, *l*'s, and *r*'s more. The word is pronounced 'were,' and not '*wewe*.' 'That is a great offer,' and not '*tat* is a *gweat offew*,'" Allan said in a kind voice.

"Big *bwotew*, it *suwe* is good to *heaw youw* voice again," Shamarra replied while hugging him tightly.

"I'm sorry for that. We, the people of planet Earth, have a weak mind. During the torture, my mind cracked—it cracked into three different parts. The person that stands before you now is what I was back on Earth. The person you saw is known as the Assassin was created from all the torturing and enhancements that the Pirates have done to this body and mind. The one Shamarra calls the 'no name' has decided with me that we will use the name of 'Ghost' because that name no longer fits me. From this day forth, we will be known as *Phantom*," Allan told her.

"*Tat* may be *twue*, but I *wiww stiww* know *wo* is *wo*," Shamarra said to him while looking up at him.

"Jack, tell me what happened from there?" the lieutenant asked.

"Let us just say that Mom, the High Grand Admiral, the Grand Admiral, Jacquelyn, and I decided to make his training as hard and unique as possible," Jack told him just as he saw his son brace himself against the wall.

"Is he going to be all right?" the lieutenant asked while noticing Phantom.

"Right now, I am more worried about the Pirates instead of him. The state that he is in right now makes him even more deadly then you know," Jack told his old friend.

"Tell me, how old was he when you adopted him?" the lieutenant asked him.

"Well, at that point, he was twelve. Now, he is turning fifteen," Jack told him just as he saw Phantom activate something on his computer.

"Faith, I need you to access the OS for those weapons. Download them into a secondary file, so I can look at them. Also, make sure you do not get caught," Phantom told the AI.

"Yes, sir. Downloading now. For what I can see, sir, they have the normal Operation System for both primary and secondary. It also looks like there is an Emergency Operation System in place," her voice echoed through his ear.

"Okay, let us see what the functions are on those weapons," Phantom said just as he activated the file and started to look through it.

Suddenly, to his father's disbelief, a smile appeared on his son's face. "That does not look pleasant," Jack said out loud.

"What do you mean, sir?" the lieutenant asked.

"Colonel, in five minutes, I want every last soldier to rush those Pirates. Do not worry. I will confront them right now. Faith, give me voice activation override on the speakers," Phantom said just as his eyes started to glow red.

"Command override is now active, sir," she replied with a confused tone.

"OS 115862 ICDU Units. Emergency override authorization P20856 HAT 30689 OM 895643, confirm voice recognition," Phantom's voice echoed throughout the station.

Suddenly, Phantom walked around the corner. To everyone's surprise, they did not hear any weapons discharg. "Sir, what does this mean? It is far too quiet for my taste, sir," the lieutenant told the colonel just as a loud humming sound echoed from around the corner.

"He has disengaged the power source to those weapons. By the way, Colonel, did you know your wife created the OS Systems for those weapons with an Emergency OS Subsystem? I bet she did not realize what the OS System would be used for. One last thing, Colonel, did you know your son is the override command for these new units?" Faith told them.

"Not unless she was ordered to in the contract she had taken with the Alliance four months ago." Suddenly, Jack started to laugh. "An Emergency OS Subsystem—nice way of saying you cannot have anything that the Alliance has made. This has to be Mom's and High Grand Admiral Calamen's doing," Colonel Calamen replied.

As Phantom turned the corner, he saw every Pirate trying to shoot at him. Suddenly, he pulled two knives out from behind his back. "Your new toys will not work without the proper command code," Phantom told them just as he shoved a knife into one of the Inanimate Charging Dispersal Units.

"What makes you think that?" a Pirate asked just as he heard the unit's power supply starting to charge up.

"Field Command, this is Daggen, we are having a problem with the ICDU weapons. Switch back to your regular blasters and finish those Alliance dogs off. Trayon will be here to help us out, shortly," Daggens voice echoed from one of the Pirate's external speakers just as the station shook.

Suddenly, a loud explosion echoed from behind Phantom followed by a blood-curdling scream. "My arm! You blew off my arm!" the Pirate screamed out with pain.

"That will not help you right now," Phantom replied just as he connected the edge of his knife with one of the Pirate's throats.

Suddenly, a loud explosion echoed from behind him, followed by another scream. "If all of the Pirates' Guilds had just left this station alone then none of you would be in this situation. Now just shut up!" Phantom told them just before throwing a knife at the person who was screaming.

After the knife connected with the screamer, he heard, "That was my little brother! You will pay for that, Alliance dog," another yelled just as Phantom saw a Pirate charging toward him.

As a smile crept across Phantom's face just then, and just then at that particular moment, he vanished. "Where . . . where did he go? Do you think he was nothing more than a halo projection?" the charging Pirate asked after coming to a complete stop.

"There is no way. Look at what he did. He killed two fellow Guild members and then just vanished. There is no way a halo projection could have done that," the field commander replied while looking confused.

"No, not a halo projection. Try chi emulation effect," a voice said from behind them.

"Who . . . who said that?" a third Pirate asked before turning around.

"Nothing more than us ghosts," the voice said, followed by a weapon discharging.

Suddenly, as the Pirates turned to look at who was talking. They noticed several bright flashes flying toward them. "Who is this guy?" one of the Pirates asked.

"My name is Phantom Breaker, a member of the fifteenth unit of the Galaxy Alliance under the command of Colonel Calamen—and your worst nightmare," the strange voice replied just as his discharged energy blasts connected with the Pirates.

"What did you just do to us?" the field commander asked as he noticed his entire body glowing.

"We are doing exactly what it was you were trying to do to *us*," Phantom replied just as he started to smile.

Just as Colonel Calamen and his troops turned the corner, they noticed all of the Pirates suddenly explode right before their eyes. "What did you do?" Colonel Calamen asked.

"Hey, son, what made the station shake?" Colonel Calamen asked just as he noticed a sudden burst of energy explod in a shockwave from Phantom's body.

"I did. We need get to the control room and the secret labs in the B section of the station. We will need to go through Lab Seven to do so," Phantom replied as he tapped a button on his arm computer.

"Sir, my sensors are picking up strange, harmonic vibrations," the sensor officer told the colonel as she activated the structure integrity of the station.

"That is because of all the explosions from inside the station and the bombardment from the enemy forces," the colonel replied.

"That is not the bad news. The sensors are indicating that the harmonic vibrations are starting to increase. Now, for the worst news, the source of the vibrations is coming from right here," she replied just as the station shook again.

"Faith, increase the dampening and absorbing fields to their maximum if they are not all ready. Now, listen up! You saw what these ICDU Units can do! Watch your backs because I don't know how many other new weapons the Alliance decided to make! Let's move!" Phantom ordered.

After the lieutenant looked at the colonel, Calamen heard, "Does he know what he is doing?" the lieutenant asked with a worried look on his face after noticing his son was returning to normal, or what you could call 'normal' for Phantom, anyway.

"Yes, he does. Phantom you said there are secret labs on this station, right? So can you explain to me how you knew that when I did not?" Colonel Calamen asked his son.

"Seventy-five percent of our Science Space Stations have a total of seven experimental secret labs. I have yet to see the schematics for this station. So right now, it would be a guess about the secret labs, except, every lab I have come across has been searched, and everything in them had been removed," Phantom replied just as he placed an object into each ear.

"Can you tell me what that is for?" the Colonel asked with a confused look.

"What did you say? I cannot hear you when I have these ear plugs in. Faith, open the communications throughout the station," Phantom replied.

"Communications are now open. You may proceed at your own leisure," she replied to him.

"Daggen, you want what this station has? If so, you will have to go through me!" Phantom cried out just as he tapped a key configure over his computer.

Before anyone could ask their unspoken questions, they heard a loud sound over the communications. "Faith, I need a block out on the communication system. I have a feeling Daggen will try to shut the system down.

"What is that noise?" the lieutenant asked while covering his ears.

"Phantom, what is going on with all of this noise?" Colonel Calamen lipped in a slow motion to his son.

"Shamarra's music, except, she does not know how to play any intstrurments, yet. So what you are hearing is nothing more than noise she calls 'music,'" Phantom replied after reading his father's lips.

"One last question, do you have another set of those ear plugs," his father asked while trying to be nice about his daughter's noisy, meaningless music.

"Sorry, sir, I only carry a single set on me," Phantom replied while gesturing toward his helmet.

A few seconds later, he only heard quiet. *That is better,* Jack thought after putting on his helmet.

"Just keep your helmet on, and you do not have to worry about Shamarra's home-made music," Phantom's voice said inside the helmet.

"I did not know there was a short wave communication system built into the new helmets," his father replied as he ordered everyone to place their helmets on.

Five minutes later, Colonel Calamen noticed every one of his soldiers were awaiting orders. "Phantom, you seem to know the way around here. I will let you lead us to the control room," Colonel Calamen told him over the helmet's communications system.

"All right, just watch out for the defense systems. If the Pirates are smart, they would have already activated them," Phantom replied just as the Science Lab Seven's door slid open.

"Someone shut that noise off!" Daggen called just as he placed his hands over his ears.

"I'm sorry, sir, someone has locked us out of that function," the person at the communications replied.

"Fine then, see if you locate the signal and block it!" Daggen ordered while thinking *Blast those Alliance dogs. How could they have done this to us without us knowing?*

While pacing back and forth, all Daggen could hear were not the sounds of the computers, nor the sounds of his follow Pirates talking, but the sounds of the noise coming from the speakers. "Sir, I have isolated the sound. It is coming from level nine, and it is right by Lab Seven," the Pirate at the security station finally told him.

"The Dogs are on this level approximately seventy-five yards away?" Daggen asked with a confused voice.

"Yes, sir, and the signal is starting to move again. Sir! They will be here in no time!" the Pirate replied after checking the security tactical sensors again.

"Fine. If they want the control room, they can have the control room. Everyone, move out toward the Sixth Science Lab," Daggen said while grinning.

A few minutes later . . .

"Sir, everyone is ready for those Alliance dogs," the Pirate at the security station told him while walking over to him.

"Good. Come on, we need to leave, as well. Except, there is something I need to do first," Daggen replied just as he fired a blast at the security station. "Now let's see how well they can track our movements," he snarled just as he ran out the door.

As the Alliance members made their way down the hall, Colonel Calamen's voice echoed through everyone's helmet speakers, "Just remember to stay on your guard. At any point in time those Pirates could ambush us again!"

"Just remember, Daggen and Trayon are mine," Phantom replied to his father's orders.

"Whatever you do, do not get yourself killed. I do not want to explain that to your mother," he replied to his son's demands.

"Whatever. She would revive me just to kill me all over again," he told him just before they both started to laugh.

"If you both are done, can we finish this mission so I can get back to my family?" the lieutenant asked just as the group stopped at the control room's door.

Suddenly, Phantom brought the ICDU unit in a defensive position with a hand up to stop the troops. Before anyone could stop him, Phantom rushed into the control room. After looking around, making sure that the room was clear, Colonel Calamen heard, "It is clear. Send them in," his son's voice came from his helmet speakers.

After he gave the signal, Phantom noticed the security station had been destroyed. Suddenly, from behind he heard, "So what do you make of all of this?" his father asked.

"Well, they destroyed the security station just so we cannot find out what they are doing. Except, Faith, give me an update on Daggen's group of Pirates. Is Trayon on the station? Can you see through the security cameras what it is that they are after?" Phantom said while plugging his arm computer into the main system.

"Sure thing, Phantom, I will tell you as soon as I can find anything out," she replied.

"What do you have in mind, son?" Jack Calamen asked his son while watching him access the main computer's information.

"Well, I am downloading a copy of the blue prints to the station. This is so we can come up with an alternate route in case we are ambushed," Phantom replied while adding the destroyed portions into the computers holographic blue prints of the Drandon Station.

"Phantom, sir, they have cleared out everything of value in every lab except for the one marked 'Alpha Science,'" Faith replied just as Jack noticed his son's muscle mass suddenly shrink.

"Thank you. Father, from this point on, you will need to be careful. I do not want to see Mom mad because I could not have protected you," Phantom suddenly told him in a calm voice while his eyes widened.

"Allan, what is wrong? This is not the time to sit here and play games," Jack whispered into his son's ears.

"Dad, I do not know why, but I feel strange. I feel as if there are people on this station right now that are in danger," he replied.

"Yeah, and those people are you and I," his father replied while looking into his hazel eyes.

"No, Dad, I mean other members of my family. I just have a really bad feeling about this," Allan replied while looking around franticly.

"Allan, I do not understand. Your mother is off the station. There are only you and I here for our family. Who else could it be on this station, and where are they if it is not us? You are not making any sense," Jack told him.

"Allan, what is it that you are feeling? Are you sure it is our extended family and not just your imagination?" Phantom asked him.

"I bet it is the boy's imagination and nothing more," the Assassin replied.

"No, I mean, they are on the station right now," Allan told the both of them.

"All right, if you say so," Phantom replied while walking away.

Suddenly, his muscle mass grew back to normal. "Sorry, sir, I do not know what had came over me. Come on, we need to get this over with," Phantom told him while looking at his father with his hazel iris and red glow.

"All right, I will let you lead the way," Jack Calamen replied while thinking, *There has to be a reason Allan is worried. But what can it be and why?*

As Phantom made his way, he heard, "Jack! Jack, do you hear me?" a familiar voice called over the family communications channel.

"Go ahead, Jacquelyn, I am reading you signal loud and clear," Jack answered his wife.

"I am back on the Academy Station. Kristy told me that she is sending you a message over a secured link. Inside the message, you will find new orders for most of your soldiers. Please hurry and come home safely. One more thing, honey, please bring our son back with you," his wife said right before the communications went dead.

"Well, boy, you heard your mother. We need to hurry up and get home," Colonel Calamen told his son just as a small sound exploded from his pocket.

"Sir, what was all that about?" the lieutenant asked.

"We just received a message from my wife telling us that she is safe. That sound was a message from my sister," he replied to the lieutenant as they made their way down the corridor. After passing through four corridors, another soldier decided to take point. "Braden, be care—" Before Phantom could finish speaking, he saw Braden slam into the wall from a blast.

"Those lousy Pirates had their blasters on stun. I am sure glad I was given this new armor to use," Braden said as his body started to glow.

No way. It cannot be. There should be no way for that to happen. Did they really make those, as well? Phantom thought as he watched Braden's body start to glow.

"Braden, I am truly sorry," Phantom told him just as he swung his arm toward Braden. However, Phantom's arm stopped a few inches from the back of Braden's neck. Without a word from Phantom, Braden's body started to fall lifelessly to the floor. "Phantom, what did you do that for?" the lieutenant demanded to know while looking at Phantom.

"Lieutenant, there must be a reason for my son to sever the brainstem of one of our own kind," the colonel replied. Then, Braden's body went flying toward the Pirates.

As everyone looked at the lieutenant and back at Phantom, they heard a loud explosion from down the hall. When Phantom looked up at the lieutenant, he heard, "Um, sir, I think you can handle it for here," the lieutenant said while noticing Phantom's eyes shifting back and forth from a hazel to a red glow.

"I can't believe that they sacrificed one of their own," the Alliance troops heard a Pirate's voice say.

"Are you going to allow him to get away with killing one of our own members, Colonel? If I were in charge, I would have him arrested for murdering a follow soldier," a junior officer said while walking up to assess the situation.

"That would be fine—*if* you were in charge. The fact is that you are not, and out of all of us here, there are only two among us that knows him the most. Lieutenant, can you tell me in your own words what the situation was that led to Braden's death?" the colonel asked while facing the junior officer.

"I think I can, sir. The weapons the Pirates are using have a different effect than a normal blaster. I would say that the weapons have the same effect as the Inanimate Charging Dispersal Unit, or ICDU. Phantom noticed it before any of us. Instead of allowing Private Braden die in a horrible way, Phantom decided to give him a quick and painless death. The Phantom launched the body at the Pirates because of collateral damage. The body spooked the unsuspecting Pirates when it exploded instead of allowing it to hurt us," the lieutenant explained to the colonel's question.

"Does that sum things up, son?" the colonel asked while turning to face Phantom.

"Most of it, Dad. The weapons, or units, that they are using right now are called OCDU's." Phantom finished.

"Tell us, what does OCDU's stand for?" the lieutenant asked.

"Organic Charging Dispersal Units, or OCDU's for short," Phantom said as he peeked around the corner just as a blast flew past his head.

"He's lying. Give me fifty soldiers, and I will prove that the greatest Alliance soldier is wrong," the Junior Officer replied.

"All right, if you truly believe that I am lying, then your wish has truly been granted," Phantom told the junior officer.

"By the way, you cannot expect any help from Phantom or anyone else," Colonel Calamen told him as he turned to Phantom. "That is an order."

"Yes, sir," Phantom replied with a snarl as he turned away from his father.

"Now I need forty-nine volunteers," the lieutenant said to the troops.

"No, I want forty-nine volunteers that agree with the beliefs of this junior officer," Colonel Calamen replied just as forty-nine hands flew into the air.

After hearing the colonel's comment, thirty-nine hands fell from view. "What? Everyone believes this liar over me?" the junior officer asked.

Suddenly, from nowhere came a snide, "YES!" from a female voice. "I have been on missions with the corporal, the lieutenant, and the colonel. Each time that we listen to the corporal, everyone returned to the station. What you are asking is a suicide mission. I, for one, will not volunteer for a stupid mission like this one," the female's voice continued.

"Flay, I appreciate those kind words. Except, you know that I will not hold feelings against anyone that thinks I am wrong—to a degree, especially if that individual is going to die," Phantom said with a grin on his face.

"I know, Phantom. Just one favor, though?" the female asked.

After a hidden chuckle, Phantom replied, "Sure, name it."

"Stay away from me while grinning the way you are right now," she replied while starting to back up.

"All right, it looks like my follow ex-recruits and I will show you old timers a thing or two," the junior officer replied as he and his twenty soldiers started their way toward the corridor.

"So how long do you think they will last?" the lieutenant asked.

"Five seconds," Phantom replied while smile.

As the junior officer looked back at his soldiers, he noticed eleven of his soldiers stopped and returned to the ranks.

"What is this? Are you all scared of one person? How many Altherians are there in the first place? How do you know if this is the greatest Altherian?" the junior officer asked them.

"Well, my older brother and sister always told me to listen to the Altherian because he would never allow anything to happen to me if it was in his ability," a male soldier replied.

"There are only two Altherian's in this galaxy. Now, listen up, there is only one Altherian in the Alliance," Phantom replied with a cold, calm voice.

"The only Altherian in the Alliance is Phantom Breaker who is standing right in front of you," the lieutenant said.

"Your brother's name is Howard, and your sister's name is Tiffani, which makes you the youngest. Your name is Shan, and you just graduated from the Academy, right?" Phantom asked while walking over to the young soldier.

"That is right. How did you know?" the soldier asked.

"Hmm, I guess I will have to honor their wishes. Shan, you are ordered to stay here while the junior officer and his group fight the Pirates that are standing in our way," Phantom replied while placing a hand on the boy's shoulder.

"How do you know my older brother and sister?" the soldier asked Phantom while noticing the different look in Phantom's eyes.

"The first time I met your siblings was during a pre-flight check for the asteroid racing one year ago. Your siblings were acting as their squad's mechanic. I just happened to walk past the fighter they were working on when my little sister noticed a large crate that had been moved over the fighter they were working on had suddenly come loose. Just before the crate fell onto the fighter, Shamarra and I were able to get everyone away from the fighter. Now, I will not even mention the second time I met them," Phantom replied with a soft, kind voice.

Suddenly, everyone heard an explosion of laughter. "If I remember right, the second time you met them you were sent on a rescue mission because the transport that they just happened to be on was attacked by a group of Pirates," Colonel Calamen said while suppressing a laugh.

"Yeah, well, that is fine. Come on, guys, we need to prove to them that we can handle this all on our own," the junior officer interrupted.

Suddenly, a fellow soldier charged toward the junior officer. "Jeb, what are you doing? Jeb, you need to get back here! *Jeb!*" Flay cried out as she saw him get hit by a bright light.

"Flay, Flay stop! Do not go to him!" Phantom ordered just as he grabbed her by the arm.

"Jeb, he's been injured. Phantom, please allow me to go to him," she said while tears streamed down her face.

"No, I cannot allow you to touch him," Phantom replied while holding her.

"You owe him your life. How are you going to repay him?" Flay asked the junior officer.

"I did not ask him to save my life. I do not owe him anything," the junior officer replied.

"You owe him because he *did* save your life," Flay muffled voice replied from Phantom's shoulder.

"Flay, look at me. I have something to tell you," Phantom said in a soft, loving voice.

"You're not Phantom. Who are you? Phantom would never talk to someone like me with love and sorrow in his heart. You must be an imposter," Flay said while trying to pull away from him.

"Jonathan, I order you to get that soldier to the other side!" the junior officer ordered.

"I am Phantom—in a sense. Flay, listen to me," Phantom said while trying to pull her back to him.

As Colonel Calamen walked up, he asked, "What is going on here?"

"Sorry, Dad, I am trying to keep Flay from being killed," Phantom replied.

"Allan, what are you doing in control of the body?" the colonel asked.

"Sorry, Dad, I didn't mean to be/ Phantom is having a hard time dealing with the deceits of the Galaxy Alliance Council. He claims that these weapons are not supposed to exist," Allan told the colonel while Flay looked at him with a confused look.

"'Allan,' Phantom, why did he call you 'Allan'? Not only that, but why did you just call the colonel, 'Dad'?" Flay asked just as Allan wiped away a tear.

"Flay, my wife and I adopted Phantom and his sister before he started to use the name 'Phantom.' Phantom has a condition that all Altherian's have. The person in front of you is Phantom, but yet he is not. Allan is the original part of Phantom, and the name 'Phantom' appeared just before he entered the Alliance Academy. I am surprised it has taken you this long to notice," Jack Calamen told her in a soft, kind, quiet voice.

"Flay, you and Allan graduated from the academy at the same time. You never noticed the difference in his body mass and the way he talked. Allan, my lad, it is nice to hear from you again," the lieutenant said in a low voice.

"Lieutenant Colonel, it is nice to see you again," Allan replied.

"Just call me Lieutenant, won't you? Allan, tell me, have you been able to suppress the third nature of yours?" the lieutenant asked.

"I am still working on it. Right now, let's just focus on the problem at hand," Allan replied while embracing Flay.

"Allan, please, you have to tell me, what is going on? You have to tell me why you don't want me to help my fiancé," Flay asked just as everyone started to hear a metallic explosion.

Meanwhile outside on the Cerberus . . .

"Commander! We are picking up a strange anomaly that is starting to enter this system!" the tactical officer suddenly announced.

"Can you identify the vessel and the pilot?" Commander Randall asked with a confused tone in his voice.

Suddenly, a fighter appeared on the sensors. "The sensors have identified the fighter as a Millowic fighter Zinggo class," B.R.A.T.T. announced.

"Why would anyone be bringing an old fighter like that to a fight? B.R.A.T.T., can you identify the pilot?" the commander asked.

"Sir, the pilot is identified as 'Phantom.' Can you tell me when Phantom left the station, and were did he find an old piece of junk like that?" B.R.A.T.T. asked.

"I don't know. Open the communications to Phantom's personal communications unit." Randall replied.

CHAPTER 12

ON THE GALAXY Alliance Station Academy . . .

"Mommy, you're back!" a young female called out.

As Jacquelyn stepped off the transport's boarding ramp, she noticed Shamarra running toward her. "My, it looks like you've grow a few inches from the last time I saw you."

When everyone heard the commotion, they turned to see Shamarra hugging her mother. "Yeah just a little," she replied.

"Here, can you carry these for me, honey?" Jacquelyn said while handing Shamarra a duffle bag.

"Welcome back, sister. Is anyone hurt?" a familiar voice asked from behind Jacquelyn.

As she turned to face the voice, she noticed High Grand Admiral Kristy Calamen standing there. "Hello sister. No, no one was injured—thanks to you brother," Jacquelyn replied while turning to look at her daughter.

"What did big brother have to do with it, anyway?" Shamarra asked.

"Let's go to Aunt Kristy's office, and I will tell you there," Jacquelyn said.

Five minutes later, while sitting on the couch in High Grand Admiral Kristy Calamen's office, Jacquelyn took a drink of water when she heard Krisy ask with a loving smile, "Can you tell me what your fearless son has done this time?"

"Well, after he rescued us from a group of aggressive Pirates, another group appeared." Jacquelyn turned on the couch and looked at her daughter. "Shamarra, can you explain to me how you were on the station when Phantom was injured?" Jacquelyn suddenly asked.

"Brother showed me how I could us my chi to project an image of myself whereever he happens to be. When the Pirates injected us with the sibling bond, we were given an invisible network that connects us together, no matter where we are," Shamarra explained.

"Wow, you must be becoming stronger than when you and I first started his training," she replied to the young child.

"Sister, as you was saying about the Drandon Station?" Kristy Calamen asked with a hint of curiosity in her voice.

A few moments later, Jacquelyn started to tell them the story again, "Phantom told a field commander about a group that he calls the Korra Guild. I extend my hand in friendship and for a pact. To my surprise, the field commander accepted the pact. After an exchanging of a few words that I do not know nor understand, the hostilities were diminished," she said with a look showing she was still trying to figure it out.

What do you mean, 'You did not know what had been said nor understood what was being said'?" Kristy asked with a confused look.

"He started to talk in a secret code and, in some cases, in a different language that I had never heard," Jacquelyn replied.

To their surprise, they heard someone talking in a language that neither one had ever heard. When they turned to look at the person that was speaking, to their astonishment, it was Shamarra. "*Codonna sho-anta molli-nowa fem-omila . . .*"

Before Shamarra could continue, her mother asked with wide eyes, "What was that, where did you hear those words, and what does it mean?"

"Our cousins taught us," she replied.

"What do you mean, your 'cousins'? Neither the Calamen's nor the Blake's have anyone that can talk like that," Kristy explained.

"It wasn't the Calamen's or the Blake's. Our cousins Tearan and Trisha were the ones who taught us the language. This language is an ancient language that only certain nobility of their race knows," Shamarra replied.

"Tearan and Trisha . . . you don't mean the prince and princess of the Korra Guild, do you?" Jacquelyn asked her daughter.

"Yes, they even taught us the other guilds' ancient languages. Except, brother is the only one who can write it and read it. All I know is how to speak it," she replied to her mother and Aunt.

"We can finish this up in the training room. Shamarra, it is time for your daily combat practice," Kristy replied.

As the three exited Kristy's office, Jacquelyn asked her, "Why did the prince and princess teach you and him how to speak the different ancient languages?"

"It was because Trayon wanted brother to be the best spy, assassin, information gatherer, tactician, hand-to-hand fighter, and a one-man-infiltration-unit that he could be. The different languages were Trayon's idea, and the ancient languages were our cousin's idea," she replied to her Aunt and mom.

"So all this time not only has Phantom been using the training the Alliance has given him, but he has also been using the training Trayon forced upon him?" Kristy asked her niece.

"Yes, with the two types of training he had, he has just become the worst kind of nightmare that Trayon could have ever dreamed of," Jacquelyn replied to the unspoken comment while looking at the smile on her daughters face.

"You should ask brother to play the halo guitar. You would be amazed how well he can play it," Shamarra replied.

"Who taught him to play that? How many other instruments does he know how to play?" her mother asked while placing a hand on Shamarra's shoulder.

"All you have to do is just hand him any instrument and he will play it. Uncle Carrag was the one who had shown him how to play the halo guitar," Shamarra replied in a loving voice that her mother was all too familiar with.

"Uncle Carrag? Who is Uncle Carrag? He is not a member of our family. By the way, honey, what is it that you have scheming?" Jacquelyn said.

"Sorry to interrupt the two of you. Can you get back to your story, sister?" Kristy asked.

Before the three knew it, the door to the training room opened just as Lieutenant walked out.

"High Grand Admiral, ma'am, what are you doing here?" the lieutenant asked while saluting.

"Well, it is time for Shamarra's combat training. Lieutenant Ericks, are the recruits done for today?" Kristy replied while returning the salute.

"Yes, ma'am," the lieutenant replied while gesturing for the women to enter.

"How is Shoanna doing with her training?" Shamarra asked the lieutenant.

A smile appeared on his face. "She is doing fine. The only thing that concerns me is that she does not show confidence in herself and her abilities," the lieutenant replied while kneeling down to face her.

"Ericks, you look exhausted. Are you getting enough sleep, or is there something else wrong?" Jacquelyn asked him.

"Third Lieutenant Ericks, I am very pleased with your training schedule. I feel that you can use a break for a while. I have decided to place the hand-to-hand combat training on someone else," High Grand Admiral Calamen told him.

"Is there something that you feel I have done wrong?" the lieutenant asked with a confused voice.

"It is not that. I just feel like you could use a vacation. You have been work extremely hard, and now you can use a break," High Grand Admiral Calamen replied.

"I do not understand. If the schedule for the recruits training is great, then tell me why?" he asked.

"I want you to prepare yourself for the upcoming elite exams. When Phantom returns from his mission, at that moment, he will become the new hand-to-hand combat instructor," she said with a smile.

"So what you are saying is, I am to rest up for the exams while Phantom trains the recruits in a more advanced style of hand-to-hand?" he replied with a hint of understanding.

"That is correct. You are very good in this field, but Phantom is even better," she replied in a friendly voice.

"I can see that. Phantom surely was a promising recruit and even a better soldier. Will he go along with the council's decision?" the lieutenant asked.

"He will not have a choice," Jacquelyn replied just as a smile appeared on her face.

Mother, what did you do?" Shamarra asked with a worried tone in her voice.

"Well, he is supposed to teach me more then he has in the field of combat, and this way I can learn at the same time the recruits do," Jacquelyn said to her daughter.

"First, you make a very rigorous training schedule while he was a recruit, and now you are making his work orders. Mom, how mean can you actually be?" Shamarra asked with a hint of being afraid.

As the four walked into the training room, the three women heard, "All right, now, listen up. You are to get to those locker rooms and change into your swimming suites! I want to see everyone poolside in five minutes!" the lieutenant ordered the recruits.

Everyone looked at each other with a confused expression as they heard, "Make it *three* minutes!" the lieutenant demanded just as all the recruits scrambled for the locker room.

"Shamarra, why did you skip your scheduled tutoring session?" Shonna asked as she approached the tree women.

"Sorry, my mom is back on the station. Shoanna, this is my mother Jacquelyn Calamen. Mom, this is Shoanna. She is my new tutor," Shamarra said while introducing them to each other.

"It is nice to meet you, but before the lieutenant becomes annoyed even more, I would go and get ready," Jacquelyn said in a soft, kind voice.

After everyone left, Jacquelyn heard her sister say, "So now finish the story. What happened after Phantom started to talk in the different language?"

"Everyone stopped what they had been doing and started to listen to what he had to say. Before I knew what was happening, we were on the way out when I turned . . ." as Jacquelyn continued the story, Kristy started to notice her sister's voice was trailing off.

"Sure. And, honey, be careful," she told him as she started to walk out of the room.

"Cousin, I just have to tell you, your son has just lost his mind," Molly told her as the two exited the room.

"Tearan, come in. Tearan, do you hear me?" the middle-aged man replied.

"Yes, I can. Now, what is it, Jon?" Tearan replied over his ear communicator.

"I am escorting five scientists and a little child to an escape shuttle, and then I will report back to you," Jon told the prince.

"Can you tell me why are you escorting them off the station, and who has given you that order?" Tearan requested to know.

"It was an order from a member of your royal family. The only thing is, I have never seen this person before," Jon told him in a soft tone so no one else could hear him.

"What are you talking about? Our family has never and will never join the Galaxy Alliance," they heard Tearan replied through the communicator.

As Jon and Tearan spoke, Jacquelyn suddenly heard, "If your son is that strong, why does he not just blast them with that kind of energy every time?" Molly asked in a low, whispered voice.

"It is because he was looking death straight in the face. He cannot just arbitrarily summon that kind of elemental energy up, and you saw how bad his arms looked. I can tell you, if he had not released that energy, we would be dead—along with Phantom. Yes, my son is very talented, and he has out maneuvered the enemy on multiple occasions, but with that look, his body was surely about to shut down, and then the poison would have killed him," she replied to her cousin.

Suddenly, they heard, "You want me to do what?" Jon asked.

"You heard me. The Korra guild does not have the habit of just going around and killing people—especially innocent people. You will allow them to leave and then return to us!" Tearon told Jon just before ending the conversation.

"It looks like today will be your lucky day after all. Come on, let's get you out of here," Jon told the scientist as he started to walk a little faster. He thought, *If Trayon found out about this, he would kill every last Korra Guild member without hesitation.*

"How far away are we from the hanger?" Molly asked as she noticed a group of Pirates rushing ahead of them.

A few minutes later . . .

"Sir, we can proceed. Both of the hallways have been disarmed," another Pirate said as Jon approached him.

"Good, now make sure that we are not being followed by any TRI Guild members. If Tearon finds out that we allowed any of these scientists to be hurt, then we will both die," Jon replied.

"Jacquelyn, what do you think they are talking about?" Molly asked her cousin.

"Us, they must be talking about us. I have a feeling that, unlike the other Pirate guilds, this one does not like to include civilian and other non-military personal," Jacquelyn replied to her.

"What are you whispering about? Don't worry. We are under orders not to allow anything to happen to any of you," Jon said just as Jacquelyn noticed him pulling the trigger on his weapon.

Suddenly, a loud discharge echoed throughout the hallway, "I thought you said you are not supposed to hurt us!" Jacquelyn demanded with a worried look on her face.

"No, we are not to allow anyone to hurt you. That shot was not meant for any of you," Jon replied while pointing toward a location far on the other side of the hallway.

When Molly, Jacquelyn, and everyone else looked down the hallway, they saw a Pirate's body with what appears to be a sniper rifle lying next to him. "We need to get moving again. Sam, split our forces up into two groups. I want one group for point and the second group covering us from behind," Jon said while looking a little worried.

"Sir, what are we going to do about these scientists?" Sam asked.

"Tearon gave us an order! I will follow his orders until the mission is done!" Jon told his fellow Pirates.

"I hope you know what you are doing. If we are caught, not only will Princess Trisha marry Trayon, but we Pirates right here and now will have our heads lying on a golden plate for Trayon's approval," Sam replied with a worried tone in his voice.

"Do not worry. I will not allow that to happen. I will not allow that power-hungry maniac win against the Korra Guild," a familiar voice said over a speaker.

"Prince Tearon, is that you?" Sam asked.

"Yes, how are the scientists doing?" he asked.

"A member of the TRI Guild just tried to snipe us," Jon told him.

"Get those people off the station and give them a full escort with our fighters. I will notify the fighter's commander of the situation," Tearon's voice finished just before a blast of static exploded from the speaker.

"You heard the prince. Now, we need to be moving," Jon said as he started his way down the hall.

"Jacquelyn. Jacquelyn, did you hear what I just asked you?" Kristy asked while trying to get her sister-in-law's attention.

"Sorry, what was that you asked?" Jacquelyn replied.

"You're telling me that the Korra Guild actually protected you, and then once your shuttle had left the hanger they made sure your shuttle had jumped into hyperspace?" Kristy asked her sister.

"That's right. I was surprised about the entire thing, as well," Jacquelyn replied while watching Shamarra run through her stretches.

Suddenly, a sound of the door to the training room opened. "Where is he? Where is that cheater?" a young man demanded to know as he walked into the room.

"Where is who? Is it not proper for a Galaxy Alliance soldier to solute a higher ranking offer?" Kristy asked.

"When you are a normal soldier, I will say yes. You should be begging to solute me! My father is the president of the Galactic Council! Now, tell me where I can find that good for nothing Phantom!" the young man asked.

To Jacquelyn's surprise, she saw her daughter walk up to the young man who was dressed in blue and red. "What makes you think my brother cheats?" Shamarra asked with a look of defiance in her eyes.

"The last Asteroid Race—there is no way he could have defeated me. I had the fastest fighter there was," the young man replied.

"Jacob, Phantom is not here. He is in a middle of a battle on the Drandon Station. Is there a message that we can deliver for you?" Kristy asked.

"Yes! That would be great!" the young man replied. Suddenly, he back-handed Shamarra and sent her slamming hard into the wall.

"How dare you lay a hand on my daughter! How about I bend you over my knee and teach you a lesson!" Jacquelyn demanded while walking up to him.

"Jacob, I would be very careful if you would like to live," Kristy said in a soft but stern voice.

Suddenly, he back-handed Jacquelyn, "Give him my message will you?" he said while looking at Kristy.

After he left, she noticed both her sister-in-law and Shamarra were not moving. "Mom, we need a medical team down here, now!" Kristy cried out after checking and noticing that they were both unconscious.

Five minutes later, as the medical team rushed into the training room, they noticed High Grand Admiral Calamen hunched over two individuals. "The child appears to be suffering when you touch her right side jaw line. The young woman here, I cannot find anything wrong with her," Kristy said while looking worried.

"Shamarra, what is Shamarra doing here? Is that Jacquelyn? High Grand Admiral, what is going on?" a doctor asked.

"Jacob walked in here looking for my nephew. When he did not find him, he did this to my sister and my niece," Kristy replied while helping to place Shamarra on the stretcher.

"Should we notify Jack and Phantom about what has just happened to them?" the doctor asked.

"Are you insane? If you tell both my brother and my nephew, there wouldn't be anything left of this station!" Kristy told the doctor and nurses with a hint of being worried once the two found out about Shamarra and Jacquelyn.

A few moments later, the doctor and the nurses rushed both stretchers in to the medical bay. "Get the scanners ready! We need to find out what happened to these two. High Grand Admiral, you need to wait in the waiting room out side," the doctor demanded from the medical staff.

A few minutes after that, the doctor walked into the waiting room. "Can you explain to me how a Drazarian child ended up with a cracked right jaw line? The skeletal structure of a Drazarian is as hard as steel. It takes a lot to damage a structure like that. What was she doing in the training room to sustain this kind of injury?" the doctor asked.

"She was back-handed by the son of the president of the Galactic Council. Will she recover?" Kristy Calamen asked with a look of worry.

"Both Shamarra and Jacquelyn will recover. Jacquelyn only has a concussion. Shamarra will be injected with medical nanites to repair the damage to her jaw. We will have to monitor her until the repairs are done. You may go and visit Jacquelyn if you would like," the doctor finished just as the door opened.

"Thank you, doctor. That would be much appreciated," Kristy replied.

"Oh, one last thing, ma'am. Try to keep this from Phantom, please," the doctor said just before disappearing behind the door.

I wish I could, except, he probably already knows, Kristy thought as she made her way to her sister's room.

A moment later, Kristy asked while entering the room, "How do you feel, Jacquelyn?"

"Sore, but it is nothing that I cannot live from. Where is Shamarra? Tell the doctor to bring my daughter to my room," Jacquelyn replied while trying to sit up.

"She cannot be moved. Shamarra has a crack in her lower right jaw, according to the doctor. She is being observed right now until the nanites are done repairing her jaw," Kristy said while taking a seat on the bed.

"I want my daughter in my room right now," Jacquelyn said with a hint of anger in her voice.

Suddenly, the nurse walked in. "Don't mind me. I'm here to check the patient's chart," she said while picking up Jacquelyn's medical chart.

"Nurse, tell the doctor to move my daughter into my room, please," Jacquelyn said to the nurse just as the nurse look at her with a confused expression.

"I cannot. She is being watched every five minutes," the nurse replied.

"I want my daughter in my room, and *I mean now!*" Jacquelyn demanded while trying to climb out of her bed.

"Easy there. If the doctors and nurses are having to monitor her healing condition, then let them. We can always have Shamarra moved into this room after the procedure has been completed," a familiar male's voice said from the door.

"Blake, when did you get back on the station?" Jacquelyn asked while looking at the door.

As he walked over to the bed, she noticed he had a serious look on his face. "Does your son know about this yet?" Blake asked her.

"We had just finished docking, and I was making my way to the hanger's elevator when the medical emergency was called. I thought I would come up here to see which recruit have made Phantom made this time," Blake replied.

"Do not worry. If it was Phantom, we would have about seven recruits in here instead of just two injured people. Reminder High Grand Admiral, do not tell Phantom about this," the doctor replied while walking into the room.

"Now, that will be too late. Once Shamarra was injured, he already knew about it because of the bond those two share," Jacquelyn said as she placed a hand over her face.

"Are you all right sister? Jacquelyn, you need to rest before you . . ." before Kristy could say anything she noticed Jacquelyn was unconscious.

"I think it is time to check on munchkin. If she is able to be moved, then we will move her in here, just like Jacquelyn wants," Blake said to his wife while walking over to her.

As they two exited Jacquelyn's room, Kristy asked, "What do you think will happen to the Alliance if Phantom harms the son of the president?"

"I do not have an answer for that. I just hope we can find someone who is able to finance the Galaxy Alliance. I do not think we will be able to stop him from killing that soldier," Blake replied with a worried tone in his voice.

"What will we be able to do? We both joined the Alliance at the age of fourteen. We dated as Alliance soldiers, and then we were married. That says the only thing that we know *is* the Alliance," Kristy replied while grabbing her husband's arm.

"I would not worry too much about it. Off record, the Galactic Council has not funded the Galaxy Alliance for the last two years. All we are doing is making it look like that they have," Mom said in a low voice so no one else could hear.

A few minutes later, just as both Blake and Kristy walked into Shamarra's room, they noticed a man in a white jacket who was checking Shamarra's chart. "You cannot be in here," the male's voice called out without turning around.

"We came to tell you, once she is able to be moved, take her to her mother's room," Kristy said to the doctor while thinking, *I just wonder how mad Phantom is right now. I know he has felt everything that had just happened.*

"All right, once we can, we will move her," the doctor said without turning to look at them.

At that exact moment, the communication's officer called out, "This is the Cerberus calling Phantom. Do you hear us? Phantom, Commander Randall needs to talk to you."

After a few minutes when there was no answer, Commander Randall said to his communication officer, "Try him again. This time, try it on both frequencies."

"What do you need?" Phantom's voice suddenly asked in a harsh tone over the communication speaker.

"Tell me, when were you able to leave the station and pick up that Millowic fighter?" the commander asked.

"What are you talking about? He has been here all this time," Colonel Calamen replied after cutting in on the conversation.

"We picked up a Millowic fighter with Phantom's indicator as the pilot," the commander replied with a hint of confusion in his voice.

"Do not worry. I have a faint idea of who that is," Phantom said just before disconnecting his communications unit.

Suddenly, Colonel Calamen and the lieutenant heard a loud beeping sound. "Phantom, what is going on?" his father asked.

Before Phantom answered, he activated a different communication unit. "Phantom here, what is it?" he asked over the silent unit.

. . .

"Feeling better, I see," Phantom said while touching his right ear.

. . .

"Is that so? Can you tell me how he was activated?" Phantom asked.

. . .

"That should not have happened. So you're telling me he activated himself, injured a few of the medical staff there, stole the second Millowic fighter, and then flew his way here?" Phantom asked.

. . .

"I think I will have to leave myself a mental note about this one," Phantom replied as a conversation continued in his ear.

. . .

"What was that? Oh, the replica? Well, I do not know how to explain this to you except for . . ." After trying to figure out how to explain it, Phantom finally said, "He is dead."

. . .

"What do you mean? What do I mean 'he is dead'? Just like I said, D-E-A-D—dead. He is dead. Do I need to spell it out for you again? Hang on, there is someone here that would like to say hi," Phantom said just as he activated his external microphone and speaker.

"Okay, Phantom! Tell me. Who is it that wanted to say hi?" everyone heard and only Flay recognized her fiancée's voice straight off.

"This is not funny, Phantom. Did you download a message from him and then decid to mess with me?" Flay said with an outraged tone.

Suddenly, Phantom activated a halo screen just as the image of Jeb appeared on it. "Now do you think I just recorded a message?" Phantom asked just as the feed showed it in real time.

"Honey, you're dead the next time I see you!" Flay said just as she turned back to the screen.

Suddenly, they heard over a second communications speaker, "This is the Galaxy Alliance Orbital Command and Training Station. Shuttle, identify yourself," a female's voice called out.

"Phantom, just be careful. That experiment of yours is incomplete," Jeb said just before disconnecting his transmission.

"Phantom, what was he talking about? And what is that thing?" the colonel asked.

"That is a bio-replica. The brain is highly sophisticated technology. First thing the doctors have to do is scan you brain patterns and then transfer it into the replica's brain unit. The skeletal structure is metallic, just like a normal robot. The doctors then place a synthetic tissue or skin over it, so that way it makes his or her bio-replica look just like you," Phantom replied while Flay turned to look at him.

"Tell me, Phantom, how long have I been living with this . . . this, this, this *thing*!" Flay asked while pointing over at the non-functioning bio-replica.

"Two days. Jeb and I were both injured on the last mission. Our mission was to map out an unknown planet for any dangers—anything that was helpful, especially any life. We found a plant that neither one of us had ever seen. It looked like a rose from the planet Earth, except, instead of green leaves, it had yellow with a blue stem. The thorns carried a potent toxin that I have yet to see. After accidently touching the thorn Jeb fell to the ground unconscious. I then picked both the plant and Jeb up and made my way back to our shuttle. By the time I made it to the shuttle, I too felt the toxin running through my body. I set the auto controls for a medical station full of medical specialists. I was out for two days. Jeb, on the other hand, was in the clear, but we did not know how long he would stay unconscious or if he would slip into a coma," Phantom told her.

"Son, when did the Galactic Council have a Medical Space Station built?" Colonel Calamen asked.

"They didn't. By the way, Dad, the Alliance has a Medical Space Station. Surprise," Phantom said while smiling.

"Then that truly means Jeb is alive?" Flay asked while looking confused. Suddenly, Phantom, Colonel Calamen, and the lieutenant heard from Flay with wide eyes, "'Dad,' 'son,' . . . you mean he is you father, Phantom?"

Before anyone could say anything, they all noticed a loud sound moving toward them at a high rate of speed. "Well, I guess it's time to show why I'm called 'the ghost of the Alliance,'" Phantom said just as his body started to glow.

"Allan, my son, just be careful, please. Your mother would not forgive me if anything should ever happen to you," the colonel said.

"There you go again. Why is it that you keep calling him 'Allan'?" Flay asked.

"I already told you. Now, go do what you have to do. Just keep in mind how much your mother, little sister, your Aunt, you Uncle, your cousins, and I will miss you," the colonel said as he placed a hand on Phantom's shoulder.

"Sure, Dad," Allan replied just as another Phantom split from the first. "Are you ready to find out how many we are dealing with?" Allan said to the look-alike.

"Let's just get these over with," the second Phantom responded just before walking out into the hall way.

A few moments later . . .

"Hey, Colonel, I don't know how to tell you this, but you junior officer and his guy are dead," the second Phantom yelled over his shoulder just as a laser flew through his body.

"How many Pirates are we facing?" Allan yelled back at the look-alike.

"Eight Pirates, and each one is holding an OCDU along with a blaster. So what do you want to do now?" the second Phantom asked.

Suddenly, everyone noticed Allan walking out in front of the Pirates, just as the sound of someone running was becoming closer. Before anyone could ask what Allan had in mind, he dropped six knives out from his shirt sleeves. "I'm only going to ask you this once. Are you going to stand down and allow us to pass, or are we going to have to kill you?" Allan asked just as he drew back into a throwing stance.

Then, the Pirate's opened fire on the two. After a few minutes, every shot they sent at both Phantoms just went through his bodies. "What are we to do now?" a Pirate asked another.

"We will stand our ground until Daggen can get here with our reinforcements," the second Pirate replied.

"Assassin, my friend—enjoy!" Allan yelled just as he threw the knives toward the Pirates.

"What? Really? I can kill them? You're not trying to pull a fast one on me, are you?" the Assassin asked.

"Now, why would I do that?" Allan asked just as six lifeless bodies fell to the floor.

"All right, just don't hold this against me," the Assassin replied just as he started to charge toward the remaining two.

Before he knew what had happened, seven more Pirates appeared from around the corner. *All right. More toys to play with,* the Assassin thought, just as he started to carve into the first two Pirates.

"Tearan, get you people ready. I am taking three platoons to help out with our forces that are engaging the Alliance. I need you, and your group will need to find away to shut off this blasted noise. Send Trisha and a group out to stop any other groups that maybe advancing on the SEL 13," Daggen said over a personal communication device.

"Fine, whatever you want! Oh, Daggen, if anything happens to my sister, I will kill you myself!" Tearan replied just before disconnecting from the conversation.

"Brother, what is going on?" Trisha asked while walking up behind her older brother.

"Daggen has ordered you and a few of our guild members to secure the hallway between SEL 12 and SEL 13. Trisha, be careful, the Galaxy Alliance is showing a stronger force of resistance then Trayon had thought," Tearan said in a calm loving voice.

"All right, I will take twelve guild members only," she replied.

"Princess, please allow me to accompany you," a guild member said while walking up.

"No, Danny, you need to stay with Tearan. If the Alliance makes it passed us, then it is up to you to make sure the future king is safe," she replied while walking toward the door.

"Danny, I want you to take three groups of our best and cover my sister in case the Alliance does show up," Tearan said just as he turned to a command computer and pressed a button.

"The noise . . . it stopped. What did you do, sir?" Danny asked with a hint of surprise.

"I didn't do anything. There is only one reason for the noise turning on and then off. He is on the station, and he is leading the Alliance troops to this location," Tearan said with a hint of being worried.

"Allan, now what are we to do? All nine Pirates are dead, and now I'm bored," the Assassin said while turning to look at Allan.

"Nothing right now. Colonel, you can advance at any time," Allan replied while walking back around the corner.

Suddenly, the person they had been hearing just turned the corner when another soldier stood up and help his palm out. When the person ran into his hand, the person fell to the floor. "Who do you think you are? Do you have any idea who I am?" the person asked while looking up at the soldier.

"You are a bio-replica, and can you explain to me how you were able to activate yourself," the soldier replied while everyone stared at him.

"What is going on down here?" the lieutenant asked as he approached the soldier and the bio-replica.

"Nothing is going on that should concern you, sir," the soldier replied just as the bio-replica climbed to his feet.

"Will you both behave yourself?" Allan asked while walking up to the lieutenant.

"Soldier, identify yourself!" the lieutenant demanded.

"Now, is that any way to talk to me, Lieutenant?" the soldier asked just as he ripped the uniform away from his body.

"Phantom? Phantom, how can this be? We just watched you split into two individuals and walk out into the hallway just as the Pirate's shots went through you and hit the wall," the lieutenant said just as the one they called Allan and the Assassin disappeared in front of them.

"Let me do my job. I was programmed with your brain wave patterns, which means when you received the stand-by, my systems told me to activate and go to this location," Bio-replica said just as he started to walk passed Phantom.

"Not so fast, soldier boy. Can you tell me why you decided not to wait until you were at one hundred percent completion?" Phantom asked just as he noticed a clump of synthetic skin fell from the bio-replica's metallic left arm.

"Because of Mother. You know as well as I . . . our mother just happened to be in danger!" the bio-replica commanded as he pushed his was passed Phantom.

"I will make this clear. Jacquelyn is Shamarra's and my mother—not yours. You were an experiment that I decided to participate in. You were designed to cover my place in the Alliance until I recovered from the injures I had sustained. You, just like bio-replica Jeb, were designed to help the Alliance. He fulfilled his duties, now why can't you," Phantom said while turning to face the bio-replica.

"I am trying to fulfill my duties. Now, allow me to handle those Pirates so you can stop Trayon," the bio-replica replied while starting to walk toward the hallway.

After regaining his thoughts, "Phantom, when was it you learned that technique, and what is it called?" his father asked.

"Shamarra calls it 'The Ghost of the Alliance.' She claims it is her favorite technique to watch me use during practice," Phantom replied while watching the bio-replica disappear down the hallway.

Shortly after Phantom and everyone started to hear, from the hallway, screams of pain, the lieutenant asked, "Do you think that bio-replica . . . do you think he will be able to handle whatever it is that the Pirate's throw at him?"

"He should. After all, he is me to a point," Phantom replied while grinning.

Before Colonel Calamen could say anything, he heard, "That is impossible. There is no way that Altherian is capable of being that strong. The hire-ups are trying to scare everyone. The other two had to be a halo-projection," a soldier said to another soldier.

Suddenly, to Colonel Calamen's surprise, "Do you really think that I am a halo-projection?" Allan's voice said just before throwing the soldier to the floor.

"Allan, Phantom, that is enough! Stop playing around and get ready. Your bio-replica is on his way back," Colonel Calamen said as he heard a set of footsteps making their way back up the hallway.

As the soldier climbed to his feet, everyone heard, "The way is now . . ." Before the bio-replica could finish his sentence, a high-powered laser blast tore through his left side.

"Are you all right?" the lieutenant asked while noticing the bio-replica was now missing his left shoulder, left side breast plate, ribs, and hip.

"I'm sorry. My systems are starting to shut down. I wish I could have done . . ." Before the replica could finish, everyone noticed his systems had finally shut down, followed by a loud crashing sound as the replica hit the floor.

"What's the matter? Did we destroy your fancy, new toy? Phantom Breaker, I know you are listening. Why don't you come out, and we'll talk about this misunderstanding," Daggen's voice called from down the hall.

"Let me think about it. I have your answer right here!" Phantom called back just as he sent a shot from his blaster down the hallway. "Over my dead body!" Phantom just suddenly blurted out with anger.

"That was the whole idea. How about allowing us to leave with all the spoils, and we will allow the Galaxy Alliance to keep the station?" Daggen called back just before laughing.

"How about surrendering, and I might just allow you to live," Phantom replied just as two shots zipped past his head. *Now, that was close. Thank god,* Phantom thought just as the blast singed the corner just before slamming into the wall.

"Help us someone, please! I don't want to become a slave!" Phantom suddenly heard a female voice scream out.

"What are you doing with those children, Daggen?" Phantom asked just as Colonel Calamen noticed Phantom's eyes starting to flash from hazel to red.

"That is not for you to worry about. These nine children now belong to us. You know spoils of war," Daggen said with a snarl.

"Daggen, you will let them go, and I mean now!" Phantom demanded.

"Over my dead body!" Daggen yelled.

"Thank you!" Phantom answered while smiling.

"What are you going to do? We cannot move from this location, or we will end up like that," the colonel asked while pointing over at both of the bio-replicas.

CHAPTER 13

"COMMANDER RANDALL, THE Pirates are starting their attack!" the tactical officer yelled.

"All fighters, prepare to engage. B.R.A.T.T., have you been able establish a connection with the computer on that TRI Guild's flag ship?" the commander asked.

"I'm sorry, sir, they have all external frequencies disabled. We cannot send any signals in, nor can they send any signals out," the AI replied.

"Then, someone tell me, why did they decide to stop their advancement?" the commander demanded to know while thinking, *All right, Pirate scum, what are you trying to pull this time?*

Suddenly, his attention was brought back to the fight when his ship shook from a direct hit. "Sir, I think they are playing with us," the communications officer blurted out just as she placed a now active conversation between the TRI Guild's flag ship and the fighters on the external speakers for them to hear.

"This is it. Activate an external channel," a strange male's voice said while Commander Randall and his bridge crew looked at each other with confusion on their faces.

"Sir, the communications are on as you speak," a female voice replied.

After clearing his throat, the male's voice said, "Attention, Galaxy Alliance, we, the members of the TRI Guild under the leadership of Trayon, have decided to let you live. The conditions are as followed: first, you must leave and not return for four standard days, second, everything on this station now belongs to us. We'll just let you keep the station itself. Third, everyone on the station right now will be our guests and not prisoners. If you do not agree to our terms, then we will have no other choice but to kill you. We have allowed your fleet to live for twelve hours because we were being nice."

Phantom's voice said, "The only reason you allow such a gracious action is because you are waiting for reinforcements. Commander Randall watch, out for possible inbound. All fighter commanders, prepare to engage the Pirates."

"Sir, we have a spacial rift appearing at the back of those Pirate's ships," the tactical officer replied.

"What in the Alliance's name is that?" the commander asked just as a giant ship appeared from the spacial rift.

"You're probably asking yourselves what that thing is. Let me introduce you to Hades, the largest assault and transport shuttle that the TRI Guild had built," the strange commander said just before laughter exploded from the speakers.

"Shut that off!" Commander Randall said just before the bridge fell silent. "Now, I want as much information as anyone can give me. I need to know what that thing uses for a power source, where it is located, how many ships that thing might be carrying, what kind of weapons that thing has, and who is in command of it!" Commander Randall demanded to know just as he noticed a small object flying from beneath the ship.

Before anything else was said, Commander Randall and his bridge crew noticed a large, glowing light emanating from Hades. "All ships, watch out for an all-out strike. We do not know what that thing is capable of," Commander Randall said just as they noticed a large beam shredded through a cruiser on their starboard side.

"Sir, we just lost the indicator for the Poseidon. If only a single blast from that thing can completely destroy the Poseidon, than, sir, we are out matched and out classed," the female tactical officer replied.

"All fighters, try to take that giant behemoth down at any cost. B.R.A.T.T., I want you to try and gain access to their computers. Try to find anything useful that we may be able to use against that thing," Commander Randall said just as he turned to his tactical officer. "Marryann, I want you to get into one of the escape shuttles. I could not look at your mother if anything should ever happen to you," the commander said while looking at the young woman with red hair.

"Father, I am not leaving my station. I am a Galaxy Alliance member, just like everyone else here. Sir, I would appreciate it more if you stop treating me like a child and remember that I am a member of this crew while on duty. You need to keep your personal affairs to yourself while on duty, sir. If you do not, I will have to relieve you from command," Marryann said while looking away from him in disgust.

"You're right. I'm sorry," the commander said while turning away from the young woman while thinking it was only yesterday he had picked her up from her first day of school.

"Do you think you were a little too hard on him? After all, he is your father. It is his way of telling you how much he cares. I just wished my father had shown me how much he cared before he died," the second tactical officer whispered to Marryann.

"No, I do not. I am not his little girl, anymore. In fact, I am supposed to be getting married next month. The only problem I have is how do I go about telling him about the wedding? He still thinks of me as the little seven-year-old who was afraid of the dark and after having a bad dream she would crawl into her parent's bed just to feel safe," Marryann whispered back.

"Do not worry. I promise that I will make sure that you will see your fiancé again," Commander Randall said just as the bridge crew noticed Marryann jumping from being startled.

"How did you know about that?" she asked him with a confused look on her face.

"I know I wasn't there for you that much, and I know that you despise me for that. I realized when your mother told me about the wedding that I allowed my duties as a Galaxy Alliance soldier to interfere with our relationship as father and daughter. I think that you would like to know, once we are back at the station, my resignation will be finalized by the High Grand Admiral. Major, you have command of the Cerberus. I am releaving myself of command," Commander Randall said just as he walked over to the bridge's elevator.

"I'm sorry, sir, you are still the commander of this ship," the Major replied.

Before he could say anything else, he started to hear, "Three cheers for one of the best commander's we have had the pleasure of knowing! Commander Randall!" when, suddenly, he heard everyone's cheering starting to get louder.

"You see, sir, even if I *did* want to take command from you, they would not allow me to," the major said while shifting her hand around the room.

"Commander Randall, your crew is awaiting your orders, sir. I'm awaiting your orders, father," Marryann said while standing up and saluting him.

"I thought . . . I thought this is what everyone of you had wanted. I overheard you in the mess hall, and then my own daughter here lately has been defiant toward my command," he said.

"No, father, you only heard half the conversation. We were talking about Colonel Calamen and his platoons. They seem to receive more off time than we do, and then there is the Altherian who calls himself 'Phantom, The ghost of the Alliance.' What makes him think he is the best out of our ranks?" Marryann said with anger in her voice.

"I don't think you all actually mean what you had just said, do you?" Commander Randall asked while looking around the bridge.

"Let me tell you something, Lieutenant, most of my own fighter Squadron owes that young man their lives. If it had not been for him and that he was just a few systems over, I would not still be here, and neither would you, father. There have been several times that boy has pulled us out of very tight situations, and there is one mission that I am truly glad that he was on our side for. Just for the record, on that particular mission, he was still a recruit," a male's voice said with disgust in his tone.

Before the male's voice could say anything else, "The same goes for my Squadron!" a female's voice said while breaking the conversation.

"Commander Luna and Commander Gale, I appreciate your words. The truth is, my entire command on this Verantix Style Flag ship owes the young man their lives. If he had not appeared with the funds to build this new flag ship, we would have been finished several times over. Before thinking or saying anything bad about that young man or his sister, you might want to think of what he has done for the Alliance. None of you may know this, but before he showed up, the Alliance was on the verge of losing this war," Commander Randall said just as a warning alarm sounded.

"Sir, we are being targeted by the new Pirate's vessel. What are your orders, sir?" Marryann cried out from the tactical station.

"Turn hard starboard. We need to try to get out of the line of fire!" Commander Randall ordered.

"Sir, someone has hacked into the computer's command codes. Some of the codes are being changed. We are currently tracking the uplink to an outside source," Marryann said while her fingers danced across the computer.

"B.R.A.T.T., try to locate the signal to that uplink. I want to know who it is that is trying to hack the system!" Commander Randall demanded of the AI.

"Sir, I do not need to. I am seeing a command code change to the systems due to an internal program that was hidden," the AI replied.

Suddenly, to Commander Gale and Commander Luna, the Cerberus started to shift from gray to black with a blue glow. "Admiral Randall, what is going on? What did you do to the Cerberus?" Luna asked over an open communication channel.

"What is going on? The Cerberus is changing as if she had different specifications to her design. It appears that she has several new cannons to her then she did before," Gale said following Luna's lead.

Inside on the bridge . . .

"What is going on, father? My station just disappeared into the wall!" Marryann cried as she heard several voices confirming the same thing with their stations.

"I do not know," Commander Randall said when suddenly everyone heard "What the . . ." just as Randall fell into his command chair.

After looking puzzled, everyone on the bridge noticed that the command chair was being raised just as they felt the floor beneath them start to lower. "B.R.A.T.T., what is happening to the bridge?" Randall asked.

"I'm sorry about the secrecy, old friend. I had placed an emergency transfer command into the system right after I found out about the new TRI Guild's new assault shuttle. The Guild named their assault ship after a planet in the Contribylus Nebula that is so unbearable because of the heat and the destruction of its primitive species. I had this new flag ship built in a factory that I could trust for its creation. This ship was created by starting with the atoms. This is not an ordinary flag ship. This was called the Cerberus for one reason and one reason alone. In a myth that I found on Planet Earth, there was a three-headed dog that guarded the gates of the underworld ruled by the one called Hades. Cerberus was named after that dog. Now, show those Pirates how hard this dog can bite. Oh, one last little detail. Don't get yourselves killed," Phantom's voice said over the speakers just as they heard B.R.A.T.T. say, "Sir, that was a prerecorded message Phantom had preprogrammed."

"Even now, you have our best interests and safety in mind. Now return to your stations," Randall said while looking at his crew and the new bridge of the Cerberus.

"Sir, I have never seen this kind of weaponry, shielding, or engine specification on any Alliance ship. How many of these flag ships do we have?" the major said after looking at the specification display.

"That does not matter. Brace yourselves. Hades is firing their main weapon!" Marryann yelled.

"What is their target? Who are they targeting?" Randall asked with a worried look.

"We are, father. We are," she replied while trying to choke the words out.

"Brace yourselves for impact," Randall said while grabbing onto the arms of his command chair.

Suddenly, Commander Luna saw the blast from Hades connecting with the new Galaxy Alliance flag ship. "All fighter Squadrons and commanders, the Cerberus has just been hit by that thing. We need to stop that thing, even if it costs us our very lives," she called over the tactical frequency.

"Don't worry about us. I'm not sure how, but it seems that everyone here is fine," Commander Randall's voice suddenly said over the tactical frequency.

"All fighter commanders in the Torus Class Fighters, right now, the Cerberus is downloading a program to your fighters. The program was designed in case anything should go wrong, and the program would automatically be sent to your Operation Systems. Unlike the Cerberus, I did not have time to build these new fighters by scratch. As of this moment, your fighters will be marked as a mercenary fighter Squadron lead by Commander Luna and Commander Gale," Phantom's voice said over a secret communications channel.

"What is going on? Commander Randall, do you know anything about this?" Commander Gale asked with a confused voice.

"Negative, we just received the prerecorded message ourselves. B.R.A.T.T., what does he mean by marked as a mercenary fighter Squadron?" Commander Randall asked with the same confused voice as Commander Gale.

"Dad! What is this? We have new fighter specifications, and it claims all the Alliance has in their control are one hundred of these so-called 'Torus Class Fighters,'" Marryann said while sitting on the floor.

"Honey, are you all right? In fact, is everyone all right? B.R.A.T.T., you have not answered my question, yet. What is going on? Why are we still here after receiving a direct hit from their main weapon, and what are the Torus Class Fighters? What is this program Phantom was just talking about?" Commander Randall asked while noticing half of his bridge crew had been thrown from their seats.

"I will explain. The program Phantom was talking about is a program to release a hidden program that was already built into the Torus Class Fighter Operation Systems. The program is an interactive Artificial Intelligence that Mom had a hand in creating. The Torus Class Fighters were designed by two of the best inventors the Alliance has ever known. Those fighters were designed for high-risk missions where the probability of anyone returning alive was extremely low or almost non-existent. The only reason that the Cerberus is still alive is because while the flag ship was being built all the way at its atomic state, all the normal flaws that you would find in a ship this size were fixed on the spot. Phantom made sure, because of the Hades, that the Alliance had a flag ship that could counter whatever that ship had to offer," B.R.A.T.T. said.

"Mercy Unit Online," a strange voice said over the tactical channel.

"Commander Randall, can you explain to us why should I be the overall commander? Isn't there anyone better qualified for this then I am?" Luna asked.

"The same goes for me. I did not volunteer for that position," Gale said just as both of the ships started to fade out of sight.

"Commander Randall! The Cerberus and the command fighters suddenly just disappeared off of our sensors. We are still able to see the Cerberus because of the glow, and that is it!" a female voice said over the tactical system.

"Marry, I want the Athena and the rest of our cruisers to open fire on that new monstrosity of theirs. All fighters, return to your transports and wait for further instructions. Commanders Luna and Gale, Phantom gave you and forty-eight other commanders those new fighters. I want you to hit anything and everything that is marked as a Pirate. The Cerberus will help to take out their new weapon. Good luck and great hunting," Commander Randall said as he turned to his weapons station. "Fire! I want that thing out of my sight now!" Randall ordered just as the Cerberus suddenly vibrated.

"But, sir, won't we hit our own fighters?" one of the gunners asked.

"You don't have to worry about that. Fire! Unleash everything we have," Commander Randall said in a cold, hard voice as he turned to the tactical station.

"Sir, our shields just took three direct hits. Dad, our shield only dropped to ninety percent. What? Our shields are starting to repair themselves," Marryann said with a hint of being surprised.

"Of course, did you truly think Phantom had not thought of an extreme all-out head-to-head battle and place it into the equation? He *did* get his training in the art of strategy from High Grand Admiral Calamen. His weapon abilities happen to come from Grand Admiral Blake, and his leadership skills came from his father Colonel Calamen. He learned how to fly from Lieutenant Colonel Melody. His science abilities, as in Genetic engineering and DNA Genetics, came from the top civilian scientist the Alliance knows. His family is the one that has taught him everything that he knows. Ever since then, he developed those abilities far better than we have seen," Commander Randall said just as Marryann looked at him with surprise.

"Dad, we just lost the identification beacons of the fighter Squadron commanders," Marryann said just as she noticed a Pirate cruiser being destroyed.

"Commander Luna, can you confirm that a Pirate cruiser was just destroyed?" Commander Randall asked over the tactical channel.

"Sorry, commander, my Squadron is making a run on that new assault vessel of theirs. Commander Gale, can you confirm the destruction of that cruiser?" she asked just the sounds of cannon blasts flew past her canopy.

"That is an affirmative. My Squadron has taken out one of the cruisers and is making a run for a second," Commander Gale said.

"Sir, I think all the Torus class fighters should make a single run on the TRI Guild's new assault ship. Then, when the shields are down or even low, we will make a second attack with every weapon the fleet has," B.R.A.T.T. said with a hint of smugness in his voice.

"Since when did you get an upgrade with emotions?" Marryann asked with a hint of confusion in her voice.

"If Mom can show emotions, then why can't her children? Open the tactical channel to the other commanders," Randall said will trying not to laugh.

"Sir, the channel is open," his daughter replied to the order.

"This is Admiral Randall. All ships are to lock onto that new assault ship with everything they have. Commanders Luna and Gale, I want your squadrons to make the first run on that ship. The rest of the fleet, as soon as I tell you that they are clear from the blasting zone, you will open fire," he said with a hint of eagerness in his voice.

Meanwhile on the Hades . . .

"Travone, the Alliance fighters have disappeared from our sensors. We also just lost one of our cruisers," a female said while looking at the tactical screen.

"Those Alliance members are nothing more than fools. Tell me, who are the pilots in those Pirate mercenary fighters, and when did they show up?" a blond-haired man said while looking into the fiery, red eyes of the female at the tactical station.

"Well, honey, what do you want us to do?" she asked him without turning her gaze from his.

"Um, sir, not to interrupt, but the last several attacks that we had done to that new Alliance flag ship didn't phase their shields. I don't see how we will be able to take them, let alone take this system," the male at the sensors station snarled.

"Well, it looks as if the Alliance is trying to push through our defenses," Travone said to the members on his bridge just as he opened a channel to his entire Pirate fleet. "All Pirate cruisers and fighters, block the Alliance from getting any closer to the station."

"Sir, it looks like they are going to ram you!" a fighter commander yelled just before the channel fell silent.

What game are you trying to play? Travone thought as he watched another one of his cruisers fall prey to the Alliance fleet. *What is it? I have to be over looking something, but what is it?* Travone continued to think when his attention was snapped back to reality from a male's voice.

"Sir, those are the Alliance fighters. If we change our friend or foe identifiers, then we would be hitting our own fighters, as well!" the man at the sensors yelled just as the Hades shook from a direct hit. "Sir, our shields are holding at ninety percent. Sir, the fighters are making another pass!" the man snarled even louder.

"One set of puny fighters can't harm the Hades!" Travone proclaimed as he heard the most horrifying news of the day.

"Sir, the second set of fighters has regrouped with the first, and the Alliance fleet is locking on to our position!" the man snarled with fear in his voice.

Suddenly, Travone felt vibrations under his feet. "Increase the dampening field to full! I do not want to feel any vibrations!" Travone demanded just as he heard a loud explosion from right outside the bridge's hall.

"Sir, I have some bad news for you," the tactical station reported.

"What is it? Can't you see that I'm busy?" Travone asked while turning to face the middle-aged man at the tactical station.

"Um, yes, sir. We just lost the transponder codes for three cruisers and fifty-nine fighters. I think that we are outnumbered," the man said.

"Fine then, target several of their cruisers and fighters. I want them dead. No, target every flag ship, cruiser, and fighter that they have and destroy them," Travone said with hatred in his voice.

"Yes, sir. This is the Hades, all ships target and destroy those Alliance ships," the tactical station relayed.

"Sir, we have received a report of a second fighter Squadron starting to engage one of our cruisers. What are your orders?" a female asked while sitting at the communications station.

"What else? Destroy them. Destroy them! Every last one of them! I don't want to see any of them left breathing," Travone said just as he heard as shriek of terror.

"Sir, our shields . . . we just lost our shields!" a female said while leaning over and looking at the tactical readout.

"All Pirate ships, withdraw now! Pick up as many fighters as you can and leave this system!" Travone said just as a smile crept across his face.

"Sir, I am picking up several anomalies right in front of us," Marryann said with a look of being surprise.

"What is it? Can you get a readout on what is causing the anomaly?" Commander Randall asked.

"It's the Pirate ships, father, their retreating," she replied while looking at him with a confused look on her face.

"All Mercenary fighters withdraw. I want you to resupply on the Cerberus," Randall ordered just as he sat back in his chair while thinking, *Phantom, I know. Make that, we owe you our very lives this day.*

"Father, Callionasus is requesting for his Squadron to be able to launch and convey a survey of the area. He thinks that there might be other Pirates in the vicinity," Marryann said while walking up to her father.

"He is just like Phantom. He doesn't know when or how to relax. The Pirates have just left the system with their tails tucked," he replied to his daughter.

"Yes, I agree, but what if he is right? Don't you think it would be wise to find out by allowing them to check the perimeter?" she replied with an inquisitive voice.

"You both may be right. All right, allow his Squadron to launch with Challious and Denieus squadrons backing him up," Commander Randall said just as he started to stand.

A few minutes after the squadrons left their ships, Admiral Randall sat back in his seat thinking. *Why did they just leave the fight? What is it that they are trying to hide?*

He heard a young female's voice approaching. "Admiral, sir, I believe there is something wrong with the system map. It is showing—" Before the voice could finish speaking, the Admiral jumped to his feet with a realization look in his eyes.

He then turned to face the female that started to report what she thought was a malfunction on the mapping system. "Tactical and sensors, I want you both to double check this system for anything that is out of the ordinary," he said while starting to feel something turning in his stomach.

"Commander, are you all right? You are looking a little nervous," the lieutenant asked while walking up to him.

"I am starting to feel that we may have landed in a trap. I think—" Before he could finish speaking, he heard his daughter's voice scream.

"Sir, we have unknown in bound. We cannot get a full reading on them. Dad, we will have contact in five, four, three, two . . ." Suddenly, her voice fell quiet just as they noticed a large flash of light erupting right in front of the station.

After several more flashes appeared and then disappeared, "Captain Callionasus, this is Commander Randall. What just happened?" Randall said just after activating the tactical channel.

"Space mines. Sir, somehow nine of my fighters hit space mines. Sir, the worst news is our sensors never picked them up," Callionasus said with disgust in his voice.

"Our sensors picked up an irregularity just before those fighters were destroyed. Be on the lookout for more enemy ships because this . . ." then, he heard Callionasus voice coming over the speaker saying ". . . could be a trap."

"Dad, Dad, Dad!" Marryann yelled after trying to get her father's attention.

"What!" Commander Randall yelled back.

"We have incoming irregularities to our portside," she said just before he noticed two of his cruisers disappear in a blinding flash.

"How are they doing this? B.R.A.T.T., I want you to recalibrate the sensors. I want to know what those Pirates are sending a few seconds before it appears out of those irregularities. I want to know before we are all killed," Commander Randall said just as he heard chatter from his communications officer and her two subordinates.

"Sir, the other commanders want to know what your orders are. They also want to know how they are to fight what they cannot see," his communications officer asked with a hint of confusion in her voice.

"Tell them to keep their staff at full red alert. We must be ready for anything," Commander Randall said just as he heard, "Sir," as her reply.

Trayone, what are you thinking in that maniacal head that you call a brain? both Commander Randall and his communications officer thought.

Meanwhile . . .

"Hey, Callionasus, we know there are Pirates inside the station. Here is the prize winning question, where are the Pirate ships that dropped them off?" a female asked.

As a face appeared on the communication screen, she saw a male in a blue uniform, and over his face was a dark-shielded helmet. "I'm not sure, Molly. We'll just have to keep a close watch out," he responded to a green-skinned, red-haired young woman while looking into her crystal blue eye.

"Sir, they're *ahhh!*" a male's voice cries out just before it faded out of existence.

"Brother! No!" Molly cried as she noticed an explosion about one hundred feet away from them.

"All fighters engage the enemy fighters. I'll try to contact Commander Randall!" Callionasus called out.

"Sir, we have movement!" she yelled with a hint of being surprised.

"Josy, where is the movement from?" Commander Randall asked while turning to look the woman in her red eyes.

"The asteroid belt, sir, it appears that the Pirates made their ships look just like the asteroids," Josy replied.

"Josyallyn, what are you telling my father? That our sensors are malfunctioning?" Marryann asked.

"Sir, we have an incoming communications. It's Callionasus," she said while ignoring Marryann's comment.

As he looked out across the battlefield, he noticed the Pirates leaving the asteroid belts to engage them. Their flag ships looked to be an asteroid itself. "Callionasus calling Commander Randall. Do you copy? Over," the male said with a hint of being surprised in his tone.

"This is Commander Randall. What is going on out there Lieutenant Callionasus?" the Commander asked.

"Sir, we just lost Lorrous, and I am afraid that his little sister is no longer able to fight. The Pirate attacked while we were conducting a sensor sweep of the asteroid belt," the lieutenant commander said.

"Tell Molly to get back to the Cerberus, and she will be relieved of duty until after we are able to give her brother a proper burial," Commander Randall said just as everyone else was surprised with his next words. "Turn around and face them. We have to try to use those mines against their own kind."

"Yes, sir, now what are we going to do about those Pirates?" Callionasus asked.

"B.R.A.T.T., why didn't you tell me about the ships in the asteroid belt?" Commander Randall asked as he turned and walked over to the tactical station.

"I'm sorry, sir, I forgot to add that possibility into my equation. I do, on the other hand, have a plan to defeat them," B.R.A.T.T. replied just as three more cruisers erupted right in front of the Cerberus.

"Fine, let's hear it!" Commander Randall said just as he heard, "Sir, I am unable to shake them!" a male's voice said just as an Alliance fighter and three enemy fighters flew past the view port of the Cerberus.

"Gunner, I want those fighters destroyed without harming that Alliance fighter!" Commander Randall ordered.

"Well, sir, I have been checking the operations system, and I have found a way to rewrite a portion of the program. This plan will have three parts to it—"

Suddenly, everyone heard Commander Randall's voice. "Stop with the babbling and just spit it out. We do not have time for just talking—we are losing our forces. What is the plan?"

"Well, sir, the plan is as follows. First, allow the Pirate's to attack our computer systems, and I will send a virus that will leave them dead where the stand. Second, I have added a tracking system on the mines to track the target. Third, we will need Callionasus to lead the mines over to the Pirate's vessels and then jump into hyperspace just for a spit second," B.R.A.T.T. said just as Commander Randall's voice interrupted him saying, "Removes him as the target and allowing the mines to target the Pirates because they will be the closes thing to attack. Commander Callionasus will never actual leave the system. Nice idea, except, how do you plan on allowing them to attack our computer systems?" the commander asked.

"That's easy. Like this," B.R.A.T.T. said just as Commander Randall and the entire crew on the Cerberus suddenly felt a serge run through the ship.

"Sir, the Pirates are trying to gain access to our computers. What would you like me to do?" Marryann said with a horrified tone in her voice.

"Nothing. B.R.A.T.T., you allowed the Pirates to think that we over-exerted our true capability and allowing them to walk straight into our trap," Commander Randall said just as a smile appeared on his face.

"Your right, and the virus has been successfully uploaded to two thirds of their fleet. In a short time, we will be able to defeat them without even using a single blast," B.R.A.T.T. said with a smug, artificial voice.

"Great, just what we need—an Artificial Intelligence with an ego. Open the communications to all channels. This is the Cerberus to the Pirate fleet. Your ships are now useless. Surrender now or be destroyed," Randall said just as he heard, "What was that comment about?" B.R.A.T.T. asked.

"What have you done to our ships?" a harsh male's voice asked.

"I didn't do anything. If I had to guess, when you tried to gain access to our computers, you might have accidently triggered a trap that was preinstalled by the company that donated this flag ship to us," Randall replied in a calm and soothing voice.

"How dare you lie to us! For that, all ships fire upon that new flag ship!" the harsh man's voice said over the audio communications.

"You do not have the ability to use your weapons, and for what I can tell, our computer is starting to show all your systems are beginning to shut down. Now, surrender now or be destroyed," Commander Randall said while smiling a devilish smile.

They're in for it. I remember how much trouble I was in when you looked at me like that, Marryann thought when she suddenly heard, "Why is he smiling like that?" a male's voice asked.

"Jassonic, when he smiles like that, you do not want to be anywhere near my father. If you are, he will release his entire wrath on you," Marryann said just as a small chuckle escaped her.

"Sir, I am starting the run. Wish me luck," Callionasus said just as his fighter started to show movement on the Cerberus's sensors.

"Commander Callionasus has just came into the mine's targeting sensors. He has just been targeted, and the mines are moving in for the kill," Marryann told her father with a worried look.

"Keep me informed of his situation as they appear, my dear. Now, Callionasus, if for any reason something goes wrong, I want you to abort with no question or hesitation," Commander Randall said while pacing back and forth.

"You don't have to worry about him, father. He is a capable pilot after all," Marryann said while wiping away her worried look as she turned to face her father.

"I know that, but what makes me worried is not the pilot of the fighter. I'm worried about those mines and if they can follow him into hyperspace," Randall said while placing a hand on his daughter's shoulders.

"Sir, Lieutenant Commander Callionasus is approaching the Pirate fleet. What are your orders, sir?" a male's voice said from the seat next to Marryann.

"He already knows what he needs to do. All members of the Alliance Fleet, stand by to back up our comrades on the Drandon Station," Randall said while thinking, *Callionasus, my boy, you best be careful, or your wife will hang me for this.*

Suddenly, Randall heard, "What are you trying to do? You just said for us to either surrender or we will be destroyed. I have not given you my decision, yet," the harsh male's voice said over the communications.

After looking around at his bridge crew, Commander Randall walked over and sat down in his seat. "True, but you never denied an all out assault. I mean, if you actually could," Randall said just as he started to hear the systems from all around him coming to life.

"Dad!" When Marryann thought that she had her father's attention focused souly on her, she spoke. "Commander Callionasus had just passed the last of our vessels. The mines are closing in on his fighter. At this rate, the mines will have his fighter in less than thirty seconds."

"My sweet but naive little girl, that fighter was given to the Alliance by a soul person that Phantom truly trusts. Do you actually think that Callionasus's fight will just fall that easily?" Commander Randall said while activating a tactical halo display in front of his seat.

"I guess if you trust that Corporal, then so should I," Marryan replied just as she noticed Commander Callionasus's fighter was now approaching the Pirate's fleet. But to their surprise, Commander Callionasus's fighter just disappeared from the sensors. "The mines have stopped. Now we will find out if our little assault works," Commander Randall said just as everyone noticed the apprehension in his voice.

"The targeting sensors are recalibrating for a new target. There. They have locked on to the Pirate's fleet, and the mines are making their move against the fleet," B.R.A.T.T. said with a hint of excitement in his artificial voice.

"Sir, one of the Pirate's flag ships was just destroyed. It also looks like the rest of their fleet is taking a major pounding," the second tactical officer replied.

As Commander Randall watched the Pirate's fleet disappear from their sensors, he could hear the confusion over the open channel. "Sir, I was wondering how soon those Pirates will realize that they have left their communication channel open?" Marryann asked her father.

"I'm not sure, nor do I care. Just make sure our communications are silent so they cannot hear us," Commander Randall said over the loud commotion from the Pirates.

"Sir, those Alliance dogs can hear us!" an older male's voice said with a surprised tone.

"You will pay for this. So help me, I will make sure of that even if I have to haunt you for the rest of your days," the harsh male's voice said.

A moment later, the channel fell silent as the members of the Alliance fleet watched the rest of the Pirate's fleet disappear in a shinning, white flash of light. "Sir, how could that have happened? There is no gravity or oxygen in the vacuum of space," a young female's voice said with a hint of confusion.

"The Pirate fleet was so close together that between all of them they had created a small gravity field. With the escaping air from the small ruptures in their hall, one little spark ignited the oxygen and created a giant explosion," Commander Randall replied while sitting back in his chair and thinking, *I am getting to old for this.*

"Sir, Commander Callionasus has informed me that his fighter has taken minor damage. He can no longer jump into hyperspace," Marryann said over the cheering of the bridge crew.

"What happened? Why can he no longer jump into hyperspace? Will everyone just be quiet so I can think?" Commander Randall said while looking around the bridge.

"Apparently, his fighter somehow scraped one of the Pirate's vessels just as he jumped into hyperspace and damaged his fighter's hyper drives," Marryann said as cheering continued.

While looking around at his bridge crew, he noticed a few crew members had stopped cheering. "Contact the Mardain. Tell her to go and pick the lieutenant commander up," Randall replied after everyone quieted down.

"Sir! Pirate vessels are inbound. What are your orders, sir?" a young male's voice blurted out.

"We are receiving a communication from—"

A middle-aged male's voice interrupted him just as a large fleet appeared behind the station saying, "We are members of the Korra Guild Fleet. Galactic Alliance, stand down. I want to make a deal."

"Dad, it appears that they have the upper hand," Marryann said while looking at the tactical screen.

"How many are there?" Commander Randall asked while trying not to show his crew how surprised he actually was.

"They have us out numbered thirty-two to one sir," Marryann said with a hint of being scared.

"This is the Cerberus, and I am Commander Randall to the Pirate Commander. Tell me what kind of a deal do you want?" he suddenly said over an open communication channel.

Suddenly, Commander Randall heard, "Sir, there is a second fleet entering the system right behind us! Dad, what are we going to do?" Marryann cried out.

"Just come down. Try to get a fix on Commander Callionasus. We cannot allow them to capture him," Randall said while walking over to his daughter.

"My name is Crolinnic. I am the commander on the Swiftloc. Alliance Commander Randall, do you hear me?" the middle-aged male's voice said over the audio communications only.

"Yes, I can hear you. What is it that I can help you with?" Randall asked.

"We will give you this station back and all of her stolen equipment that the TRI Guild, along with the other guilds, has taken. All I want is to be able to remove any members of the Korra Guild from the station. You may even take the surviving members from the other guilds as your prisoners," Crolinnic said kind, gentle voice.

"Let me think about it and I will—" Before he could finish his sentence, he suddenly heard a different langue familiar voice.

"Commander Crolinnic, we accept your generous offer. I warn you that if you try anything under-handed, I will personally kill you," the voice said over the open channel.

"Who is this and how is it that you know our guild's langue? By the way, I have a gift for you. It seems that the fighter was damaged, so we gave the pilot a lift back to the Alliance Fleet," Crolinnic said in a surprised voice.

"Admiral Randall, is there anything wrong with any of the fighters?" Phantom's voice suddenly said in normal langue.

"Well, yes, sir, Commander Callionasus's fighter just happened to have been damaged after he moved the mines in range of the other Pirate's Fleet. It appears that the Pirates have transported his fighter back, and it also appears that he is fine," Commander Randall said as he noticed Callionasus maneuvering his fighter back to the Cerberus.

"All right. Alliance ships, stand down. I want to allow them to pick up the surviving members of their guild as long as they do not show hostility," Phantom said just before the communications channel exploded with static.

"All ships, you have been given your orders. Stand down until further notice!" Commander Randall said while thinking, *Phantom, what are you planning?*

CHAPTER 14

"SHAMARRA, ARE YOU awake yet? Shoanna is here, and she says that you have a test to take this morning. Come on, Shamarra, don't tell me you're still in bed," Shamarra heard her mother's voice from the kitchen.

"Yes, Mom, I'm up. I was trying to find something to match the blue shirt brother had given me," Shamarra said just as she walked out of her bedroom.

"Well, good morning, sleepy head. Did you sleep well?" Jacquelyn asked her daughter.

"I slept somewhat decent. Mom, when is big brother going to be home?" she said just as she sat next to Shoanna.

"It only has been fifty-six hours since I have returned, and that means he still has fourteen more hours to go before he is late. Now, don't worry about your brother. He can take care of himself. Her you go. Now, eat up. I want to hear how you did on that test later," she replied while placing Shamarra's breakfast in front of her.

"All it will be over is Earth's ancient history. That will be a breeze," Shamarra replied with a mouth full of food.

"Shamarra, you know better than talk with your mouth full. Didn't your father and I teach you better manners then that?" Jacquelyn asked with a scorning looking on her face.

"Come on, kiddo, we better get you to that test. Thank you for breakfast, Mrs. Calamen," Shoanna said while starting to stand up.

"I know that you are a recruit and you are supposed to be formal with the officers and their families. My name is Jacquelyn—not Mrs. Colonel Jack Calamen, not Mrs. Jack Calamen—it is just plain, old Jacquelyn. Please call me Jacquelyn, all right?" Jacquelyn said as Shamarra stood up and while giggling.

After the two walked out of the apartment, Shamarra heard, "You mother is really nice. You are lucky to have a mother like her. My mother and father were mad with me the day I told them I was joining the Galaxy Alliance Military," Shoanna said.

"Why were they mad? They should have been happy for you, instead. What is it about the Galaxy Alliance that people hate?" Shamarra asked.

"They say that the Alliance Military is nothing more than a legalized group of Pirates. If you cannot pay the Alliance to render assistance, then you are on your own. Unlike everyone else, I've started to see a change in the Galaxy Alliance three years ago," Shoanna said while walking down the hall.

As the two walked, Shoanna started to notice that Shamarra and she were being stared at by other Alliance members as they walked passed. "Did you know my aunt, High Grand Admiral Kristy Calamen, became the leader of the Alliance under Mom three years ago? Not only that, did you know the Galactic Council has new member in charge of the Galactic Council? And that was three years ago. Besides, my brother joined the Alliance three years ago," Shamarra said with a grin on her face.

"I didn't know that. What I *do* know is that I had to make a deal with my parents so they would allow me to join the Alliance," Shoanna said as the two stepped onto the elevator.

"Oh, what kind of a deal was it?" Shamarra asked while looking up at Shoanna.

To her surprise, she noticed a sad look on the young woman's face when she suddenly heard, "I cannot believe they allowed someone like her in the Galaxy Alliance. Look at her. She doesn't even resemble our species. It sickens me that someone from our species was born with that color of hair. The Alliance must be hurting for recruits if they allowed a 'Muddy' in the Alliance," Shamarra heard two Shamoran's say.

"What's wrong with both of you? Just because she is different does not mean you have the right to treat her like an outcast. Yes, she has crystal blue eyes and blond hair. So what? Don't others have the same look among the Shamorans?" Shamarra asked with defiance in her voice.

"No, there is not. With her eye color and hair color, the only way it could have happened is if her DNA was altered. Yes, there are a few people among the Shamoran species who have blue eyes, and then there are others with brown eyes. There are no others other than her with crystal blue eyes unless they were altered. Most of our species will either have brownish-red or reddish-green hair, and not that blonde color. If her family has that kind of money, they would not be poor farmers, now would they, recruit?" the Shamoran with a lieutenant rank demanded.

"Come on, recruit, you have to answer a superior ranking officer. Now, answer my big brother," the second Shamoran said.

"You don't have to explain anything to them," Shamarra said in an angry voice.

"He is right. I must answer my superior officer, even if it is untrue," Shoanna said just as shamarra noticed Shoanna's eyes starting to tear up.

"No, you don't. I order you not to answer them," Shamarra said just as she noticed Shoanna's eye widen from being surprised.

"You little runt. Who do you think you are? You are a Drazarian, aren't you? Except, your hair color is redder then a normal Drazarian, and your eyes are a different color green than the other Drazarians," the second Shamoran asked.

"Do not call me my brother's nick name! My brother calls the color of my hair 'fire red' and my eyes 'emerald green,'" Shamarra demanded as she turned to face the two.

"Your brother! Ha! If your brother is anything like you are, he is nothing more than a good-for-nothing wannabe soldier that is only good for target practice. There is no way he could be anything less than bait to lure the Pirates into an Alliance trap. Why, looking at you both, your brother, you, and the Muddy next to you would be worth less than the paper his contract was written on!" the lieutenant said just as he started to laugh.

"How dare you talk about my big brother like that! For your information, he is not a Drazarian. If he was here right now listening to the way you just talked to me . . ." Before she could finish, she heard.

"What? If he was here right now, what would a loser like him be able to do to someone with the amount of advanced skills that I have?" the lieutenant asked.

"He would make you run home crying to your mother!" Shamarra said just as tears started to run down her face.

"How dare you talk to me like that! Recruit, what is your name?" the lieutenant asked just as the elevator stopped.

"Shoanna. Shoanna Malnerva. Why do you want to know?" she asked as tears ran down her face just as Shamarra hugged Shoanna.

"You see, little brother, she is the right person I was telling you about. I will make sure the time in the academy will be rough," the lieutenant said just as the doors opened.

As the door opened, Shamarra's eyes widened after hearing, "That mission was a little challenging. I just wished little brother had been there," a familiar voice said.

"Yeah, I know what you mean, except, he is off running an ambush simulation," a second familiar voice said just as she heard, "Oh, the elevator is finally here."

"You might not want to ride this one," the lieutenant said just as he stepped off.

"Yeah, the air in that elevator has a really nasty stench to it," the second Shamoran said as he stepped off right behind his brother.

"Oh, really? By the way, we haven't seen you on the station before. What are your names if you don't mind me asking?" a tall, reddish-skined man said.

"That is because we just arrived to the station four hours ago from the planetary academy. Why should we tell you what our names are?" the lieutenant replied.

"Does the planetary academy forget to train the recruits to salute an officer that out ranks you?" a tall, bluish-skined man asked.

As the two looked back, they both noticed the rank of Lieutenant Commander emblems on the men's shoulders that they had just passed. "Sorry, sir, we didn't realize . . . My name is Gronnica, and this is my little brother Cronnicer," the lieutenant said just as the two Shamoran saluted the superior officers.

"Hey, kiddo, what's the matter with you? Is everything all right?" the bluish-skinned man asked.

"Daniel, those two called Shoanna and I a 'muddy,'" Shamarra said just as she turned to face them.

Suddenly, the reddish-skinned man caught the elevator door just before it completely closed. "Hey, Lieutenant, the next time you make someone cry or feel bad, I would check the Alliance records and make sure her last name is not Breaker. I will only warn you once. The next time you make this child cry, you will be wishing my big brother and I are the ones punishing you. Instead, if you make either one cry again, I will personally take care of you. Do I make myself clear?" the reddish-skinned man said.

"Do as you wish. Just remember one thing. My uncle is a major, and he will bust you back to privet faster—" Before he could finish, he noticed the bluish-skinned man bend over and embrace the child. "What are you doing hugging a filthy muddy like that?" the lieutenant asked.

"She is of pure blood. I have seen her medical records myself. In fact, both of these women are. I was helping out in medical, and this recruit had her physical, and there were no signs of any kind that indicates her as having filthy DNA. By the way, you can tell the major that Lieutenant Commander Daniellericmoja is awaiting his visit. He can also find me in the office of the High Grand Admiral," Daniel said while Shamarra began to cry again.

"By the way, lieutenant, my name is Lieutenant Commander Ianistiolla. Tell your uncle to be in the High Grand Admiral's office in one hour," the reddish-skinned man said just before the elevator door closed.

"Brother, what are we going to do?" Cronnicer asked.

"Don't worry. They're bluffing us. We will tell the major, and he will cover for us," Gronnica said as the elevator door finished closing.

"Daniel and Ian, I would like you to meet my new tutor, Shoanna Malnerva," Shamarra said as she wiped her face on Daniellericmoja hair.

"It is nice to meet you, Shoanna," Ianistiolla said as he placed a hand on Shamarra's head.

"It's nice to meet you, Lieutenant Commander Daniellericmoja, and you, too, Lieutenant Commander Ianistiolla," she said while saluting.

"Just call him Daniel and me Ian. Shamarra and Phantom does," Ianistiolla replied.

"If I could have hit him, I would have," Shamarra said as she backed away from Daniel.

"You do know if you had hit the guy, your brother would be mad. You know you are on restrictions when he is not around," Ian replied as he started to smile at the two women.

"Yes, I know I can handle the way that they treat me. I just cannot stand here and listen to the way those nobodies can stand there and disgrace my brother like that," Shamarra said.

"Um, excuse me, I didn't know that the Alliance had a Grownolith among the ranks. By the way, what does that symbol on your right shoulder say?" Shoanna asked while looking at Daniel's uniform.

"There aren't that many Grownoliths in the Alliance. So that does not surprise me that you didn't know about our species being members," Daniel said with a smile on his face.

"Daniel, may look like a normal Grownolith, but he joined the Alliance after being a bounty hunter. So you see, with his incredible sense of smell, he can tell us pinpoint danger. That symbol, little lady, is the crest for the Special Operations Unit. Luckily for the Alliance, there are a total of three members to the Special Operations Unit for the Alliance," Ian said.

"Why is that?" Shoanna asked while looking confused.

"Don't worry about it, kiddo. Where were you going just now?" Daniel asked.

"I was supposed to be taking a test on Earth's history," Shamarra replied as she wiped away the last remaining trails of her tears.

"Why are you studying Earth's history?" Ian asked.

"You know, my brother decided to study the Planet Earth. He is the only one that is knowledgeable about planet Earth's history. He wants me to be just a knowledgeable as he is," Shamarra replied.

"How can you take a test when he is not here to give it to you?" Daniel asked while standing back up.

"He gave the test and the answers to the teacher. Once my test is done, Shoanna and I must report to Lieutenant Ericks for hand-to-hand combat," Shamarra replied as a smile appeared on her face.

"You know, your brother doesn't like you training with the recruits. Lieutenant Ericks will need to find someone else to help him with all of the examples," Ian said while starting to chuckle.

"You know, he will ground you if he catches you training with the recruits," Daniel added.

"Yes, I know. He doesn't want me holding the recruits training back. They're way better than I am when it comes to the whole hand-to-hand combat," Shamarra said just as the elevator stopped.

"Why did we just stop? We need the twenty-first floor, not the fifth floor," Shoanna said while looking at the lit number displayed on the elevator.

"Sorry, I had to run an override command, so our number took priority over yours. We will see you later, Shamarra. We must debrief

High Grand Admiral Calamen about our mission. Shoanna, I will see the two of you before Shamarra is done with her test. I have something to show the two of you," Daniel said just as Ian and he exited the elevator.

"You sure know some strong people in the Alliance. I cannot believe you know the Special Operation Unit Daniel and Ian. By the way, didn't they say there were three members? Do you know who the third member is?" Shoanna said with a confused voice.

"My brother," Shamarra said in a calm voice.

"Oh, is that so? Your brother! What do you mean your 'brother'?" Shoanna said just when she realized what Shamarra had just said.

"Yes, my brother. We're here," Shamarra said a few minutes later.

As the elevator's doors opened, they noticed the teacher standing in the doorway to her exam room. "Shamarra, you're late. I told your mother to make sure that you were here on time," the lieutenant commander said just before turning and walking into the room.

"Sorry, ma'am, I just couldn't decide on what to wear. Now that I am here, I am ready for this week's test," Shamarra said as she walked into the room.

"I'm glad to hear that. Take your normal seat, and then you may begin. Now, class, while our youngest test taker gets prepared for her test, you will need to prepare for your Alliance entry exam that I will hand out here shortly," the lieutenant commander said as Shamarra stopped at her designated seat.

"Shamarra, you may start. You may leave after you are finished. The rest of you will remain in your seats until I pick the answer pads up," the female said while handing Shamarra her test. A few minutes later, everyone heard, "Recruit, you may take a seat by the door, but I warn you, if you tell them any answers, you will be dropped from the Alliance," the lieutenant commander said as she turned to face Shoanna.

"Instructor, may I have a word with you before you begin?" a male's voice said just as a middle-aged male walked into the room.

"Sure, Major, I will be right there," the lieutenant commander replied to the major just as she saluted.

"I mean now!" the major ordered.

"I will be right back, class. Shamarra, go ahead and continue. If you have any questions, I will be back to answer them shortly," the lieutenant commander said while picking the exam question up.

"Oh, look, a muddy thinks that she can be an Alliance Soldier. I'm sorry, sweet heart, but you will never become an Alliance member because I will have my father make sure that you will never pass the exam," a male's voice said.

"Just because she is a Drazarian, what makes you think that she is not of pure blood?" Shoanna asked while sitting in her seat.

"Great, I cannot believe that the Alliance allowed a muddy like that as a soldier. What is your job? Decoy? No, wait, I know—fluid girl. Fluid girl, I'm thirsty. Get me something to drink! And, muddy, my feet hurt. I want you to rub them now," the young Shamoran male child said.

"She will be a member of the intelligence officers. Once she has completed the academy, she will be a higher ranking officer then you will be," Shamarra said while looking at her test.

"Just what we need in our Alliance, one muddy that is in love with another muddy," the boy replied.

As the candidates started to make more snide comments, Shamarra heard, "I know how they will finish their training. When these two graduate, their bodies will be launched into the nearest sun," the Shamoran boy said while smiling.

"May I ask, and if not, I will do it anyway, what is your name?" Shoanna asked.

"Kachellic, my father is the person our instructor is talking to right now," the boy replied.

"Great, another ignoramus who is unable to look past his own nose. I guess it is 'like father like son,'" Shamarra said as she started to stand.

Suddenly, the lieutenant commander walked back into the room. "What is going on in here?" she asked with a stern voice.

"Here is my test, ma'am. I will just have to finish it later," Shamarra said while handing the lieutenant commander her test.

"You *do* know that your brother wants this done by eleven o'clock Galactic Standard Time?" she replied.

"Yes, just like all the other tests. This room is so noisy right now that I cannot concentrate on my test," Shamarra said just as Shoanna and she walked out of the room.

"All right, I will see you later then," the lieutenant commander said just as she turned her attention back to the candidates. "For those of you who pass the entrance exam, we will have a new hand-to-hand combat instructor here on the station," she said just as the major walked into the room.

"Kachellic, what is going on in here?" the major asked.

"That child was picking on me. She even told me that she could get you kicked out of the Alliance. She also said that you know nothing about hand-to-hand combat and that a baby could defeat you and I. Dad, are you going to take that from her," the major's son replied with a sorrow voice.

"No, start the test, instructor. I have a few things to take care of," the major said just before leaving the room.

"What are you planning on doing to that child?" the lieutenant commander asked as the major walked out of the room.

Suddenly, she heard from outside the door, "I will teach that muddy that it is improper to talk to a pure-blooded Shamoran the way she just did," the major said.

"Leave that child alone!" the lieutenant commander said just as she ran into the hallway.

As both Shamarra and Shoanna turned to see what the commotion was all about, they noticed the major walking toward them when the two suddenly heard, "You best not lay even a figure on that child. If you do, you will have to deal with her brother!" the lieutenant commander said while running up on the major.

"How dare you talk to my pure-breed son that way!" the major said in a snide voice as he drew his right hand back.

Suddenly, a loud noise echoed throughout the hallway. "How dare you get in my way!" the major said while looking at Shoanna.

"It's because I will not allow you to harm this child. Go ahead and throw me out of the Alliance, but I will not allow you to even lay one finger on her," Shoanna said while looking at the major with intense hatred.

"Shoanna are you all right?" Shamarra asked just as Shoanna placed a hand to her check.

"I'm fine. I have been dealing with people like him all my life just because I look different. Everyone clams that it is because my parents decided to alter my DNA. My family doctor was surprised to see when I was born that I had blue eyes instead of brown and blond hair instead of brunette. So all my life I have been fighting arrogant people like this man," Shoanna said while staring into the major's eyes.

Suddenly, Shamarra noticed the major connecting a second punch into Shoanna's solar plexus. "How could you? How could you do that to her? You are a major, and she is just a recruit. You saw it yourself. She tried to dodge your attack, but you are better then she is," Shamarra said just as she noticed Shoanna's unconscious body hitting the floor.

"What did you just do, sir?" the lieutenant commander asked.

"Teaching this recruit a lesson, a lesson on how to respect her superiors!" the major's snide voice said.

"You realize she is one of Phantom Breaker's recruits, and he does not take this lightly?" the lieutenant commander said while checking Shoanna over.

"Hey, brat, what is your name?" the major asked.

"My name is of no concern to you, but if you must know, my name is Shamarra Breaker Calamen," the young Drazarians girl said while glaring at the major.

"How dare you!" the major said as he drew back his fist.

Suddenly, the major felt someone holding his fist back just as he started to move it toward Shamarra.

"You better not even think about striking her! Once you do, that will be the last thing that you will ever do!" the lieutenant commander said.

"How dare you restrain me! You do understand that I can terminate your service in the Galaxy Alliance!" the major said as he turned and connected a back hand to her face.

"How dare you hit her! My brother will punish you for this! By the way, if you try to get rid of her, my Aunt, Uncle, and brother will promote her and demote you!" Shamarra replied while the lieutenant commander held her hand to her cheek.

"I will not allow you or anyone to harm this child. You can try to demote me or even get rid of me. Just listen to me carefully. The next time you even think about harming this child, I will personally teach show you that you cannot just go around and punish anyone that you wish," the lieutenant commander said just as the major started to walk off.

"One last thing before I take this insubordination to the Alliance council. Do you know who this child's Aunt, Uncle, and brother are?" the major asked in a harsh voice just as he stopped in mid step.

"Her Aunt is High Grand Admiral Kristy Calamen, her Uncle is Grand Admiral Blake, and her brother is, like I said, Phantom Breaker.

Both Phantom and Shamarra are the adopted children of Colonel Jack Calamen. By the way, I think that you should know both Kristy and Jack Calamen are my mother's cousins," the lieutenant commander said in a calm voice just as she turned her back to the major and started to walk toward her classroom.

Great, not only do the leaders of the Alliance allow a boy to do whatever he wants, they also allow this girl and her entire family to run the Alliance Academy Station. If I didn't know any better, the Alliance will only have a few more months before we are over-powered by those blasted Pirates, the major thought just as a young doctor walked by.

"What happened here?" the young doctor asked.

"This recruit was assaulted by the major you had just walked past," Shamarra told him while wiping Shoanna's hair away from her face.

"Great, the worst person to ever become an instructor will take over the hand-to-hand combat classes next week, and we now have a major that is assaulting recruits as punishment," the young doctor said while picking Shoanna up in his arms.

"Will she be all right?" Shamarra asked in a calm voice.

"We will find out once we get her to medical. By the way, what is your name?" the doctor asked.

"My name is Shamarra. The young woman in your arms is named Shoanna. What is your name?" the young girl asked.

"Well, my name is Derrik. I am the medical doctor from the Planetary Academy. Between you and me, if the hand-to-hand combat instructors cannot help these recruits to defend themselves, then they may want to be transferred to the Planetary Academy for better training," the young doctor said.

Meanwhile in High Grand Admiral Calamen's office . . .

"I'm glad that your recovery mission went so well. I am truly sorry that I could not allow Phantom to help you out this time. Mom has analyzed the data and found out that the Pirates are trying to recreate an experiment that had failed three years ago," High Grand Admiral Kristy Calamen said.

"Well, if they succeed, we'll just have to destroy it," Ian said just as Daniel looked at the time.

"Is there somewhere else you would rather be right now, Lieutenant Commander?" Kristy asked.

"No. Sorry, ma'am. Ian and I ran into kiddo on the elevator. Both a recruit and she were crying," Daniel said.

"Oh, do you know why they were crying?" Kristy asked.

"Two newly graduated recruits, sorry soldiers from the Planetary Academy, were calling the recruit and Shamarra both 'muddy.' I told the two that I wanted the major their uncle in your office so we all could talk. Ma'am, that was almost fifteen minutes ago," Ian said just as Daniel stood up.

"Where do you think that you are going?" Kristy asked while watching him walk toward the door.

"You do not need me here. I'm going to check and make sure Shamarra and the recruit are both fine. For some unknown reason, I just feel uneasy about it," Daniel said while looking through the transparent steel windows.

"That sounds like a good idea. We are having the entry exams for the Planetary Academy today," Kristy said while standing up. As she made her way to the door, both Daniel and Ian heard, "Well, are you boys coming along, or do I check on my niece by myself?"

"Sorry, ma'am!" the two said in unison as they ran out behind her.

Before Daniel and Ian realized only a couple of minutes had passed, they were standing in front of the exam room. "Lieutenant Commander Jolania, sorry to interrupt, but is Shamarra still in here?" Daniel asked after opening the door.

"Why should anyone care about a Drazarian muddy like her?" a young male asked.

"Kachellic, you're done. Turn your exam in and leave the room. I will grade what you have done up to this point," Lieutenant Commander Jolania said while Daniel stepped into the exam room.

"Why should you care about a muddy like her? And further more, why should you have a muddy Drazarian teach anyone hand-to-hand combat? My father would kill him in a fight," the boy said.

"Her brother just happens to be my cousin and is not a Drazarian at all. He is an Altherian," the young woman said.

"Where is your father? I want a word with him about the way you are misbehaving," an older female's voice said from outside the door.

"When I see the major I will let him know that you are wanting to speak to him," the young man said.

"Daniellericmoja, can you help this young man in locating his father, please?" Jolania said.

"That would be my pleasure. And so would watching Phantom take care of the smug look on your father's face once and for all," Daniel said to the young boy.

"Yeah, right. My father will kill this Altherian with ease. This Station Academy has never produced a decent soldier from the get go!" Kachellic said while throwing the test at Jolania.

"I think that your father needs to teach you better manners than that," Kristy Calamen said while walking into the room.

"Who do you think you are, old lady?" the boy asked.

"Ma'am it sure is great to see you today, ma'am," Jolania said while saluting.

"It is nice to see family once in a while, isn't it cousin?" Kristy Calamen replied while walking over and hugging the lieutenant commander.

"Yes, cousin, it is. By the way, High Grand Admiral, your niece needs to finish her test before her brother arrives from the training exercise," Jolania said while pulling away from her cousin.

"Well, that may be longer than we think. Right now, he is leading a team against a group of Pirates that have taken the science station Drandon for themselves," Kristy said in front of the-would-be new recruits.

"If my father was there, the station would be ours once again," the boy replied.

"You're probably right, except we had to send the Altherian on a rescue mission to save your father once before. I honestly think that we have sent the right person to take care of this problem," Kristy Calamen replied.

"High Grand Admiral Calamen, you are needed in the medical bay. Your niece is there," Mom suddenly said.

Meanwhile . . .

"Derrik, what are you doing here?" a familiar male's voice said while walking up.

As the young man turned to look at who just spoke with a hint of being surprised, Derik asked, "Uncle, what are you doing here?"

"Doctor Collingan, please you must help her?" Shamarra said while tears ran down her face.

"What happened to this recruit, Shamarra?" the doctor asked while walking over to Shoanna.

"It was a major from the Planetary Academy. He started to hit me, and she stepped into the path of his fist," Shamarra said just as Derrik placed Shoanna on the exam table.

"You don't have to worry. My uncle is the best doctor that the Alliance has ever seen," Derrik told the young child just as they heard Doctor Collingan say, "Now let's see what the problem is."

"I know he is the only one that my brother allows to exam me when I am sick. Now when my brother needs an examination everything becomes top secret," Shamarra said while smiling.

A few minutes later, everyone heard the doctor ask, "Shamarra what is her name?" while checking the recruit's skull.

"Her name is Shoanna. Is she going to be all right, sir?" Shamarra asked while looking calmer then she just had been.

"She has a split skull, and it looks like she might have a little brain damage from the punch. All I will be able to do is just make sure that she is comfortable until the specialized surgeon arrives," Collingan said while injecting the recruit with a relaxing agent.

"Uncle, you are the best doctor the Planetary Academy has. The Station Academy is unable to handle something like this," Derrik said while have urgency in his voice.

"For this kind of damage, there is only one person that is capable of handling the procedure. Phantom is unable to do anything while he is handling an assault on a science station outpost. Derrik, I know the reason you joined the Alliance. Do not consider the Station Academy's Commanders as weaklings. If it had not been for the High Grand Admiral Calamen, the Galaxy Alliance would have been destroyed three years ago. They were able to handle a situation, even though we called them weak. Neither the Planetary Academy nor the Station Academy could have produced a person anything like the Galactic Frontier has. The greatest achievement this Academy has ever produced is Phantom Breaker and his little sister," the Doctor said while kneeling down and placing a hand on Shamarra's head.

"I do not understand, Uncle. What do you mean by that?" Derrik said with a confused voice.

"Instead of training a unique individuals like the Altherian on the Station or the Planetary Academies, High Grand Admiral Calamen decided to allow the Galactic Frontier to train him. They set up the very best instructors in every known fighting style, medicine, tactics, ambushing, etc., to train this individual and to allow him to grow," Doctor Collingan said while examining the test results.

"What does it say, Uncle?" Derrik said while walking closer to Doctor Collingan.

"While physically there is nothing wrong with her, her interior energy flow is being obstructed," the doctor replied while walking over to a computer and sitting down.

"What do you mean, 'obstructed'?" Shamarra asked while walking up to the computer.

"In Phantom's terms, her entire inner energy, or chi, is being blocked without any apparent reason. All I can tell you is in theory she has been poisoned with harmful chi or energy. The procedure is too complicated for someone like me. I just hope Phantom is able to get back here in twenty-four hours standard galactic time," Collingan said just as the door opened behind them.

"Mom, Aunt Kristy, Daniel, and Ian, what are you doing here?" Shamarra asked while turning to see the four walking into the room.

"We heard that you were again in the medical bay, and we decided to check on you," Jacquelyn said as she walked up to her daughter.

Suddenly, the door opened again. "Ma'am, is everything all right in here? We saw the four of you running into the medical bay," a familiar male's voice said.

"Ericks, everything is fine, right doctor? The three of you may leave now," Jacquelyn said while placing a hand on her daughter's shoulders.

"No, everything is not fine. This recruit is dying unless we are able to find a cure," Collingan said while placing a hand to his face and exhaling in frustration.

"What do you mean she 'is dying'? How can this be possible?" Kristy asked with a worried look on her face.

"Somehow, a major from the Planetary Academy stopped her life force or energy. The man meant to hit me with the attack, and Shoanan decided to stop him by stepping in front of me," Shamarra said as tears ran down her face.

"So her very life energy that gives her reason to live is depleting?" Kristy said just as she noticed a bright orange light flash from Shamarra's hand.

"Shamrra, honey, why is your hand glowing that color?" Jacquelyn asked just before noticing the empty look in her daughter's eyes.

"We have a message for you from Colonel Calamen Kristy," Mom said while startling both Kristy and Jacquelyn and Shamarra fell to her knees and then to the floor.

Before either one could confirmed that they heard Mom's artificial voice, they suddenly heard, "What is happening there?" Jack's voice suddenly shot from the communications unit in the medical bay.

"What do you mean, Colonel? Everything is fine," Kristy said in a calm voice.

"Phantom's acting stranger than normal, and his right hand is glowing brightly. He is reacting to Shamarra's emotions, and I can accept that, but what I can't accept is why he is reacting to them," Jack replied while both his sister and his wife smiled.

"Jack, tell me how is our son doing!" Jacquelyn blurted out with a worried intense look on her face.

"That is why I am calling. Phantom does not appear to be responding to any orders that we have issued him. All he keeps saying is, 'They made you cry, and I will punish them for it,'" he replied to his wife with a worried sound to his voice.

"Shamarra has been crying because her new tutor has been attacked by a major from the Planetary Academy. I'm sorry, honey, her condition doesn't look good," Jacquelyn said in a saddened voice while kneeling down next to Shamarra.

"All right, try to keep her calm, and I will handle the boy. Hey, Phantom, wait, what are you doing? Faith, try to increase the wall absorbers," Jack said just before the communications ended.

CHAPTER 15

"SIR, THERE IS something wrong with the corporal!" a young male's voice cried out with terror.

"What, what is it?" Colonel Calamen yelled while running toward the direction of the voice.

After turning the corner, both the lieutenant and Colonel suddenly stopped in mid run as the two heard, "We need something to douse out the fire! Don't worry, Corporal, we will help you!" a young male soldier said.

"Lieutenant, start evacuating the troops," Colonel Calamen said quietly to his old friend while looking at what appeared to be red and blue flames radiating from his son.

"Yes, sir," the lieutenant replied just as Colonel Calamen heard Phantom's harsh, cold voice, "They made her cry. I will not allow them to live for this."

"Everyone, we will back track look a way to get around those Pirates!" the lieutenant said while walking back down the hall way.

"Lieutenant Major, how do you expect us to find a way around when we all already know this hall way is the only way in and out of this section?" a female recruit replied.

"Just do as you're ordered!" the lieutenant replied while thinking, "I just hope Jack knows what he is doing."

"Academy Station, Mom, can you hear me? It's Jack Calamen. I need to talk with my wife!" Jack said urgently into his personal communicator.

"Yes, Colonel, I can hear you. What is wrong?" Mom said with a confused tone.

"I need to talk to my wife! I need to talk to Jacquelyn!" Jack said with more urgency in his voice.

"Calm down. I will transfer you to the medical bay," Mom said while Jack thought, *Medical bay . . . Why would she be there unless something has happened to Shamarra.*

Just as Jack heard a familiar clicking sound that confirms the communication was now active, Jack blurted out, "What is happening there?"

"What do you mean? Colonel, everything is fine," Kristy said in a calm voice through his ear speaker.

"Phantom's acting stranger than normal, and his right hand is glowing brightly. He is reacting to Shamarra's emotions, and I can accept that, but what I can't accept is why he is reacting to them," Jack replied while looking at what appears to be stronger flames radiating from his son's body.

"Jack, tell me, how is our son doing?" Jacquelyn blurted out.

"That is why I am calling. Phantom does not appear to be responding to any orders that we have issued him. All he keeps saying is, 'They made you cry, and I will punish them for it,'" he replied with a tone worry.

"Shamarra has been crying. Her new tutor has been attacked by a major from the Planetary Academy. I'm sorry, honey, her condition doesn't look good," Jacquelyn said in a saddened voice.

"All right, try to keep her calm, and I will handle the boy. Hey, Phantom, wait, what are you doing? Faith, try to increase the wall absorbers," Jack said just as he disconnected the communications.

"Shamarra, what is wrong? Why are you crying again?" a familiar voice said.

As Shamarra frantically looked around, she suddenly noticed a tall male standing in front of her. "Allan, they hurt her. They hurt big sister," she replied as tears streamed down her face.

"Calm down and speak to me more clearly. Now, who hurt her? Who are you calling 'big sister'?" Allan said while pulling Shamarra closer to him.

"Shoanna was attacked by a major from the Planetary Academy. The major drew his hand back to strike me, but Shoanna stepped in the way and was hit instead. The major then used an attack that I have never seen before. You must help her before she dies, big brother," Shamarra said while embracing her brother.

"I need to know what happened before I can do anything. Do you remember what kind of an attack it was?" Allan asked her while looking into his sister's miserable eyes.

"All I know is his hand was glowing just before he touched Shamarra in the solar plexus. Can you help her? No, you *must* help her, please, big brother?" Shamarra cried out in pain.

"I will try my best, but you know I cannot promise you that I will be successful. Just relax yourself. I will use your body to help the person that you call Shoanna," Allan said just as he disappeared.

"Shamarra, Shamarra honey, can you hear me? Please say something," a familiar voice echoed through Shamarra's head just as her eyes opened to see her mother kneeling next to her.

"Something," Shamarra replied as she started to stand.

"No you must not move. You might have injures from the fall," Jacquelyn said while trying to keep her daughter still.

"Mother, let me go! I must tend to the injured recruit," a strange but yet familiar voice replied just as Jacquelyn's eyes widened.

"You're burning up. Doctor, get over here quickly. She is burning up," Jacquelyn cried out.

"How can she be burning up when there is nothing to cause it?" the doctor asked just as Shamarra's body erupted into strange looking flames.

"Shamarra is fine. Now, get out of my way and allow me to tend to the injured," the strange voice said just as the flames started to take on an appearance.

"Who are you, and what have you done to my daughter?" Jacquelyn asked with fear in her voice.

Without a word, the body of Shamarra and the strange entity walked toward the bed where Shoanna was laying. As the two moved closer and closer, the entity could hear the alarms from the monitoring units. "Recruit, you better not give up on us. Just hang in there. We will have the cure soon," another doctor said.

"Sir, I just had a talk with the major that had done this. He refuses to cure this recruit. His comment was, 'She should have never gotten in my way,'" the nurse said as tears started to form in her eyes.

"Then, there is no hope for her," the doctor said in a hopeless voice.

"Move out of my way," a young child's voice and a male's voice said from behind their backs.

As the doctor and nurses turned, they noticed Shamarra standing there with a strange glow about her.

"I said get out of the way," the voices said as Shammar's body started to walk passed them.

"What can you do that we can't? The only other person that might have a chance is over twenty light years away," the doctor said as she walked by him.

"I can't believe how pathetic simple-minded people actually are," the voice said just as Shamarra's body stopped at Shoanna's bed side.

"What are you talking about?" Jacquelyn asked with a hint of being curious.

As the entity looked at him, a sudden green flash of light left from his right eye. "Phantom, Phantom, is that you?" Jacquelyn asked while thinking, *Only one person would do wink at me like that. Allan, how are you doing that?*

"She is suffering because she is unable to breathe. She has also sustained injures to her lower internal organs and brain. Let's see if I can relieve some of that pain," the strange voice said just as both the entity and Shamarra reached out for the injured recruit.

"What do you think you are going to do with her?" a nurse blurted out.

Suddenly, a quick, blinding light erupted out into the room. Before everyone could see what had happened, they suddenly heard a loud gasping sound. "There. Her internal organs are working properly now. It will take a few days to heal, so I would not let her leave the medical bay for two days. Now that *that* problem is done, how are we going to fix her neural damage?" the strange voice said as Shamarra picked up a data pad.

"What do you think she is doing?" a nurse asked Jacquelyn as the two watched her typing information onto the pad.

"I really don't think my daughter is the one doing that. I don't know why, but I have a feeling that, somehow, Phantom is the glowing entity standing right before our very eyes.

"That can't be! He is several systems over at the Drandon Station," the nurse replied just as the two noticed Shamarra and the entity walking toward them.

"This should fix the problem, but if not, give her a cure-all that the Alliance uses to treat all poison," the strange voice said just as the entity started to fade away.

"Shamarra, are you all right? Can you tell me what happened?" Jacquelyn asked her as she noticed her daughter's beautiful crystal blue eyes looking at her.

"He did it, Mommy. He helped Shoanna just like he said he would try to do. Now, I really feel sorry for those Pirates on the Science Station," Shamarra said with a worried look on her face.

So that was Phantom after all . . . No, it had to have been Allan, Jacquelyn thought just as she heard a loud noise entering the medical bay. "Go get something to eat, honey, you must be hungry by now. I will do what I can, and when Phantom arrives, I'm sure he will check on her himself," Jacquelyn said to her daughter.

"Where is she? Where is my daughter?" an unfamiliar male's voice said.

"May I ask who you are, and what brings you to the Galaxy Alliance Station Academy?" High Grand Admiral Calamen asked the middle-aged man while a middle-aged woman stood by his side.

"I am Sholena, and this is my husband Maulla. Shoanna is our daughter, and we would like you to tell us what happened to her?" the middle-aged woman asked.

"I would like to, but we need to perform an important operation on her," Jacquelyn said just as she started to put on a surgeons outfit.

"You need to leave right now. You can see your daughter in three days," High Grand Admiral Calamen said while Grand Admiral Black and she ushered them out of the room.

"We have come here to talk our daughter out of this nonsense of hers one last time. If you don't understand what we are saying, we are taking our daughter back to Delta Grega, and that's it," the middle-aged man said.

"Sorry, her commanding officer is not her right now, and you will need his permission to withdraw her from the Alliance. Until you can talk with him, I would not plan on leaving the station for three days," Blake said just before the door closed behind him.

"Who do you think you are for holding my daughter as a hostage? We are her parents, and we know what's best for our little girl. We have found her a husband, and now it is time for her to keep her promise to us," Maulla replied to the Grand Admiral.

"What you are talking about is the same thing as turning your own daughter into a slave. In fact, my wife and I were able to talk with her since she is tutoring our little niece while her brother is away. She told us that the reason why she joined was to help you out with your money problems. Now you are talking about selling her off as someone's bride. That sounds an awfully a lot like turning her into a slave."

"Don't you dare tell me what it sounds like or not. Fine, you're right, we basically did sell her as a slave just to pay our debts off. That is the price that our family has to pay," Maulla said with a sad voice.

"Grand Admiral Blake, how is she doing? Will she be alright?" a young child ran up to the Grand Admiral.

"Jacquelyn is starting the procedure now. Don't worry, everything will be fine," Blake said while kneeling down to Shamarra.

"What is wrong, child? Is the big, nasty Galaxy Alliance keeping you from seeing your mother or another family member?" Mualla said while glaring at Blake just as he noticed a smile on the Grand Admiral's face.

"Are you insane? If it wasn't for these nice people, my brother and I would have been dead a long time ago. Isn't that right, Uncle Blake," the child said while looking at both Sholena and Mualla.

"That's right, kiddo. I will make you a promise. As soon as you can see Shoanna, I will personally find you and bring you here. For now, you need to finish up that test of yours," Blake said while placing a hand on his niece's head.

"Do you really promise?" she replied to her uncle.

"Yes, as soon as your mother is done, I will come and find you," he said while standing back up.

As the child ran off, he heard, "That child is as Drazarian, if I am not mistaken, and yet you are not, but she called you her uncle. Why is that?" Sholena asked with a confused look on her face.

"That is because she was adopted into my wife's family. The person that is performing the operation is her mother and my sister in-law," Blake said in a sad voice while watching his niece run down the hallway.

"Hey! Watch it, kiddo. You need to slow down!" a lieutenant commander said just as Shamarra ran past her.

"Uncle, I was worried about the recruit. How is she doing?" the lieutenant commander asked.

"Jolania, I would like to introduce you to Mualla and Sholena," Blake said just as his niece walked up to him.

"It is nice to meet you. Uncle, we have a really big problem about what has happened to the recruit—"

Before Jolania could finish, she heard Blake reply, "She has a name, and that name is Shoanna."

"Sorry, sir. Like I was saying with what had happened to Shoanna and the fact that she is Shamarra's tutor, her new hand-to-hand combat instructor will not be pleased. Some of the other members are talking about the instructor will be demanding the people's heads for this one once he finds out," Jolania said while ignoring both Sholena and Mualla.

"I think we can talk about this later. These two individuals are the parents of recruit Shoanna Malnerva. They are here to withdraw their daughter and take her back home for her wedding," Blake said.

"This can't wait. For all we know, he could be finding out about what has happened right now. You know just as well as I do that once he finds out about this, the mission that he is on will be over in about one galactic standard hour," Jolania said with a worried voice.

"He *does* know about what has happened. He was the one that was able to get the young lady to breathe again. I'm sorry. We will find a place for you to stay," Blake said while gesturing for the two to leave the waiting room.

"You don't have to act like you care about our daughter. We know what you Alliance commanders like to use the women of the Alliance for. Undercover roles like servants, maids, entertainment, and who know what else. We also know that your commanding officers will take advantage of young recruits like my daughter," Mualla said with a harsh voice.

"The people that take on those roles do so at their own discretion. I chose to help out with an undercover mission myself," Jolania replied just before she turned and started to walk off.

Jolania, honey, what has made you feel so badly about what has happened? Blake thought just before saying, "Please follow me, and I will help you get settled in."

"I think they knew that we were coming, and the Alliance is trying to put on an act," Mualla told his wife as the two followed a few feet behind Grand Admiral Blake.

"Commander, what are you orders?" the lieutenant asked Colonel Calamen.

Before anyone else noticed it, the colonel noticed Phantom had stopped glowing except for his hand. Suddenly, he reached around the corner and discharged a burst of energy. After the station stopped shaking, a soldier asked the lieutenant, "What was that? Are we under attack again?"

"Not at all. I think our Corporal is starting to make his—" Before the lieutenant could finish, he suddenly saw Phantom jump to his feet and charge down the hallway. Before anyone could look to see what was going on, everyone started to hear horrified screams.

"Let's get going!" Phantom's voice demanded just as a blaster shot zipped past the corporal's head. *Daggen, finally you're mine,* Phantom thought just as he jumped sideways out of Daggen's sight.

"There the Alliance dogs are. Stop them at all costs!" Daggen demanded.

As Phantom was able to get back to where he was originally, the soldiers heard one discharged weapon after another as each blaster shot slammed into the wall. "Faith, pull up the schematics for the station for me," Phantom ordered as he started to type one his computer.

"Great, he took care of one group just to land us in a mess with another," a soldier said.

"Where did they find someone like him? He's cute," a female soldier said.

"Who said that? Soldier, identify yourself," Colonel Calamen said after overhearing a few soldiers taking.

"I did, sir. My name is Sarah," the soldier said while standing up.

As the soldier stood up, Colonel Calamen noticed a young woman with green hair, light-blue skin, and gray eyes. *Wow, only if I was a teenager again,* Colonel Calamen thought just as he said, "Soldier, you *do* know my son is off limits, right? The only one we will allow to get close to him is his sister," the colonel said as he walked up to the soldier.

"I'm sorry, sir. It just slipped. To be honest, sir, most of the young, female soldiers that do not have boyfriends or are to be married soon have a crush on him," Sarah said while looking past the colonel and at Phantom.

"For those of you that may want to ask, I will tell you now. No, he does not have a girlfriend . . ." As the colonel talked, Sarah though to herself, *Great, I may actually have a chance. I see how he treats his little sister. He treats her like a family member. This means I have a chance.*

"Yes, he does have someone that he loves dearly who is actually his little sister. For the last time, he is off limits," Colonel Calamen said just as he turned his back and started to walk off.

After taking two steps, he suddenly heard as he turned around, "That's not fair. How can someone *that* cute be off limits?" The Colonel heard a lot of different female's voices say.

I hope we can keep this 'off limits' working. If it does, not we will have a huge problem in the Alliance, Colonel Calamen thought. "Phantom, what is the best plan of action here?" Colonel Calamen asked while walking back toward the front of the hallway.

"Well, with Daggen, a frontal approach will not work. I would suggest a sneak attack," Phantom replied while sliding closer to the hallway entrance. While peeking around the corner, several shots flew past his head. *One, two, three, four, five and six . . . So Daggen thinks that he can stop us with only five Pirates and himself? I guess you're a bigger fool than I thought,* Phantom thought as he started to move away from the entrance.

Suddenly, Phantom heard, "Well, do you have a plan or not? What is wrong with you?" a soldier asked just as Colonel Calamen placed a hand on the soldiers shoulder.

"How many are there, and are we outnumbered?" Colonel Calamen asked his son.

"We are out-gunned, but not out-manned. If we try to rush them, we will take a lot of casualties. I suggest we try a more quiet approach," Phantom said as he peeked around the corner again.

"All right, how many soldiers will you need?" Colonel Calamen asked with a worried tone to his voice. Phantom held up four fingers.

"Four Platoons? What, are you mad? We have seven here, and they still have us pinned down," the soldier said.

"Is it platoons? Phantom, you need to be more specific than that," the colonel replied.

"Not platoons—men. Faith, I need you to access the data on the station," Phantom said. As he walked away from the entrance and sat down on the floor, his father noticed he was doing something on his arm computer.

"If I have not told you yet, happy fifteenth birthday. Now, let's see you live to see sixteen," Jack said as he noticed a grin appear on his son's face.

"Faith, I have the data I was looking for. Now father, look at the holographic outline of the station and the level that we are on. Here, about twenty yards back, there is a maintenance crawl space that will run above and below that particular group of Pirates. I will need two people to follow me above the Pirates and two people to crawl below the Pirates. I will want another person as a decoy," Phantom said just as the picture highlighted the paths Phantom was talking about.

"All right, I think that will work. Now, what kind of weapons will you need?" the colonel asked.

"All I will need are four smoke grenades and flash grenades," Phantom said just as he looked up and noticed objects moving upon them quickly.

"What about the men that you will be taking with you?" the lieutenant asked.

"Our volunteers have just arrived," Phantom said as everyone heard, "Death Commander, we have found them," Phantom heard a familiar voice say.

"My name is Lieutenant Commander Ericcan, and don't you dare call me anything else," everyone heard a high demanding voice said just as Phantom looked back down the hallway where he knew the Pirates were.

"Just so you all know, after this mission, most of our ranking officers will be training the new recruits at the Station Academy. Corporal Breaker, you will be handling the hand-to-hand combat training. By the way, do us a huge favor and don't hurt the recruits to badly," the colonel Calamen said.

"I will not waste my time training children," Phantom replied to his father's statement.

"This is an order from your Aunt High Grand Admiral Calamen and the AI Mom," Colonel Calamen replied.

"Fine then, all I can promise is that those recruit's won't be hurt too much. That is fortunate for them, unlike these boys back here," he said as his smile turned into a concentrated look of determination.

As Phantom peeked back around the corner, he noticed nine large creatures each holding large laser cannons. Each cannon looked to be twice the normal size of a normal cannon and possibly being nine times stronger than the normal cannons. *Great. Reinforcements. That's just what we need around here—more Pirates!* Phantom thought while the other twelve Pirates disappeared. A few minutes later, a Lieutenant and five other soldiers came running up to the group.

Suddenly, all five soldiers that had arrived with the lieutenant saluted Phantom. "You ungrateful worms, you would rather salute a-non commissioned officer then your own commander?" the lieutenant demanded.

"That's right, sir. We will live longer with him around then we would with you any solar day. He is the top hand-to-hand combat fighter, and he is also a close range fighting master. He will get us past these Pirates without a single life being lost," a low ranking soldier said.

"Nicholas, how are you doing? The last time we saw each other was on graduation day at the academy. By the way, do me a favor and don't salute me. Do you understand?" Phantom replied.

"I guess all the rumors were true. You hate rank, even though you should be a lieutenant," the boy answered back.

"Colonel Calamen, I have found my four soldiers. Come on, guys, let's move out, and I will explain on the way," Phantom said while moving away from the wall.

As he turned away from the hallway, everyone heard nine more blasts hitting the wall behind him. "Jake, Michael, Michelle, and Nicholas, you're going to be with me on this plan. Jasmine, you'll cover our movements by launching a flash grenade and then a smoke grenade. Now, here we are on this station. I was thinking about running to this crawl space over here. It is just a few meters around the corner behind us. One team will be climbing the ladder to the crawl space above these Pirates while the other team will be climbing down to get beneath them. Once in place, both teams will send a flash grenade toward each other first. I hope all of you have been practicing your aiming because this is the crucial part. We need the grenades to connect with each other. Then, in a twenty-second interval, both teams will launch the smoke grenades. I will finish the rest of the plan myself. Don't worry, this will be an easy walk from here on out. Now, Colonel Calamen, no one will be allowed to rush down that hallway for any reason. Those Pirates will open fire as soon as they are blinded. They will expect us to rush them and to try to overpower them. Here is where it gets tricky. Jasmine, you can ricochet the grenades off these walls at this specific angle. Does everyone understand what the plan is? Just remember this—no one is allowed to die while I am here. My team, go ahead and move out. Everyone else, just wait here and relax," Phantom said well reaching over and grabbing his backpack.

As he pulled out a pair of different shoes, he heard, "Um, what are you doing?" Jasmine asked from behind.

"You never enter into a blind gun fight without a set of knives. These shoes are made with knives hidden in the bottom of the boots," Phantom said while grinning.

As the five soldiers walked away, Jasmine pulled her weapon out and started to examining it when she heard, "Hey, Mikey, I was wondering what planet is the corporal is from?" a young female soldier asked.

"Phantom is an Altherian. Except, he may not be a typical Altherian, but he is the only one that we know of," Jasmine answered while continuing to examining her gun.

"Wow, is that true? Do you really know him? What is he truly like? Does he have a girlfriend? Do I even stand having a chance with him? Oh, my, he is extremely cute," a young, female voice said.

"Soldier, what is your name?" Jasmine asked while turning around and looking the young female.

"My name is Sarah," the young lady answered.

"Well, Sarah, Phantom, at the age of twelve, lost his entire family. At the age of thirteen, he joined the Galaxy Alliance. He *does* have a Drazarian sibling. He will do anything to protect her because he loves her dearly and will die just to keep her safe. No, he does not have a girlfriend. He is more of the loner type, which is due to his sister," Jasmine said just as she loaded a grenade into the chamber.

"Does that mean I have a chance?" Sarah asked with hope in her voice.

"No, his sister is only four, and he means everything to that little girl. As a Parralian, I know what family means. We may look like every humanoid—even possibly an Earthling. Except for our strength just happens to be six times stronger than theirs, and our minds use about sixty-five percent more than most humanoids. He never really had friends back at the Academy, except for Nicholas who shared a dorm room at the academy with Phantom. Now, is that enough information for you about the corporal, or do I need to go on? Just one more thing, solder. He is off limits for all us women who may have the bright idea of dating him, especially for those who think of him as a prize or trophy," Jasmine said just as she closing her eyes and leaning her back to the wall.

"Do you know anything else about him?" another female soldier asked.

"I do not know much about him except for what I told you. I found that much out from his father Colonel Calamen over there. Michelle, Michael, Jake, and I were on a mission under a different commander. At that particular time, we were only supposed to be gathering information about a group of Pirates who thought that they could hide near the station Academy. Two days into our mission, we were discovered, and we sent out a distress signal. By the time anyone could help us, we had two members of our platoon badly injured, and the Pirates had been hunting us for four days straight. When we just happened to run out of supplies, we heard a sound outside of the cave we had been hiding in. When we went to see what had happened, a dark figure was walking into our cave—straight toward us. Phantom then took the shirt off his own back and started to cut the shirt up. He used it to cover the exposed wounds of our comrades. Afterward, he told us to gather our things because it was time that we went back to the Alliance Station. When we weren't moving fast enough, we heard 'Hurry up and move.' Before we knew it, we were standing in front of a ship that was to evacuate us from the planet. The four of us were able to talk with him for three days. Because of that, I was able to know a few things about him. His sister and he think if anyone becomes too close to them, that person will end up dead," Jasmine said in a calm, sad voice as she placed two fingers to her ear.

Suddenly, everyone heard, "Fire in the hole!" Jasmine yelled as the first grenade was launched.

Meanwhile . . .

"There it is. Michelle, you, and Jake will get below them. Nicholas, Michael, and I will be above. Remember, we must be sitting above and beneath the Pirates before we can move. We must get to the locations that I showed you in a maximum of five minutes," Phantom said as the five ran toward the crawl space.

A matter of seconds, Phantom, Michael, and Nicholas started to climb their way up the ladder, just as Michelle and Jake started to descend to their crawl space. A few seconds later, both teams started to crawl through the tunnels of the Science Station. As Phantom moved through the crawl space, he thought, *I don't have time for this.*

"Phantom, we have a problem. Which way are we supposed to go?" Jake said over a private channel.

"Jasmine, we need the flash grenade to mark our goal," Phantom called over their communications while looking at a split in the tunnel.

Suddenly, he heard the sounds of a grenade ricocheting off the walls, followed by a quick flash at a distance ahead of them to the left. "This way—to the left. We are behind schedule now. We need to move it!" he replied.

"Just lead the way, sir. We are right behind you," Nicholas responded.

"Sir, what is going on down there?" Michael asked just as he heard a loud multiple discharge of blasters.

"The Pirates are shooting at our allies," Phantom replied while thinking, *I just want to know about the weapons they have that makes this station so valuable for them to strike.* Then, Jasmine heard in her ear from Phantom, "Launch the smoke grenade."

As both groups moved through the crawl space, Phantom heard the second set of ricocheting sounds coming from behind them suddenly explode. "Sir, those Slag Dogs hit the smoke grenade, and now I am out of ammunition. Now what can I do to cover your movement?" Jasmine said with a worried tone in her voice.

"Nothing. I will handle the rest from my end. Just get away from the hallway entrance before they try the exact same thing that I had you just do," Phantom said as he continued to move through the crawl space.

Suddenly, she dropped to the floor just as a blast shot flew past her head when she heard "Michelle, Nicholas—now! The flash grenades!" Phantom called out while opening a drop hatch above and behind the Pirates.

"All we need is a few more seconds, and then lights out for those Pirates," Nicholas said as he opened a second crawl space hatch directly in front of the Pirates.

"Hey, Daggen, when is Trayon supposed to arrive with our backup?" one of the Pirates asked.

Trayon, I swear, this time you're mine for sure, Phantom thought just as he heard, "Ready in five, four, three, two and one," Nicholas said through a short wave communications device just as Phantom heard the discharge of his weapon.

As both soldiers shot their grenades Phantom dropped down out of the shaft. Suddenly, Daggen started to rub his eyes just as he heard, "What is going on? Are the Alliance dogs trying to counter our forces?

Or are they just trying to make it *look* like they are while the rest of their forces retreat for a second strike?" a Pirate asked.

"I don't know. All I am able to do right now is up-close things. It appears that the Alliance dogs want us to play hid and seek," Daggen said just as his fellow Pirates started to laugh.

"That's right, and I'm it," an unfamiliar voice said from behind them.

"Who . . . who are you? I don't remember hearing your voice among our troops before," Daggen said just as he heard someone gasping for air.

"What just happened? Can anyone see what is going on?" Daggen asked just as he started to see a dark figure standing right in front of his eyes.

Well, TRI Guild Dog, one of your fellow men decided to betray you and shoot one of his own comrades," the unfamiliar voice said while looking around.

"Blast those Alliance dogs. If I had my eyes closed when the second flash grenade went off, I would be able to see right now. All right, you tell me where the traitor is, and I will kill him myself," Daggen said while holding up his blaster.

"There he is over there! Hurry, he is trying to get back to the Alliance soldiers!" the unfamiliar voice said.

As Daggen noticed the dark figure pointing to his left, Daggen swung around and shot one of his own men dead in the chest. Suddenly, Daggen heard something hitting the ground followed by, "It wasn't me, boss. It wasn't me . . ." the Pirate said with his last dying breath.

"You missed him. I can't believe you missed him. There, on you right! What's this? The traitor has followers? Quickly, all four of them are trying to get down the hallway," the unfamiliar voice said just as Daggen started to become red in the face.

Daggen then quickly turned around and started to shoot at any dark objects moving. "Trying to kill me now are you?" Daggen said just as he noticed a dark figure moving closer to him.

As Phantom watched Daggen shooting his own men, he was counting to himself, "Five, six, seven, eight, nine and ten."

"There, let that be a lesson to all you traitors," Daggen said with a grin on his face.

"Um, Daggen, the traitor is you for shooting all of your men. Now launch the smoke grenades!" the unfamiliar voice said as Daggen opened his eyes.

There, right there in front of him in the Alliance red, blue, and black colors was a member of the Alliance. "Now, Daggen, how could you have killed all those innocent non-traitorous Pirates that you once called 'friends'?" the Alliance soldier said with a grin on his face.

After looking around and noticing that all his fellow Pirates had horrified looks on their faces just as they died, Daggen looked back at the Alliance soldier and snarled, "Who are you so I can leave the Alliance your name? What you have done here today is unforgivable!"

"For what you had done to my little sister and family, the only sentence is death to be carried out immediately," the soldier replied just as Daggen heard a loud explosion from behind.

Suddenly, the entire hallway was filled with smoke. "What is happening si—" Before the only sole survivor of Daggen's unit could finish his sentence, Daggen heard a loud noise when something connected to the floor.

"Shommaun, Shommaun, are you still with me?" Daggen asked just as he felt someone touching his back. After only hearing a small acknowledgement, Daggen leaned to the left. "As soon as we can see the soldier, open fire at him," Daggen ordered.

"Great idea, except . . ." Before Daggen could hear what the exception was, he felt something sharp being plunged into both of his arms and something sharp cutting through his leg.

"Who . . . who are you?" Daggen asked just as he noticed the smoke covered hallway had started to dissipate.

"Tell me, Daggen, where is Trayon?" the soldier asked while looking into Daggen's eyes.

"He will be here soon, and then you will be killed," Daggen replied while feeling warm liquid running down his arms.

"I already know that. Where is he right now?" the soldier demanded to know as his eyes started to glow red.

"What makes you think that I will tell you? He will kill me once he finds out I said anything to you Alliance dogs!" Daggen replied with fear in his voice.

"*He* will kill you? *I* will kill you if you don't, and then I will revive you and then kill you all over again. Now where is Trayon?" the soldier demanded once again.

"If you want Trayon, his real name is 'Tearan' and is from the Korra Guild. He would like other people to think there is someone else in charge of the TRI Guild. Tearan is in the science lab Alpha Omega Delta," Daggen replied with a grin on his face.

"Thank you for telling me where the prince and princess of the Korra Guild are. That still does not tell me where Trayon is, or maybe my cousins will be willing to tell me," the soldier said as Daggen noticed hatred had appeared in the soldier's eyes.

"Your cousins . . . Tell me before you die, who are you?" Daggen asked a second time.

As the soldier closed in next to Daggen's ears, the soldier whispered into his ear, "You used to call me 'the runt.'"

"No, it can't be. No, you can't be him. Your dead! I saw it myself! The science ship was destroyed by the Alliance dogs, and I saw you die. Trayon even has a copy of the archive of your death. Someone . . . help me . . . this Ea . . ." before Daggen could cry out for help, Phantom snapped his neck lick a twig.

"Son, are you all right?" Colonel Calamen asked while walking up to Phantom.

"Why did the Alliance decide to build these weapons that the council clammed were too dangerous? If anyone had been hit with this Inanimate Charging Dispersal Unit, their entire clothes would become a bomb," Phantom told him while holding a weapon three times bigger than their ordinary blaster.

"What do you suggest? You know we have to run the Pirates off of this station," Jack told his son.

"Father, take the troops back to the shuttles and get off of the station. I will only need two platoons for the remaining task," Phantom said as he stood up.

"You don't know how many more Pirates there are waiting ahead of you," Jack Calamen told his son.

"Yes, I do. Those Pirates belong to my cousin's guild. I will be able to handle this, so don't worry," Phantom said while turning to looking at father.

"What makes this so important to you that you are willing to risk everything for it?" Jack asked him while noticing his son's red iris.

"What would mother say if you decided to try the same thing I am doing right now?" Phantom asked him with a hint of hope in his voice.

"She tried to stop me, and I still proceeded with my orders knowing that I would be the only one that could accomplish the task at hand," Jack replied to his son.

"'What make this so important to me,' you asked? I am trying to end my sister's nightmares," Phantom said as he turned away from his father.

"All right, you're my son, and I trust in your judgment. Just be careful. I don't want to explain to your mother or sister that I allowed you to die," Jack told his son.

"Michelle, Nicholas, Jasmine, Michael, and Jake will be my lieutenants for this part of our mission. My platoons, prepare to move out," Phantom said as he made his way down the hallway.

"All right, you heard the corporal. Now, both units move out," Jack Calamen told everyone as he watched his son disappear into the darkness of the forward hallway.

CHAPTER 16

"I HAVE SOME bad news for you recruits. Your hand-to-hand combat instructor, General Marrus, has become very ill. Mom and the Alliance council have made a decision and have chosen a replacement instructor for you, except, he will not be back for a few days. I will still be your instructor until he returns from his mission," Lieutenant Ericks told them as he entered the room. After looking around at the recruits, he noticed a familiar child was sitting among them. "Shamarra, honey, what are you doing here? I had not been notified that you were going to be in my class today," the lieutenant said while walking up to the child.

"General Marrus was allowing me to watch and at times join in with the training of these recruits. Besides, my tutor is in this class, and I need her on hand to help me out with my homework," Shamarra told the lieutenant.

"For the next few todays, your lessons we will be reviewing for the new instructor. Now, let's begin and, Shamarra, stay in your seat," the lieutenant told her.

Meanwhile back on the station . . .

"Phantom, how far we going to go?" Nicholas asked while looking left and right as he walked past open hallways.

"You don't need to be on high guard right now. We won't even need our weapons for this part of the mission. We will need to walk through the science labs labeled 'Bio-Engineering One and Two' before we get to where we really need to be," Phantom said as he turned the corner and continued to walk down another hallway.

"How do you know where to you are going?" Jack asked him.

"This is not my first time here at this Science Station. Besides, I was the one that helped test out the security systems. I told them one and half years ago that the system they had would not hold up to an all-out assault," Phantom said as he looked at his arm computer.

"So you helped them design the security protocols, then?" Nicholas said as he noticed Phantom walking through the hallway with out looking at where he was going.

"I'm sorry, but I can't give you that information," Phantom said as he looked up and noticed a door saying 'Top Secret. Authorized People Only. All Others Stay Out." "This way and don't touch anything," Phantom said as the group approached the door.

"Yeah, you never know what those crazy scientists are cooking up in there," a soldier said.

"Yeah, you never know. They could be trying to create a better soldier than our corporal here," another soldier added just as laughs started to echo through the hallway.

"Will all of you keep those mouths shut?" Nicholas ordered as he watched to see any reaction from Phantom. A few minutes passed when he realized that Phantom was either ignoring the comment or he had not heard it. *Well, that's a relief for now. I wonder what Phantom is thinking about,* Nicholas thought to himself.

"Trisha, I know you want to help by keeping a look out for the Alliance soldiers, but I would feel better if you were back here with me," a male's voice said over her personal communications device.

As Trisha looked up one hallway and down the other, she replied to her brother, "Tearan, I don't think anyone is on the station anymore. We've been keeping an eye on the monitors, and I have yet to see anyone from the Alliance since the first group of soldiers were killed trying to find alternate way into the station."

"Just be careful, will you? I will not allow you to see Mother before me or Dad does. In fact, get back here now. I must be losing my mind. I can't believe you talked me into allowing you to be the lookout *or* the fact that I agreed to it," Tearan said suddenly as she heard, "Prince Tearan, what do you think this could be?"

"What? What is it? What did you find?" she asked her brother.

"Some sort of canister. I'm not sure what it is," Tearan replied "Just be careful on your way back here, all right?" he added just before silencing his personal communications unit.

"You don't have to be so overly protective of me. You know that, don't you?" she yelled at her communicator.

Back inside the lab . . .

"What is that thing?" Tearan asked one of his guild members.

"I'm not sure sir we were able to get inside the vault, but this is all we found," the Korra Guild member replied while holding up the canister.

"Fine, I'll just hold on to it until we can figure out what it is," Tearan said while clipping it to his belt. *It must be a weapon. Why else would there be a clip attached to it?* Tearan thought as he returned to the computers database.

"Phantom, did you hear something?" Michelle whispered as she spun to look down the different hallways.

"Don't worry about the noise. What you heard is straight ahead of us. From this point, I don't want anyone making to much noise," Phantom told them as he placed his back to the wall.

"What are you doing?" a soldier asked him.

As Phantom slid closer and closer to the front hallway, he told them, "We're close to the remaining Pirates." Then, he thought, *What did the idiots do? Take the names off of the doors?*

"How can that be? I didn't see anything marked as 'Bio-Engineering One and Two,'" another soldier said with a hint of anger in his voice as he watched the corporal move closer and closer to the edge of the hallway.

Suddenly, they noticed Phantom raising a single fist. "What . . . what is it?" a soldier asked with fright in her voice. Then, everyone noticed the so-called lieutenants placing a hand over their mouths as the five shuffled to the two sides of the walls. "Sir, what do you want us to do?" Michael asked Phantom as he noticed both Nicholas and Phantom looking around.

"Just stay here, and don't allow anyone to use their weapons. I mean *no one,* for any reason, is authorized to use their weapons for any reason with out me ordering them to," Phantom said just as he ran down the hallway.

"What is he trying to do, get us killed?" Graggen asked Jasmine.

"I don't know, but I do know he will not get us killed," Jasmine replied just as she looked around the corner and noticed Phantom closing in on a female Pirate.

Just as the female Pirate turned to check the hallway a second time, she suddenly felt a hard object slamming into her body, and her feet were no longer touching the ground. Just before the darkness covered her, she heard a faint, sad, "I'm sorry."

"All clear. Let's move out!" Jasmine said while noticing Phantom picking the female Pirate up in his arms. "What are you doing? She's still breathing," Jasmine said as she approached him.

"Let me have that Pirate. I will make sure that she will stay dead," Graggen said with anger in his voice.

"You will lower that weapon before I take it from you," Phantom said while looking at the soldier.

"You can't deny me my vengeance for them killing my little sister. This is my right, and I will not allow anyone to stop me, especially a young hot shot like you," the soldier replied.

"Revenge is one thing, but I will not allow you to kill a helpless, young, innocent woman. Can you tell me how sure you are that this young woman and her Pirate Guild were the ones that killed your sister?" Phantom said as he approached the soldier.

"Boys, are you forgetting something?" Jasmine asked while stepping between the two.

"I will deal with you after this mission is over. Now, let's move out!" Phantom demanded as he turned and walked away.

"I hope your medical is good. The next time you talk to him, I would not make him mad," Jake said as he walked past the soldier.

Twenty floors below Phantom and his platoons, Colonel Calamen and his group entered the hanger. As the colonel looked around, "What happened here?" he said while looking at the empty spaces that once housed their ships. "Jacobs, what is going on? Where are the ships?" he asked while feeling confused.

"Sir, I think I found them, or I'm looking at what appears to have been your missing ships. It looks like the Pirates were able to steal them out from under your nose and then destroy them just so no one could escape," Jacobs answered with an angry tone.

"Alright, I guess we don't have a choice. We'll have use that old SF Ninety-Two. Lieutenant, we'll need someone to cover our movement to that freighter," Colonel Calamen said as he noticed a few Pirates walking around in the hanger.

"What kind of cover fire do you need?" the lieutenant asked while looking through his backpack.

"Anything, I don't care. Just cover us and do not worry about the damage. Do you understand?" Calamen said while pointing to the star freighter.

"All right, how about this?" the lieutenant asked just as he threw a grenade.

Before anyone could ask what kind of grenade it was he had just thrown, the grenade exploded and unleashed a mist. "Put your breathers on. If you inhale any part of that mist, you will fall unconscious," the lieutenant said just as the first Pirate fell to the hanger floor.

"All right people, you heard him. Get those breathers on and then make your way to that star freighter," the colonel ordered just before his face disappeared behind his breather.

A few minutes later, Phantom stopped at a security monitor and noticed an old SF Ninety-Two shuttle launch from the hanger. "Phantom, what is it? What do you see?" Nicholas asked as he noticed a few of the soldiers looking at them confused.

"Nothing, we are almost there," Phantom said as he turned from the monitor and started to walk away.

"Phantom, I need a word with you, please," Nicholas said as he noticed the way he was holding the female Pirate.

"Make it quick," Phantom said as he shifted her weight to make her more comfortable.

"The way you are holding her is the exact way you hold Shamarra when she is unconscious. I'm sorry to notice, but tell me, who is this young woman? Allan, please, I need to know," Nicholas said in a low voice.

"I told you back in the Academy not to call me that. Only my sister can. For the record, the identity of this woman is not of your concern," Phantom said as he walked away.

"Okay, what's made you moody?" Nicholas suddenly spoke out.

"What do you mean? He's always moody. What makes this time any different?" Michelle asked while walking up to him.

"I know he's always moody, but there is something else that has made him even worse than normal," Nicholas replied as his eyes grew wide.

"What? What is it?" Michelle asked when she noticed his eyes.

"Whatever you do, don't make any hostile attempts against that Pirate," Nicholas said as he started walking again.

"Come on, sleeping beauty, it's time to wake up," Phantom said as he looked at her face.

After a short moan, "What happened to me?" the female Pirate asked just before realizing she was in the arms of the enemy. Suddenly, to Phantom's surprise, he heard, "Please don't kill me. I don't know who you are, but don't hurt me," she said with a scared voice.

"Don't worry. I promise you won't be harmed. You're a Jalleen are you not? What is your name?" Phantom asked in soft kind voice.

"My name is Trisha, and yes I am a Jalleen. How did you know? Do I know you from somewhere?" she asked him while looking past the red glow and into his hazel eyes. "You look familiar to me," she added.

"Now, where's Tearan? I know he must be around here somewhere," Phantom said in a low voice.

"I can't take this anymore. Let me kill her. Let me kill her now!" Graggen demanded as he pointed his weapon at her again.

"I have given you an order, and I expect you to follow it. She will not be harmed for any reason, and if you or anyone else thinks that my orders aren't worth following, then I will consider you as a traitor to the Alliance," Phantom said as he stopped in mid-step.

"I don't care about your orders. You will allow me to kill this Pirate," Graggen said as he brought his black furry hand up and aimed his pistol at her.

Before anyone could stop Graggen, Phantom spun around and connected with a tornado spin straight to the back of Graggen's head. "Get up. Get up now. That's an order," Phantom said while looking down at the soldier.

"How can I follow orders from someone that will protect a Pirate? Sir, you're the traitor and not me!" Graggen replied as he lay on the floor motionless.

"Fine then, you two pick him up and carry him. Jasmine, disarm the soldier. Make sure you have all of his weapons," Phantom said in a cold, harsh voice that no one had ever heard before. As he turned and started walking, "If I allow you to kill this young woman, we would be no better than Trayon and his TRI Guild Pirates. Besides, if you had killed her, then we would have been killed," Phantom said just as he turned the corner.

"Sir, what just happened, and what does he mean 'we would have been killed'?" Graggen asked in a confused voice.

"You better be grateful that he just spared your life. He just saved all our lives, you ignoramus. Don't you think before you act? Just look around. We are surrounded by Pirates, and here you are trying to kill a helpless, unarmed, young, female Pirate. Knowing our luck, most of those Pirates probably think of her as either a potential wife or a younger sibling, but here you are trying to kill her," Nicholas said while noticing about one hundred different Pirates with angry looks on their faces and weapons drawn.

A moment later, all four hundred and forty soldiers were standing in front of the door marked as Alpha Omega Delta. As they entered the room, they noticed the room was full of Pirates. Phantom stepped forward. "I'm holding Trisha. Now, Tearan, come out and reveal yourself," Phantom said in a language that the Alliance soldiers had never heard.

"How is it that you know our native language?" a male's voice asked with while showing that he was surprised.

There, between two towering Pirates, stepped a male with bluish-green skin and brunette hair. A moment later, after Phantom closed his eyes, they snapped back opened to reveal Phantom's natural hazel eyes. "Here you go. Now, walk over to your brother. Just watch out for both the Pirate spies and the Mantises that are in the room," Phantom whispered into her ear as he placed her back on her feet.

"Do I know you? Your face looks very familiar to me?" she replied as she started backing away.

"Are you all right, sister? They have not hurt you, have they?" Tearan asked her as she approached him.

"No, they have not. He would not allow them to," she replied just as she heard in a surprised voice, "What is he doing now?" Tearan asked just as Phantom knelt before the two.

"It is good to see the two of you have all grown up, Prince and Princess of the Korralla. If you mind me asking, can you tell me as how King Carrag is doing?" Phantom said while looking up at Prince Tearan and Princess Trisha just as he pulled out a pendent from under his shirt.

"How is it you know so much about us? There is no one in the Alliance or any other factions that knows that much information about our guild," Tearan said while walking up to his so-called enemy.

"I know more about you and your guild than you actually think, my lord and lady. For example, I know three years ago you, Prince Tearan, would wear red, green, and blue clothes. Your sister, Trish, would keep her hair no longer then her shoulders. When your father would introduce the two of you, he would joke around and tell everyone that he has two sons instead of a son and a daughter. Trish always seemed be get mad at King Carrag for doing that," Phantom said with a familiar smile only to Trisha.

"I don't understand why, brother, but I actually feel that I know him somehow," Trisha said with confusion in her voice while wide-eyed.

Suddenly, to everyone's surprise, "All Alliance soldiers, you will shoulder your weapons now!" Phantom demanded while rising to his feet.

"I'm sorry you have more information on us, but I have none on you. Tell me, stranger, what is your name so I may address you properly?" Tearan said while trying to figure out who the stranger was.

"I'm the number one enemy on the Pirate guild's assassination list. My name is Phantom Breaker," Phanotm replied while smiling and looking smug.

Suddenly, Trisha noticed a dark shadow charging for her brother, "Tearan, look out!" Trisha cried out with fear.

Suddenly, Tearan felt a hand pushing him out of the way just as a knife flew past him. "If I still had been standing there, I would have been killed. What is going on here?" Tearan said with a confused look while noticing Phantom had a mantis by the leg.

"Nice try, Mantis assassin. Can you tell all of us what it is that you are trying to do?" Phantom asked out loud.

"My mission is to kill this worthless boy. Can you tell me who it is that will stop me?" the Mantis asked with a harsh, cold voice.

"I will not allow you to harm either the prince or the princess. If you want them that badly, then you will have to kill me first," Phantom said just as he kicked the creature's foot out from underneath itself.

As the creature fell, Phantom shoved his knee into the creature's spine, followed by an elbow connecting to the creature's breast plate. As the elbow connected with the breast plate, everyone heard a loud cracking sound just as the creature screamed out in pain. Before anyone could see what had happened, the Mantis's head exploded. After looking at the lifeless body, everyone in the room looked at Phantom and noticed half his face was covered in the Mantis's blood. "Thank you, but how do you know the move that is only taught to my family?" Tearan asked with wide eyes.

After wiping the blood from his face, Phantom replied while looking at the Prince and Princess, "Hybrid Mantis Assassins—their bite is worse than their bark."

"Please tell us, how do you know our family's favorite attack?" Trisha asked as second time.

"What? You don't remember me from back then?" Phantom said with a hint of confusion as he closed his eyes. Suddenly, he snapped them back open. "Runt!" Phantom finished before anyone else could ask another question.

As soon as he said that, Trisha started to cry. "Can it really be you? We were told that your science shuttle had been destroyed by the Alliance," Trisha said ran to him with her arms extended.

To everyone's surprise, he embraced her. "That's not true. The Alliance saved me just before the science shuttle was destroyed. Tell me, cousins, why are you here? What is it that Trayon is after?" Phantom asked as he felt the tears from Trisha running down his neck.

"I'm wondering if the Drazarian girl made it out alive, as well," Tearan asked with a hint of hope in his voice.

"Shamarra is doing well, actually. She looks like she is nine now. In fact, she has been asking when it would be the best time to see our long-lost cousins," Phantom said just as the Alliance soldiers noticed Tearan making a hand gesture and the Pirates lowered their weapons.

"The royal family is back together once again. Boy, will father be surprised," Tearan said as he held out his hand.

"Phantom, you're kidding me. These two are your cousins? I remember you telling me something back in the Academy, but I never thought that you were serious," Nicholas said while letting out that he was surprised.

"I must know, what is it that Trayon is after?" Phantom asked a second time while looking into the teary eyes of Trisha.

"We have to bring him every new weapon that the Alliance has been working on," Trisha told him just as he heard, "You and your family are nothing but traitors. You will die for this!" a harsh male's voice said.

Before everyone realized what was happening, a knife appeared out of nowhere, flying straight for Trisha's head. "Sister, no!" Tearan yelled out just as he closed his eyes from the fear of losing his younger sister.

Suddenly, to his and everyone else's surprise, a hard, metallic sound echoed throughout the room. "At times like these, it does not pay to climb out of bed," Phantom said as he looked down at Trisha. "Are you all right?" he asked her.

"Yes, but what happened?" she replied as she turned her head and noticed a thin, clear sheet was extending from Phantom's arm.

"How did you do that? What are you wearing?" the harsh male's voice asked.

"It's called a specialized uniform that is designed for one thing and one thing only—hand-to-hand combat," Phantom replied as he rotated her around to his back as his shield disappeared. "Nicholas, Michelle, Jake, Jasmine, and Michael, make sure nothing happens to her," Phantom ordered just as two knives appeared in his hand.

"What are you going to do, sir?" Jasmine asked him as she stepped in front of Trisha.

"I'm going to be taking care of an unwanted pest better known as an assassin," he replied as he started to walk forward.

"These two runts are mine. If they don't finish their mission, then I must kill the boy and take the girl to her husband to be," the harsh male's voice replied.

"Then humor me, will you? What was their mission, and what makes this station so important," Phantom asked him as he walked around the entire group of Pirates.

"This station has a secondary use called 'making new weapons for the Alliance.' This was a joint effort for all the guilds to gain more power beyond the Alliance's imagination. The problem is that you pesky Alliance dogs just had to show up and foil our plans," the harsh male's voice replied just as Phantom walked past him.

"All right, I might believe that story. Now, tell me, what do you mean about Trisha having a husband to be?" Phantom asked as he stopped in front of Trisha.

"The deal was if our mission was successful, then Trayon would be able to over throw our father," Tearan said just as Phantom turned to look at him.

"The second part of Trayon's deal was if our mission was unsuccessful, then I would have to marry his younger brother, Travon. He wants the Korra Guild's rich recourses and personnel," Trisha said just as a tear ran down her face.

Suddenly, he turned and looked deep into her bronze eyes and he touched her chin. "I would rather see you dead than having to know that you are married to him!" Phantom said in a harsh cold voice.

"What? What are you saying, Allan? You know you can't kill her because she is your cousin, and you care for her!" Nicholas cried out in horror.

"I will not have any family of mine married to that man!" Phantom replied with hatred in his voice.

"I knew of a boy in the Alliance Academy who was hated, laughed at, was made fun of, and had no friends just because of the way he looked. That boy was always kind, no matter what the situation was. He slowly started to disappear and reappear during his training, and yet every time I was able to talk with him, he was always worried about his cousins. When I first met him, he had the name of Allan, even though he later changed it. Now, what has happened to that boy that would make you say such things and do such hate-filled things even to your cousins?" Nicholas asked while all the Alliance soldiers looked confused.

"It's all right. My sister and I already know why he acts and talks with such hatred toward one man. Everything that has happened to Phantom was caused by only a single person. I would have killed you myself, sister, except, it is not in the nature of our family or our guild to kill innocent blood, no matter what the cause is," Tearan said as he hung his head in shame.

"You don't have to be ashamed, I would be more than willing to take my own life than to be married to a man that would take a child and turn them into a weapon for his enjoyment," Trisha replied as more and more tears ran down her face.

"Then it is settled. After I deal with the last few remaining spies, I will then kill you myself," Phantom said just before connecting an elbow into an unsuspecting Pirate's face.

"Would he really be capable of killing her? I mean, I know she is a Pirate, but would it be possible to call her 'innocent'?" Jasmine whispered to Nicholas.

Before Nicholas could even say a word, he wrapped his arms around the female Pirate. "Don't worry. I will not allow him to harm you," he whispered into her ear.

"You won't even have a chance of stopping him if he truly wants to kill me. You can let me g—" Before Trisha could finish Nicholas felt her flinch.

"What wrong with you?" he asked while looking down and feeling something warm running down his arm. As he looked at his arm, he noticed some yellow substance there just as Trisha's body fell lifeless. "Phantom, I thought you were joking! Couldn't you have waited until after we had talked some more!" Nicholas demanded as he pulled a dagger from Trisha's side.

"Sorry to disappoint you, old friend, except, I was not the one who did that. I would have killed her in a different way than just assassinating her," Phantom replied just as threw a fist passed a second Pirate's neck.

Suddenly, blood busted out from the area where Phantom's fist had flown past. "Not bad for an Alliance dog Puppet. Now how about trying to kill a real assassin? I was told my predecessor was killed while trying to create an ultimate assassin. Unfortunately, they could only enhance my body by eighty-nine percent," a strange male's voice echoed in the room in reply.

"I was wondering when you were going to reveal yourself. Were you the one that took out the hybrid Mantis's secondary killing knives? Now you just tried to assassinate my cousin," Phantom said with a hint of delight in his voice while looking up after throwing a knife into a third Pirate's head.

"Yes, I am. Is there anything else you would like to tell me before I kill you and then slaughter your fellow Alliance dog soldiers?" the strange male's voice asked in turn.

"What's your name?" Phantom demanded as everyone noticed the red glow of Phantom's eyes had turned green.

"I do not have a name. You could say I was an orphan before I was taken in as a volunteer test subject for Trayon's experiments. Enough talking. Let's get down to business shall we?" the strange male's voice echoed around the room.

"Well, why not? I always wanted to know what it felt like having to fight an enhanced assassin," Phantom replied as a smile appeared on his face while looking up into a shadowy corner.

To everyone's astonishment, a darkly dressed figure suddenly appeared in front of them with the crest of the TRI Guild on his right arm. "Let me guess, you have the other guild crests across your back, right?" Phantom asked as he took a strange stance.

"Oh, ho! What's this? The little puppy wants to dance? Sorry, boy, I don't do dancing lessons!" the dark figure replied.

"Just humor me and let's see how go you think you are," Phantom replied as he motioned with his right hand for the stranger to advance.

"Fine, it's your death. Just remember that I warned you," the assassin replied just as he charged toward Phantom.

Before Nicholas, Tearan, or anyone else could follow the assassins movements, Phantom and the stranger were locked in a struggle of life and death. "Not too shabby for an Alliance puppy. How old are you, boy?" the stranger asked.

"If you must know, I just turned fifteen. What's it to you?" Phantom asked just as he blocked a kick from the assassin.

"Well, happy birthday. I'll make sure to plant flowers on your grave as my gift to you," the assassin said just as he blocked a punch. Suddenly, he felt something worm running down his cheek. *How did that puppy cut me?* the stranger thought as he touched his cheek and looked at the blood.

While grinning, "You must be wondering how I was able to do that, right?" Phantom asked just as he jumped into the air with a fist drawn back for a strike.

"You're not going to stop me, boy!" the stranger replied as he placed both arms into a blocking position.

A few seconds had passed when the stranger realized the attack had not connected yet. He quickly lowered his arms to see what was happening when he suddenly felt a hard object connecting with his solar plexus. "You're too overly confident," Phantom said when Tearan and the rest suddenly noticed the air starting to pick up.

"What did you just do?" Tearan asked his cousin with confusion in his voice.

"First attack of the Elemental Wind—'Pressuring Winds,'" Phantom replied just as a circular motion of wind appeared on the assassin's solar plexus.

"What is this, a child's play thing?" the stranger asked while watching the circle starting to grow.

"I do believe it is called a dirt devil on the desert of Colipsa Three," Phantom replied as his grin grew with the sudden rage of winds. Suddenly, everyone saw the assassin fly off his feet and into a large computer station. "That is why you never underestimate your enemy," Phantom said as the body fell to the floor motionless.

"Phantom, I don't think she is breathing anymore!" Nicholas yelled in horror as he placed her motionless body on the floor.

"Give her here!" Phantom demanded as he picked her up and started to walk toward an emergency medical bay.

"Tell me you can save here. Our father lost our mother four years ago, and now he's about to lose his only daughter," Tearan replied as he followed Phantom.

"Don't worry. She will be fine even if I have to drain every ounce of my life force to save her," Phantom replied just as a hidden door suddenly opened.

After Phantom placed her on the examining table, he pulled out a bag with fluid in it. "What are you going to do with that?" Tearan asked as Phantom ignored the worried tone in his cousin's voice.

"This will cure anything that is wrong with her," Phantom replied just as he shoved a needle into Trisha's arm.

"How long will this take?" Tearan asked just as he heard a commotion outside.

"Will you keep it down? We're trying to save Tris—" Before he could finish, Tearan noticed the assassin's body was missing from the floor. As he looked at both the Alliance soldiers and his own men, he noticed both groups were backing away from something. Suddenly, he heard the door close behind him, followed by, "Where is that low-life Alliance puppy? How dare he. How dare he use such an underhanded trick against me!" the strange male's voice proclaimed.

"Watch out, sir. He has a strange kind of knife," one of the Korra Guild Pirate's told him.

"Bring him out! Bring out that Alliance puppy!" the assassin demanded with blood running down the side of his mouth just as the others backed into the wall.

"Someone just shoot him and get it done with," Tearan replied just as he heard the door open back up.

"Now, what is going on out here?" Phantom asked from behind Tearan.

"The assassin is still alive, and he welding a strange weapon," Tearan replied just as he saw Phantom walking toward the assassin's location. Suddenly, after dropping his hinds at his side, Tearan felt the strange object that had been left inside the locked case. "Phantom, I don't know what this is, but I hope that you can use it," Tearan said as he threw Phantom the silver canister.

"What is it? Do you—" Before Phantom finished his sentence, he suddenly remembered a gift his mother told him about. *Can this truly be it?* Phantom thought as he rotated the object around. Suddenly, he noticed what appeared to be five small sensors on the object. *I wonder what this does?* Phantom thought as he placed his fingers on the sensors.

Suddenly, the entire room heard, "Phantom, this message is only imprinted to your DNA. If you are hearing this recording, that means that either you have found your birthday present from your father and I, or I told you where it was because something dire has happened. This is a new nanotech weapon that your father and I thought you might like. We call it a 'Virbrent Blade.' Once you grasp the canister like a normal hilt, the nanotech exterior will reveal the functions. This is a nanotech sword that is able to cut through most objects. I have also added a special feature to the nannites. There is a switch that will allow you to heat the sword up for a stronger cut. Your father and I hope that this will come in use. Happy birthday, son, and always remember that we love you very much," Jacquelyn's prerecorded voice said just before falling silent.

"Wow, it looks like you have found someone that truly cares about you," Tearan told Phantom just as he noticed Phantom tightening his grip on the cylinder.

"Yeah, I have. Even considering my past, they still love me for me and not what I can do," Phantom replied just as the nanotech cover started to fade away to reveal a hilt.

Suddenly, Tearan and Phantom both noticed the assassin charging toward them. "Phantom, whatever you do, make your next attack count, or we will all be dead!" Tearan told him just as the assassin lifted his blade up over his head for a head-on attack.

As the assassin brought the blade down everyone, they suddenly heard a metallic object hitting the ground. Suddenly, everyone heard the assassin cry out, "How is this possible? This can't be possible! You broke my Cllinirt Blade! This blade is unbreakable! How did you break it?"

To Tearan and everyone else's surprise, Phantom was holding a full length sword in a blocking position. "The only thing that I know is that nothing is indestructible—and I *do* mean nothing," Phantom replied in a harsh, cold voice as he looked the assassin right in the eyes.

After moving as far back as he could, both the assassin and Phantom's eyes focused on one another. "No, this can't be. Stay away.

Just stay away from me. Someone help me! He's going to kill me!" the assassin cried out in horror as he watched Phantom walking closer and closer toward him.

"You tried to kill me," Phantom said in a soft, friendly voice. "You first tried to assassinate my cousin Trisha. Then you turned on both the Korra Guild and my soldiers. After there is no one else left to protect them, you were going to kill Tearan and then finish Trisha off. I will not allow you to hurt my little sister. I will not allow anyone to hurt my little sister ever again. When I see Trayon, I will make sure I give him you regards," Phantom said as he closed in on the assassin.

"No, stop, please, someone help me! He's a monster! He's going to kill me!" the assassin cried out in horror.

"You asked me who I was, so I think I might as well tell you before I take your life," Phantom said as he grabbed the guy and pulled him in close. In a low whisper, "I was once a hostage who watched his family being killed, tortured, branded, forced to kill innocent people against my will, and forced to live as an exile for the rest of my life. Who am I? You really want to know? I was once captain to Trayon's secret arm of elite assassins, 'The Ultimate Assassin,' and your predecessor," Phantom whispered into the assassin's ear.

"No, that is impossible. There has to be a mistake. You're supposed to—" Before the assassin could say anything else his head fell to the floor.

"When did Phantom do that? Nicholas, were you able to see Phantom give that assassin the finishing blow?" Michelle asked with confusion in her voice.

"I didn't see his arm move even an inch," Nicholas replied as he watched Phantom return to the medical bay.

After the door closed, both Tearan and Phantom heard, "What is going on? Why am I in a medical bay?" Trisha asked just after she opened her eyes.

"It's all right. You're fine now. Tearan I will take Trisha and return to the Galaxy Alliance Head Quarters. You can go back and tell Trayon that she was killed trying escape from the station. Once we are back at the Alliance, I will place her under my protection so don't worry. Besides, I know someone that would be happy to see you—to see both of you, in fact," Phantom said as he sat down next to Trisha on the right side of her make-shift bed.

"All right, but what am I going to tell our father?" Tearan asked while sitting on the left side of Trisha's bed.

"Do I get any kind of say to this plan?" she asked the two while trying to sit up.

"No!" they both demanded while looking into a surprised young woman's eyes.

"Phantom, we have a problem!" Faith suddenly blurted out.

"What is it? What's—" Before Phantom could finish his sentence, he heard, "This station will self-destruct in five minutes," the automated voice called out.

"Tearan I will make you a deal. I will give you half of the weapons here, but I will set them to explode the first time someone tries to use them. I want the most dangerous ones, and in return I will give you the blue prints to the Alliance's new fighters. I will not allow them to get away with this. The Galactic Council members are nothing more than idiots. What makes them think that they can do as they please?" Phantom said as he helped Trisha to her feet.

"Deal. Now how are we going to get out of here?" Tearan asked while looking at his sister.

"Faith, open all the hallways from here to the Pirate ships!" Phantom demanded as he picked Trisha and started to carry her.

"By the way, I was not able to tell you, but we still have scientist prisoners. We placed them over in the secondary mess hall. Make sure you take them with you," Tearan added just when he noticed Phantom using his arm computer. "What are you doing?" he asked Phantom.

"Your blue prints and the other information have just been downloaded," Phantom said while handing Tearan a data crystal. "Just do me a favor. Make it look like this station was just a true science station and nothing more," Phantom added as he walked out carrying Trisha in his arms.

"Sir, what is going on?" Michael asked while looking around.

As Phantom looked over at the computer where the assassin had landed, he noticed a red, flashing light. "Somehow, this lab was designed as a secondary command post for the Admiral. I think when I attacked with the elementals and launched the assassin into that computer, somehow he landed on top of the self destruction button. Our new mission is to get the remaining Alliance prisoners out of here. You will find them in the secondary mess hall," Phantom told the soldiers as he turned to Tearan and said, "Cousin, good luck and don't worry about your sister. I will make sure nothing happens to her," Phantom said just before turning around and walking out of the lab.

"Sir, there is no way you will be able to get back to your shuttles," Faith suddenly said into his personal communicator inside Phantom's ear.

"Is there any other shuttle that we can use? I don't care if it's an older ship or not as long as it can fly," Phantom replied just as everyone turned and looked at him with worried faces.

As the alarm sounded, the Alliance soldiers went from a medium stride to an all out run toward the second mess hall. A few moments later, the door to the so-called cell block opened, and there stood a middle-aged woman. "Doctor Sherrie, tell whoever is in there with you that we need to move and move now," Phantom said stopping right next to her.

"Phantom, what is going on?" Sherrie asked with a confused look on her face.

"The station is going to self-destruct. Are you still working on the Eagle's Shadow?" He asked her just as they both heard, "Sir, we have three minutes before everything is destroyed."

"We just finished it yesterday, and we were going to make the test run today. What do you mean 'going to self-destruct'?" she asked him.

"No time. Let's move. Faith, download yourself to my arm computer and erase your programming from the station's computer. Make sure you download everything with your program," Phantom said as he looked into the mess hall and noticed two other scientists sitting at a table.

"All right, you two, you heard him. Let's get to hanger SVH!" Sherrie ordered just before running out of the mess hall.

"Nicholas, take the soldiers to the SVH hanger. I am sending you a map on how to get there," Phantom said into his communicator as he started to walk again.

"Is she a prisoner?" one of the scientists asked as he ran by.

"No, she is a guest. Now just shut up and run!" Phantom demanded just as he started to quicken his steps.

"I've been wondering, what does SVC stand for?" Nicholas asked as he turned the corner.

Suddenly, he heard, "Two minutes before self-destruction. All personal please evacuate now," the automated voice called out.

"Downloading is complete, sir. Phantom, how are we going to be able to get off this station in less than two minutes?" Faith asked from his arm computer.

"The SVH stand for Secret Vehicle Housing. Now stop asking questions and move. Sherrie, if my memory serves me correctly, the SVH is just up ahead, is it not?" Phantom asked as he noticed his soldiers suddenly stopping.

"Yes, in fact, it is right ahead of us now," Sherrie replied just as she bumped into a solder.

To everyone's amazement, there sat an odd-looking shuttle. "What is that thing? It's too big to be a cruiser, and yet it is too small for a small vehicle transport shuttle," Jake asked as he turned to help Sherrie to her feet.

"From the blueprints, this shuttle has room for two fighters and will still be able to get us all home with room to spare," Phantom said as he walked over to the boarding ramp. "I want all of you on board in less than twenty seconds," Phantom replied just as he heard, "One minute left before self-destruction."

After looking at each other, the soldiers started to push and shove their way into the shuttle. A small moment later, Sherrie, Nicholas, Jasmine, and Michelle noticed Phantom placing Trisha into an empty seat. "You will be all right now. Go ahead and try to get some sleep," Phantom said as he buckled her in.

"What are you going to do?" Trisha asked him as he started to stand.

"I will have to fly the shuttle. Don't worry, you're safe—I promise," Phantom replied as he walked toward the cockpit. Just as he reached the cockpit, he jumped into the pilot's seat and began to warm the engines when he suddenly heard, "This is the Korra Guild, and my name's Tearan. The station will self-destruct in a few moments. All vessels must leave the area now," Tearan's voice said over the communications.

"I am Commander Randall. Tell me, boy, where are our soldiers? Where is Phantom?" Commander Randall asked.

"Don't worry. We will be leaving the station in ten seconds. Now get out of here before it's too late," Phantom said over the audio communications only.

As both the Alliance and Pirates' vessels started to leave the area around the science station, they noticed a strange shuttle launching out from one of the station's hangers without an identification responder active. "Sir, we have an unknown shuttle leaving the station. What are your orders?" a female said from the tactical station.

"Don't worry about it. I suggest we worry more on our hyperspace jump instead of that shuttle. Get a hold of Mom and tell her what just happened," Commander Randall replied just as he felt a slight shutter from his ship moving into hyper space.

Now standing on his flag ship, Tearan thought, *Little sister and cousin, please be safe until I see you both again.* "Make the jump now!" he demanded just as he took a seat in the commander's chair.

"Sir, what are we going to do about Trayon?" a guild member asked in concern.

"What do you mean? For the information I found, all that station was, was a normal science station and nothing more. If Trayon does not like that answer, then he can look at the data crystal for himself. That also means that the arranged marriage is off because, for all we know, Trisha was not able to be saved," Tearan replied as a smile appeared on his face.

"Yes, sir, very good," the Pirate said, refusing to pry any further.

CHAPTER 17

WHILE WATCHING THE recruits sparing with each other, he suddenly heard a load crashing sound. A moment later, he noticed a recruit was lying on the floor. "Shoanna, what is wrong?" Lieutenant Ericks asked while walking up to her.

"I don't think I'm ready for any advanced training just yet?" Shoanna said as she started to climb to her feet.

"Why can't you just stop thinking about how to defend yourself and just do it? Shoanna, you are a nice, young woman that can't just let her past go. You are now an Alliance soldier in training, and that means you have a new start in life. Instead of—" Before Lieutenant Ericks could finish, he heard, "Shoanna, why are you in here training? You should be in your room packing!" a male's voice demanded to know.

"I'm sorry. Civilians are not allowed in here. I must ask you to leave," Lieutenant Ericks told the man while straightening up.

"I will not leave without my daughter, and there is nothing that you or anyone else can do about it!" the man replied while walking up to Shoanna.

"Lieutenant Ericks I would like to introduce you to Maulla my father," Shoanna said as she turned to face her father.

"You are coming home right now, and that is the end of it!" Maulla said while grabbing his daughter's arm.

As he started to walk away, he heard, "Ouch! You're hurting me," she cried out as the two started to walk away.

After a few more cries, Maulla heard, "Let her go! You claim to be her father, but yet fathers are not supposed to hurt their children, especially their daughters!" a child's voice demanded.

"What do you know, you're only a child. If you act as disobedient as my daughter does, I truly hope that your father shows you what obedience is. I'm done talking to anyone else. Let's go. Your husband to be is waiting," Maulla said as he pulled Shoanna along with every step he made.

"Guards red alert, one of my recruits is being kidnapped," Lieutenant Ericks called over the communicator just as the alarm sounded.

"You can't stop me from taking my daughter!" Maulla demanded as he turned to face the lieutenant.

"Actually, yes I can because her instructor is not present at the time and I am his fill in. You will let her go before I order these nice people to throw you in the brig," Lieutenant Ericks replied while looking at seven members of the Alliance security personal.

"You would not dare to touch me!" Maulla demanded as he let go of Shoanna's arm.

"Recruit, walk toward me. Guards, if that man makes any kind of movement toward her, I want you to stun—" Before Lieutenant Ericks could finish his sentence, High Grand Admiral walked in with a women dressed as a scientist and a civilian female.

Look at that. She recovered quickly, the civilian thought while walking into the room behind the High Grand Admiral.

On her way back to the lieutenant, Shamarra ran out and wrapped her arms around Shoanna's waist "Everyone, stand down. Recruit Shoanna Malnerva, I think it's time for my niece's nap. Please see to it," High Grand Admiral Calamen said while noticing everyone was standing at attention with a solute except for Shoanna.

"Yes . . . yes, ma'am," Shoanna replied while trying to pull Shamarra away from her waist.

Suddenly, to everyone's surprise, they heard, "I'm not tired. Besides, are you going to allow this old fos—"

Before Shamarra could finish her last word, she heard, "Shamarra! Shamarra, you're only four years old. You need your sleep! Now be a good little girl and do as I tell you to," the High Grand Admiral replied.

"Honey, do as Aunt Kristy says. I will be there shortly to tuck you in," the woman dressed in the scientist's uniform said in a loving voice.

"All recruits will take a rest. We will pick this up in a few hours," Lieutenant Ericks ordered while glaring at Maulla.

Before Shoanna's parents could say a word to her, they heard, "This is my life now, and I don't need you here to tell me what I need to do, father," Shoanna said in a sad voice just before she left the room.

Before Maulla could reply, he heard, "If you ever interrupt my recruits' training again, I will have you thrown off this station, and I don't care if there is a shuttle ready or not! You don't realize how special your daughter truly is, do you?" Kristy Calamen asked.

"Now I understand why she has a hard time feeling confident in herself. I don't care what you say. This is her place. I can tell you this, if her instructor can see in her what I do, than he will not allow her to be quiet! I'm sorry, High Grand Admiral. If you need me, I will be in the medical bay. I suddenly started to feel ill," Lieutenant Ericks said with hatred as he walked past.

"Are you trying to insult me? If there is something you would like to tell me, then you can tell me in a sparring match!" Maulla said as he turned and looked at Lieutenant Ericks with hatred.

"Lieutenant Ericks, don't you have something else you need to take care of?" Kristy Calamen asked as she turned to see the lieutenant trying to suppress a grin. "This topic is done. You will not interrupt any more of Shoanna's training until we are able to talk with her true instructor!" High Grand Admiral Kristy Calamen finished.

"Ma'am!" Lieutenant Ericks replied while saluting. As he turned for the door, he suddenly stopped. "My recruits will be back here in two hours, and when they are, I don't want to see you here! The next time you interrupt my training, I will not allow it to slide!" Lieutenant Ericks said.

"Lieutenant!" the woman in the scientist uniform yelled just as Ericks left the room. A moment later, the door closed. "I would like to apologize to you for his behavior. I think he's been hanging around my son to long," the woman said in a kind voice.

"Maulla and Sholena, I would like you to meet my sister-in-law Jacquelyn. The young child you just met, Shamarra, is Jacquelyn's daughter, and just so you know, her son will be Shoanna's new instructor. I will give you a single warning. Watch what you say and don't make him mad," High Grand Admiral Calamen said with a worried look.

"Can you tell me what kind of a person your son is?" Sholena asked Jacquelyn as she turned to face the woman.

"Telling you how this station works is easy, but trying to describe my son, now *that* is hard. Well, like Kristy says, he can get mad easily, and he is very moody and deadly. Yep, I think those are the only words that I can use to describe him, all right," Jacquelyn said before starting to suppress a chuckle.

"What do you find funny?" Maulla demanded to know as he turned to face her.

"Talk to me like that, and I might just kill you myself before my son can!" Jacquelyn said as she turned and walked out of the room while leaving Maulla with a look that could only say, "What did I just do?"

A few moments later . . .

How dare he talk about my family like that! She isn't just lacking self-confidence, she is totally afraid of him, Jacquelyn thought as the door to her apartment opened. As she walked past Shamarra's room, she stopped and noticed Shoanna was lying next to Shamarra, asleep on the bed from exhaustion. *Poor thing. You're giving it your all, aren't you?* Jacquelyn thought while looking at Shoanna. Suddenly, she heard her communicator chime, "This is Jacquelyn. What can I help you with?" she replied to the chime.

"Jacquelyn, I received a communications from Commander Randall. The Drandon Station has just exploded. He reports that both Jack Calamen and Phantom were able to get away from the station, and they are both heading here," the AI Mom said in a soft, caring voice.

"Can you tell me how soon they will be here?" she replied with a sigh of relief.

"I'm not sure . . . six maybe seven hours if they are taking a cruise through hyper space. Phantom must be back here for the first part of the exams, though, so I don't think that it would be too long before they are back," Mom replied.

"Thanks for the update. I'm exhausted. If you need me, I'll be taking a nap," Jacquelyn replied as she closed the door to Shamarra's room. *You're safe here. Go ahead and sleep,* she thought as she walked toward her bedroom.

"Computer, can you identify that unknown DNA yet?" Odin asked while climbing out from a medical regeneration unit.

"DNA has been confirmed. The unknown DNA is of Atlantian origin. For what I can tell, this DNA matches that of the royal family," the automated voice said.

"Are you sure? How can that be? I was told that there were no surviving Atlantian left," Odin replied with confusion in his voice while looking at the findings.

"I'm seventy-five percent confident about this, sir, but I would like to run further tests before I can be sure," the automated voice replied.

"You're pretty sure that he is of Atlantian origin, but you are also saying that if somehow his DNA had been altered, he could have come up with the same DNA makeup as me," Odin said while trying to figure out who the individual named Phantom truly was.

"Yes, I will try to run a more conclusive test just to be sure," the automated voice replied just as Odin started to hear the chime and beeps from the old computer's mainframe at work.

"Now how will I be able to get away from those people, who ever they are?" Odin thought just as he walked over toward the weapons on the far right side of the wall.

"May I ask what you are planning on doing?" the automated voice asked.

"Well, first things first, you will analyze that DNA I gave you. Second thing on the agenda is I need to get out of here and back into space. The last thing I need to do is get help and stop them from using our old technology for creating more destructive weapons," Odin said as he started to load up with every piece of weapon that was there in the room.

"I'm sorry, sir, the results are inconclusive," the automated voice said as Odin walked over and took the blood sample from the machine.

Suddenly, a few minutes later, Odin started to hear faint sounds. "Computer, can you tell me what is happening?" Odin asked as his eyes flew to the far left wall.

"In a matter of hours, those people will be inside of this room. You better have a plan and get out of here," the automated voice replied.

"I already have one in mind," Odin replied while running over to the analyze machine. After grabbing the DNA sample, Odin then started to run toward the same location where he picked the weapons up. "Computer, open the secondary door, and once it is closed, you will encrypt *all* the activation codes and then shut down!" Odin demanded just as door began to open.

"Sheena, ma'am, we need your opinion on these right away," a male's voice said while walking up the hallway.

"I'll take a look at the data when I have the chance, Nicholi," she replied as she stopped and turned to look at the young man.

"General Glen wants the information in the next hour," Nicholi said. "Now, since I have fulfilled my orders, how about a dinner date, Sheena?" Nicholi added with a lopsided grin.

"Sorry, maybe next time. I better get started before General Glen decides that I'm taking too long," she replied as Nicholi started to walk down the hallway. *Now, why would I want to have a dinner date with someone like you? After all, your uncle is the General,* she thought.

"All right, I will take you up on that offer. I will see you later," Nicholi said just before turning the corner.

Suddenly, Sheena felt a hand cover her face and pull her to the side. "Shhh! If you make a sound, I will kill you. Do you understand me?" a familiar male's voice whispered into her ear.

After shaking her head in agreement, he lowered his hand. "Odin, is that you?" Sheena asked with a sigh of relief.

"Sorry, I didn't realize it was you. I'll need your help if I am to get out of here," Odin told her as he looked up and down the hallway.

"Sure, but only on one condition. You must take me with you," she replied just as Odin released his hold on her.

"I can't—your place is here and mine is with my own kind. This discussion is over," he told her just as he moved back into the shadows.

"What? What's wrong?" she asked when she suddenly heard footsteps approaching her.

"Sheena, who were you just talking to?" an unwanted male's voice asked.

"General Glen, I don't know what you are talking about. I was just on my way to your office," she replied as the general and she started walking down the hall.

"You're lying to me, Sheena, I can tell. What is it that are you hiding?" General Glen asked while turning around to look back up the hallway.

"I swear it was nothing. I was just thinking out loud, is all," she replied while continuing walking around the corner.

I'm sorry. Even if I wanted to take you with me, I just can't. I'm going to need some help with this one. I can't allow them to turn our old technology into their personal arsenal, Odin thought just as he slightly peeked around the corner.

Suddenly, he noticed a few guards walking past his location, and he wiped sweat from his forehead. *That was a close one,* he thought just as he began to sprint from his location to his fighter. *I better use the secret passages before I get caught again,* he thought as he stopped and lifted a secret hatch from the floor. After a sudden splash, he closed the hatch and began to sprint down the half-lit tunnel. *All I need is a few hundred meters, and then I'm out of here,* he thought while checking his distance from the hanger.

As he continued on his way to the hanger, he thought, *I hope my fighter is still there in one piece. If it's not, I'm in serious trouble,* just as he heard "How will you get out of here?" a familiar female's voice asked.

As he turned, he noticed Sheena was standing right there. "Very carefully. Now, what are you doing here?" he asked with a hint of concern in his voice.

"I'm going to help you escape. The main question I have for you is how you are going to stop the military once you've left?" she asked him with fright in her voice.

As he started to walk again toward the hanger, "There is one person I can ask, but no matter what, I'm going to need help," Odin replied as he turned down another corridor.

After looking backward to make sure no one was following them, he noticed a sour look on Sheena's face as he heard, "May I ask who that could be?" she said with a hint frustration in her voice.

"Just a young man I met a few hours ago," Odin replied as he stopped.

"Why did you stop?" Sheena asked just as she heard voices a few meters in front of them.

"We're here. I want you to wait until I have their attention before you exit the passageway. You must not allow them to harness the technology of Atlantis," Odin said as he looked into Sheena's eyes.

"Why? What will happen if they do?" Sheena asked him with confusion in her voice.

Before she could say anything, Odin rushed out into the hanger. *Go. Go on, and don't worry about me,* Sheena thought as she watched the guards running after him.

"Stop, or we'll shoot!" one of the guard demanded just as he took aim.

Without any hesitation, she charged the guard. "No! Stop! You mustn't kill him!" she cried out in mid charge.

Just as the guard turned to see who screamed, her body connected with the guards. "What are you doing? We can't allow him to leave!" the guard demanded just as he noticed Odin climbing up the ladder of his ship.

Within seconds, both Sheena and the guard watched Odin climb the ladder and take a seat in the cockpit just as the canopy started to close. "Don't look at me, just get out of here!" she screamed out just as their gazes connected. With a nod to confirm his understanding, both the guard and Sheena heard the engine roaring to life. *Go! Go on! Get out of here,* Sheena thought just as Odin looked like he was contemplating shutting the engines off.

Suddenly, the engines became louder. "Why did you do that? Don't you understand the general will have you thrown into the brig?" the guard asked with confusion in his voice.

A moment later, the fighter shot out of the hanger. "I know what will happen. I just couldn't stand by and allow you to kill a sole survivor of a lost civilization," Sheena finally said after a few moments in a calm, soothing voice.

On his way back into space, "Sir, what are you going to do?" the AI asked in a worried voice.

"I'm going to need help to stop them. I don't have a choice but to save that young woman," Odin replied as he noticed the color of the sky starting to fade.

Meanwhile, on the Eagle's Shadow . . .

"Sherrie, I thought you fixed the problem with turbulence while flying through hyperspace?" Phantom asked as he felt the bucking and shuttering from the pressure of hyperspace.

"Yes, we have. You just forgot to activate it," Sherrie replied as she started to chuckle and flipped the switch.

Suddenly, the ride smoothed out. "Nicholas, take over as the pilot, and once we are near the Alliance Academy, I will finish piloting the Eagles Shadow," Phantom said as he heard his arm computer beeping at him.

"All right, but where are you going?" Nicholas asked with confusion in his voice.

"I'm going to check out those fighters in the shuttle hanger, and afterward I'm going to check on my cousin," Phantom said after climbing out of the pilot's seat.

After Phantom walked out of the cockpit, he heard, "My name is Sherrie, and I'll be your co-pilot for this flight," the female's voice said from the shuttle's cabin.

A few moments later . . .

"Trisha, how are you feeling?" Phantom asked after waking her up.

"A little more sleep should help me. Do you know of any place that I can lie down?" Trisha replied as she tried to stand.

"Don't try to stand, yet. I have given you the cure and something that would help you heal, but it will take time," Phantom said as he picked her up.

"You don't have to carry me. I'm more then capable of walking on my own," she replied while placing her arms around Phantom's head.

"Just let me carry you to the medical bay. If you try to walk now, you will be seriously harmed," Phantom replied as he walked out of the cargo hold.

"Fine, but the next time you will do as I tell you, or I will have to show you why you should listen to me," she replied just before she heard him blurt out with laughter.

"What? Is everything all right in here?" Michael asked as he ran in from the second cargo hold.

"Yes, everything is fine. Come on, I should get you to the medical bay so you can sleep in a bed," Phantom said after calming himself down.

Wow, he laughs, Michael thought as he walked back into the cargo hold. A few minutes later, he returned to his seat. "Hey, Michelle, have you ever heard Phantom laugh?" Michael asked right out of the blue.

"No, Michael, what made you suddenly ask about that?" she replied with confusion in her voice.

"He laughed. I actually saw and heard him laugh. He doesn't laugh. There is no way that laugh was his, but he did! I saw him actually laugh," Michael said while sounding confused.

"I think you might want to get checked out once we are back at the Academy, Michael," Michelle replied while hearing him mutter.

"I'm fine no thanks to your comment," he replied while leaning back and closing his eyes.

While Michael and Michelle talked, Phantom walked into the medical bay. "Here you are. Now try to sleep, and if you need me, here is a communicator that will only contact me," Phantom replied as he laid her on the bed and placed a communicator in her hand.

"What are you going to do?" she asked while looking drowsy.

"I have a few things that I need to do. You should get some sleep before trying to do anything else," Phantom replied as he stood back up and started to walk for the door.

"Are you going to be here when I wake up? I'm sorry, all of this feels like a dream," Trisha said him while trying to fight to keep here eyes open.

"Yes, I will still be on the shuttle unless there is trouble. Now, sleep and we can talk some more after you recover," he replied in a soft, loving voice as he turned the lights off and exited the room. After standing out in front of the door for a moment, *Now I can look at those fighters,* Phantom thought as he started to walk away from the medical bay.

As walked past both cargo holds heading for the hanger, "Hey, Phantom, I was wondering, were you laughing a few minutes ago?" Michael asked as he and Michelle stepped out form one of the cargo holds.

"I don't know what you are talking about," Phantom replied without looking at them as he continued to walk toward the hanger.

"See? I told you it was only your imagination. Now if you would excuse me, I'm going to take a nap," Michelle replied as she let her hair fall to its normal length.

"Oh, thanks, some girlfriend you turned out to be, honey," Michael replied as Michelle walked over to her seat and leaned back.

"Any time, dear, any time," she replied as she closed her eyes.

That should keep them from eavesdropping from now on, Phantom thought as he entered into the hanger. A moment later, Phantom looked inside of the fighter's cockpit. *I know this system. We had simulations on the prototype last year. I wonder if they realized I threw the test results on purpose,* Phantom thought as he jumped down from the fighter. "Computer, if you need me, I will be taking a nap," he said while walking toward the hanger's exit.

"Affirmative, sir," the automated voice responded.

Four hours later . . .

"Prince Marko, here is your update. We will be at the Galaxy Alliance Head Quarters in about three hours going at this speed," the female pilot said over the interior communications.

"Then pick up the speed! I don't want to wait for three hours!" the Prince demanded as he sat in his seat.

"I'm sorry, sir, at this speed and with an unmarked shuttle, we will not be a target for the Pirates. Remember, your parents received a message that the Pirates will try to abduct you," the female replied just before ending the communications.

"Unknown shuttle, I know what you are carrying for cargo. Surrender it now before we disable your engines."

"There is no way I would ever give you our cargo," the pilot replied as she started to increase the shuttles speed.

"Sir, they're trying to run," a male's voice said over the open communication channel.

"This is the freighter Tango Minka. All Alliance ships in the area, we are under attack by Pirates. I repeat, all Alliance ships in the area, we are under attack by Pirates. We are requesting your immediate help," the female pilot called out over all emergency channels.

"Sir, I'm starting to jam there communications," another Pirate replied just the communications fell dead.

"Nicholas, I think you should hear this," Jasmine said from the communications station as she activated the interior speakers of the cabin. "This is the freighter Tango Minka. All Alliance ships in the area, we are under attack by Pirates. I repeat, all Alliance ships in the area, we are under attack by Pirates. We are requesting your immediate help. This is the freighter Tango Minka. All Alliance ships in the area, we are under attack by Pirates. I repeat, all Alliance ships in the area, we are under attack by Pirates. We are requesting your immediate help," the message looped as Nicholas heard, "The communications just fell silent," she suddenly said with a worried look on her face.

"Go find Phantom and tell him what is going on," Nicholas replied as he looked to see where the communications came from.

After finding out where he was, Jasmine walked into the captain's quarters. There, she saw Phantom asleep in the chair. The way he looked, he had been without sleep for days. *I hate to do this. It looks like he could use the rest,* she thought as she walked toward him. *Oh, how cute. He looks like a little child sleeping like that. I know it's against the rules, but one quick kiss and no one will know the difference,* she thought as she stopped next to him. "Phantom are you awake?" she asked in a normal voice.

Suddenly, to her surprise, she noticed he was taking in his sleep. "Sherrie, why do the controls look familiar?" he muttered as he sat there sleeping.

Oh, look, he's dreaming. How cute, she thought as she knelt down next to him.

"Sherrie, why do the controls look familiar," Phantom asked while jumping into the pilot's seat.

"This shuttle is the HAD—the Hybrid Assault and Defensive shuttle better known as "Eagle's Shadow." We are invisible to radar and sensor locks," Sherrie replied.

"Phantom, wake up! We need you!" Jasmine said as she pulled out red lipstick from her pocket. A few minutes later when it looked like he had not heard her, *Fine, then how about this,* she thought as she started to apply red lipstick to her lips.

"Sherrie, you mean this is the same control system that I saw last month?" he said as he started to role to his right side.

"Phantom, wake up now!" Jasmine demanded as she bent forward to kiss him.

Suddenly, his eyes snapped open, and with a quick motion he pushed her to the floor. "Thanks for the friendly jester, but I think you need to save that for someone more deserving like a boyfriend. No woman should waste a kiss on me," Phantom replied as he stood up.

"Now, did you really have to throw me to the floor?" Jasmine asked as she started to stand.

"Sorry. Shamarra doesn't even wake me when she has a nightmare and she crawls into my bed. If you're coming, I'm on my way to the cockpit," he said as he started to walk toward the door.

He didn't recognize me. How could he have done that without recognizing me? Was that a reactionary reflex, or was it something else? Besides, what was up with that look he gave me when he first woke up? I must know, Jasmine thought while running up to him.

"Sir, we have received a distress call from a freighter that is being attacked by the Pirates," Jasmine finally said after falling into step with Phantom.

"How far away are they?" Phantom asked as his steps started to quicken.

Before she realized what was happening, she noticed he was in an all-out run. "Hey, sir, wait up for me!" she yelled just as she saw him round the corner. *Man, he can move,* she thought as she chased after him.

As Phantom entered the cabin, "Nicholas, update. What is going on with that freighter?" he asked just as he stopped right behind the pilot's seat.

As Nicholas climbed out of the pilot's seat, "The freighter is about three light years ahead of us. I'm not sure how many Pirates there are. All communications fell silent a short time after the distress signal went out," Nicholas told Phantom just as Phantom started to buckle the web harness.

"I want Jake and Michelle on the aft gun turrets, and I want Michael and you on the forward gun turrets," Phantom told Nicholas just as Jasmine entered the cabin. "Jasmine, when I find out the situation, you will take over as the pilot. Next to Nicholas, you are the best among the soldiers here," Phantom added as he started punch the new directions into the navigational computer.

"What happens if there are more than the freight and the Eagle's Shadow can handle?" Jasmine asked him.

"Then I will have to use one of those fighters in the back hanger, won't I?" Phantom added just as he noticed the conversion from hyperspace to real space. "Hold on. Here we go," Phantom said as he heard confirmation that all four turrets just came online.

"What is going on here? Where did all those fighters come from?" Jasmine asked as she counted six fighters and a freighter being attack by twenty Pirate fighters.

"I don't know, but I think it is time that we helped them out. Don't you?" Phantom said.

Before Jasmine and Sherrie knew what was happening, Phantom had unbuckled his webbing belt and was already half way toward the hanger when the two suddenly heard the turrets sound. "Hurry up and take your seat. We are nothing more than a target like this," Sherrie said as she noticed the cruiser turning to meet them head on.

"It's fine. We can out run them," Jasmine replied just as the sound of engines echoed throughout the insides of Eagle's Shadow.

"Doctor Sherrie, open the hanger doors for Phantom!" Jasmine demanded as she took the controls and dodged the first assault wave from the cruiser.

Moments earlier as Phantom ran down the hallway to the hanger, he activated his interior communications with the AI he had stored. "Faith, after I check the fighter's OS system out, I might need you as my co-pilot. Once we engage the enemy, I will need you to send the freighter and their escorts into hyperspace with the Eagle's Shadow,"

"What if the diversion does not work? What will we do then?" Faith asked him.

"Now, have I said anything about a diversionary tactic? I plan on taking as many of those Pirate fighter's out before we have to jump into hyperspace," Phantom said as he dashed into the hanger. As he ran, he heard shot after shot from the gun turrets. *Don't worry. Help will be there shortly,* Phantom thought as he climbed into the fighter.

"Phantom, I heard the engines warming up, so we are opening the hanger door as we speak," Jasmine's voice said over an audio internal speaker inside the hanger.

Great, a fighter that warms itself up, Phantom thought as he placed the helmet on. "I copied Jasmine. If you receive any orders through Faith, I want you to take it as a priority one order," Phantom replied just as the hanger door showed empty space.

"Will do, and good hunting, sir," Jasmine said just before she disconnected the interior speakers.

Now, let's see what this baby can really do, Phantom thought just as he noticed the fighter had already removed itself from the hanger. "Faith, I don't think you will be able to handle this fighter," Phantom said as a smile appeared on his face.

"Who do you think you are? This is Pirate space," a male's voice called over an open communications channel.

"I'm sorry. Your passport has been rejected. You may leave now or be destroyed," Phantom replied to the male's voice.

Before the Eagle's Shadow knew what was happening, a black-and-gray fighter flew pass them and started to engage the enemy. "Now, Faith!" Phantom called just as he dodged the first wave of missiles.

To everyone's surprise, they noticed the fighter maneuvering into a barrel role. "How is that possible? He has never touched that fighter, and yet I have never seen a person maneuver a fighter like that. If Phantom is not careful, he'll redline the engines," Jasmine said as she watched with wide eyes.

"I'm not surprised, considering," Sherrie said as the two watched Phantom charging toward a group that was bombarding the freighter.

"I will not tell you again, fighter, this is Pirate space. Everything in this space belongs to us. You better leave before we decide to kill you, too," a male's voice said.

"Computer, where is that communications coming from?" Phantom asked as he started to increase the fighter's speed.

Without any words, a picture of a red fighter appeared on the indicator. "This is the Galaxy Alliance. You are currently in Alliance space. You will disengage and leave before I decide to change my mind," Phantom replied.

"Oh, and who is this I'm speaking to?" the male's voice replied after a short but harsh laugh.

"Sorry, I don't have a rank. I guess you can call me a recruit that somehow was separated from his unit," Phantom replied as his grin started to grow.

As Jasmine looked at Sherrie, "What do you mean? How is that possible?" she asked with confusion in her voice.

"Sorry, I didn't say a word. You're just hearing things," Sherrie said not realizing that she had accidently spoken out loud.

"Sorry, sorry, how can you sit there and tell me that I didn't hear what you said? You know something, and I want to know what it is," Jasmine said as she turned her attention back to the battle.

"I don't know much, but what I *do* know is that the harder he pushes himself, the faster he learns the new system. You should have seen him in the simulations. The odd part was that he asked to see the manual for the controls. When we started the simulation training, he was able to maneuver the fighter better than the other candidates. He was able to do things that the other candidates could not," Sherrie said while smiling. Suddenly, she looked at a light indicator that showed the readouts on the fighter. "What? How can this be? The fighter should not be able to do that!" Sherrie said wide eyed.

While the two were puzzled, "Computer, increase the fighter's speed by ten percent and activate multi lock indication on those Pirate's fighters as an enemy and that freighter as an ally. Computer, lower the true fighter's helmet. Acknowledge all orders," Phantom said while taking a normal helmet off. Before the computer could acknowledge the orders, seven Pirate fighters started to charge toward Phantom just as his fighter's speed started to increase again. As the helmet lowered onto Phantom's head, he lowered the visor to it. *Now, let's see if they can keep up*, Phantom thought just as he read all the acknowledgements from the computer. A moment later, Phantom plugged a cord from his arm computer into the fighter's computer. "Faith, I want you to keep track of all of those Pirate fighters. Tell me when we have been targeted," Phantom said.

"Yes, sir. At the moment, seven fighters are attacking the freighter and nine fighters are after us. The Eagle's Shadow is currently under attack from the cruiser," Faith replied.

"No, this can't be! How is he doing this?" Sherrie said as she stood up and slammed her hands onto the co-pilots control panel.

"Um, what's wrong?" Jasmine asked just as she dodged a set of begrudges of cannon fire and missile attacks from the Pirates.

"He has already maxed out the fighter's speed, and yet his speed is increasing," Sharrie said with confusion in her voice.

"You're telling me that Phantom was able to bypass the limitations and has maxed out the fighter's capability? Does that mean the fighter will explode?" Jasmine asked with a worried voice as she watched the Pirate's fighters closing in on Phantom's fighter. Suddenly, they noticed Phantom placing the fighter into a forward spin just as he launched eight missiles toward the oncoming fighters. "What is he doing? We need to help him," Jasmine said while looking amazed at his flying.

"Hold on, we are receiving new orders. We are to escort the freighter to the Alliance Station Academy," Sherrie said while reading the new orders that had just appeared on the tactical station.

"Prince Marko, we just received orders from an unknown source to jump into hyperspace. We are to head straight for the Alliance Space Station. What is your order, sir?" the female pilot said over the interior speakers.

"Do it. I just hope the person that told you to do that is capable of handling those Pirates," Marko replied as he saw a Pirate's fighter suddenly explode from a missile.

Within a single minute, the Eagle's Shadow watched the freighter disappear into a blurry white light. "I hope he knows what he's doing," Jasmine said just before noticing the area starting to blur out of existence.

As the Pirates continued to press their advantage, Phantom slowed the fighter down. "Computer, on my command, you will release the spare parts from their containers and release hidden mines," Phantom told the computer while grinning. *This will teach them a thing or two. The next time they think about messing with anyone, they should truly find out who the pilot is,* Phantom thought just as he heard his alarm echo through the cockpit.

"Now we have him. All fighters, fire!" a male's voice called to his fellow pilots.

"Don't allow even a single piece of that ship to escape," a familiar voice replied.

While Phantom heard the enemy pilots making jesters at killing him, he watched the missiles approaching his fighter quickly. "Computer, now release the flash decoys followed by the extra parts and mines," Phantom ordered just as he finished typing in his Alliance Space Station's location for hyperspace jump.

Suddenly, the Pirates noticed a large explosion and bright lights. "It looks like we succeeded in destroying that fighter, sir," a female's voice said while looking at her fuel level. "I'm returning to the cruiser. I'm leaking fuel somewhere," the pilot added as she veered away from the rest.

We'll check the wreckage, and then we'll be returning, ourselves. I will see you back on the cruiser," the pilot of the red fighter replied as he approached the debris field.

Suddenly, to the cruiser and the single fighter's disbelief, the entire fighter Squadron just disappeared with a bright flash. "How, how can this be possible? Commander, can you hear me? Commander, please respond. Can you hear me? What has happened?" the female pilot asked while only hearing static as a response.

"Just give up and return to the cruiser. We will head back to the base," a male's voice replied after awhile.

"Travon, sir, what about my squad members?" she asked him as she approached the hanger.

"What about them? They're dead. Once you've secured your fighter, I want you to get some rest. I'll visit you later," Travon replied while walking away from the communications station.

"Oh, Commander, you will. I'll be looking forward to it," her voice replied just before the channel fell silent.

"The commander must be feeling awfully lonely. I can't believe he just came out and said that," the communication officer replied to his partner.

"I want this cruiser back at the TRI Guild's headquarters now!" Travon demanded just before exiting the bridge.

"Ma'am, I received a report from Faith. Phantom and his group have made it off the science station before it exploded. His group had just engaged a group of Pirates that were attacking a freighter and her escort. Both the freighter and her escorts survived—barely. Phantom and his group are escorting them here as we speak," the female communications officer said after a message had appeared on her screen.

"All right, I will let High Grand Admiral Calamen know of the situation. Now what about the High Priestess? Have you been able to locate her yet?" a female's voice said.

"Yes, Lieutenant Major, the High Priestess is currently in the officers club enjoying a meal," the female communications officer added.

"Fine then, I will notify the High Grand Admiral both the special package and her nephew are on their way here," the lieutenant major replied just before leaving the control room. Suddenly, the tactical officer noticed an unknown fighter and an unknown cruiser that just appeared in the system. With them came six fighters and a freighter showing identification as being from Molios System. "I think we should get the lieutenant major back here for this one," the male at the tactical station reported.

"This is field Commander Lieutenant Jasmine with the Eagle's Shadow requesting permission to land myself and the 'chuckling,'" a familiar voice said over a communication channel.

"Request granted. You might want to tell your fighter pilot to slow down. They're heading toward the hanger awfully fast," the communications officer said as she noticed the unknown fighter designated as "chuckling" shooting passed the Eagle's Shadow toward the main hanger.

"I will allow you to tell Phantom what he can and can't do," Jasmine replied with a small chuckle before disconnecting from the open channel.

What? Phantom is piloting that strange fighter? the communications officer thought as she hurried to open the hanger doors before Phantom and the fighter became a permanent, black scorch mark on the station's exterior.

Before the hanger doors were completely open, the fighter had already cleared the doors and started to land. Phantom reached over and disconnected the cord from the fighter's computer. "Faith, well done," he said out loud as he allowed his back to slam against the seat.

"Thank you, sir, but your quick thinking and piloting skills were what really saved us—not me," Faith replied with what appeared to be confusion in her voice.

"No, Faith, a pilot, as well as a commander, is only as good as those who are willing to follow his orders. That even includes me," Phantom said as he lifted the canopy and started to climb down from the fighter.

"Mac, who do you think that hot shot is? Why did the pilot fly in here as fast as he did? He could have killed us," a young male's voice asked while he turned to look at his middle-aged boss.

Before the young man knew what to do, he noticed Mac walking toward the dark figure who was climbing down from the fighter. "Who do you think you are—"

Before Mac could finish his sentence, he heard, "Mac, calm down. It's not like you haven't seen me fly even faster in here," the stranger's voice said just as Mac noticed the man starting to take his helmet off.

"Phantom, is that you?" Mac asked as a familiar face appeared from behind the helmet.

"Yes, Mac, and when you see Sherrie, I need you to give her this back and tell her that I'm sorry for ruining the insides of that fighter," Phantom said as he handed his old friend the helmet.

"So it was that bad, then? You know you can always talk to me," Mac said while looking at Phantom's expression.

"Yeah, the mission went that badly," Phantom replied while think of all the soldier's lives that had been lost and the stench of blood from his soaked cloths and hair.

"Phantom, there are more people than just you in the Alliance. You don't have to try and save the galaxy all by yourself," Mac replied as he noticed Phantom running his hand through his hair.

A moment later, he pulled his hand away from his hair and looked at it. Before Mac could even ask, Phantom flicked his hand just as multiple colored liquid flew from it. After a few minutes of silence, "Yes, Mac, I know that, but it seems like I'm the only one that can save the galaxy," Phantom said as he started to walk passed his old friend.

"I'll see you later, kid, and we can *really* talk then," Mac said.

Phantom waved hand his hand in return and said, "We'll see. Bye for now."

As Phantom walked off, Mac thought, *Either you're one lucky fellow, or you're the unluckiest of people that I've ever known.*

"Sir, look at that freighter. Who does it belong to?" one of his crew members asked.

After looking at the freighter and the fighter escorts, "That symbol you see on both the fighters and the freighter? That symbol is the crest from the System Molios, and for what I have heard, we are expecting the youngest Prince from the royal family on Molios today," Mac said just as both the freighter and an unknown cruiser landed in the hanger.

A few moments later, "Mac, have you seen Phantom? He's acting weird," Jasmine said while running down the ramp.

"Yeah, I think he's going to get cleaned up. By the way, here the helmet for that fighter. He says it needs a clean-up job," Mac said while handing Jasmine the helmet.

"I'll take that," a female said while walking up to Jasmine and Mac.

"Sherrie, I presume? Phantom says you need to have the fighter cleaned up, and same thing for the helmet," Mac replied just before he turned and started to tell his mechanic crew what they need to do.

CHAPTER 18

AN HOUR LATER...

"Phantom, you need to get to your hand-to-hand combat class," the AI mom said as Phantom started to take his ragged shirt off.

"I could use a clean up, but it looks as if my new uniform has now arrived. Fine, I'm on the way, but I want to observe the student for this week before I start the actual training," Phantom replied as he walked out of his apartment.

As he walked down the hallway, a few of the soldiers walked out of the mess hall and were talking. "Did you here what the major did to that recruit, brother?" one of the soldiers asked the other.

"Yeah, our uncle is not a person to mess with. I hear that this pathetic station academy had a soldier graduate from here with the title 'The Best Hand-to-Hand Fighter.' What I think is that they are trying to scare us," the other soldier replied.

"Excuse me, I just arrived. Can you tell me what happened?" Phantom asked while stopping in mid step and looking at the two soldiers.

"There was a brat that tried to get our little brother kicked out of the academy exams. Our uncle tried to talk with her, and she started to disrespect him, and then she tried to attack him. When he tried to defend himself, a recruit intervened and was hurt because of it. If I were in charge of this station, that brat and her family would be relocated to another post," the second soldier said.

"So your uncle defended himself, right? When he tried to stop the child from hurting him, he some how injured a recruit. Am I right?" Phantom asked with anger in his eyes.

"Yeah. So? What's it to you?" After looking at the rank on Phantom's uniform, he said, "Corporal, tell me why are you getting so defensive? I'm a lieutenant, and I think that the brat deserved what she received for intervening in something that did not apply to her," the lieutenant replied with disgust in his voice.

"I take it that you are both newly graduated from the Planetary Academy. If I were you, I would be careful with they way you talk around here, or the best fighter on this station might show up and teach you boys and your uncle a few things in hand-to-hand combat," Phantom said as a lieutenant colonel started walking toward them with a salute.

After the lieutenant and his brother realized Phantom hadn't saluted the lieutenant colonel, "What, are you insane? She is a higher ranking officer than you are. You're supposed to solute her," the younger brother of the two replied.

"One last question, if you don't mind. What are your names?" Phantom asked while looking at the lieutenant colonel.

My name is Gronnica, and this is my little brother Cronnicer. Tell me, what is you name, recruit?" Lieutenant Gronnica demanded to know.

"One, he's not a recruit, and he needs to get moving, don't you?" the lieutenant colonel said as she pointed down the hallway.

"Yes, fine, all right, Jolania. You know you don't have to talk to me like our aunt and Mom does," Phantom said wile walking toward the far hall way.

"Is that any way to talk to a lieutenant colonel? Before you leave, what is your name, Corporal?" Cronnicer yelled at Phantom as he continued to walk.

"Hey, cousin, I'll see you later, all right, Lieutenant Commander?" Phantom said just before he turned the corner.

Suddenly, from another direction, Phantom heard, "Recruit, slow down before you hurt yourself again," Jolania's voice ordered just as he heard, "Yes, ma'am," a female's voice replied. As the recruit ran past, Phantom heard two male's voice breaking out in a hard laugh. *I think those two need a lesson in how to treat my sister and other people with respect,* Phantom thought as he stopped and watched the recruit running down the hallway. A few moments later, he started to walk toward the training room labeled "Training Room A" once again. As he approached the room, he noticed two soldiers standing in front of the doorway. "What is going on here? Why do we have the Planetary Academy personel on the station?" Phantom asked as he walked up.

After turning to see who had spoken to them, one of the soldiers recognized the person. "Corporal Breaker, Phantom, what are you doing back here?" one of the soldiers replied.

I'm here to see what my so-called recruits have learned in hand-to-hand combat so far," Phantom replied as he stopped in front of the two.

"Hey, brother, who is this?" the second soldier asked with confusion in his voice.

"Sorry, Phantom, my young friend, I would like to introduce you to my little brother, No-li-congen, but I call him Gen. Gen, let me introduce you to the best soldier the Alliance has ever had," the first soldier said.

"Come on, Lieutenant Sergeant Dra-li-ta. Dra, I'm not that good of a soldier. I have been lucky when it came to my training, and now I think that the Alliance council has decided to give that training to the new recruits," Phantom said while looking around at the Planetary Academy personal.

"Have you been told High Priestess Tralinea has returned to the station? Also, can you tell me what your last few missions—"

Before the lieutenant Sergeant could finish, all three suddenly heard, "If our council had control of this station, these recruits would be a lot stronger, and did you know the new hand-to-hand combat instructor for the station is a recruit himself?" Someone in group of four planetary soldiers said.

"Well, that must be impressive for a lonely recruit to become the top hand-to-hand combat of the Alliance—"

Before Phantom continued, he heard, "Sir, what are you doing? Are you trying to make the Planetary Academy Alliance hate the Space Station Academy Alliance even more?" Dra asked in a low and confused voice.

"How about we all meet in the training room to see this new instructor?" Phantom finished as a smile appeared on his face.

"Why should we listen to a Station Alliance memeber? How about you listen to me? We will never listen to a filthy Station Alliance member! Good day!" one of the soldiers replied.

As the four soldiers started to pass them, both Phantom and Dra noticed Gen's face starting turn red. "Do you even know who this—"

Before Gen could finish, "Just let it go, little brother, just let it go," Dra said while placing a hand on his brother's shoulder.

"Do as you're told. They are not worth the trouble the three of us would get into when it should only take one of us," Phantom said as he ran his hand through his hair and then looked at it.

"Is that blood, sir? Are you bleeding?" Dra asked while looking at the discolored fluid on his hand.

"Don't worry, it's not my blood. I need to be more careful when I slaughter my enemies," Phantom replied as he shook his hand and the blood flew off his hand on to the floor.

With a shocked look, both Gen and Dra noticed Phantom walking toward the information board. Dra heard, "What does he mean when he slaughters his enemies?" Gen asked while turning to look at his brother.

"I'm not sure what he means by that," Dra replied just as Phantom stopped in front of the information board.

After a few deep breaths, Phantom activated the information and started to look for his training room. Without thinking, Phantom tapped a spot on his shirt. A moment later, his uniform went from a normal soldier's uniform to a civilians outfit. Suddenly, Phantom heard a male's voice say, "Slow down before you hurt—"

Before the sentence could be finished, Phantom suddenly heard, "Watch out! I can't stop!" a female's voice yelled just as Phantom turned to look at the person yelling. Before Phantom could finish, the turn he suddenly felt something or some one colliding into him.

As he finished the turn and looked down, Phantom noticed a young woman lying on the floor. As he bent over, "I think you should be more careful next time and walk instead of run," Phantom said while holding his hand out.

"I'm sorry, it's just that I'm running late to my hand-to-hand combat class," the young woman replied just as she took Phantom's hand and started to pick herself up. A moment later, after looking at the young man who helped her to her feet, "By the way, I'm Shoanna. Are you a new recruit?" she asked while looking at him.

"You can say that. I'm Allan, Allan Martin, and can you tell me why you're staring at me?" the young man asked just as he heard the computer shut off.

"I like your different colored hair. Did you change the color of your hair, or is that all natural?" she replied just as she noticed that she had been blushing.

"I'm looking for the hand-to-hand combat training room. Do you know where it is?" Phantom asked just as he activated the computer again.

"I can take you. I was on my way there," she replied just she moved her hand through her hair.

"Can you tell me why you're trying to cover up that almost-healed scar?" Phantom asked her just as he noticed her face went into shock.

"How did you know?" she asked him as she started to walk down the hallway.

"That's easy. You tried to cover the scar up by moving your hand through your hair and placing the hair over that particular spot. Will you tell me what happened?" Phantom asked while turning back to the computer.

"Sure, but my question is, are you coming?" she asked him while turning around to look at him.

As he looked up at her, he noticed that she started to blush again. "Sure, as long as you know where we need to be," he replied in a confused voice while looking at her red face. "Are you feeling all right?" he asked her just as started to walk toward her.

"I'm feeling fine, and the training room that you need is the training room labeled 'Training Room E,'" she replied in a snide voice as she started to walk away.

At least she is doing better, Phantom thought just as he watched her walking away.

"Hey, Phantom, is that you? Oh, man, it's been a while. How are you doing?" a female's voice said from behind him.

"Oh, hi, Jessica. How are things in the infirmary?" Phantom asked after turning around to see a familiar face standing before him.

"I was on my way to the training room to tell Shoanna's instructor to take it easy with her training until she is fully healed. But since you're here now, my job is done," Jessica said as she and Phantom started to walk.

"Don't worry. She will be fine, and I don't want the recruits to know who I am just yet. Tell me, why is the Planetary Academy Alliance here?" Phantom replied as he turned his focus back to the different soldiers walking passed them.

"The Galactic High Council is starting the written test this week for the elites. For my understanding it is the same test you took six months ago. Now, tell me, you were the pilot of that new fighter, right?" she asked in an excited voice.

"Yes, I was," Phantom replied as they continued to walk down the hallway.

"Tell me, how did it feel?" Jessica asked with more excitement as she stopped.

As he stopped and turned to look at her, he stopped to think for a few minutes. "If I had to compare it with anything, I would say the Vortex. The Vortex was designed to fly thirty percent faster then anything the fleet has to offer. Now the new fighter seems to move twenty percent faster then the Vortex. That's fifty percent faster then anything that the Alliance has. The Vortex was designed to maneuver thirty percent more efficiently than the other ships. The new fighter is also twenty percent more efficient then the Vortex. All in all, I would say that the new fighter is fifty percent better then anything the Alliance has to offer," Phantom said with a hint of appreciation. *But once I'm able to look at the designs for the new fighter, I think I will be able to make it even better,* Phantom though as he watched Jessica walk toward him.

Who does that man think he is to question me? she thought as she made her way to the training room. Suddenly, she found herself at standing in front of the training room door, and after a few deep exhaled breaths, she thought, *Here we go. Just another day. Nothing happened. It's just another day.* As the door opened, she walked into the room. She suddenly heard, "Look, it's Shoanna! Look, everyone, it's the fool!" a male's voice suddenly yelled out.

"Nock that off!" Lieutenant Commander Ericks ordered. After walking over to the young woman, he said in a low, kind voice, "Shoanna, go ahead and take your seat." Suddenly, he turned to face all the recruits. "I have a few things I need to finish up for your new instructor, and then I will be ready to teach you a new style, and we will have a guest that will help out for today. For now, just sit there and behave yourselves, or you can practice your basics until I'm done," Ericks said just as Shoanna walked over to her seat.

"How are you feeling, Shoanna?" a young child's voice asked.

When Shoanna turned to her right, she replied, "I'm feeling fine, Shamarra. Thanks for asking. So what have I missed?"

"I wish my brother were here to teach those Planetary Academy Alliance guys a few things about hand-to-hand combat," Shamarra replied while looking at a group of Planetary Academy Alliance members.

"Hey, look, it's the Station Academy Alliance recruits. I know, how about we teach them how to fight," a lieutenant said while walking up to the recruits.

"Sure, I'll fight with you," a male recruit replied while smiling.

"Shoanna, isn't he the one who injured you?" Shamarra asked while looking at the lieutenant with hatred.

"Yeah, he is," Shoanna replied with a hint of fright in her voice.

"Oh, look, it's our favorite recruit. Do you want to learn to fight some more?" the lieutenant said just as he turned to his friends and started to laugh. As he approached Shoanna, Shamarra noticed a frightened look starting to appear on her face.

"Are you all right?" Shoanna asked while starting to feel a little worried herself.

"Don't worry about me. As long as that lieutenant leaves you alone, then everything should be fine," Shoanna said while placing a hand on Shamarra's shoulder. After looking at the lieutenant for a few minutes, Shoanna stood up. "I will spar with you this once, but after this is done and over with, you will leave us alone," Shoanna said while walking out on to the mats while Shamarra returned to her school work.

Suddenly, everyone heard the door opening. "No, the lieutenant will leave the training room right now. The next time you pick on anyone, I will medically discharge you from the Alliance," a female's voice said while walking into the room.

"Who do you think you are?" the lieutenant asked while turning around to see who spoke.

"My name is Jessica, and I'm a nurse for the Alliance. Unless you really want to see what I said would come true, then I suggest that you leave. Leave now!" the woman said as she walked passed the lieutenant.

"What is this Alliance going to? Egotistical morons?" the lieutenant said to his friends as they turned and started to walk out. Suddenly, the lieutenant and his friends stopped at the door. He then turned around and noticed the recruits starting to act normal again. "Look at them. They think that they are better then you or I," the lieutenant said while standing in the doorway.

"I would leave the recruits alone for now on," a familiar male's voice said from behind them.

After turning around and noticing the familiar face of the corporal they spoke to earlier, "Oh, look, it's the puny corporal," the lieutenant said while the other three started to laugh.

"How about joining me back into the training room? How about it, children?" the young man said while walking into the room.

From inside the instructors' office, Lieutenant Commander Ericks started to hear a loud uproar from the recruits. After walking out of his office, "What is going on out here?" he asked just as he noticed Phantom walking toward the bleachers.

"Now since you're here—"

Before Lieutenant Commander Ericks could finish, he noticed Phantom giving him a look that told him, "If you say anything, you will regret it." While walking, he noticed four planetary academy graduates walking into the room, and he was thinking, *What does he have planned for those graduates?* As the lieutenant commander continued toward the recruits, he noticed Phantom was standing by the bleachers. Before he could ask what was going on, Phantom touched a finger to his lips. "Alright, everyone, you should start reviewing your basics. Just remember this is practice, and you should not hurt each other. I think you graduates should stay here, and maybe you could give them a few pointers," Lieutenant Commander Ericks said while keeping his eyes on Phantom.

"Sorry, my name is Allan, sir. What can I do?" Phantom asked with a smile appeared on his face. Suddenly, Shamarra's head shot up and right there, in flesh and blood, stood her brother. Before she could say anything, she watched him walk over to her. "And what's your name, kiddo?" he asked as he moved toward her.

"That's far enough. This is Shamarra, and you will not harm her," Shoanna said while stepping between Phantom and Shamarra. Suddenly, she watched Shamarra walk past her with a smile on her face. "All right, what's made you happy all of a sudden?" Shoanna asked with a confused voice.

"Stop talking and begin your exercise. Now get to work," Lieutenant Commander Ericks told them just as he noticed the graduates walking over to another recruit. As the lieutenant commander walked toward the lieutenant and his three friends, he thought, *Now what are they up to?*

As the lieutenant commander closed in on the small group, he heard, "I'm surprised that your mother and father are allowing the Station Academy to train you. I think you should talk to our uncle and transfer to the Planetary Academy," the lieutenant said just as the lieutenant commander stopped right behind them.

"Just because you are from the Planetary Academy does not mean that you know what you are talking about," Ericks said just as he noticed Phantom taking a seat on the bleachers.

"I wish they would just leave the station until they learn what manners are," Shoanna said just as she noticed the other recruits started to pair off.

"I don't care who your father or uncle is. Take a seat over on those bleachers. Now, the rest of you should get to work," Lieutenant Commander Ericks said while turning and walking back to the instructor's office.

"Allan, wasn't it? Come on, you can practice with me," Shoanna said while walking over to an unused spot on the mats. "Allan Martin, did you hear me? I need you to stand over here," she said while placing her hands on her waist.

"Huh? Oh, sure, just don't go too easy on me," Phantom replied while looking at Shamarra. After touching his hand to Shamarra's cheek, he walked onto the mats. After a few minutes, "Now what should I do?" he asked her just as his smile disappeared.

"Just show me what you are capable of doing," she replied just as she dropped down into a basic stance. "Ready or not, here I come," she said just as she threw a punch. Just before the punch connected, Phantom side-stepped to the left. *How was he able to read my attack?* she thought just as she jumped up with a spin kick. To her surprise, he dodged the attack by bending backward, followed by a right-sided side flip. *How could he do that? Did I show him what I was going to do?* she thought just as he landed on all four. "Come on, you must counter my attacks with your own attacks," she said wide-eyed.

"Not too shabby," Phantom said as he started to stand up from his crouch. As he started to walk toward her, he placed his hands behind his back. "Now stop playing around and show me what you are able to do," Phantom said just as a small flash of light escaped from his eyes.

"What was that?" Shoanna asked while taking a step back. Without another word, she started to charge him. As Phantom looked around, he noticed half the recruits were watching Shoanna and his match just as he ducked, dodged, and blocked Shoanna's punches, kicks, jabs, and her unsuspecting tornado kick. Attack after attack, Phantom dodged her attempts with ease, just as he heard her say, "What is wrong with you? You have to counter me."

"Stop holding back and connect a punch or something, will you?" Phantom said while looking and waiting for Shoanna to catch her breath.

Suddenly, they heard a loud thud just before Shoanna turned to look see what had just happened. They noticed a recruit sliding down the wall. To everyone's surprise, Shamarra ran over to her brother's side. "Hick is out again. Charles, you know you're better then he is!" Shamarra demanded while looking at the recruit.

"Well, I'm sorry that there is no one here that can touch me," the recruit said as he noticed Allan walking up to him.

"I'll spar with you," Phantom told him as a grin appeared on his face.

After looking Allan up one side and down the other, "Sure, except, I will only spar with you if it is full contact," Charles said as he started laughing. "I'm sorry. Allan, right? How can you, a brand new recruit, think that you are a challenge for me?" Charles finally said.

"What's the matter? Are you an Earthling?" Phantom said as he walked over to the middle of the mats.

After a few minutes of the recruits laughing at him, Charles walked over to his cousin. "You know you can call me what ever you want, but I would kill you. Sorry but I will have to decline," Charles said as he turned to face Phantom.

"Fine, then. If you won't face a challenger, I will have no other choice but to take this to your superiors and have you decommissioned from the Alliance," Lieutenant Commander Ericks said just as he stopped next to Phantom. "Phantom, I don't understand what you're planning, but that recruit's father is a lieutenant colonel, and his uncle is the general of the Planetary Academy," Ericks said in a low voice.

"So what? That just means sooner or later I will have a run in with both of them. Acting as a recruit is helping me to see how irrigate the recruits truly are," Phantom replied while glaring at Charles.

Before anything else could be said, they heard, "How dare you threaten me. Both my uncle and father outrank you, and if you do that one more time, then I will have you decommissioned from the Alliance," Charles said with hatred in his voice.

"Neither one of them can save you if your instructor decommissions you. I don't care if your father and uncle are in command of the entire Galactic Alliance or if they are the sole donators to the Galactic Alliance payroll. Fight me or leave the Galactic Alliance in shame," Allan said with a hit of arrogance in his voice.

Meanwhile, in the hanger as an old SF Ninety-Two freighter landed, Mac and a group of security personal started to approach the old freighter. "Lower the boarding ramp and prepare to be boarded!" the commander of the security group demanded.

As the ramp lowered, the security group and Mac suddenly heard, "Stand down! I'm Colonel Calamen. We will be disembarking shortly," a familiar voice said over the exterior speakers as they heard a second set of foot steps.

Before anyone could ask any questions, they heard a hard, mature laugh erupting. "Like father like son. I guess this is why Phantom is the way he is," Mac said while laughing.

"I don't understand, sir," a lieutenant in the security group asked in confusion.

"Well, Phantom is the kind of person that if he can't get back to his fighter or if it was destroyed, he would find another way back here," Mac said as he turned and started to walk toward his work station.

A few seconds later, Colonel Calamen walked down the ramp as five soldiers ran over to the shuttle. "Sir, we'll escort the prisoner to the brig," the lieutenant said as he brought his blaster to bare, just as a strange-looking, young woman, walked down the Eagle Shadows ramp.

"I would lower your weapon before you make Phantom mad," Jasmine said as her foot touched the hanger's floor.

"What are you talking about? Why would Phantom get mad at me?" the soldier asked while looking confused.

"Sir, I would like to introduce you to Trisha. She is Phantom's cousin and guest while on the station," Jasmine said while grinning.

"Speaking of my son, where is he?" the colonel asked after looking around and not seeing his son's face.

"He is in the training room with the recruits," Mom answered.

"He's what?!" the colonel cried out just as he started running toward the elevator's door.

"What is he worried about? For what I can tell, my cousin can handle himself very well," Trisha said while looking confused.

Suddenly, the hanger went up in laughter. "No, no, the colonel isn't worried about what the recruits will do to Phantom. He's worried about what Phantom will do to the recruits," Jasmine replied while gasping for air.

"You know, I've never seen the way he treats the recruits," Michael said with a hint of being curious.

"I know. Let's all go and take a look," Michele added just as she started to walk toward the elevator.

After everyone looked at each other for a few seconds, they suddenly ran after Michele. "So how does my cousin treat the recruits?" Trisha asked in mid run.

"Well, I think he treats them the same way that recruits and instructors treated him while he was in the Academy," Michael replied just as the doors opened.

Meanwhile, back in the training room . . .

"I will not allow anyone to leave if you don't accept my challenge. You think that you're better than anyone here, and now you have the chance to prove that statement. Instead of proving your boast, you are cowering like a baby behind your father and uncle," Phantom said while walking around the recruit and the four graduates of the Planetary Academy.

"You believe you're better than we are? Then prove to us how good you really are by fighting my uncle, the general," Charles said while watching Phantom's every movement.

"Fine, then. I will fight you for five minutes without even throwing a punch," Phantom replied to the boy's sarcasm.

"Go ahead and fight him. The match will be over in less than twenty seconds, anyway," the graduate lieutenant said.

"Fine. If he ends up dead, it's not my fault," the boy replied to his cousin while walking toward the mats.

A few seconds later, both Allan and Charles took sparring stances when they heard, "Other than no weapons, there are no rules," the lieutenant commander said as he approached the two fighters.

"I don't need any weapons to kill this new recruit," Charles replied with sarcasm while looking at Allan.

Just before the match started, Phantom heard, "We're now taking bets," one of the graduates said while smiling.

"I'll bet my entire allowance on the new guy. Can you tell us what your name is?" Shamarra said while smiling.

"Well, I'm sorry, little one, but we don't accept small change. The opening bets are starting at one hundred credits. My name is Dra-li-ta but you can call me Dra for short," Dra said while talking to her like a little baby.

"Well, I'm sorry that you think that way, cry baby. If you must know, my allowance is three hundred credits a day. I know—how about one week's worth of allowance?" Shamarra said in a mocking voice. As she looked at Allan, she noticed that he was looking displeased at her. "Um, never mind. I will only bet one hundred credits," she suddenly said.

"Sorry, baby, you said one week's worth, so you will owe us fifteen hundred credits once this match is over," Dra replied with a smile that said "easy pickings."

"Alright, how about this; she bets fifteen hundred credits and each one of you bets the same amount. If you do, I will match your bets with the same amount once I lose," Allan said as he started to laugh.

"Alright, that's a deal," Cronnicer replied just as everyone heard Gronnica's friends start to cheer.

"I'll take that bet myself," Lieutenant Commander Ericks said just as he held up a credit chip.

"Sure you can. And that just means more credits for us. How about that recruit?" Gronnica said as he started to count the credits he had written down.

"Um, sure, I will bet nine hundred credits on Allan," Shoanna said while looking worried.

"If you're not going to match the other bets, then you can't place a bet," Cronnicer said while laughing.

"She will bet fifteen hundred credits, as well," Shamarra said just as a devilish smile appeared on her face.

"I don't have that amount of credits," Shoanna whispered into Shamarra's ear.

"Just don't worry about it," Shsamarra said just as a devilish grin took the place of her smile.

"That's enough. No more bets. Now, are both recruits ready?" Lieutenant Commander Ericks said as he motioned everyone else off the mats.

A moment later, Phantom watched the recruits walk back to the bleachers just as he heard the mats shift. *Does he really think I'm that gullible?* Phantom thought just as he bent backward.

"How did you know?" Charles asked just as his fist connected with the emptiness of air. After he flipped backward, everyone heard, "I would call it pure luck," Phantom replied as he started to stand up from crouching.

"Pure luck. Yeah, sure, um, okay. I mean, everyone gets lucky once in their life time," Charles said as he crouched into a stance that no one else had ever seen.

"The Crowlin Style of Martial Arts. That stance indicates a lightening chi attack," Phantom said as the two started to circle each other.

"How did you know that? There aren't very many people that have seen this style," Charles said just as he charged toward Phantom.

Just as Charles kicked at Phantom, everyone noticed Phantom block the kick with his arm. After Phantom moved a few steps backwords from the connection, "What's the matter, Allan? You can't handly a love tap?" Charles asked just as he punched at Phantom.

"Sure I can, but I just lost my balance, is all," Phantom replied just as he side-stepped the punch.

As the matched continued, everyone was in awe as Phantom blocked or side-stepped every kick and every punch Charles threw at him. *I think I've proven my point. Besides, Shamarra could hit harder then this guy.* Phantom thought just as he stepped out of the way of the tornado kick Charles tried to connect.

Ten minutes later, everyone suddenly noticed Charles throwing a quick punch that had actually connected with Phantom's face. As Phantom fell to a single knee, "What's the matter, Allan? After boasting like that, I will admit that you're good, but I'm even better," Charles said while walking around Phantom.

"No, the truth is I allowed you to connect with me. Now I'm tired of this game, and I'm going to finish it," Phantom said while beginning to stand up.

Suddenly, everyone in the training room started to laugh—all except three. "I think you should yield, Charles. I believe you should, and right now," Lieutenant Commander Ericks said.

"Ericks, it won't do you any good. This boy knows nothing about yielding or submitting," Phantom said while take a stance that the galaxy has never seen before.

"You can't. That stance is secretive. You can't use the Shadow Style," Shamarra cried out from the bleachers.

After turning to look at the child, "Shadow Style . . . What's the Shadow Style?" Shoanna asked with confusion in her voice.

"I shouldn't tell you this, but that recruit is no recruit. The young man is my brother, Phantom, and your new combat instructor," Shamarra said in a low voice while noticing Phantom's right arm starting to glow.

With wide eyes, Shoanna turned back to the match just as Phantom charged toward the recruit. "What, you actually think you can defeat me?" Charles replied just as he noticed Phantom closing in on him.

Suddenly, the training room doors opened just as everyone heard, "Phantom, stop! You're supposed to be training them, not injuring them!" Colonel Calamen said as he rushed into the room. With all the commotion, Phantom finished his attack and turned to look at his father. "I was teaching this recruit a lesson. You know that I would only injure him and not kill him," Phantom said just as everyone noticed Charles falling to the ground.

"How is it possible? How did you hit me when I didn't even feel the connection?" Charles said as he held his side and solar plexus.

"What are you talking about? I missed my mark. What you felt was the aftermath of my chi," Phantom said while looking at the recruit.

"I would like my credits now," Shamarra said with sarcasm in her voice.

"Recruit, I would like to introduce you to your new hand-to-hand combat instructor. He is Phantom Breaker and Shamarra's older brother," Lieutenant Commander Ericks said while stepping in front of the recruits.

"Shamarra, tell me, who is the one that threatened you and injured your friend there?" Phantom said while looking at the Planetary Academy graduated recruits just as his eyes started to glow again.

"It was those two and their uncle. It was the lieutenant and general who really injured her," Shamarra said while pointing over at Gnnicer and Cronnica.

"This time next month, you will fight this recruit in a combat match," Phantom said as his eyes started to flash from red to green.

Suddenly, everyone heard the door opened a second time, and the general walked into the room. "Where is he? Where is the recruit that was picking on my nephew?" the general asked with hatred in his voice.

"I'm not a recruit but a corporal," Phantom said just as he turned to face the general.

"Fine, then. I demote you to a recruit status," the general replied while getting into Phantom's face.

"I will advise you to get out of my face before you regret your actions," Phantom replied just as he started to push buttons on his arm computer.

A few moments later, "Phantom, please reactivate the coding for the weapons and ships. I don't know what makes you think that you can come to my station and order these people around general, but the corporal will stay as a corporal, and he will train these recruits in the arts of combat," Mom said as her voice echoed throughout the training room.

"I can. Neither you nor the council can stop me. Remember, my contract is not a normal one. I can leave at any time," Phantom replied as his eyes started to shift color. With confusion on their faces, everyone turned to look at Phantom. "This matter is not over with. If you want a piece of me, then here is your chance general," Phantom said as a smile appeared on his face.

"If I have to fight this recruit, then what's in it for me?" the lieutenant asked while walking up to his uncle.

"Odin calling the Galactic Alliance. I'm requesting clearance to land. I need your help," Odin voice said over an open communications channel.

"Jackson, tell High Grand Admiral we have a visitor asking for clearance to land in the hanger," the commanding officer said.

"He has clearance to land. Once he has landed, escort him to High Grand Admiral Calamen's office," Mom replied.

"Yes, ma'am. Jackson, I will leave the escort to you," the commander said just as he activated the communications. "Odin, you have clearance to land in the hanger spot Alpha Charlie Tango 23. Once you've landed, you will be escorted to High Grand Admiral's office."

"Thank you, and I understand," Odin said just as his fighter approached the station hanger's doors.

Three minutes later, after the fighter's engines shut down, Odin started to emerge from his fighter. "I'm Jackson. If you would follow me, I will take you to the high grand admiral's office," the soldier said as he motioned toward the elevator.

I'm great. Thanks for asking. Now I know why he is the way he is, Odin thought while thinking of Phantom as he climbed down the ladder.

A moment later, Odin was standing in front a door labeled "High Grand Admiral's Office." "This way. High Grand Admiral Calamen is awaiting you," Jackson said as he left.

Meanwhile in the training room . . .

"If you win, I will resign from the Galactic Alliance, but if she wins, then you and your uncle will be losing your ranks. That means you will have to go back through the Academy, and I will train you in the art of combat," Phantom replied while looking at the general.

"Just for that, I will fight you here and now!" the general demanded just as he swung at Phantom.

Before realizing what was happening, he found himself on the mats with Phantom's knee in his chest. "Listen up! Lesson one: don't underestimate you opponent. It could be a deadly mistake," Phantom said as he stood up.

After walking over to his little sister, he heard, "This is not over yet!" the general said as he climbed to his feet.

After locking eyes, both Phantom and the general charged each other. "I have you now!" the general demanded just as he increased his speed.

Suddenly, the general flew back into the wall. "How? How is this possible? No one has ever beaten me," the general said just before blacking out and sliding down the wall onto the floor.

"You have great speed, but it's not fast enough," Phantom said as he heard a hard swallow from the lieutenant.

"You actually beat our uncle," the lieutenant said while looking at Shoanna.

"Computer, activate one of the combat droids," Phantom said while pacing back and forth.

"I think you should take some time off and prepare yourself for the elite exams," Colonel Calamen said while walking up and placing a hand on his son's shoulders.

Before the colonel could say anything else, everyone heard a metallic sound moving toward them. "Ah, there you are! Lieutenant, I want you to punch a hole into the chest of that robot," Phantom said as he pointed at the combat droid.

"How do you expect me to do that?" the lieutenant asked after looking at the robot.

"Your fist. I said, lieutenant, punch a hole in that robot!" Phantom demanded as he walked over to the bleachers and sat down.

"Fine, sir!" the lieutenant said as he walked up to the robot.

"Phantom, son, did you hear what I told you?" Colonel Calamen said with annoyance in his voice.

"I heard you, and I've told you before, I will not go through with the orders of taking the elite exams," Phantom said just as he heard a metallic sound followed by, "Ouch! That hurt!"

"Lieutenant, are you all right?" Phantom said while walking over to the lieutenant.

"This is impossible. How do you expect me to punch a whole in the chest plate of this robot?" the lieutenant asked while holding his hand.

"That's easy. Like this!" Phantom said just as he shoved two fingers into the robot's chest plate.

Before anyone could say anything, they watched the robot fall to the floor. "When I'm done with you, each and every one of you will be able to do what I just did," Phantom said as he turned around and looked at the recruits.

"This is why the High Grand Admiral Calamen and Mom chose him to be your new combat instructor," Lieutenant Commander Ericks told the recruits as he walked over to Phantom.

"Class is dismissed for lunch. When you return, Ericks will continue as your instructor until the elite exams are over next week. The elite's exams for the recruits will be in one month from now if you think you're capable of handling the ruoghest missions," Phantom said as he started for the door.

"Phantom, you are needed in High Grand Admiral Calamen's office," Mom said just as the door opened.

"I'll be right there," Phantom said as he left the room.

Back inside the High Grand Admiral's Office . . .

"Ma'am, I need your help. All the lost technology my people of Atlantis had is being taken by the military. We must stop them before something bad happens," Odin said as he took a seat.

"Odin, right? You're telling me that the people of Earth are harvesting the lost technology of Atlantis?" Kristy asked the strange male sitting in her office.

"Yes, that's why I need your help. Can you help me or not?" Odin asked just before taking a drink.

"I can't make that decision just yet. What would happen if the Earthlings *do* use the technology that they had stolen from your lost city?" Kristy Calamen asked while pacing back and forth.

Suddenly, there was a knock at the door just before the door slid aside. "Ah, Corporal, please enter," the high grand admiral said to her nephew.

As Phantom walked into the room, he noticed a familiar face sitting at the table. "Odin, what are you doing here? How did you find this place?" Phantom asked as walked toward the briefing table.

After taking a seat, he heard, "I placed a tracking device on you and the grand admiral. I was puzzled when I followed them both to this station. Now, can the Galactic Alliance help me or not?" Odin asked just as he slammed his hands onto the table.

After a few minutes of listening about what was happening to Atlantis back on Earth, he heard, "Well, can you help him or not?" High Grand Admiral Calamen said to her nephew just as she took a seat.

After standing up and walking over to the door, they heard, "Aunt Kristy, I don't know if I can help him or if I can't—I just don't know," Phantom replied as he stopped at the door.

Suddenly, both Kristy Calamen and Odin looked at each other just as the door to her office closed. *What is on your mind? Are you afraid of your humanity or what?* Kristy thought just as she heard, "Order him to keep his sister's tutor by his side at all times. If he will not embrace his humanity, than we will force it upon him," Mom's voice said while breaking the awkward silence.

Kristy replied, "Yes, ma'am. I will make sure the order is followed . . ."

Phantom Family Tree

- Shamarra (Little sister)
- Colonel Jack Calamen (Adopted Father)
- Jaquelyn Calamen (Adopted Mother)
- High Grand Admiral Kristy Calamen (Aunt)
- Grand Admiral Blake (Uncle Kristy's Husband)
- Lieutenant Jolania (Blake and Kristy's Daughter)
- Catherina Melody (Blakes sister's Adopted Daughter)
- King Carrag (Korra Guild) (Uncle)
- Tearan (Korra Guild Prince) (Cousin)
- Trasha (Korra Guild Princess) (Cousin)